MW00559279

Traveling Through the
Valley of the Shadow of Death

Traveling Through the Valley of the Shadow of Death

Margaret Turner Taylor

Llourettia Gates Books, LLC
P.O. Box #411
Fruitland, Maryland 21826

Paperback ISBN: 978-1-7347347-1-3
Hardback ISBN: 978-1-7347347-0-6
ebook ISBN: 978-1-7347347-2-0
Library of Congress Control Number: 2020905253

Cover design by Jaime L. Coston
Photography by Andrea Lõpez Burns
Interior design and layout by Jamie Tipton, Open Heart Designs

*This book is dedicated to my mother
and the other women who traveled
with her to Germany in 1938.*

CONTENTS

PREFACE

In the summer of 1938, on what was ostensibly an academic trip to study mathematics, my mother, Geneva Regina Burkhart, and other women dared to travel into the heart of Nazi Germany. They did learn mathematics, but they also learned what Hitler's regime was doing inside the Third Reich. The stories my mother told me when I was growing up and the few artifacts that remain from that summer journey, lead me to suspect her trip to Germany was, at least in part, an intelligence-gathering mission.

One question that has puzzled me is why my mother chose to go to Nazi Germany in 1938? Why that place and that particular time in history? Whenever I shared my mother's story with others, everyone had the same questions. There are the obvious answers. She wanted to travel; she wanted to study with distinguished mathematicians at German universities; she was given a scholarship that paid for the trip she could never have afforded to make otherwise.

Columbia University, a prestigious academic institution, sponsored the trip and offered credits towards her master's degree. It was her chance of a lifetime. Mathematics was my mother's passion, and the opportunity to hear lectures given by professors with gifted mathematical minds was unquestionably a draw for all the women in the travel group.

Columbia University had to know that Germany in 1938 was a dangerous place. Germany had reoccupied the Rhineland and gobbled up Austria. The Sudetenland of Czechoslovakia was next on the menu of the voracious Nazi beast. Wise professors at Columbia chose this time to take a group of American women to Germany to study mathematics. Sophisticated in the ways of the world and well aware of what was happening in Europe, why would the Columbia University Teacher's College organize such a trip? What were they thinking? They must have had an ulterior motive.

My husband subscribes to the view that "they didn't know in 1938 what a bad man Hitler was going to turn out to be," but I'm not satisfied with that answer. I suspect there was some other reason to spend a tremendous amount of money on an elaborate trip for a group of female mathematics teachers.

How had my mother, as a graduate of Ohio University, learned about this tour of Germany that was sponsored by Columbia University with its accompanying scholarship? How did she learn that such an opportunity might be available to her? Who told her how to apply to be a member of the group? I'm surprised she had the nerve to participate in something which was so far outside of her comfort zone and so far outside of her information zone. New York City was a world away from Belmont, Ohio, and Germany might as well have been on another planet.

I've always wondered why my mother's parents allowed her to go on the trip. Even though she was twenty-five years old and had been teaching and earning her own way for several years, if her father had told her not to go, she would not have gone. She had that much regard for his opinion.

Did my mother and her parents not realize in 1938 how evil Hitler was and how brutal the Nazis were? Were they unaware of what was happening in Europe? A terrible civil war was raging in Spain, and in March of 1938, Hitler's aggression resulted in the Austrian Anschluss. I'm shocked that my mother would so innocently seize this opportunity. On the other hand, maybe the risk that she was taking is magnified through the retrospective of history.

ᏬᎮᎯᏬ

PROLOGUE

*"All that is necessary for the triumph of evil
is that good men do nothing."*
— EDMUND BURKE

Geneva Burkhart's trip to Germany in 1938 is not just about what happened more than eighty years ago. It is a story for now and for all times. Her experiences are pertinent to what is happening in our world and in every one of our lives today. We as individuals and collectively as a society are inevitably in the process of writing our own histories. The choices we make today determine our tomorrows — for ourselves and for the lives of our children and grandchildren.

The rise of Nazi Germany and the cataclysmic wickedness the Nazis brought to the world are examples of the temporary triumph of evil. But evil never sleeps. It can never be defeated "once and for all." It is forever and eternally out there, always ready to overtake us when we aren't paying attention, always ready to take advantage of weakness.

The world in 1938 was broken. The obvious crumbling of European politics obscured an even more destructive decay in the underlying social fabric and moral sanctions which keep humanity in check. Civilization was about to collapse in upon itself, and evil would rule without limits. The unease of impending disaster permeated everything.

Geneva was at the beginning edge of her grown-up life.

She was bright and had a college education, but she was also painfully naive, very religious, and scarcely aware of the geo-political events of the times in which she lived. A public school mathematics teacher, who hoped to marry her childhood sweetheart, she chose to leave the safety of her prescribed life and travel into the devil's lair — Germany in 1938.

☙❧

I AM A JEW

NOVEMBER 1937
FRANKFURT, GERMANY

THERE WILL NEVER BE ANOTHER HAPPY morning. I used to greet the first moments of awakening with a kind of vague and hopeful anticipation. Each new day welcomed the next episode in my life. I allowed myself to luxuriate in the last few seconds of sleep and slowly pulled my mind into awareness. That time, when I looked forward to living, is no more. My first feeling now is overwhelming sorrow, followed by anger, and then by fear. A terrible weight oppresses and suffocates me. My brain lags behind, and it's a moment before I remember why I am so wretched. When reality dawns and I remember what burdens me, I know why I am drowning. The gray shroud of despair engulfs me and drags me down. I don't want to be awake or alive. I don't want to feel anything at all. I try to talk myself into existing. Why has death not found me and taken me away from this hell on earth? The anger comes when I realize I will never live a normal life. I am no longer master of my destiny.

I am Max Meyerhof, a Jew living in Germany in 1937. Hitler came to power in 1933. Anyone who was paying attention and read his book *Mein Kampf* would have known what was coming. Hitler never hid his views. The Nuremberg Laws of 1935 took everything from German Jews — their citizenship, their assets, and their ability to earn a living. These cruel laws redefined what it meant to be Jewish. If one of your grandparents was born a Jew, even if you'd been a Catholic or a Lutheran all your life, Hitler's obsession with Aryan purity has determined that you are a Jew.

But I really am a Jew, not just a Jew defined by genealogy. When it became clear what Hitler and his Nazis had in mind for us, I considered leaving Germany. But I didn't want to leave my home and family and my university education. Now, I have lost it all; everything is gone. I have waited too long.

My father was a rabbi, the best of men who spoke out against injustice wherever he saw it. He denounced Hitler and the Nazis. Rabbi Joachim Meyerhof's words of protest, the declarations of a patriot who fiercely loved his country, were his attempt to save Germany from a madman. The rabbi was murdered because he told the truth.

The Gestapo took my soul on a sunny November afternoon. They came to our home as we sat down to tea. I'd finished my classes early and was looking forward to an evening with my parents and sisters. Mother had just served our cups of strong tea and returned to the kitchen to take the strudel out of the oven when there was a knock at the door. Mother made the best strudel in the world, from preserved blackberries and plums, with a dusting of sugar crystals on the top. She brought it to the table on a blue and white Meissen platter. My sisters and I sat at the tea table, and my father answered the door.

They didn't ask if they could come inside. Viciously pushing my father out of the way, the brutes displayed no manners or common courtesy and stormed up the stairs. My father ran after them. One of the three Gestapo thugs grabbed him and held his arms behind his back. The policeman who smelled like schnapps pointed a gun at my mother and sisters and me and told us to stand in the corner of the room and not to move. The third man took out his gun and held the barrel in his hand. He beat my father's face and head with the handle. I started to go to my father, but the man who kept us in the corner pushed his weapon in my face. My father's head was bloody and rolled to one side. When he dropped to the floor, my mother rushed to hold him in her arms. The man pointing his gun at my sisters and me, turned and shot my mother twice in the back and a third time in the head. Seeing our mother lying on the carpet gasping for breath, the blood flowing from her body, my sisters began to scream. I knew these men who had come for my father were without mercy. We were all going to die. They threw my father down on top of my mother, as if discarding a bundle of soiled laundry.

Screaming profanities at the three of us children, the men circled the room, throwing my mother's collection of fine china onto the floor and smashing every piece to bits. Our musical instruments were beside the piano, and one of the Gestapo asked which of us was a musician. Both of my sisters, Greta and Annika, stunned but afraid not to answer, acknowledged that they were.

"And what do you play, little Jew girl?" the schnapps drinker asked Annika. Annika, only seven, whispered that she played the violin. The man told her to put her hands on the tea table. She put both of her hands out with her palms down and looked up at the man, terrified for her life. He laughed and said, "I will fix those little Jew fingers so they will never be able to play the violin again." He held her small wrists down on the table with one of his huge hands and smashed her fingers with the butt of his gun. I can still hear the cracking of those tiny, fragile bones. I can still hear her screams. He kept pounding and pounding until her hands were nothing but bloody stubs on the ends of her wrists. Blessedly, she passed out from the pain and collapsed on the floor. My sister Greta, who was twelve, reached out to help her, but she was restrained by one of the policemen.

"Are you also a musician? What instrument do you play?" Greta was in such a state, she couldn't speak. She vomited on the front of the Gestapo's jacket and fell against him. Angry at having his uniform ruined, he pushed her to the floor and shot Greta in the head. Then he fired his gun at Annika whose bloody fingers were dripping on the Persian rugs my family had always prized.

"Filthy Jewess swine! Look at what you've done. I'm going to have to have my uniform laundered."

I was paralyzed with horror. My mind has replayed the terrifying display of unrestrained violence and brutality a thousand times. My family was dead, everyone destroyed in a few life-shattering moments. I knew the Gestapo would kill me next. It didn't matter that we'd done nothing wrong. They would never let me remain as a witness to the unspeakable things they'd done to Rabbi Meyerhof and his family.

When he'd spoken out against Hitler and the Nazis, my father knew he was putting himself and our family at risk. We'd talked about it and agreed my father had to do what he felt was right, what God was telling him to do. He worried that he might be arrested and even jailed, but none of us imagined that the recriminations would be so absolute. He was a moral man who couldn't remain silent. I don't know what his conscience would have told him to do if he'd had a crystal ball and been able to look into the future to see what would happen to his family.

The drunken Nazi who'd crushed my sister's fingers eyed the strudel on the tea table. It was still warm, and he grabbed a large piece and pushed it into his mouth. Purple juice from the berries dribbled over his fat fingers and ran down his face and chin. The other two Gestapo were beside him in an instant, wanting to taste the delicious pastry. As they passed the plate of strudel back and forth, stuffing it into their mouths like animals, I saw my opportunity.

There was no time to be sickened that these madmen could brutally maim and murder one minute and eat strudel the next. I could not allow myself to experience the shock and disbelief of what these devils had done to my loved ones. I couldn't acknowledge the grief and the despair of the overwhelming losses. The destruction of everyone in my life whom I held most dear had taken only a few minutes, but the slaughter was imprinted forever on my heart and in my memory.

Knowing I would be dead before they left the house, I picked up a heavy wooden chair and threw it at the men. The chair got the attention of the barbarians who were gorging themselves on pastry. One of them reached for his luger, but the strudel saved my life. Because he'd been holding the sticky dessert, his hands couldn't get a proper grip on the gun. I shoved him out of my way and ran to the sitting room window. I grabbed another chair and threw it hard, knowing this was my only chance to escape. The window shattered in front of me as I jumped through the breaking glass and fell to the ground below. I heard shots fired behind me and felt the sting of bullets in my arm and in my leg. The sitting room was one floor above the entrance to our house, and it was a considerable drop to the ground. I just missed the brick front walk and landed in a thorny bush that broke my fall.

The bush that saved me had already lost most of its leaves, and I suffered scratches and cuts from its sharp stems. It was cold outside, and I didn't have a coat. Bleeding from at least two gunshot wounds, I had no plan and no place to go. I refused to fall before the Gestapo's assault. I was determined to escape and survive. I had to live on for those I'd lost, to exact revenge for this unspeakable tragedy.

The Gestapo had to go down the steps to get out of the house. I was already on the ground and had that small advantage, but I was limping and bloody. My adrenalin surged and propelled me forward. I ran, and then I ran some more. I'd grown up in the neighborhood and knew the woods. I knew which buildings were abandoned and where the secret places were. I knew there was a boat house by the lake. I knew who lived in the houses. I needed a refuge and time to take care of my wounds. I was leaving a trail of blood and didn't want to lead the Gestapo to my hiding place.

I ran to the lake and threw myself into the water. I struggled to reach the center of the lake with my one good arm and dove below the surface. Swimming under water, I returned to the shore to give myself a chance to rest under the wreck of a wooden dock. The water was excruciatingly cold, but it was a healing balm as it numbed my pain.

I ducked down when I heard the Gestapo talking close by. "He can't get very far. He has to be injured after going out the window, and I know I hit him with at least one bullet before he jumped. He made it to the lake. I expect he'll die there. We have to search, but we'll be dragging his body out of the water in a couple of days."

Hiding under the collapsed dock, I could hear their conversation as I drifted in and out of consciousness. I had to get out of the cold water soon, or I would die from hypothermia. I had to attend to my bullet wounds before I bled to death.

Where could I go to get warm? The Gestapo would look for me and wouldn't give up until they found me and killed me. Would they search all the houses in the neighborhood? How long would they search? I couldn't stay in the water or wait to treat my wounds.

Two Gestapo continued to walk around the lake, and the third man went for reinforcements to join the search. I had to get to dry land and find a place to hide while there were still just two men searching, before there were twenty men looking for me.

~ CHAPTER TWO ~

PEACE!

NOVEMBER 1937
JACK TREVANIAN (NEW YORK) ON THE PHONE
WITH NIGEL BARNABY (LONDON)

"PEACE? OF COURSE HE WANTS PEACE. EVERY-body wants peace! There's nothing wrong with peace. Peace is a wonderful thing. Peace is, well, peace isn't war. The best thing about peace is ...," Jack Trevanian paused as he tried to think of something to say about peace that he hadn't already said, "...it's peaceful. I know he makes speeches and calls himself a pacifist and an isolationist. He's just trying to be a more sophisticated Woodrow Wilson. He's a Democrat. All Democrats are pacifists. We have to change his mind. We have to completely enlighten his upper class behind and show him what the Nazis really have in store for us."

. . . .

"You and I are in agreement, and those who think there won't be a war with Germany have their heads in the sand. It's

8

wishful thinking, and they're allowing their own naïve view of the future to get in the way of seeing the facts."

. . . .

"That's why we're planning to take a study group to Germany, to gather information. The tour will be designed to collect court-worthy evidence, hard facts that Hitler is planning war, a really big war. The President is a lawyer. He understands what building a case is all about. I think he will pay attention to ours when we present it to him."

. . . .

"No, Nigel, I don't think he really is like Woodrow Wilson. I think he's more pragmatic than Wilson, less of an idealist. That's my opinion. And who knows how much of that League of Nations thing was Woodrow's idea and how much was Edith's. I know Edith, and I like her. She's a fine, intelligent woman, but, damn it, she was never elected President. She had no right to pretend to be the President. She had no right to take on the authority of acting for the President of the United States, even when he had a stroke. That's what Vice Presidents, not wives, are for." Jack was in attack mode.

. . . .

Jack's shoulders relaxed and his jaw unclenched. "You're exactly right; I digress. And yes, I know I do that more than I should. Ha! This is about Roosevelt, not about Wilson. And okay, I admit it, the League of Nations is a good idea. It's a good idea like Socialism is a good idea. They're both good ideas, and they both don't work!"

. . . .

"I'm saying that, if confronted with the reality of what the Nazis are already doing and what they're planning to do in the future, Franklin will come around. What you may not realize about Franklin is that he really loves cyphers and codes and all of the spy and secrecy stuff. As an assistant Secretary of the Navy during the Great War, he was in charge of the ONI, the Office of Naval Intelligence. He adopted the ONI as his own project and used his personal influence to make the department more powerful than it had ever been. In fact, he became somewhat obsessed with the threat of internal subversion, even before the U.S. got into it in 1917."

. . . .

"He was a great admirer of 'Blinker' Hall, director of Britain's Naval Intelligence. Because Blinker was able to decode the Zimmerman telegram and leaked it to President Wilson, Franklin idolized Blinker as a blooming genius, which he was. Franklin thought intelligence gathering was essential to winning, and by the end of the Great War, Roosevelt had built the ONI into a pretty darn good intelligence-gathering network. The current head of the Intelligence Division in our War Department is an old fogy who doesn't do a damn thing. Everybody knows that. Franklin hasn't really fought for an intelligence organization since he was elected President, but I know he thinks it's important. It's politics, and it's resources that are holding him back. Franklin's obsessed with all his social welfare programs, and he hasn't given espionage any priority at all."

. . . .

"Yes, Nigel, I know. When one is the President of the United States, everything is politics. My personal opinion is that Franklin knows there will be war with Germany. He may be hoping that the British and the French can take care of the little Austrian bastard, but Franklin's a smart man. I may not agree with his politics and all of that socialist baloney he's so entranced with, but I do respect his intellect. Everybody in the whole USA, both Republicans and Democrats … they're all afraid to even think about saying the word 'war.' Franklin can't say it publicly, at least not right now, but he knows at some point, to defeat the Nazis, the United States will have to get into the fight."

. . . .

"We have to provide him with the information he needs but doesn't know how to get. Currently, he's preoccupied with things in the Pacific. He's sent his good friend Vincent Astor to sail his yacht, the *Nourmahal*, around the South Pacific to snoop on the Japs. Franklin wants Astor to get a look at what's happening in the Marshall Islands. Supposedly, Astor's on a secret mission, but it's not really much of a secret to anybody. Astor is supposed to look for signs of a military buildup by the Japanese, as if anybody needs a secret mission to figure out what's going on with that. Of course they're building up their military. They've been grabbing every piece of territory in the Pacific they can get their hands on, and nobody is doing a darned thing about it."

. . . .

"You Brits have also been trying to get a look at what's happening in the Marshall Islands, and Vincent Astor isn't going to be able to get any closer than your people did. I understand why Franklin is fixated on the Pacific, but he ought to be paying half as much attention to what's going on in Germany. Whether he wants to hear it or not, we're going to bring him hard evidence about what's happening in Europe.

In spite of what he says, I think he really does want to hear it. He wants the information but doesn't know how to go about finding it. Bringing back the facts will force him to look at the reality of what Hitler is up to. We have to do everything possible to make sure Franklin and Churchill know the truth. Eventually, they will be thankful to have the information, to save the world from the Nazi bullies and that strutting, shouting, unseemly little vegetarian pervert."

Jack Trevanian was a big man in every sense of the word. He was six feet five inches tall and had girth to match his height. He was a big-time lawyer in a big law firm in the biggest city in the United States, New York City. He handled big, high-profile cases. He had a big voice, and he had made very, very big money investing in real estate. He was a big player in the world of big business. He personally owned several big houses and gave big parties. The expression "larger than life" was coined to describe someone like Jack. But Jack also had a big heart, and what many people didn't realize was that he was a very big patriot and cheerleader for the United States of America. For years he had spent countless hours and huge amounts of his personal fortune to try to keep his country safe.

Sir Nigel Barnaby and Jack Trevanian had become friends during the Great War when they were both young officers fighting the Germans in France. Their friendship was based on mutual respect and shared values and had endured and grown stronger over the years. They'd joined forces in several fights the rest of the world would never know anything about. Neither man needed public recognition, and both were determined that Germany would not ride roughshod over the world again. They intended to do whatever they could to stop Hitler, or rather, everything they could do to convince their respective governments to stop Hitler.

Nigel Barnaby was as quiet as Jack Trevanian was sometimes loud and brash. With Eaton and Oxford in his background, Nigel was brilliant, brave, and deceptively soft-spoken. Jack knew that if Nigel made a decision, it was almost impossible to change his mind. It could be done but rarely happened. When Nigel came up with what might seem at first to be a wild and crazy way to solve a problem, and if he decided his approach was the right one, he dug in his heels. It amazed Jack how often Nigel turned out to be right. The two men had tremendous affection for each other. Jack liked to tease his friend, and Nigel was a good sport about it. Jack thought he secretly enjoyed the joking humor, even when it was at his own expense.

CHAPTER THREE

PEMBERTON

FALL 1919
PEMBERTON MANOR, HAMPSHIRE, ENGLAND

JACK TREVANIAN HAD NEVER VISITED AN English country house before Nigel Barnaby invited him to spend a weekend at Pemberton Manor. Jack knew Nigel's home was surrounded by acres of land and had a staff of servants, but he was still impressed when the taxi drove through the gates of the estate and dropped him off in front of Nigel's enormous stone mansion. Nigel and his wife Portia and some other friends were playing croquet on the lawn, and Nigel hurried to welcome Jack. Clearly delighted to see his friend, he put his arm around Jack's shoulders and led him to the croquet court.

"Portia, Portia, come and meet Jack." Nigel called to his wife. When she turned around and walked toward them, Jack was startled by Portia Barnaby's beauty. She wore a kilt in her Lamont clan tartan and a sweater that exactly matched the blue in the plaid. A whirl of color, she hurried to join her husband. She glowed with good health and happiness, and her hair was a riot of strawberry blond curls falling unconfined and blowing in the September breeze. She was so lovely and so full of life. Jack was surprised by the vibrancy of her personality as she reached out to bring him into her world. Her eyes were dark violet, a color Jack had never seen in anybody's eyes before, and he was captivated by the intelligence, sweetness, and generosity of spirit that lay behind those violet eyes.

She grabbed his hand in both of hers, and he was moved when she said how happy she was to finally meet him and have him visit them at Pemberton. He was introduced to the other guests whose names he quickly forgot.

As they walked back to the house for tea, Jack told Nigel what a lucky man he was. Nigel clearly adored his wife and told Jack with great pride that they were expecting a child. Jack was affectionately jealous of Nigel who seemed to have everything any man could possibly want. Jack knew he would never have a woman in his life who was as lovely as Portia.

There were other guests, but Jack was always seated at Portia's right for meals. She asked him all about himself and seemed to be genuinely interested in what her guest of honor had to say. She and Nigel regaled their friends with stories in a charming back and forth manner that kept everyone laughing and entertained. Portia's mother, as everyone knew, had read Shakespeare in her university days. Nigel and Portia had met at Oxford and had humorous tales about the antics they'd been up to when they were younger. They enjoyed their lives and laughed about the difficulties of running a large estate with many animals, tenant farmers, and drafty rooms. They never mentioned the Great War, a subject Portia would not allow to be discussed at her dinner table.

Jack wished the weekend would never end, and he put off

his departure as late as he could on Monday. Nigel said his goodbyes early because he had a meeting, and Portia walked with Jack while they waited for the taxi to drive him to the station.

"Jack, do you know why Nigel was awarded his Victoria Cross? He won't tell me anything about it, and I thought you might know, if anybody did."

"I don't know anything for sure. He would never talk to me about it either. Whatever it was, it happened before the U.S. got into the war. I asked once, and he was angry with me for bringing it up. He nearly bit my head off. I'll tell you what the rumors were, but I can't stand by any of these stories as being true. I was told about two events, both of which demonstrate exceptional bravery on Nigel's part. One incident was early in the war when he and his men set dynamite charges under a strategic bridge in Belgium. Their mission was to destroy the bridge and keep the Germans from crossing a river. For some reason, the fuse didn't work properly, and the dynamite didn't explode. Enemy fire was heavy all around, but Nigel left his hiding place and crawled back under the bridge to reset the fuse. He returned to where his men were concealed, and the bridge was destroyed on the second try. He could have been blown to bits. The faulty fuse could have engaged, or German gunfire could have set off the dynamite. It was a remarkable thing, according to the stories."

"Why in the world would he not tell me about the bridge? What was the other story?"

"The other story, I think, is the one that probably resulted in his being awarded the Victoria Cross. Nigel was in charge of coordinating an attack across German lines. His men were to engage in a flanking operation out from the Maginot Line to destroy a German artillery post that was raining terror on British troops. Nigel's job was to stay close behind and direct the two groups of infantrymen who were trying to get behind the Germans. When one group of his men was ambushed not far from British lines, Nigel left his position and ran into enemy fire to rescue them. Several were hurt, and supposedly he dragged them back into British territory two at a time. Barraged with bullets, he went back into the line of fire to bring more men to safety. He did this four times — the last time bringing back three badly injured fellows. He dragged a man with each hand and had the third on his back. Three of the men he rescued were already dead or died shortly afterwards, but he saved the lives of six injured soldiers. It makes one wonder if he had a death wish. The odds were huge against his living through all of that, but he did it anyway."

Portia turned pale when she heard the story about her husband. "He was quite foolish to do such a thing, wasn't he? I'm shocked by his behavior, if the story is true."

"In war, men sometimes do superhuman things without thinking about the consequences. They see something that has to be done, and they do it. I think Nigel acted from the noblest of impulses. He saw his men were going to die unless he acted, and he made a decision to do whatever was necessary to save them."

"I've always trusted Nigel's good judgment to temper his tendencies to take risks."

"Nigel is the bravest and most brilliant man I've ever known, and he has superlative judgment. He can figure out incredibly complicated situations before the rest of us have even begun to think about them. I've never known him to be wrong —either about the analysis of the situation or about the solution. He listens to criticism and doesn't have an ego that gets in the way of accepting suggestions and alterations to his plans. He is a genius at what he does."

"Thank you for telling me what you know. I now have a better idea about why Nigel won't talk to me about his medals. He's a complicated man. You see many sides of him, but there are parts of Nigel he hardly ever shows to anyone. Even I don't know all there is to know about Nigel Barnaby."

Portia continued and Jack paid close attention, "Nigel has many different kinds of friends and acquaintances. He has childhood friends, school chums, business and professional colleagues, friends at his London office, friends with whom he plays cards at his club, social, and so on. But you, dear Jack, are special. For Nigel, you are a friend of the heart. You are one of a kind. I've known about his very high regard for you since he first met you. Now that I've spent these past few days with you, I'm tremendously relieved and pleased that you reciprocate that friendship. For you, also, Nigel is a friend of the heart. Cherish this relationship, Jack. It's worth more than almost any of the other treasures you will have in your life." When the taxi arrived, she kissed him on the cheek and waved him away. Both believed there were a lifetime's worth of weekends to look forward to at Pemberton Manor.

Several months later, Jack received an exuberant telegram announcing the birth of healthy twin boys Chester and Charles, named after their grandfathers. The new parents asked Jack to be godfather to both boys, and the telegram was signed: "Much love, Portia and Nigel." Less than two weeks later, Jack received another telegram. It read: "Portia died from systemic infection after Caesarean section. Please come to England. I am desperate. Nigel."

Jack dropped everything and sailed on the next ship. He spent six weeks with Nigel at Pemberton Manor. Nigel had prevailed on his cousin Rosemary Barnaby to come and stay temporarily to take care of the babies, the house, and himself. Rosemary never left Pemberton. Eventually, Nigel went back to work at MI6, and Jack returned to New York. They wrote each other lengthy letters every week. Once transatlantic radio telephone became available to the public, they spoke often, and never mind the cost.

During his visits to Pemberton Manor over the years, Jack had come to know Nigel's boys. They had their father's stature and distinguished aristocratic looks, but the color of their hair and the color of their eyes had to be a constant reminder to Nigel of the love he'd lost. Strawberry blond curls and violet eyes are a rare combination. Because of Nigel's secret and sometimes dangerous work, when the boys enrolled in boarding school, he legally changed their last names to Lamont, Portia's maiden name. He was protective of them at all costs. They were the tangible progeny of his life's most precious gift, as well as a reminder of how cruel and unpredictable life can be.

CHAPTER FOUR

SAVING MAX I

NOVEMBER 1937
FRANKFURT, GERMANY

IT WAS FINALLY DARK ENOUGH FOR ME TO CLIMB out of the marsh and make my way to a warm place. The two men who were searching for me were far enough away from where I was hiding, so I slipped onto the land and crawled through the grass toward a large house a few hundred feet from the lake's shore.

When I reached the garden, I heard more Gestapo soldiers arrive to join the hunt. It was completely dark now, and I ran to the basement door. I knew the house was empty. The family who'd lived there had left Frankfurt for the summer as they did every year, but this fall they'd not returned. They were Jews who had attended my father's congregation, and they'd urged my parents to leave Germany with my sisters and myself. My mother had wondered out loud if the family would ever come back to their house in our neighborhood. I knew I would be welcome in their home if they were here, so

I assumed I could intrude on their hospitality while they were away. The basement door was locked, and I couldn't enter that way. If it was discovered by the Gestapo, a broken pane of glass in the door would reveal my hiding place.

I'd been to this house for parties in the past and knew the layout of the interior. A large sun room at the back had a wall of windows and doors that opened onto a terrace. I might be able to get inside that way. With so many windows to examine, the Gestapo might not notice if one pane was broken. I climbed to the terrace and felt my way along the outside wall of the solarium. There was one French door at the end of the room that was closed but wasn't locked. The carelessness of a servant was going to save me, and I slipped through the door and locked it behind me. If the Gestapo came looking for broken panes of glass and other signs of entry, they wouldn't find any here. They would find only tightly locked doors and windows at this house.

My leg and arm were bleeding. The cold water had staunched the blood for a while, but as soon as my skin began to warm up, the bleeding began again. I knew the Gestapo would search all the houses in the area, and I couldn't leave a trail of blood. My clothes were soaking wet, and I was dripping water on the floor of the solarium. I grabbed a blanket from one of the couches and wrapped it around myself. As I mopped up the water, I noticed it was beginning to turn pink with blood. Covering my tracks as best I could, I prayed the water would be dry by the time anyone came to search the house and my blood wouldn't leave stains on the slate floor.

Holding the blanket around me to keep from dripping bloody water in my wake, I stumbled as I climbed the circular staircase. It was dark and difficult to avoid tripping over my wrap. I kept going until I reached the top floor of the house where the servants used to stay. I knew there were attics full of old furniture and a trunk room where I might be able to hide. I limped down the hall to a servant's bedroom and found a closet where I could bury myself under a mound of clothes.

I needed to tend to my wounds, but most of all I had to stay hidden from the Gestapo. I peeled the torn shirt sleeve off my arm. Because my body was warming up, I was now bleeding profusely. I tore a strip of cloth from my shirt and tied it around my arm to try to stop the bleeding. Because there was no exit wound, I was afraid the bullet was still imbedded in my right upper arm and would have to be removed. I pulled down my trousers to examine the gunshot wound in my thigh. I found an entrance wound and an exit wound. I was thankful the bullet had gone straight through and was not still inside my leg. I'd been shot from the rear as I was going out the window, so the exit wound was in the front of my thigh. The damage was severe, and I was amazed that I'd been able to walk at all. I struggled to tie a tourniquet around my leg, but the bleeding didn't stop as it had when I'd applied pressure to my arm. There was no heat in the house, and I was wet and cold.

As my body continued to warm up, the blood flowed more freely, and the pain, which had been numbed by my immersion in the icy water of the lake, surged over me in waves. I grew woozy and knew that if I didn't stop the bleeding, I was going to pass out in the closet and bleed to death. I searched in the dark and found a pile of servants' old uniforms. I tore the fabric into strips and packed my thigh as tightly as I could. Bloody rags were everywhere, but finally the bleeding in my leg slowed. I was growing weaker and lay down as close to the back wall of the closet as I could. Hiding the blood-soaked rags under my body, I covered myself with the pile of discarded uniforms. The clothes smelled musty and unwashed, and I could only hope that I'd hidden myself well enough.

I was chilled to the bone and in a lot of pain, but most of all, I was afraid of being discovered. I'd tried to cover my tracks as I had climbed the stairs to my hiding place, but I'd been in shock and not thinking as clearly as I should have been. What telltale signs had I left behind? I gave in to my exhaustion. Sleep finally came and temporarily took away the pain and horror of the day.

I was awakened by the sound of loud boots tramping up the stairs. The leader of the Gestapo search party was shouting directions to his men as they went through all the rooms on this upper level. The electricity was turned off, and the men carried large battery-powered torches. I stayed as still as I could. They came to the small servants' bedroom, looked under the bed, and opened the closet door. Frustrated and tired of searching this large house with its many rooms and closets, they knew they had more houses left to search. One of the Gestapo kicked at the pile of dirty clothes on the floor. When the man's boot struck my injured thigh, I almost cried out in pain. A steel-toed boot can be a dangerous weapon. One searcher picked up a few of the servants' uniforms with the barrel of his rifle and poked at the pile of clothing on the floor. Thankfully, they decided there was nothing but a bunch of old clothes in the closet. It was the middle of the night, and the men were eager to go home.

"There isn't any sign he's here. There aren't any broken windows or broken locks on the doors. Nobody could get in here without a key. Everything was locked up tight, and we had to break a window to get in. We should focus only on houses and buildings where he might have broken in. It's a waste of time to search every house."

"Would he go for help to a house where he knew someone, or would he go to an empty house?"

"Who knows? We have to search both occupied and

unoccupied houses. And what are we supposed to say to people when we wake them up at four o'clock in the morning? Do we give the usual reason — that we're searching for a dangerous criminal and need to check their house for their own safety? How many times do you think people will believe that? We're looking for the rabbi's son. I think some Jew family would take him in and lie about it,"

"If he's taken in by other Jews, we'll find him soon enough. Non-Jews won't take the chance of harboring a Jew. Anyway, I'm sure he drowned. We'll find him floating in the lake in a few days. Mark my words."

One of the men gave the pile of clothes a last poke and a few more kicks. They left the closet and traipsed back out into the hall and down the stairs. I tried to hold my breath while they were searching the closet. If it hadn't been so dark and if they'd paid more attention, they might have seen the bloody rags they'd turned up. Thank God they'd not yet brought the dogs, as dogs certainly would have been alerted by the smell of fresh blood. I felt a huge sense of relief, amazed they'd not found my hiding place. I might be safe here for a few days, but when my body failed to float to the surface of the lake to prove I was dead, the Gestapo would be back to search the house again.

CHAPTER FIVE

SAVING MAX II

NOVEMBER 1937
FRANKFURT, GERMANY

T HE NEXT MORNING, I WAS SHIVERING IN THE unheated house and knew I had to clean and bandage my wounds. Since the Gestapo had searched and left the house, infection was my most immediate threat. I gathered up all the rags that had any blood on them so I could get rid of them. If the Gestapo came back with the dogs, they would sound the alarm if they found the slightest trace of blood in the closet. I rummaged through one of the bathrooms on the second floor for antiseptic to clean my wounds. I found a cloth laundry bag and filled it with bandages and towels, tweezers, and bottles of astringent. In the largest bedroom I found clean underwear, shirts, and a pair of trousers several sizes too large for me. They would have to do. I was dangerously weak as I made my way down the stairs to the kitchen.

I found a small pile of sticks beside the wood burning stove and decided to risk starting a fire to boil some water.

I stripped down to my skin and made a bundle of my torn, bloody clothes and the bloody rags from the closet. I intended to bury all of it in the garden, to hide the evidence that I'd been inside the house. It seemed to take forever to heat the water. I washed my entire body with soap I'd found by the kitchen sink and dried myself with clean towels.

I examined my thigh as I sat at the kitchen table and filled a bowl with boiling water. I used a dishcloth to cleanse my leg wound with the scalding water, and then I poured antiseptic on my thigh. The burning in my leg made me cry out loud. I wrapped knitted cotton bandages tightly around my leg. I knew I'd have to change the dressings often and wondered how I would manage to keep infection away.

While I still had water boiling, I turned my attention to my mangled arm. I sterilized the tweezers and probed my arm for the offending bullet. Because the pain was so acute, I put a screwdriver in my mouth to keep from biting my tongue. Unable to locate the bullet with the tweezers, I dipped a paring knife I'd found into the boiling water and cut into my arm. After a few minutes of painful digging, I realized I needed to find a doctor. If the bullet stayed inside my arm too long, the wound would become infected. My arm was in terrible shape. I tried to sterilize the bullet hole with rubbing alcohol and bandaged it as best I could. I was exhausted from the pain and from the effort of trying to take care of my wounds, and I was light-headed and hungry.

I stumbled to the pantry and found some jars and tins of food left behind when the family had gone away for their summer vacation. I opened some cans, warmed some lentil soup, and ate a quart of white beans. Nothing I'd ever eaten in my life tasted as good as the soup and beans I ate that day.

I washed my spoon and the empty jars and decided to make myself a bed in the closet of one of the upstairs bedrooms.

I wouldn't come down to the kitchen until the next day when I would need to eat again and boil more water to change my bandages. It wasn't yet noon, but I couldn't stay awake any longer. I was losing track of time. I wanted to stand guard against another search of the house, but fatigue overwhelmed me.

It was dark outside when the pain woke me. I couldn't find any pain-killing drugs in the medicine cabinet, so I looked for brandy to help me cope. I was hungry, but told myself I couldn't plunder the pantry again until the next day. I wondered how closely the Gestapo were watching my parents' house and when it would be safe to go back there to get some clothes. There were drugs for pain in our medicine chest, and I knew where my parents kept money. I could gather the things I needed to continue to survive. There was no reason to stay in Germany, so I began to make plans to leave. The Gestapo would realize soon enough that my body wasn't going to float to the surface of the lake.

The first thing I had to do was find a doctor who could remove the bullet from my arm. Dr. Jacob Engelman took care of Jewish patients and practiced in my neighborhood. He had been stripped of his medical license by the Nuremberg Laws, but he continued to attend to those who came to him for help. The Gestapo might be watching the doctor's house, but I had to get to him as soon as possible. If I could gather my strength, I would go to his house tonight. I decided to eat again before going outside into the November cold.

The coat I found in a hall closet was much too large, but it was warm and had a pair of gloves in the pocket. Keys to the house were hanging on the wall in the pantry, so I would be able to easily come and go. No broken locks or window panes would give away my hiding place. After another meal of lentil soup, beans, and tinned fish, I left the house by the basement door and locked it behind me. I planned to return that night after visiting the doctor.

The bitter autumn wind assaulted my face, and freezing rain drenched me. It would soon turn to sleet or snow. At first, I was so stiff I could scarcely move at all, let alone move quickly. If anyone stopped me on the street, it would be obvious that I was badly hurt. I made my way to the doctor's house, walking through backyards, crawling painfully over walls and under fences, and hiding in the bushes whenever I heard the slightest noise. When I reached the doctor's house, I threw some stones at the window of the room where I thought he slept. I watched and trembled in the cold until he finally raised the window. I shouted that I was the rabbi's son and needed to see him right away. The long hike through the neighborhood had drained me of my strength. At last, Dr. Engelman opened his back door for me.

"The Gestapo have already been here, asking about you. What's happened?" As we made our way to the secret part of his house where he conducted his surgery, the doctor asked me questions.

I told him. "The Gestapo came and killed my family. They're all dead — my mother, my father, and both of my sisters. I'm alive only because I jumped out of a window. I was shot in the leg and the arm as I was escaping. A bullet went through my thigh. I tried to dig the bullet out of my arm but couldn't get it. I'm afraid I've made a mess of it by trying to doctor myself. I need medical care, and I need something to take the pain away." Dr. Engelman began to remove the soiled bandages from my leg. I broke down in tears as I told Dr. Engelman what the Gestapo had done to my family. I tried to be brave, but in many ways I was still just a boy.

"These Nazis are the most brutal of bullies. I don't under-stand why they would maim and kill those beautiful little girls." Dr. Engelman's emotion made it almost impossible for him to choke out the words. "I don't understand any of it except that evil now rules in this country of mine,"

Dr. Engelman looked at my wounds. "The bullet is deeply embedded in your arm and will be difficult to remove. I'll have to debride the wound in your thigh and put in some stitches to help it heal." Engelman looked at me with concern, and I knew he was wondering if I had the strength to undergo the treatment he intended. "I will use sulfa powder on your wounds, but you must be very careful to avoid infection. You did a good job of bandaging yourself, but even my best efforts can't guarantee you won't get an infection. I'll have to give you anesthesia while I poke around in your arm, and you'll have to stay here for a couple of days so I can keep an eye on you."

"I can't stay here and put you in more danger." I desperately needed Dr. Engelman's help, but I was afraid for him. "The Gestapo think they're going to find my body in a day or two. I've only got that much time before they come around to question everyone again and search for a second time. I have to get out of the country as quickly as possible."

"And where do you think you will go when you leave? You can't possibly get out of Germany. The Gestapo can't afford for you to live and tell others what they did to your family. You have to be silenced, and until they find your dead body, they'll keep looking for you. They've already put out the rumor that your family has left Germany. I expect they will have cleaned things up inside your house, and they have a guard outside. For how long, I don't know. You can't go back there, if that's what you're thinking."

"I have money and clothes and a French passport at my house. If I'm going to make my escape, I need money and my own clothes."

"How do you happen to have a French passport? Will it

fool the Germans? Or the French? Will it fool anyone? Where will you go?"

"My father got all of us French passports a few months ago. He wanted my mother and my sisters and me to leave Germany. My mother refused to go without him, and look what good that did all of us. I can get a job on a cargo ship that's sailing someplace outside of Europe — to South America or to the United States."

"Let's get those bullet wounds healed before you start to make plans. You're not going anywhere for a few days."

"You can't keep me here. It's not safe for you or for me."

"Do you think you're the first person who's come to me with bullet wounds? I have a very secret recovery room where my special patients stay after they've had surgery and before they're able to go out into the world again. What good would it do for you to escape the Nazis and then die of sepsis? You'll stay until I decide you're out of danger."

I assured Dr. Engelman that I'd boiled the tweezers and the knife I'd used to try to remove the bullet from my arm, but he was very concerned about the way my wound looked. I took off my clothes and lay down on the narrow operating table to allow the anesthesia to take me to a place where physical pain and the pain from terrible memories couldn't touch me.

When I regained consciousness, I didn't know where I was or what day it was. Overcome at first with those familiar feelings of fear, helplessness, and anger, I didn't understand why I felt as I did. Then I remembered everything and I wept. When my thoughts cleared, I looked around the tiny recovery room. The space was just big enough to hold a mattress. I was on a bed inside a cupboard. The doctor would have to stand outside the cupboard to examine me. I drifted back to sleep.

The next time I awoke, the doctor was standing by the bed watching me. He examined my wounds and changed the bandages. He told me I was "doing nicely" and asked if I was ready to eat something. I wasn't. I was nauseated and still woozy from the ether. The doctor made me drink a few sips of water, and I fell back asleep.

I had no idea whether it was day or night when the doctor brought me some clear broth and insisted I drink it. He said I needed my strength if I was going to recover. Except for getting out of my cupboard to use the chamber pot, I slept all the time. I assumed the doctor was giving me pain medication and something to keep me resting. He brought me more substantial food, and I grew stronger. Ready to put my escape plans into effect, I demanded to know how long I'd been in the secret cupboard recovering from my wounds.

"Three days. The Gestapo have been searching the lake and will begin dragging it today to try to find your body. They've gone to all the houses and other buildings in the neighborhood and found nothing. They're convinced you're dead, but they don't understand why your body hasn't surfaced. There's still a Gestapo team watching outside your house. You can't go back there — even with a beautiful French passport waiting for you."

"I have to go to my house. My life is over if I can't escape from Germany."

"After what you've been through, I can't say you're still a boy. But please stay here one more day, and I'll help you with your escape. I agree you must leave the country. The Gestapo will come looking for you eventually, and they will come back here soon enough to search my house again."

CHAPTER SIX

THE WORLD SLEEPS

NOVEMBER 1937
NEW YORK AND LONDON

"GENTLEMEN DO NOT READ OTHER PEOPLE'S mail," was the statement made by Secretary of State Henry Stimson in 1929, and his opinion officially defined United States' policy with regard to spying during this period in history. It was a time of well-earned peace after the brutality of the Great War. The U.S. did not have a dedicated intelligence-gathering arm of government. Acquiring confidential information was delegated to the Department of State, and they learned what they could through their embassy personnel around the world. The United States Army and Navy were under the War Department in the 1930s and had understaffed intelligence departments tasked with finding out what was happening in the armies and navies of other countries. The Intelligence Division of the War Department was headed by someone with a great deal of seniority but insufficient imagination.

Jack Trevanian could hardly contain his agitation and disbelief when he read the encrypted cable Nigel Barnaby had just sent to him:

"On November 5, 1937, Hitler met secretly in Berlin with Göring and other members of the Nazi leadership. He declared to this inner circle his intentions to take European territory by force, by threatening to go to war and by actually going to war if necessary. Hitler is determined to follow through with his passionately held views about Lebensraum and his vision for the inevitable destiny of the German people. Hitler believes that the German people represent the best of Europe's Aryan race and that the confines of Germany's current borders do not allow its people to have the standard of living they deserve. He stated again that Germany's future absolutely depends on finding 'a solution to the problem of the need for living space.' Knowing that Germany's neighbors will not give up their territory willingly, Hitler has stated his intentions to take the necessary territory by force."

"This is all the proof anybody needs. Nigel, I don't know how you got this information or how you got it as quickly as you did, but this makes Hitler's intentions unequivocal. Who can possibly believe that he honestly wants peace? He doesn't, and this communique proves he doesn't. This is a crisis of the first order, but you're fully aware of that. Even over here in the land of the pacifists, there are many of us who are very worried about what's happening in Germany. Nobody in our government or in the public wants to hear about European problems, let alone wars." Jack felt strongly but acknowledged that his opinions were the minority view.

Nigel was heartened to hear Jack speak out so forcefully. Nigel didn't understand why everyone who believed in freedom wasn't alarmed by Adolf Hitler's meteoric rise, his aggression in the Rhineland, and his secret wars ... the current ones he was already fighting at home and the future ones he had in store for the rest of the world. "Your oceans have always protected you Americans. They kept you out of the Great War until 1917. Not that we in Britain are unappreciative that you finally got into it, and no one will ever deny that we couldn't have won it without you. You spent millions and paid a great price in terms of young American lives, but the cost to the United States was relatively small compared to what the British and the French sacrificed, either in treasure or in human cost."

Jack was completely on Nigel's side but felt compelled to emphasize the reality of the political climate in the U.S. "You know our military budgets and personnel have been declining since 1918. Americans accept that our intervention in Europe's difficulties was a necessary entanglement of the past, but most people on this side of the Atlantic are adamant that, from now on, Europe will have to manage its own infighting and settle its own spats. The all-pervasive view here is that we want no part of your intrigues and your troublesome bad boys. The U.S. government officially dismisses any alarmist talk about what's happening over there as 'not our problem.' I hate it that my countrymen feel this way, but they do." Jack was not proud to have to admit all of this.

"None of what you say surprises me. You Americans always have your heads in the sand and want to pretend that what's happening in the rest of the world won't affect you or is going to go away on its own. Well, it isn't going away on its own this time." Nigel wasn't angry with Jack. He was angry that neither the U.S. president nor the Congress seemed to grasp how dangerous the world was becoming.

Nigel continued. "Nobody needs an intelligence gathering organization to realize that Germany's war against its Jews began years ago. The Nuremberg laws don't leave a shred of doubt in anybody's mind about that. The Versailles Treaty and international law specifically forbid Germany to rebuild its military. MI6 has solid facts about the pace of Germany's military rearmament. With the whole world watching, Hitler is thumbing his nose at all of us and doing exactly what he wants to do. We seem powerless to do anything to stop him." Nigel didn't often sound discouraged, but today he did.

"You may be the pot calling the kettle black." Jack did not hesitate to point out to Nigel that the British had their heads in the sand, too. "Your politicians have to know, in spite of not wanting to say so publicly, that sooner or later there's going to be a war with Germany. Why do they lack the will to take a stand against the Nazis?"

"I'm fighting an uphill battle, even in my own country and even armed with overwhelming evidence of Hitler's misbehavior. Government officials in my country have chosen to ignore the growing mountain of incriminating information our intelligence services have presented to them about Hitler. Those who hold power in Britain believe, against all evidence to the contrary, that they can reason with Hitler and talk him out of imposing his will on his neighbors. I'm ashamed to have to say it, but the truth is, they believe in appeasement."

"We don't have *any* official intelligence gathering organization in the U.S. — none at all. You Brits have been in the spying business for a long time and are much more sophisticated than we are about how to collect covert information. But what good is all that, if you don't do anything with the secrets you've uncovered? If nobody is going to pay attention, is it of any use to gather more information about what's happening in the Third Reich?" Jack sounded discouraged, too.

"The Europeans continue to pretend that our latest madman isn't really mad. We refuse to believe that the world is moving inexorably toward another terrible conflict. Even if the world is in denial, it is essential that those of us who will be Germany's future enemies learn as much as possible about what Hitler is plotting. It's not a secret to anybody that Germany is rearming with breathtaking speed, but there are many specific questions that need to be answered. What new weapons is he developing, and how far along is the production of these secret terrors? How many men are the Nazis training and arming for a future war? What is the state of the German economy as a whole — its industry, its agriculture, its raw material supplies, its labor force and people? How many Germans support Hitler because they agree with his policies, and how many are silent or passively support him because they're afraid to speak out against him? Are the Nazis really rounding up Jews, intellectuals, the feeble minded, the handicapped, and the insane and holding them in camps against their will? Or worse, is Hitler destroying them in the name of purifying the Aryan race? All of these questions need answers." Nigel was passionately pleading the case to Jack, his friend who already agreed with him.

"You don't have to convince me, Nigel. You know that I'm already on the same page with you. The dilemma for me is what we can do about it. I believe that indisputable facts ought to carry the day, but then I'm a lawyer, not a spy. Since my government refuses to do any spying, I say we do some spying on our own. We go after the specific information we need to know. There have to be people who disagree with their Fuhrer and would be willing to talk to us, albeit in secret. We must connect with those individuals in positions of power and responsibility who aren't sympathetic to the Nazi cause. We especially want to meet with physics and mathematics experts who are working in the German atomic energy program. We want to talk with engineers who are working in Germany's weapons development programs — scientists who are helping Germany invent and produce the implements of the next war. We have to get to them." Jack was determined to find a way.

"It's become increasingly difficult for British Intelligence to get information out of Germany. Professors at German universities are closely watched, and many have disappeared. Scientists essential to the growing German war machine are threatened and intimidated and not allowed to leave the country. Germany and Britain are already in a psychological war, a war of wills. The Nazis have been watching British visitors for some time, and Brits are not able to move freely in Germany any more. British citizens who travel in Germany are followed and are forbidden to travel to certain areas. We're not allowed to meet with Germans who hold sensitive positions. The Germans have uncovered and executed British spies who've tried to gather intelligence about the country's intentions and war readiness. The truth is, I can't get any of my operatives into and out of Germany any more. It's going to be up to you Americans, I'm afraid."

"I agree. It is up to us. We won't have any official status, of course, and we will have to fund whatever we do out of our own pockets. That's okay. There are former members of the military and other concerned citizens who want to do something to help. We're a bunch of amateurs, but with your help, Nigel, we just might be able to pull this off. What do you think?"

"I think our efforts will be overwhelmed when we are up

against the well-organized Nazi enemy. We probably won't be able to accomplish much of anything. The truth about what is happening in Germany today cannot be discovered by ordinary means. The Nazis show the world a false face. The intentions they advertise are lies. It's a last resort to be sure, but, if you're willing to try this, I will give you all the help I can. To say I am thrilled to have you on board is an enormous understatement, my friend."

Jack was eager to share his plans with Nigel. "I am making it my urgent and immediate mission to put a group into Germany to do some snooping. I know that one or two people traveling alone, even from the United States, would be too obvious and easy to follow, and the Nazis are keeping their eyes on all non-Germans. Every contact between a foreigner and a German citizen automatically places that person under suspicion. A group is always more difficult to keep track of than one individual, and the Germans will be less suspicious of a group from the United States. We need an excuse to travel around the country. I'm determined to put a travel group together, and it will be made up of Americans."

"You're biting off a great deal with this, Jack, but your idea sounds tempting. The press and the decision-makers in both the United States and Britain are clueless. If we can show irrefutable evidence about what's going on in Germany, no one will be able to ignore the accumulating body of facts. Even if our very persuasive case does not change any minds, the wealth of information we collect will be incredibly useful once hostilities begin." Nigel was beginning to work his way out of his gloom.

"I owe you a dinner at Keen's the next time you're in New York."

"Invitation accepted."

CHAPTER SEVEN

SAVING MAX III

NOVEMBER 1937
FRANKFURT, GERMANY

D R. ENGELMAN WALKED DOWN THE STREET to Franz Hartmann's house. Before the Nuremburg Laws had taken away his medical license, Engelman had delivered Franz and Margot's two children. The doctor knew his friend Franz was willing to help when there was trouble. Engelman knocked on the door, and Franz himself answered and greeted him warmly. The doctor suggested that they take a walk around the block, and Franz stepped back inside his house to get his coat and tell his wife Margot he was going out.

As they walked, Engelman told Franz about the tragedy at the rabbi's home and that Max was at the doctor's house recovering from surgery. "He's been through a lot and is determined to make his escape from Germany. He intends to go back to his house to get the things he needs to leave the country. Is there anything you can do to help him get away?

He's a very bright young man, but his death warrant was signed when he watched the Gestapo murder his family."

"I'll do whatever I can to help. Is he strong enough to ride in my car? If he's that determined, I have a place where he can hide until he's recovered enough to leave the country. I'll be sure he's warm and has food."

"Can you drive him there tonight? The Gestapo will be back at my house soon. They may be knocking on my door at this very moment. They know I'm a doctor, and they know our young friend is hurt. When they don't find his body in the lake, the first place they'll come is my house."

"Let's go to the garage and get my car."

They parked around the corner from the doctor's house and entered through the back door. When the doctor went to his secret recovery cupboard, it was empty. "I shouldn't have left him alone. I know he went back to his house. He could collapse at any time. He's still under the influence of the pain-killing drugs I gave him, and he isn't thinking clearly."

"Where is his house? As you know, I am a Jew only by decree, and I'm sad to say I don't know where the rabbi's house is."

"You are a good Catholic Jew and a good man, whatever your religion. We'll walk to the rabbi's house the back way."

Dr. Engelman went around to the front of the Meyerhof house to see if the Gestapo guards were still in place. Two men sat in an official-looking car at the curb. Franz tried the basement door and found it unlocked. They assumed Max had entered this way and was still inside. Franz said, "Find the boy and get him to leave immediately."

Engelman entered through the basement door and climbed two flights of stairs. He found Max doubled over, about to be sick, in the darkened drawing room. The smell of death was overwhelming. A sliver of moonlight that shone through the windows enabled Dr. Engelman to see. He, too, was repulsed by the stench and the sight of copious amounts of dried, darkened blood on the floor and rugs. The Gestapo had taken the bodies away, but they'd not done a very good job of cleaning up the scene of their crimes. Someone had put cardboard over the broken window where Max had jumped to the ground below. Engelman helped Max stand up and tried to move him toward the back steps and their escape through the basement.

He couldn't turn on any lights or use a flashlight, but Max knew his way around his own house in the dark. Once his nausea had passed, he was able to move quickly in familiar territory. He pulled away from the doctor and ran to his father's library. The Gestapo hadn't found the secret compartment in the woodwork of the bookcase. The passports and the German, Swiss, and French money were all there. Max quickly stuffed everything into his knapsack, and Dr. Engelman told him they had to leave at once.

Again Max refused and hurried to his bedroom. He took a suitcase and a duffle bag from the closet and packed some clothes. He threw in cherished photographs of his family and as many other mementoes as he could take with him. When his packing was finished, he made the room look as it had before he'd arrived. The Gestapo wouldn't notice a few missing picture frames. Max and Dr. Engelman headed for the basement exit. The back stairwell was dark and steep, and they had to tread carefully.

Franz was waiting outside the basement door. It seemed as if Engelman had been in the house forever. Franz heard a car door slam and crept around the side of the house. Two Gestapo watchers were out of their car, walking toward the front door. The door was unlocked, and they pushed it open and went inside. Max and Dr. Engelman either had to hide inside the house or get out immediately. Franz was desperate to warn them, but there wasn't any time.

Max and Dr. Engelman heard the front door open and the heavy boots of the policemen stomping through the house. The rabbi's son and the doctor were almost away, and now this had happened. As they were going down the back steps, the Gestapo were going up the front stairs. They were within yards of each other. If they were caught, Max knew that he and Dr. Engelman would be killed on the spot. If they were seen, the Gestapo would know that Max hadn't died in the lake and would never stop looking for him. They had to make a break for it, but they absolutely could not betray their presence in the house. Max tapped Dr. Engelman on the shoulder and motioned for him to take off his shoes. This wasn't an easy thing to do as they stood in the middle of a steep and narrow staircase, but finally both Max and Engelman were rushing toward the basement door in their stocking feet.

When they reached the basement door, Franz was waiting for them. He grabbed the key from Max and locked the basement door behind them. Taking the heavy bags from Max, Franz urged them both to run. They went as fast as Max's condition would allow. He was limping and slow and struggled to keep up with the two older men. Dr. Engelman put his arm around Max's waist and dragged him along, as they made their way back through the neighborhood yards and gardens to Franz's car.

"Get into the boot of the car. Hurry!" Franz told the boy.

"I have to go back to the house where I was hiding. I have to bury my bloody clothes and bandages and the cans and jars I left. I have to get rid of the rags that are covered with blood. I made myself a bed in the upstairs closet, and the Gestapo will know I'm still alive if they find any evidence that I was staying there."

"The most important thing right now is for you to get as far away from this neighborhood as you can. If the Gestapo realize you've been back to your house, they will come looking for you with tracking dogs and lots of men. Do you have a key to the house where you were hiding? Tell me the address, and I will get rid of any traces that you were ever there. I'll do it tonight."

The boy was relieved to have Franz's offer of help. "The Gestapo will never know I was inside my house. I was very careful to leave everything as I found it." Too weak to argue with Franz and Dr. Engelman any longer, Max needed their help to climb into the boot of the Mercedes. Franz drove them to a very different part of Frankfurt, a neighborhood where neither the boy nor the doctor had ever been before.

Whenever Franz went to the room he rented under the false name of Theo Stocker, he always changed into his railway worker's uniform. Because the room had a separate entrance to the outside, he very rarely saw his elderly landlady. He was scrupulously careful to keep his alternative identity intact, but tonight Franz decided he didn't have time to change into his disguise. He had to risk smuggling Max into the room as quickly as possible. With the doctor in the passenger seat and Max in the boot of his car, Franz drove as close as he could to the back alley entrance of his rented room. He unlocked the boot, and he and Engelman helped Max climb out. The boy was pale and weak, and they had to carry him inside. Fortunately, there were no steps, and Max immediately collapsed on the hard mattress of the cot in Theo Stocker's very humble home.

"Max, you must listen to me carefully. You're staying in a room I have rented under a false name, the name of Theo Stocker. You will need to remain here for several days. You cannot answer the door under any circumstances. The landlady is almost blind and hardly ever bothers to come to the room. If she knocks on the door, tell her you're ill, and she can't come in. The rent is paid ahead, and that's all she really cares about. There should be no reason for her to want to talk to you. The only thing that could get her attention is that I'm almost never here, and she might notice that there's someone staying in the room. I expect she'll leave you alone, but don't open either the door to the hall or the door to the alley for any reason. I'll give Dr. Engelman a key to the alley door, and he will always use that door to come and go. I will come back later to check on you and bring you food, and I will always enter by the alley door, too. Do you understand what I'm saying to you?"

"I won't answer either door, and you and the doctor will come to see me through the alleyway door. Thank you for hiding me, Mr. Stocker. I will recover quickly and leave your room as soon as I can."

"You may stay as long as you need to. Just don't answer the door. Dr. Engelman and I will return in a few hours with medical supplies and food. Don't leave the room for any reason. There are crackers and some cans of soup. I will bring real food later. Give me the address and the key to the house where you've been staying."

Max searched for the key in his pocket. He told Franz he didn't know the exact address of the house by the lake, but he described its location. He told Franz he'd pushed the bundle of blood-soaked rags and clothes under the kitchen stove with the empty food tins and jars. Franz promised to bury it all in the garden. He promised to get rid of the makeshift bed Max had made for himself in the second floor bedroom closet. When Franz had assured Max that all traces of his presence would be removed from the house, Max fell asleep.

Two hours later, Franz and Engelman returned. Franz

brought a large basket of food to the room, and Dr. Engelman arrived with his doctor's bag of bandages and antiseptics and other supplies. Engelman was worried about Max's arm. Franz unpacked the basket of food and set it out on the table. There was half a roasted chicken, slices of ham, homemade bread rolls, two kinds of cheese, apples, pears, some boiled eggs, and a large wedge of chocolate cake.

Max was barely able to sit up on the bed while the doctor changed his bandages. As soon as the doctor finished wrapping his leg, Max hobbled to the table and grabbed at the chicken like a starving man. With his mouth full of food, he apologized for his bad manners. Neither the doctor nor Franz cared about his manners. They were delighted that Max was feeling well enough to eat.

The doctor gave Max an injection and told him he was going to have to lance and drain the infected wound in his arm. Engelman cleaned out the pus, cut away the dead tissue, and taped the wound back together.

One of Theo Stocker's landlady's rules for renting the room was that there was never to be any trash or garbage left there. Every tenant was responsible for getting rid of his or her own refuse. Franz gathered the used bandages and the other garbage. There was more than enough food for Max, so Franz and Dr. Engelman left him alone for the night. It was very early in the morning, and both men were exhausted as they slipped out the back door into the alley. Franz drove the doctor home and then made his way to the house where Max had been hiding.

CHAPTER EIGHT

CONVINCING VEERE

NOVEMBER 1937
NEW YORK

JACK TREVANIAN'S CHILDHOOD FRIEND, DR. W.D. "Billy" Veere, was a professor at Columbia University. Columbia enjoyed an excellent academic reputation, and any group sponsored by the school would be held in high regard. Billy Veere was a well-known researcher, author, and world expert on the subject of teaching mathematics. He knew Germany and had traveled there several times with student groups. After his last trip, he'd sworn he would not return as long as the Nazis were in control of the country.

"I'm not going back. I've already told you that. It's dangerous, and it's too depressing for so many reasons. Two good friends, one at Freiburg and one at Tubingen, have been dismissed for their political views. The professor from Freiburg has now disappeared completely. He would have been the first to speak out against the growing militarism and repression. I suspect he said or did something the Nazis didn't like, and they've put him in a camp or killed him. As of 1935, all of my Jewish colleagues, many brilliant mathematicians and physicists among them, have lost their jobs at German institutions of higher learning. I've heard that 'special camps' for intellectuals and socialists are bursting at the seams. The Nazis are building more as fast as they can. I'm sorry, but my answer is 'no.' The summer of 1938 is definitely not the time to be taking a tour group to Germany. It's foolhardy to even think of doing such a thing."

Jack didn't give up easily. "I'm going to be shameless and appeal to your patriotism and overwhelm you with reasons why you must do this for your country and for the free world. It's an emergency, and you are one of the few people with the credentials and the skills to lead this group. It's vital that we get an information-gathering unit of some kind into Germany as soon as possible. The U.S. has no official intelligence agency, and we are essentially deaf, dumb, and blind when it comes to what is happening in the Third Reich right now." Jack told Billy Veere everything he knew and used all his powers of persuasion to convince his friend.

"But I'm not a spy. I'm just a college professor. You are asking me to do things about which I know absolutely nothing. I know about teaching mathematics. I don't know about your world of cloak and dagger."

"Don't worry too much about that part of it. You are absolutely critical to our plan. Besides your knowledge of Germany and your experience leading study groups over there, you know Franklin Roosevelt. Roosevelt respects your opinion. If you come back from a trip to Germany with the facts, Franklin will listen to you. Your abilities to organize and lead the trip are vital, but your credibility with the most important man in the world makes you indispensable. He will believe the information you bring him, and you will participate in the debriefing we will give to the U.S. President after the trip."

Billy Veere told Jack Trevanian repeatedly that he would not participate in what he considered a dangerous undertaking. But few could stand up to Jack Trevanian when he put on the full-court press. He shared with Billy the classified documents that Nigel Barnaby had sent to him. If Nigel ever found out what Jack had revealed to Billy, Nigel would be furious. In addition to the patriotic card, Jack played the guilt-trip card. Billy Veere had planned to spend his summer on the coast of Maine writing a book. Reluctantly and begrudgingly, he became convinced of the urgency of the situation and agreed to organize and lead a tour group to Germany.

Once Veere was on board, he insisted on being in charge of working out the details and practicalities of the trip. He told Jack frankly that he feared it would be difficult to get permission to take a study group to Germany. "I'm certain the Germans will never allow us to bring in a group of men to tour their country, so we're not even going to try that. A group of women teachers will be much less conspicuous and will be viewed by the Nazis as less intimidating than a group of men would be. The ministry with which we will be working to arrange the trip believes, mistakenly of course, that women, even mathematicians and teachers, are not as smart or as observant as their male counterparts. These misogynistic opinions are completely erroneous but will work to our advantage. For several reasons, we will be sending only women."

"I hear what you are saying, and I tend to agree with you. But I'm going to have to think about this and get myself used to the idea that the group will be made up of women." Jack, who was almost always very sure about everything, was having some trouble coming around to Billy Veere's point of view. He knew Veere was right, but Jack was worried about what Nigel Barnaby would have to say.

Billy Veere outlined his plan. "We will select only single women, and all of them will be mathematics teachers. Each woman will be required to have several years of teaching experience. The study group 'curriculum' and itinerary of professorial lectures will lend itself to making contact with mathematicians, physicists, engineers, and others knowledgeable about weapons innovation and rearmament. Our group of women will be able to travel around Germany, visit German universities, and interact with scientific experts who have the information you're so eager to get."

Jack explained to Billy that some of the members of the group would be assigned covert roles. "Not all of the women will have secret responsibilities. Those who don't have special assignments will serve as 'cover' for the group. Those who are cover are just as vital to the success of the mission. They will be exactly the mathematics teachers they appear to be, and their only motivation for joining the group is to learn mathematics and to travel."

Taking all of this into consideration, Billy Veere realized that in order to get exactly the right individuals as well as a group that was composed of a satisfactory combination of teachers, they would have to offer incentives. "We will give master's degree credits to all who participate in the tour. Each woman who wins a spot in the group will be on a scholarship."

Jack enthusiastically supported his friend's suggestions. "All expenses will be paid, presumably by Columbia University. In reality, much of the cost of the trip will be covered by me and my network of wealthy American patriots who agree that Hitler is a threat to the entire world, not just to Europe."

Dr. Billy Veere, using his own considerable powers of persuasion, was able to convince Jack Trevanian that their best chance for success was to select women for their tour group. "Who will suspect a group of female mathematics teachers of being spies? Much can be learned during informal conversations at lunches and cocktails and during breaks between the talks. Some members of the group will be in place to gather intelligence, but most of the members will be as advertised, nothing more than the mathematics teachers they claimed to be. To me, our group of women teachers seems like almost perfect camouflage."

Jack was worried. "Quite frankly, I don't know why they would allow us to send anyone at all. My best guess is that there must be some people in power who are misguided and believe that the United States could be persuaded to enter into a future conflict on the side of the Nazis."

"That's ridiculous, of course, but if they think that, so much the better. It won't be an easy thing to get permission from the Nazi government for us to make this trip. There's the ever-present and almost insurmountable mountain of paperwork, as well as the many restrictions the Nazis will put on everything, including the composition of the tour group. If the group is allowed to travel to Germany, we will be told where we can travel and what we can see."

In spite of the fact that the number of Billy Veere's friends and colleagues who worked at German universities had dwindled, a few of his contacts from the days of the Weimar Republic had been able to hang onto some important positions in the Nazi government. Bernhard Rust was the current Nazi Minister of Science, Education, and National Culture, the Reichserziehungsminister. This was the Ministry that would give the thumbs up or thumbs down for Veere's tour to go ahead. Rust was a former school administrator with whom Veere had enjoyed a passing acquaintance years earlier.

Once Billy Veere was on board and convinced of the

importance of taking a group to Germany, he was determined to make it happen. "I am going to use all of my prestige and influence to make the trip a reality." He appealed to the political vanity of Minister Bernard Rust and spun a convincing yarn about how important it was for Germany to present a positive image to the world. It took considerable guile to convince the Nazi Education Ministry that this trip could be a real "coup" for Germany. Veere stressed the value such a trip could have for influencing public opinion in the United States.

Veere's advocacy for his group finally paid off. In the end, the ministry was convinced it was important to make a good impression on the Americans. There were enough people in the German political hierarchy who believed that the Americans would stay neutral in a war or even come into the war on the side of Germany. For some within the Third Reich, who were helping to get the okay for the Columbia study group to come to Germany, the United States was still a plum to be harvested in the upcoming global conflict. Someone within the bureaucratic maze eventually made the decision that it was important to show these female Yanks the best of what Germany had to offer. Negative impressions would be avoided.

The Nazis placed many restrictions on the members of the tour group. There were rigid guidelines regarding the women's backgrounds. These limitations would complicate the process of selecting the participants. "I don't like all these rules and restrictions one bit." Jack Trevanian never liked being told what to do.

"I don't like it either, but if we're going to receive permission to travel through Germany, we have to accept their conditions. That's the price of admission." Veere had been in Germany in 1936 and had run into the Nazi's oppressive regulations then. The German government's ridiculous directives were one major reason Veere had vowed not to return until the Nazis were out of power. "Of course, they know I speak German, but they have definitely said that no one else in the group can know how to speak, understand, or read German. As with every group that travels to Germany these days, a government 'guide' and translator will be provided. He will accompany us at all times, wherever we go. He's really a Nazi 'minder' — a Nazi assigned to spy on us and report back everything that is said and done. This is the worst of their rules, but we don't have a choice."

"What are they afraid we will see? It's downright creepy, I think, to make us have a pretend guide, who in fact is spying on us all the time." Jack definitely did not like the idea of having a Nazi minder.

"It's creepy all right, but I can deal with that problem. Your job is to lay out all of this for Nigel Barnaby and convince *him* that the traveling group of female mathematics teachers will work as a cover for the intelligence gathering activities he has in mind."

Jack knew Nigel Barnaby would scream bloody murder about the female composition of the study group. "It won't be easy, but I think I'll be able to talk sense into Nigel Barnaby on the women issue. It's hard for Nigel not to be running the whole show. He can't be in the field this time, and he hates that." Jack explained to Billy Veere why it was so important to keep Nigel Barnaby's role in their venture under wraps. "Barnaby can't be connected with this American group in any way. You are our front man, and Nigel and I will advise you. But we have to stay in the background, out of sight. The Nazis know Nigel is MI6, and he's not welcome in Germany. There can be no inkling that Barnaby has any association with the Columbia group. The trip will never get off the ground if the Germans have the slightest suspicion that Barnaby is involved. Because I'm known to be a friend of Nigel's, I am also suspect. I cannot participate openly in the project either." Billy Veere nodded his understanding. He was now completely committed and would do everything he could to be certain the trip went forward.

CHAPTER NINE

SAVING MAX IV

NOVEMBER 1937
FRANKFURT, GERMANY

W HEN FRANZ AND DR. ENGELMAN WENT to Theo Stocker's room the next night, they found Max delirious with fever. Dr. Engelman tried to rouse him. "Max, Max, can you hear me? Tell me you can understand what I'm saying."

Max could only mumble a few incoherent words. He was in and out of consciousness, and Franz was alarmed to see how worried Dr. Engelman was.

"Is he going to be all right?" Franz asked.

"I don't know. He's critically ill and should be in hospital. Max has systemic sepsis. The sulfa powder I've been putting directly on his wounds hasn't been sufficient to prevent infection from spreading throughout his body. I'm going to have to treat him with sulfanilamide pills. Prontosil is a relatively new drug, a sulfa-based wonder drug produced by the pharmaceutical company Bayer."

"Will the Prontosil work? Can it fight the infection and save Max's life." In just a few days, Franz had become emotionally invested in saving Max. He'd grown fond of the brave young man.

"I don't know if it will work or not, but it's his only hope. Nothing else has a chance of combating his septicemia. I have to treat Max with Prontosil, but the drug has serious side effects that can be extremely dangerous, even fatal. He might be allergic to Prontosil. Some people are. He could easily die, you know, either from the side effects of the drug or if the drug doesn't work."

"How were you able to get hold of this miracle drug? I've never heard of it."

"It isn't easy to get. Because I'm a Jew and can no longer practice medicine legally, I can't get life-saving drugs like Prontosil for my patients. I have to depend on the kindness and generosity of my non-Jewish physician colleagues to supply me with what I need — the sulfa powders, the drugs, everything. They want to help, but these new drugs are in short supply. Those who are willing to share what they have are putting their lives in danger by assisting me. I don't have enough of the medication to save Max, and if Max is to have any hope of surviving this, I'll have to go begging from physician to physician, asking for just a little bit more Prontosil from each one. "

"What can I do to help? Is there any way I can get the drugs for you?"

"No, I don't want you to be involved in this. I know what to do. Once I begin giving him the medication, I'll have to stay here with him to be sure there are no adverse reactions. I want to determine if the Prontosil is working. I'm going to spend the night here tonight and for as long as it takes. I've not come this far to give up trying to save the life of the rabbi's son. You go on home. I don't want Margot to become more suspicious than she already is."

"I have a confession to make. I wasn't going to tell Margot anything about what is going on, but she asked me last night about the food that's been disappearing from the house. The cook complained to Margot that food she thought she had in the larder was missing when she went to get it."

"I'm not surprised Margot and the cook noticed the missing food. Margot keeps a close watch on everything."

"She said she knows I have something going on at night, something I'm not sharing with her. Margot knows nothing about this room or anything at all about Theo Stocker. I'll tell her everything about Max once he's made his escape from Germany. I hate lying to her, but for now, I've told her that some friends have fallen on hard times. I told her I was taking food to them to help out, and she seemed satisfied with that explanation. She said she would smooth things over with the cook." Franz paused. He needed to share his concerns with Dr. Engelman. "When we married, Margot and I promised we would never lie to each other. What has happened in Germany in recent years has forced me to tell her many lies and keep many secrets from her. I wonder if I will ever be able to live with the guilt of that."

"The Nazis have forced all of us to live lives filled with deceit. I know God will forgive you for the lies, but I can't say what Margot will do." Dr. Engleman smiled a faintly sympathetic smile at the disheartened Franz.

Engelman spent the night applying cold compresses to Max's body to keep his fever down. The doctor slept off and on, dozing in the one comfortable chair in the room. He heated water on Theo Stocker's hot plate to make tea for himself and Max. Franz had made sure there was plenty of tea and sugar and arrived the following evening with two additional baskets of food. He included some bottles of wine from his own well-stocked wine cellar. He brought a box of chocolates and some other special foods for Max and the doctor.

Although Engelman couldn't say yet whether or not Max was responding to the Prontosil, Max was conscious for brief periods. Franz spoke to Max but wasn't sure if Max understood what he'd told him. "I've been to the house by the lake, where you were hiding after you were shot. I found the blood-soaked rags and soiled bandages and your dirty clothes. I buried everything in the backyard with the empty tins and jars." Franz paused to see if Max had heard him.

Max was so ill, so pale, lying on the narrow cot. Franz wondered if the vulnerable young man would have the strength to make it through his illness. Even if he recovered physically, Franz doubted he could he ever recover from the psychological trauma the Nazis had inflicted on him. "I went from room to room to be sure I'd removed all traces that you were ever there. I put the bedding away that you'd arranged in the closet and left everything exactly as you found it. No one will suspect a thing. I locked the door and put the key under a planter in the garden." Max was not fully aware, but Franz thought he detected a slight sigh of relief when he told Max that he had taken care of everything.

Max's voice was a raspy whisper, and Franz had to bend over the cot to hear what he was saying. "Thank you Mr. Stocker. For going to the house and cleaning up my messes."

After several days, Max's color had improved, and his temperature was down. He appeared to be responding to the Prontosil. He was awake more and more every day and finally began to eat again. Once Max was out of danger, the doctor went back to his own home to sleep at night. He brought clean bandages and antiseptics twice a day to care for Max's wounds.

Finally, Dr. Engelman said the words Franz had been waiting to hear. "I'm pretty sure Max will be able to travel next week."

Knowing the Gestapo would come to his house sooner or later, Engelman told Franz that he'd decided to leave Germany with Max. "Even though I'm confident Max is going to live, he's not strong, and he has several painful months of recovery and rehabilitation ahead of him. He needs someone to care for him until he is back on his feet. My own days in Germany are numbered. I've been officially forbidden to practice medicine since 1935, but I'm certain the Gestapo know I'm still treating patients. One day they will knock down my door, tear my house apart, and find my secret surgery and hidden recovery cupboard. I'll be arrested and taken to a camp. It's just a matter of time before that happens. This is no longer the country I once loved so dearly. It's time for me to leave. I am not welcome in my own homeland." Tears ran down Dr. Engelman's face as he told Franz he had decided to leave Germany.

Max had brought with him all the French passports his father had secretly purchased months earlier. Engelman hoped to use the rabbi's passport to escape from inevitable death at the hands of the Nazis. "I don't look anything like the photo on the passport the rabbi purchased for himself, but I'm determined to make it work. It's my only chance. I'm about the age of the rabbi, and with some alterations to the passport and if no one looks at it very carefully, it might pass muster. I want to go to England or Scotland. I want to live someplace where I can openly practice my profession again."

Max wanted to join the crew of a cargo ship and get as far away from Germany as he could. Franz had already been working on a plan to get them out of the country.

Franz's wife Margot was French, and the Hartmanns had friends and resources in France. Franz arranged for a Citroën with French license plates and registration to be driven to Frankfurt. Dr. Engelman and Max were going to leave Germany as two Frenchmen, father and son, so it made sense to have a French car.

CHAPTER TEN

SAVING MAX V

DECEMBER 1937
ON THE ROAD TO AACHEN

ON THE NIGHT MAX AND DR. ENGELMAN were planning to leave the country, Franz parked the car behind Theo Stocker's room. Leaving most of his worldly possessions behind in his Frankfurt house, Dr. Engelman had packed his precious medical instruments, a bag of gold coins, and some important keepsakes he wanted to take away with him. Franz had removed the rear seat of the Citroën and hidden the doctor's valuables in the empty space. The car would be searched at the border, and hopefully, no one would know that the "Frenchman" who was driving the French car was a German doctor.

Max was using a crutch under his left arm, and his right arm was in a sling. Tendons and muscle tissue had been damaged by the Gestapo bullet as well as by Max's crude attempts to remove the bullet from his arm with a kitchen knife. He would need months of therapy if he hoped to be

60

able to use his arm normally again. Engelman helped Max put on his winter coat. During Max's illness, Dr. Engelman had grown very protective of Max. Engelman had never married or had any children, and Max was now without a family. Dr. Engelman regarded Max almost as an adopted son. Engelman was determined that this young man who had suffered so terribly was going to have a future.

They gathered up the leftover food to take with them and collected the trash. When they left, Theo Stocker's room looked exactly as it had the night Dr. Engelman and Franz had arrived with their very sick patient.

Both Max and the doctor had warm clothes and several kinds of money. They prayed they would be able to use their French passports to get out of Germany. The doctor's French was not very good, but Max's was excellent. Max's mother had taught French at a private academy for girls before she was fired from her job because she was Jewish. She'd made sure that Max and his sisters learned French from the time they were young children, and they'd all spoken it fluently. Max's father's second language was English, and he spoke English often with his children. The rabbi had loved to read biographies in English, theology, and American detective stories. Now Max was the only one in the Meyerhof family left to speak French or English or any language at all. Max was confident he could convince a German border guard that he was really a young Frenchman.

Dr. Engelman and Franz hoped that the hunt for Max had not spread very far outside Frankfurt. "Even though they haven't found his body, the Gestapo think Max drowned in the lake or bled to death. They don't know the rabbi's son has had people helping him. If they believe he's still alive, they think he's on his own." Franz was more confident than the doctor was.

They considered various escape routes and decided the best chance was for Max and the doctor to leave Germany for Belgium at the border crossing south of Aachen. If they could get into Belgium, the doctor had friends there who would help them with the next stages of their journey.

Max's passport was perfect. The doctor's passport had been carefully altered. Because it was a French passport, they were hoping the German border guards wouldn't be looking at every detail like they would if it were a German passport. The passports had all of the correct entry and exit stamps. Max's father had paid handsomely to be sure the papers were in order.

They planned to arrive at the German-Belgian border late at night. Darkness would make a close comparison with their passport photos more difficult, and the alterations in the doctor's passport would be less likely to be noticed. Their story was that they'd been in Koln for the funeral of Max's cousin, the older man's niece. They were returning to their home in France. Max's elderly grandmother was quite ill. It was a plausible story. If the Gestapo expected Max to be traveling alone, Dr. Engelman's presence as his father provided camouflage. If the Gestapo was looking for Max all over Germany or even in the western part of Germany, they could be in trouble. They were counting on the fact that a missing rabbi's son, who had probably drowned in a lake in Frankfurt three weeks previously, was now old news.

The weather conspired to make driving on this December night difficult, even without the Nazis to worry about. It was cold and snowing hard, long before they reached Aachen. Unfortunately, before they arrived at the border crossing, their car slid off the road and got stuck in the snow. An accident was the last thing they needed. German patrols were everywhere, on all the roads, especially at night and near the border.

Max wasn't strong enough to dig the car out of the snow. Dr. Engelman was a physician, and he'd never had to dig a car out of the snow. They didn't even have a snow shovel. The snow was coming down thick and fast as Dr. Engelman desperately tried to get the car back on the road.

As he struggled to free the motorcar, a truck full of German military men approached them on the snowy roadway. They weren't Gestapo, just a rowdy bunch of foot soldiers who'd been out drinking and were on their way home to their barracks for the night. They stopped and asked Engelman and Max if they needed help. They were shouting in German at the stranded motorists, and Engelman quickly made the decision that since they had a French car stuck in the snow, they would have to act like Frenchmen. The Germans don't like the French, and the French don't like the Germans. But maybe these drunken fellows would overlook that fact and give them a tow out of the ditch.

Max spoke German as he imagined a Frenchman would. "Hello, we have run off the road and can't get our motorcar going again. Can you give us a tow?"

"What are you doing here, you and the old man?" One of the tipsy soldiers was curious about why they were out in a snow storm so late at night.

"We've been to my cousin's funeral in Koln and are heading for Belgium. We weren't expecting snow and don't have a snow shovel."

A few of the soldiers were sober enough to make a decision and had a brief conference. Max's heart was pounding in his chest, and Dr. Engelman's face was ashen as he sat, silent as a stone, in the driver's seat. Several of the Germans climbed out of the truck and got behind the car. They were whooping and hollering with glee as they slipped and slid through the snow, in and out of the ditch. It was an adventure for them, a continuation of the boisterous fun that had begun in the beer hall a few hours earlier.

"What's wrong with the old man?" One of the soldiers called out. "Why doesn't he talk?"

"He's hard of hearing. I mostly have to tell him what people are saying with sign language." This answer from Max seemed to satisfy their curiosity about Engelman's failure to speak.

After much noisy horseplay and falling down in the snow, the car was pushed back onto the roadway. Max waved and shouted his thanks to the drunken bunch as Dr. Engelman guided the car slowly down the road, heading for their next challenge, the border crossing at Aachen.

There were no other cars at the border. They drove up to the crossing as if they were arriving from Koln and positioned the Citroën so the guards would have to approach the passenger side of the car. Max did the talking and conversed with the border guards in French-accented German, trying to sound like he imagined a native French speaker would sound to these German guards. He'd already practiced his accent with the truck full of German soldiers. As frightening as the encounter had been, it had built Max's confidence that he could pass himself off as a Frenchman.

"Passports, please. Where are you going? Why are you driving on this dark road in the middle of the night? It's snowing like hell, in case you hadn't noticed. You could easily skid off the road and get stuck in a ditch." The border guard was not polite.

"We've been to a funeral in Koln and are trying to reach Belgium tonight. My grandmother is very ill with pneumonia in France, and she may not live long enough for us to reach her to say goodbye. We would have preferred not to travel in this terrible weather, but we didn't have a choice." Max's heart was pounding in his chest. He had already used his cover story with the drunken foot soldiers, and it sounded more believable the second time around. Max tried not to hold his breath. He was cold and weak and terribly afraid, but he put on a good show for the German guards.

One of the guards took their passports into the border shed. This unexpected move alarmed Max and the doctor because it meant their passports were going to be examined under brighter lights.

The guard seemed as if he was gone a long time, but he eventually returned without the passports and asked to see what was in the boot of the car. Unless the guards took the car apart, they wouldn't find Engelman's medical instruments and valuables that were hidden under the car's back seat. Max and Engelman had been careful to put only valises and rucksacks in the boot, and when the guards searched their bags, they found nothing but clothes and toiletries. There were two bottles of good French wine that Franz had left on the back seat with the basket of food. One of the guards picked up the bottles of wine and exclaimed over the vintage.

"You are welcome to the wine." Max joked, "When we get back home, we will have more excellent wine to choose from, and we'll never miss those two bottles." One guard laughed, and the other frowned as though the comment was somehow disparaging to German wine. Both guards were happy enough to accept the gift. A third guard came out of the shed, bringing the two French passports. He handed them to Max, leaned into the car, and eyed Dr. Engelman's face with suspicion. When the guard began scrutinizing the doctor, Max was sure they'd been found out and would be arrested momentarily. He wondered if he had the strength to run into the nearby woods. He would be outnumbered. He knew he did not have the stamina to get away but decided he would rather freeze to death in the snow than to give up and go quietly to a German death camp.

To their shock and surprise, the guards raised the barricades and waved Dr. Engelman and Max through. They were on their way to Belgium. The two Jews who had just escaped death at the hands of the Nazis, glanced at each other as the barrier of the German border came down behind their car. Although they were too exhausted to say much, the look of relief and joy that passed between them said more than words could express. At that moment, they knew they'd made it. They would have another chance at life. They passed through Belgian border control without any trouble and headed for their hotel in Liege. They were free men at last.

Dr. Engelman and Max stayed at the hotel for a week and then moved to a small rental house outside the city. Dr. Engelman had connections in the medical community and hired a physical therapy specialist to work with Max to restore full use of his leg and to improve his ability to use his right arm. Because of nerve damage, Max's arm would never be fully functional.

Dr. Engelman arranged for Max to legally change his name. It was a security precaution. The doctor made plans to move to England and set up a medical practice there. Max made some inquiries about a position on a ship that traveled to the United States and South America. He knew he had a very long way to go in terms of his recovery, before he could hope to go to sea. Max accepted that he would always walk with a limp. He knew he couldn't establish a new life or begin to work against the Nazis until he he'd regained his strength and rebuilt his stamina. He grieved for his lost family, and he'd not forgotten his vow to avenge the deaths of his loved ones.

CHAPTER ELEVEN

DINNER AT KEENS

DECEMBER 1937
NEW YORK

"WHY ARE WE DOING THIS? YOU'RE ASKING *me* why we're doing this? You know *exactly* why we're doing it. We don't have any MI5 or MI6 or Room 40 or any of that other fancy folderol that you Brits have," Jack Trevanian punctuated his words with a shrimp fork fully armed with a shrimp and a copious amount of cocktail sauce.

"Jack, how many times have I told you we can't get any of our own 'fancy folderol' or anybody else into Germany these days," Nigel Barnaby wasn't really upset with his friend, although he was quite angry with a lot of other people in the world. "The Gestapo has every one of our embassy and consular people under observation at all times, and I do mean at all times. Telephones, houses, hotel rooms, and tables in restaurants — all are bugged. Every foreigner who enters the country has minders and watchers with him or her, all day every day, all night every night — from the minute they cross the border into Germany until the minute they leave. We tried to send in a man from Budapest last week. All he had to do was take the train to Frankfurt, pick up a package in the station's left luggage department, get back on the train, and travel on to France. He'd made this same trip many times in the past, but this time he got off the train and never got back on. His body was found in the river the next day."

"My God! Do you have a mole someplace? It's that Philby fellow. I know it. I met him once and didn't like his shifty eyes. Everybody knows he's a socialist and a communist and is married to a communist woman. He's a Bolshevik, for God's sake, even if he is against Hitler. Why do you trust him? "

"Kim Philby isn't the point, and we don't need a mole. The Nazis have eyes and ears everywhere — in cities and small towns and at all stops in between. Their border people are secret police, and they're taking down every name. We're paralyzed."

"Isn't that exactly why we're organizing this travel group?" Jack dug into his salad with gusto. "Come on, Nigel, I'm paying for this meal, and I'm not paying for it if you don't eat it."

"All you Americans think about is food." Jack started to interrupt, but Nigel wouldn't let him. "And don't even think of making any remarks about British food."

"You're the one getting defensive. I never said a word ...."

"Let's get back to the subject at hand." Nigel was losing his patience. "What makes you think a busload of old maid school teachers is going to accomplish what none of our professional intelligence services can accomplish? I agree it has to be Americans, but why does it have to be women?"

"I had one heck of a time convincing Billy Veere to take on this project, and it was his idea to use women."

"These women are amateurs. We need professionally trained people in the group, and there aren't many well-trained women spies sitting around waiting to go to Germany for the summer. There might be some British women spies, but I seriously doubt if you could find even one American woman who has been trained to be a spy."

"You make my point exactly. Who would ever suspect these middle-aged women of spying? And most of the group will be exactly what we say they are — spinster mathematics teachers. No one can deny that fact. They will be traveling around the country, learning from famous mathematicians and scientists at German universities. Columbia is a very well-respected institution, and these women really will be earning graduate level course credits. For all intents and purposes, this is a legitimate trip. And, Nigel, you might be surprised who I can turn up, in the spy category, when I really need to." Jack cut into his enormous rare T-bone steak, blood seeping from it as he stabbed a piece of meat.

Jack had more to say. "Why do you order roast beef here? Don't you get enough of it in England? And what the heck does your Prime Minister Chamberlain think he's doing? He's acting like a Frenchman or a yellow-bellied sap sucker. He's acting like he's a member of the Labor Party, not a Tory."

Nigel glared at Jack, "I like roast beef, and it's nicely prepared here. And, you know I've never have been a fan of Neville Chamberlain."

"I'm just pulling your leg, Nigel. Enjoy your roast beef. Uncle Sam doesn't know he's paying for this dinner, but he is."

Nigel's voice changed, and he became somber. "There's something I need to talk over with you, something that has been weighing on my mind for some time." Nigel paused until he was certain he had Jack's full attention. "My sons will reach their eighteenth birthdays next year. Chester is reading classics at Cambridge, and Charles is reading history at Oxford. They are terribly bright and thoroughly good young men. You know them and what good lads they've turned out to be. They are my last human link to Portia. I would die for them."

Nigel continued. "I think the world stumbled into the Great War without giving it the critical and deliberate consideration that a decision to go to war must always demand. An enormous amount of thought has to precede such a decision. I don't want the world to stumble into another war. You and I are working very hard to convince the leaders of our countries that war with Germany is inevitable. We know we will eventually have to fight a war against Hitler. I feel more strongly about this than I've ever felt about anything in my life. I know my own sons will join the war effort when the time comes. I could be selfish and try to keep them out of it. I have the clout to find them safe positions where they could participate in the war effort but avoid the shooting. But I would never do that. To interfere in their lives and deny them the opportunity to choose their own destinies would go against everything I believe in. In advocating for another war, a horrible war in which thousands of young lives will be lost on both sides, I must be able to say to myself that I'm willing to have my sons die fighting *this* war to destroy *this* enemy. Only by being willing to sacrifice my own precious children can I argue in favor of a war and try to convince others to make the decision to send their own beloved sons to die."

Jack remained silent.

Nigel continued. "When I was a young man, I had a friend who was a poet. I still remember a poem she wrote about peace. It was a naive poem, a kind of argument or negotiation with God about promising each other things. She would live a certain kind of life and do certain things if God would promise her there would be no more war. It expressed the idealism of the very young and was not a particularly good poem, but two lines have stuck with me all these years. 'Give me no sons to send away to die. Give me no daughters who stay at home and cry.' One does not bargain with God, Jack, but I know to the depths of my being that I will send my sons away to die to bring down this madman."

Jack hesitated before he said anything. "I don't have children, so I can't begin to fathom the sacrifice you're willing to make to fight this fight. I do understand how deeply you believe that this war must be fought, and I am with you all the way. Nothing else I ever do in my life will matter as much as this matters."

They were both quiet, trying to find a way to turn the conversation back to the practicalities of what was ahead.

Jack broke the silence. "Speaking of going to war, I'm incensed that the Japanese sank the *Panay*. Bombing an American gunboat would be an act of war under any other President. I know the Empire apologized and said it was all a big mistake. Does anybody really believe that? I sure don't, and the American people don't believe it was an accident either. 'Bull Roar' is all I have to say about that apology! I'm very discouraged that Franklin let it go without more of a fuss."

"He has to pick his battles, and the timetable in which to fight them. He's not ready yet. Unfortunately, it's a fact that none of us are ready yet. That's why this mission is so important. We have to show the world that the Nazis are getting ready and the rest of the world needs to get ready, too. Now, tell me what I can do to help."

The two men continued to talk late into the evening. The fire in the fireplace that had brightened their dinner on this cold and snowy December night was now embers in the grate. Nigel returned his small notebook to his jacket pocket, put on his elegantly tailored overcoat, and left the steak house. He walked down the narrow back steps from the Lambs Room, which tonight had been their own private dining room, and exited unobserved through the restaurant's side door.

It had started to snow in earnest and would be inches deep by morning. The limo waiting down the street pulled up to the curb and drove Sir Nigel Barnaby to a nondescript apartment at 34 East Sixty-second Street in New York City, known to those who visited there as The Room. After a brief meeting with several members of this cloak-and-dagger group which prized the clandestine and the secret, Nigel Barnaby's car drove him to Grand Central Station. He was heading for Washington, D.C.

Jack Trevanian hailed a cab and went home to his New York brownstone, pleased with the results of his meeting with Nigel Barnaby. Jack had a good idea about how they could execute their plans and now thought they had a better chance of success. In spite of his feelings of satisfaction and optimism, there was always that something at the back of his mind that nagged at him. He hoped he wasn't getting in over his head.

CHAPTER TWELVE

CHANCE
OF A LIFETIME

FEBRUARY 1938
ATHENS, OHIO AND BELMONT, OHIO

D R. CUTTER, GENEVA BURKHART'S MATH advisor at Ohio University, had asked her to come to his office, and she was nervous about why he wanted to speak with her. Geneva had received her teaching certificate after studying for two years at Muskingum College in New Concord, Ohio. She'd taught school for three years and then decided to go back to get her Bachelor's degree at Ohio University, with a major in mathematics. She had all A's in Dr. Cutter's class and was probably his best student, so she didn't think the summons to his office could be anything bad.

"You know I have a very high regard for your mathematical abilities." Geneva tried to look modest when Dr. Cutter praised her. "Through a friend of mine in the mathematics community, I've become aware of an opportunity that might interest you. I don't know if you have ever wanted to travel to Europe, but if you've ever thought about having an adventure, there's a wonderful scholarship and travel opportunity that's just become available to women with your mathematical talent."

"I've always wanted to travel, and my fiancé, who graduated from Ohio University a few years ago and is now at Harvard Medical School, has urged me to expand my horizons and learn more about the world. He thinks I'm too provincial, too much of a country girl. I'd love to hear about the scholarship and the chance to travel."

"The program is sponsored by Columbia University Teacher's College in New York City. It's for the upcoming summer, the summer of 1938, and is specifically for women who teach mathematics. If you are chosen to participate, all of your expenses will be paid, and you will earn credits toward a master's degree in teaching from Columbia. I know you have talked about working for your master's, and as you must know, Columbia is one of the country's finest institutions of higher learning. Are you interested?"

"Oh, yes, I am more than interested, but the competition for something like this must be fierce. Do I have any chance of being accepted?"

"You have an excellent chance. You have a great deal of natural talent in mathematics, and you work hard. I will write a letter for you, and you will have my highest recommendation."

Dr. Cutter continued. "There's a formal application to fill out, and you will be required to have two interviews. You won't have to go to New York for the interviews. Someone will come to Ohio to interview you, or you might have one of the interviews over the telephone. Would that be all right?"

"Of course. This will be my chance of a lifetime. Tell me more about the program."

"Ten women, all mathematics teachers, will be selected to travel to Germany this summer. The trip will be for thirteen weeks, including one week of orientation in New York City, ten weeks in Europe, and two weeks at sea. The trip will be organized as a lecture tour, and the group will travel to several German universities where you will learn from outstanding mathematicians. Besides the academic and intellectual experience, there will also be plenty of time for sightseeing and having fun. The itinerary is still being arranged. It won't be all work."

"I grew up on a dairy farm in Eastern Ohio, and I never dreamed I would have the chance to travel abroad on a scholarship."

"The five days of orientation will be on the Columbia University campus. You will have to be in New York by June 1st. Travel arrangements are still being organized. I am sure you will love every minute of the experience. There's a great deal of turmoil in Europe right now, and Germany's government under Hitler is very controversial. What will your fiancé and your family say if you're accepted into the program? You will be spending the entire summer in Europe."

"I hope they'll be thrilled for me. Thank you Dr. Cutter. I'm honored to have this opportunity. I hope my application will be solid enough to get me into the program."

After she submitted the paperwork, Geneva's interviews were scheduled. Dr. William Veere, a professor from Columbia University, and another big and very talkative man, a Mr. Jack Trevanian from New York City, traveled to Ohio University to interview her in person. During the interview, they questioned her about a story Dr. Cutter had included in his letter of recommendation.

"I want to know more about these blackboard challenges that are such a hallmark of Dr. Cutter's math classes. Can you tell me something about these contests?" Dr. Veere wanted to hear directly from Geneva how she would describe her mathematical prowess.

Geneva laughed, a little bit embarrassed. "Dr. Cutter has two students stand at the board and race each other to see who can solve an intricate calculus problem in the shortest amount of time."

Veere had already heard that part of the story. "Yes, and I hear that whatever student you competed against, you always won. Is that true?" Geneva nodded. "Because you always won, someone in the class suggested that you and Dr. Cutter go head to head." Geneva nodded her head again. "Well, Geneva, who won that competition?"

Geneva smiled. "I solved the problem more quickly than Dr. Cutter." She hastened to explain. "Dr. Cutter's chalk broke, or I don't think I would have finished before he did."

"So, you bested the teacher in the contest?"

"I don't want to toot my own horn, but I'm sure my ability to solve calculus problems was one reason Dr. Cutter recommended me for this trip."

After Dr. Veere and Mr. Travanian had finished asking all their questions, Geneva felt as if she'd performed well during the interview. Now she just had to wait to hear if she would be accepted.

ᏆᎢᎬᏗᎾ

The German Cultural Ministry had set rigid requirements for the women in the group. All of them had to have been born in the USA. Participants could not have any family members who currently lived in or who had ever lived in Germany. The women were allowed to speak and understand "restaurant German," but none of them were allowed to be anything close to fluent. There were age and other kinds of restrictions. The most important specification was no surprise to anyone who'd been paying attention to what was happening inside Nazi Germany — none of the women in the group could be Jewish.

Veere felt he'd selected a nice mix of Catholics, Methodists, and Lutherans. There was even one Episcopalian. It really infuriated him not to be able to include well-qualified female Jewish mathematicians, but he felt the safest thing was to agree to the no-Jews restriction. Once he'd agreed to take it on, he had worked tirelessly to put the trip together and was willing to do almost anything to insure that it went forward.

When he reviewed Geneva Burkhart's paperwork, he noted that she'd written on the line for religious preference: Chestnut Level Church. Not being familiar with that denomination, he called Miss Burkhart on the telephone for clarification.

"This is Dr. William Veere, Ms. Burkhart. I need to verify something you've written on your application for the summer program. You listed 'Chestnut Level Church' as your religious preference. I am not familiar with that denomination. Can you enlighten me?"

"Of course, Dr. Veere. Chestnut Level isn't a religious denomination. It's just the name of my local church. It's up on a hill that's flat on top and has chestnut trees all around it. It's a lot like the Methodists because we do so much singing. But Chestnut Level is better than the Methodist church because we not only allow both dancing and playing cards — we encourage them. I love to dance, and I'm very good at all kinds of card games."

"I have to have a denomination listed for the paperwork."

"Just write down Methodist. I'm going to marry my childhood sweetheart next year. He's a Methodist, and we'll be attending the Methodist Church after we're married. We're going to live in Connecticut, and there isn't any Chestnut Level Church in New Haven."

In addition to the limitations the German Cultural Ministry had placed on the women in the group, Veere and Trevanian had their own selection parameters that narrowed the pool of participants even more. There would be no married women or widows in the group, hence the "old maid" or spinster description. Trevanian wanted a wide-ranging geographic distribution of the women's hometowns. He didn't want any of the women to have known each other before the trip because he was concerned that knowing friends of friends might accidentally reveal the "sleepers" in the group or unravel their cover stories. He wanted women of all ages. A couple of the women in the group were a bit "long in the tooth," and Miss Burkhart was definitely on the young side.

Veere insisted that all the women be extraordinary mathematicians and have real experience teaching mathematics. For the most part, at least on paper, they'd been able to abide by these requirements. Trevanian didn't want there to be any question about their qualifications for acceptance into the Columbia Teacher's College's graduate school or for the scholarships each one had been given. The group had to be "above reproach" in terms of intelligence and academic excellence.

After much deliberation, Dr. Billy Veere and Jack Trevanian were satisfied with the composition of the group as a whole as well as with the individuals who were in it. The group of ten spinster mathematics teachers was finally chosen, and the letters were sent.

It was official. Geneva's official acceptance letter arrived in the mail welcoming her to the Columbia University Master's Degree Study Abroad Program for mathematics teachers. Geneva was thrilled as well as apprehensive about being admitted to the program. Geneva knew she loved math, and she thought she would love to travel. Other than sleeping in her college dormitory room, she'd only been away from home overnight when she'd entered yearly 4H contests at the Ohio State Fair in Columbus. Once she'd spent a weekend in Pittsburgh. She hoped she would be able to understand the German professors and hold her own with the other members of the exalted study group.

Dr. William Cutter, her college advisor, brought Dr. William Veere and Mr. Jack Trevanian, the two men who had interviewed Geneva, to the farm in Belmont, Ohio to talk to Geneva's parents about the trip. Geneva's father closely questioned each of the men who came to have lunch with the Burkharts. Dr. Veere would be in charge of the tour. Geneva liked him very much and was pleased that he was going to lead their group.

Jack Trevanian promised Geneva's father that he would "bring his girl home safe." Jack hoped and prayed he would be able to deliver on that promise. It was a dangerous time to travel anywhere in Europe, and he wondered several times a day if it was worth it to put innocents at risk to achieve his critical goals. Each time he questioned his judgment, he answered his queries with a resounding "Yes!"

Although she was twenty-five and paid her own way financially, it was important to Geneva that her parents support her decision to take such a momentous journey. Her father had been skeptical from the beginning. He insisted that nothing was free and didn't understand how it was possible that his daughter's trip abroad would cost her nothing. Why was Geneva being offered this very costly opportunity without having to pay for any of it? He wanted to tell her she couldn't go. Geneva's mother, however, told him in no uncertain terms that their daughter was going on the trip and that Theodore was not to say anything more about it. Geneva's mother had come to her rescue. This was not Mae's usual role in the family, but once she had spoken, no one argued with her. Geneva was going to Germany.

Geneva was excited to receive several additional communications about the upcoming trip. Dr. Veere and Columbia University sent detailed itineraries, schedules, and lists. Geneva was told to arrive in New York City before June 1, 1938 for five days of orientation on the Columbia campus. Housing would be provided. The group would sail on the French ocean liner, the *Normandie* on the afternoon of June 6th, and they would arrive in France five days later on June 11th. They would go directly from La Havre to Paris on the train. Paris! Geneva could scarcely believe she was going to spend a week in Paris. The group's tour of famous German Universities and lectures by important mathematicians and physicists was carefully laid out over a period of eight weeks. The women would spend a week in London at the end of the trip, and Geneva would return to the United States on a German ship, the SS *Hansa*.

The communications from Columbia told her how much luggage she was allowed to bring with her and what kinds of clothes she should pack. There were other lists, including a list of things she was not allowed to take abroad with her and a list of things she could expect to encounter when traveling in a foreign country. It was a lot to absorb.

Even with all the lists, Geneva worried about the practicalities of the journey. She'd never been to New York City. Once they arrived in Europe, they would travel by train and by bus. Geneva had never dreamed she would sail on an ocean liner or travel on a European train.

Would she be able to eat the food in Europe? Spoiled by her mother's excellent cooking and baking skills, Geneva was used to good, plain food. Except when she had been away at college, almost everything she'd ever eaten was grown on her family's own land. She knew she was unsophisticated, but she was determined not to let anyone guess how really apprehensive she was.

Geneva worried that she might not have the right clothes for traveling to New York and to Europe. She was confident that she looked good in clothes, but most of hers were homemade. Would the other women in the group have trunks full of expensive and fashionable outfits? As soon as Geneva was chosen to go on the tour, her mother had taken her to Wheeling for the day, and they'd carefully chosen patterns and material. They'd shopped at Stone Thomas for shoes, a raincoat, and even some store-bought dresses. Her new underwear, hand-sewn travel clothes, a long black silk skirt, and an evening gown filled the trunk and one suitcase Geneva was allowed to take. Geneva's mother was usually very, very tight with a penny, but for this special time in Geneva's life, her mother had dipped into her own private cookie jar savings and made sure that Geneva had everything she needed to make her feel confident enough to take on the world. The local seamstress in Belmont had done a rush job with suits, blouses, and skirts that would allow Geneva to feel as if she were one of the best dressed among her fellow teachers.

Geneva didn't speak or understand German, and she didn't know much about Germany, other than what she'd learned in history and geography classes in school. She bought a short history of Germany so she could read about the country she would visit in a few weeks, and she bought a small German dictionary and a *Baedeker's Guide*.

In addition to her *Baedeker's*, her German-English dictionary, and her book about German history, Geneva bought Emily Post's etiquette book. Much of the etiquette book had to do with a butler's responsibilities, the footmen's outfits, how to address royalty, and other things Geneva would never in a million years need to know. Reading about arcane lifestyles was interesting if not pertinent, but some of the etiquette information was useful. If nothing else, it built her confidence that she would not make a faux pas at the table.

She read newspapers and magazines and listened more carefully to the radio. She wanted to learn everything she could, and there was always something in the news about what was going on in Germany in the spring of 1938. None of it sounded very good to Geneva.

CHAPTER THIRTEEN

CHOOSING GENEVA

MARCH 1938
JACK TREVANIAN (NEW YORK) ON THE PHONE
WITH NIGEL BARNABY (LONDON)

"YES, SHE IS VERY PRETTY, AND YES, SHE'S A bit flirty. And what's wrong with that?" Jack Trevanian was tuned up.

Sir Nigel Barnaby, at the other end of the line, rolled his eyes and sat down in his wooden desk chair. This was not going to be a short telephone call.

Jack continued. "Miss Burkhart is a mathematics scholar and can more than hold her own with the group. Dr. William Cutter, who is a professor, a mathematician, an astronomer, and a very well-known and well-respected person in Ohio and even nationally, would not have recommended her if she didn't have the qualifications. She has three years of teaching experience. She attended Muskingum College in Ohio for two years, got her teaching certification, and left college to teach. Then she went back to finish her undergraduate degree at Ohio University, which is where she met Dr. Cutter. Billy Veere thinks she's a great addition to the group, and I don't think it hurts at all to have one of the women be a little bit younger and a little bit more attractive than the others."

"A little bit more attractive, Jack?" Nigel knew he wasn't going to convince Jack to drop Miss Burkhart from the group.

Jack continued to advocate for the very attractive young woman from Ohio. "Okay, Nigel, so she's a lot more attractive than the others. This is a good thing. She's a distraction from some of the older, frumpier women in the group. With Miss Burkhart to look at, who's going to be paying attention to some of the others in the group who are not exactly what they appear to be? In case you've forgotten, some of our women have 'special assignments.' We don't want any attention pointing in their direction. In fact, Nigel, one of the reasons we chose Miss Burkhart is because she is young and pretty ... and flirty. We want her to attract attention. We're going to be assigned some kind of Nazi minder or tour guide or translator or whatever they are calling their snitches this month. We know, of course, that this fellow's main job will be to spy on us. We're hoping Miss Burkhart will charm our Nazi flunky, so he won't have time to watch the rest of the women too closely."

"Could she be a security risk?"

"Of course she's not a security risk. Who the heck is saying that, for God's sake? That's by far the most ridiculous thing I've heard you say yet. I went to her home town and talked to her family. Cutter and Veere both went with me. Her folks had us to their house for lunch. The lunch was more like a dinner. Her mother is a heck of a good cook. It was simple country food, but it was first-rate, all grown on their farm, including the pork chops!"

"You can't judge a family by its food, and you're easily distracted by food, Jack."

"Cutter was her math professor and advisor at Ohio University. He says, if anything, she's quite unsophisticated. He says she voted for Alf Landon but otherwise knows nothing much about politics outside of Ohio."

"What about her father's political views. Could he be some kind of subversive?" Nigel wasn't giving up without a fight.

"No, no, no! Her father is a well-educated farmer who used to be a school teacher. He runs a farm and a small business, a dairy that bottles and delivers milk to the whole town of Belmont, Ohio. It's a very small town. And, yes, he's a Republican, and he doesn't like Roosevelt. Mr. Burkhart says Roosevelt is a socialist. So what? Lots of people don't like Roosevelt. If Franklin weren't a friend of mine, I probably wouldn't like him either. And Mr. Burkhart is correct; Roosevelt is a socialist. So what? It's all there in the written report Veere sent you. It sounds to me like her dad is the opposite of a Bolshevik, if that's what you're worried about."

"Mr. Burkhart is very open about his disagreement with Roosevelt's policies."

"Yes, it's true, her father said he thought Roosevelt's Social Security Act was 'the work of the devil,' and maybe it is? He said, and I am reading directly from the report now: 'This Social Security nonsense will bankrupt the country. It won't be in my lifetime or in my children's lifetimes. But my grandchildren and great grandchildren will be in a hell of a mess because of it. Just wait and see.' What's wrong with that? We have free speech in this country. The man has opinions. Not liking some silly program FDR thought up doesn't make him a traitor to his country and doesn't make his daughter ineligible for this trip. Roosevelt is not the Queen of England. We're allowed to criticize him if we don't agree with what he's doing."

"I'm worried you made promises to her family you may not be able to keep." Nigel was still making his case.

"So now you are angry that her father made us promise to 'bring her home safe.' What do you want me to tell him — that we won't bring his daughter home safe? Germany may be at war before they arrive or go to war while they're there. Of course Burkhart wouldn't be silent if anything happened to her. That's what any father worth his salt would say about his daughter. Is the promise to her father any reason to leave Miss Burkhart out of the group? I didn't think so."

Nigel was silent on the other end of the line.

"So, what else do you have on your list of objections about Miss Burkhart?"

"Burkhart sounds like a German name." Nigel was grasping at straws.

"It doesn't matter if her name sounds German to you. The Germans know her name is Swiss, and the Swiss know her name is Swiss. I know her name is Swiss, so maybe you are the only person on earth who's worried about her name sounding German. For God's sake, why does it matter? One of the restrictions that Nazi culture guy was adamant about was that no one in the group be able to speak more than 'restaurant German.' She doesn't even know any of that, Nigel. She took a few years of French and says she didn't do very well with it."

Nigel's silence on the line indicated he'd admitted defeat.

"She's staying. She'll be a perfect addition, as well as a tremendous asset, for several reasons. Anyway, we don't have time to look around for anybody else at this late date."

"Don't say I didn't warn you."

"Quite right, you'll have to get used to the idea and learn to live with it. Now, about this harebrained scheme you've thought up for getting a German scientist out of Germany. Have you finally gone utterly and irrevocably mad? This is by far the worst idea you have ever come up with. "

"Don't go off half-cocked, Jack. Hear me out on this."

"Okay, go ahead and convince me that dressing up a German physicist, who is a man, in women's clothes and putting a blond wig on him is going to convince anybody anywhere that he's a female schoolteacher. My frequent and excessive hyperbole notwithstanding, this is wrong-headed and will only end in disaster. Mark my words. Don't say I didn't warn you." Jack Trevanian was completely serious about what a bad idea he thought Sir Nigel Barnaby had come up with this time.

CHAPTER FOURTEEN

OVERLOADING THE CART

APRIL 1938
JACK TREVANIAN (NEW YORK) ON THE PHONE
WITH NIGEL BARNABY (LONDON)

"**N**IGEL, WE ALREADY HAVE WAY TOO MUCH going on with this trip. I just don't think it's a good idea to try to put another 'pretend' teacher into the group. She's going to stand out, and the other women will be suspicious of her. We're trying to accomplish a great many things in a very short period of time."

. . . .

"I understand it may be one of the last chances we have to get people into Germany. But why do we need a bookkeeper? And before you start to lecture me, I know you can give me a hundred reasons why it's vital to world security that we include this woman."

. . . .

"I'm sure you have many unbelievably clever ways to make her appear and disappear. We're not planning to be anywhere near Hamburg. I think we may be overloading the cart, Nigel."

. . . .

"I know she's a brilliant mathematician. They all are. I have her curriculum vitae right here in front of me. But she's not really a teacher, and these women are smart cookies. They'll figure out she's not who she says she is in about five minutes."

. . . .

"I know you don't like to put things down on paper, but how am I supposed to understand how important this woman's mission is if you don't lay it out for me."

. . . .

"Yes, I do need to know. I am putting my people at risk, and I think this additional person you want to add is increasing that risk beyond what's acceptable. I'll talk to Veere, but he's always much too agreeable. He takes on more than he should. We're asking him to do too many things he's not trained to do. I agree that if he were doing these things in the United States, it wouldn't be a problem. The whole point is that Germany is a dangerous place to be doing anything."

Two days later, the encrypted cable arrived from London, and Jack knew before he'd even begin to read it that Nigel Barnaby was going to have his way, as he almost always did. He had to chuckle when he read the heading of the memo and realized that his friend Nigel had referred to him as "Cowboy" and to himself as "Thinker."

TOP SECRET TO COWBOY FROM THINKER

A strategic naval plan is currently being drawn up in the Third Reich. Several versions of the plan are proposed, and we want to influence which one is adopted. We have a contact in the German navy who is very high up in the command hierarchy. He needs a native-speaking German woman to serve as a bookkeeper under his direction. She will be a member of the group that's developing and presenting the three plans. Our navy man does not have the requisite mathematical skills and needs someone who can, to put it bluntly, "cook the books" in favor of one of the competing plans. Three variations of the plan will be submitted for Hitler's and Goering's approval, and we want to be sure they choose one plan over the other two. The plan that is selected will determine what Germany's navy will look like in future years. It will establish how many of each type of naval vessel will be produced for the future. It's no secret that Hitler is preparing for war. One of these strategic plans will determine how many battleships, destroyers, U-boats, etc. will be built for Germany's future navy — that is, the composition of the navy Hitler will take to war against us and our allies.

The British know their vulnerabilities. They know that U-boats, of all the German vessels, will be the most damaging to the

British Navy when war begins. The British feel the RAF can handle the battleships, destroyers, and other surface ships. Pertinent to that, dollar for dollar, pound for pound, and Reichsmark for Reichsmark, the Germans can produce about two U-boats for the same amount of time and money it takes to produce one large surface ship. Their capital would be better spent building as many U-boats as possible. We have to keep them from making a decision to do that.

Each of the plans being considered includes a different ratio of U-boats to various types of surface ships. We want Hitler to decide on Plan Z which calls for a greater number of surface ships and fewer U-boats. We need high-ranking German naval officers and others who can influence Hitler, to advocate with our man for Plan Z. Hitler seems to understand that there are limitations on materials and natural resources, but he will not accept that financial resources are also scarce. He says to print more money or pay everybody less for the battleship or the railroad car or whatever it is. Some of the men who have influence with Hitler will take into consideration how much each vessel costs and how long it takes to build. If we can show that a U-boat costs more and takes longer to build than it really does, the U-boat loses its attractiveness relative to other types of ships. If we can show that a battleship or a destroyer costs less and takes less time to build than it really does, the attractiveness of the surface ship increases relative to other choices.

Hitler doesn't like U-boats, and he loves surface ships — the bigger and more ferocious-looking the better. It's a matter of vanity. U-boats are under the water. You can't see them, and they are ugly little things. He loves to see the huge, graceful surface ships. They feed his image of Germany's greatness, and the more guns on it the better. We think he will make a decision in favor of surface ships because of his own narcissistic preferences. We have to make sure that there are hard numbers to support the choices he makes because of his personal whims.

Our agent can do this work. She understands all aspects of accounting and bookkeeping, unusual for someone who also has her exceptional grasp of theoretical mathematics. She can literally spin numbers into gold or into anything at all, and she can write up a cost analysis that would persuade even Hjalmar Schacht.

Gretchen Haldemeyer was born in 1903 and lived the first nine years of her life in Dortmund in Westphalia, Germany. Her much

older parents immigrated to Davenport, Iowa
in 1912. Gretchen attended local American
schools where she learned to speak English
without any accent. She speaks American
English as well as she speaks her native
German. Gretchen's father died when she was
fifteen, and her mother died not very long
after Gretchen graduated from high school.
Gretchen was her class valedictorian.

Gretchen was brilliant in math and received
a scholarship to attend MIT, where she
graduated Summa Cum Laude in mathematics. After Gretchen finished college, she
came to Britain to study at the London
School of Economics. She was recruited
by MI6 ten years ago. She speaks perfect
"American," with a little bit of an Iowa
accent, perfect "Westphalian German," and
perfect "English English." She also speaks
a few other languages. She's always wanted
to be in the field and wants to return to
the country of her birth to work against
the Nazis. Hitler is destroying the best
of German culture and tradition, and she
wants to do what she can to help bring him
down. Best, Nigel.

Nigel and Jack spoke on the telephone again a few days
later. Nigel summed it up for Jack, "What it boils down to is
that we need to have a person, skilled in arithmetic, statistics,
bookkeeping, and cost analysis. We have the opportunity to
place her in a position where she can help manipulate decisions

that are being made. She will provide convincing numbers to guarantee the outcome we want. Hitler pays no attention to what something costs. If he wants it, he gets it. Other more rational people, who have important decision-making roles, recognize the necessity of taking costs into consideration. We need someone to prepare reports and put together the budgets and timelines to convince these more rational decision makers."

Nigel continued, "There's an individual working with us who's in a very high position in the German military. He can influence these choices, but he needs numbers to present with his arguments. He needs a report, pieces of paper, and hard evidence to support his recommendations about what future needs will be and what the alternative choices will cost. He can convince key people, but he can't prepare the budgets, the paperwork, and the technical information he needs."

"Who is this guy, the one who's in such an important decision-making position?" Jack was curious.

"You wouldn't believe it, even if I could tell you who he is, which I can't."

"So, Nigel, how are we going to add another woman to the group?"

"Well, that's more of my good news, Jack. We don't have to add another women. She's already in the group, and her cover name is Grace Davis from Cedar Rapids, Iowa. You're looking at her real name on my memo. Grace Davis and Gretchen Haldemeyer are one and the same woman. "

"Now I smell a rat, and I don't like it. You and Veere or somebody put this woman into the group. All along you had an ulterior agenda for her, but you didn't tell anybody about it until now! Can I trust you, Nigel? This looks and smells like skullduggery. Does Veere know about this?"

"Veere knows she's in the group and has a 'special' assignment. She's going to leave the others very early in the trip.

She can't be seen as a member of the group once they're in Germany. She'll be extracted and go on to her assignment when the group arrives at their first stop after leaving France. And, Jack, I wasn't hiding anything from you. You knew I always intended to put a 'sleeper' into the group, someone who would leave the group and remain behind in Germany. You've known from the beginning that was a goal. I wasn't certain the plan to employ Gretchen as a bookkeeper with the German Navy was going to work out. I just got the word that both our German navy 'friend' and MI6 have agreed to that part of the operation."

"Good news, Nigel! She's already in the group! Once again you've scored a brilliant coup! You never cease to amaze me." Jack had to admit Nigel was right, but he was still miffed.

"One more thing, Jack, it turns out she's a second or third cousin or something of our important person in the German Abwehr! He's delighted that he's found her and will have a chance to work with her. He's bringing her into the job he has in mind by saying she's a member of his family, which she is. The Germans have no problem with nepotism. So she's a win-win all round. As you Americans say, how about them apples?"

"You really are too much, Nigel. I plead no contest."

"There's one last thing which makes this a perfect match. There are real records in Dortmund in Westphalia that a Gretchen Haldemeyer was born in 1903 and attended primary school there. The reason those records are there is because our Gretchen really was born there and really did go to school there. Our German friend currently has a very important position in German military intelligence, and he's going to be sure there's an appropriate paper trail, i.e. records for Gretchen Haldemeyer, all the way up to and including the present day. It is fortuitous that German records show, for real, her birth in Germany thirty-five years ago, and it is likewise fortunate for us that our navy man is in a position to invent and insert paperwork that shows she's been going to school and living and working in Germany continuously since she was born there. This is going to work."

"You said she'll be leaving the group early. What's going to happen to her?"

"Why don't I let that be a surprise for you?"

"I don't like surprises, and you know that!"

"Speaking of surprises, do you think any of the women will refuse to go on the tour because of what has just happened in Austria? With all that's going on over there, I'll bet Mr. Theodore Burkhart is having a fit since he gave his daughter permission to go so far away from home."

"We all should be having a fit because of what just happened in Austria, but not many world leaders are speaking up to complain about it. What are we coming to, Nigel, when a bully marches in and takes over an entire country, and nobody does a damn thing about it?"

CHAPTER FIFTEEN

LEAVING GERMANY

APRIL 1938
FRANKFURT, GERMANY

"MY DARLING MARGOT, YOU AND THE children must leave Germany for good." Franz had tears in his eyes and desperation in his voice. They'd argued about this so many times before, and he'd run out of words to plead his case. "I work for these people, and I know what they're planning to do, what they are already doing. You're French, and you and the children must leave Germany while you still can, before it's too late." Franz had insisted Margot walk with him outside in their garden to have this conversation.

"Germany is my home now, Franz, and I love this place, Nazis or no Nazis. Our children are safe. They're Germans. Just because you had a Jewish grandmother doesn't make you a Jew. We're a family of good Catholics, and we, or at least I, go to mass more than once a week." Margot gave him a small smile. "I want to stay here in Frankfurt in my beautiful house with my beautiful children and my beautiful husband."

During the past few months, Margot had made her argument to Franz with decreasing conviction. She knew in her heart that her position was a lost cause, not only with Franz but also with herself. For years, she'd watched what the Nazis were doing to the Jews. Some of her friends had disappeared. She'd heard the rumors about the concentration camps and the killing of retarded children and crippled people. She knew all of these things and could see the direction life in Germany was taking. She was no longer able to convince herself that her world could remain intact.

"Margot, you need to know that I've helped Max Meyerhof and Dr. Engelman leave Germany. They're now safe in Belgium, but Max's story is terribly tragic. The rabbi and his wife and Max's two sisters are all dead, murdered by the Gestapo."

Margo gasped and the color drained form her face. "All dead? Murdered? What happened?"

"It's a brutal story, and I don't even want to tell you about it." But Franz proceeded to tell Margot what had happened to Max and his family.

Margot began to cry when Franz told her what had happened to Max's sisters, Greta and Annika. "I used to see them playing in the neighborhood park when I went there with Frederick and Chloe. Those beautiful little girls were so sweet. I can't believe it. How could this happen?"

Franz told her about Max being shot as he fled from the Gestapo and jumped through the window of his house. "He almost died from a systemic infection, but Dr. Engelman saved his life. Max uses a cane and probably will never regain the full use of his right arm." Franz told her how the two had escaped to Belgium. Margot thought the world of Dr. Engelman who had delivered both of her babies.

"Oh, Franz, these were the best of people. They did nothing to deserve this."

"I am as devastated by these deaths as you are. I've wanted to tell you about Max's family, but I had to wait until Max and Dr. Engelman were safely out of Germany. I still don't think you fully grasp the new reality we are living with in this country. One does not have to practice Judaism to be considered Jewish in Germany these days."

The terrible story about Max's family hit Margot very hard, but she didn't really see what these horrible events had to do with her. It was impossible for her to think of Franz as Jewish.

"We are Catholic, and we have always been Catholic. In spite of the fact that you don't attend mid-week mass very often, you are a much better and more devout Catholic than I have ever been." Margot, who was raised in France, had attended mass on Christmas, Easter, Ash Wednesday, and a few other important Holy Days. After her marriage to Franz, she began to appreciate the depth of his devotion to his religion. "You know I respect you, and I have tried to make sure our family observes all of the Catholic cultural and religious traditions. You have made me a much more religious person, and I have started to attend mass on my own, not only on Sunday when we attend as a family, but also during the week. I find comfort in the words of the priest, the ceremony, and the tradition of the liturgy."

"You aren't hearing what I'm saying. You are missing the point entirely. It doesn't matter how often any of us attends mass. Anyone with a Jewish grandparent is considered to be Jewish. I'm pleading with you. I know what's planned for the future for anyone who has any Jewish blood, no matter how little blood that might be. It doesn't matter to the Nazis what religion one actually practices or in what church one was baptized. They decide who is or is not a Jew."

Franz continued. "I didn't think the Nuremburg laws or their disgusting proclamations applied to me. It never occurred to me to think of myself as a Jew. I know very little about the Jewish religion or culture. I do know Hitler is determined to destroy the Jews in Germany and all over Europe, even those of us Jews who are devoutly Catholic."

Margot knew in her heart that he was right, and in spite of wanting to believe otherwise, she knew the Nazis would never stop their pursuit of evil. Hitler and the Nazis had to be defeated. She dropped her head and began to sob. She grabbed hold of Franz and beat her fists against his chest in anger and frustration. He tried to comfort her and held her as she flailed her arms at the enemy she so detested but couldn't touch.

"I will never leave without you, and you know that."

"I promise I will leave Germany when you and the children are safe. The Nazis need me right now for their uranium program, but I will soon become expendable. When they have finished with me, they will send me to a concentration camp or kill me. Many Jewish scientists have already been sent to these camps. We are near the end of a research project for which my expertise is absolutely required. When this work is completed, they will move me to one of those places for Jews, communists, and others who are politically personae non grata. The Nazis still need our brains and our knowledge to continue to build their war machine. When they have finished exploiting everything we know, they will kill us."

Margot tried to stop sobbing and focus on what Franz was telling her. It was too horrible, but the signs were everywhere. In spite of always being a positive person and looking on the bright side of things, Margot admitted to herself that Franz was right, that unspeakable things were in store for the Jews and for the non-Jews of Germany. She was worn out from the argument with Franz and with herself.

"You're right, of course. We will go to France for the summer as we have always done. I will think about everything you've said, and we'll stay in Burgundy and not return to Frankfurt when the fall comes. The children and I will miss you terribly."

"Things are moving very quickly, my dear, and we must be ahead of events. I am near the end of my value to the Nazis, and when I'm no longer useful, they will make me disappear. We must work together to make plans so we all are safe. Please work with me."

"I will do whatever is necessary to save you and our children."

"I hadn't wanted to tell you before, but I know I'm being watched and have been for some time. I was told months ago I couldn't leave the country. Whenever I go to Berlin or Freiburg, any time I leave Frankfurt for even one day, there's always someone following me and watching my every move. When I travel, I know someone is listening in to everything that is said in my hotel room and on the hotel telephone. I'm afraid our telephone here has also been tampered with so the Nazis can listen in on our calls. They have planted other devices in the house. That is why we can only talk about these things when we are outside in the garden. We cannot ever talk about any of this inside the house. And you must be very careful, especially as we plan our escape, to say nothing compromising over the telephone."

Franz continued. "Several of my colleagues have been taken, and no one knows where they are. Catholics and Lutherans, whom the Nazis have now decided have Jewish blood, as well as the intellectuals who have communist or Bolshevik leanings, are all disappearing. Lise, who is the most brilliant of all of us on the Uran Projeckt, has told me she will leave whenever her escape plans have been finalized. My turn is coming soon. Because I have special knowledge of physics, information that Germany's enemies would like to have, I will never be allowed to leave Germany. The Nazis fear I might escape the country and tell their enemies what we are doing here. That's why they watch me so carefully, and this is why you and the children are also at risk. The Nazis know they can keep me silent and in my place because they can threaten to harm you. This is why you must promise me that you will get ready to leave at once. You must be prepared to go to Switzerland when I tell you it's too dangerous to stay in France."

Margot could not believe her ears. "Too dangerous to stay in France? What are you talking about?" Margot's blue eyes blazed with alarm. She shook her head of blond curls and turned away from her husband. "I have agreed to stay at my family home in Burgundy. Why would we be in any danger there?"

"There's going to be a war, Margot. I know this because I'm one of the people who is helping Hitler rebuild the Germany military and prepare for a terrible future war. I'm not proud of what I'm doing, and I'm planning to leave as soon as I know you and the children are out of danger. Hitler won't stop with the Rhineland or Austria or even the Sudetenland. I've read his vile little book, *Mein Kampf*, in which he lays out his plan to conquer all of Europe. He wants to take over France, the Low Countries, Russia, Britain, and even Africa. No one knows how long it will be until war begins, and I plan to join you as soon as I can make my own escape. I believe with all my heart that ultimately France will not be safe from the Nazi war machine. That's why I want us to be living in Switzerland when war comes."

"How do you know the Germans won't invade Switzerland? Where would we be then?"

"Switzerland and America will be the only safe places during the next world war. You must tell me that you believe I know what lies ahead and what we must do to prepare for it. We are fortunate that we have means and property. I have already moved a great many of our assets out of the country. Most who are in danger don't have the money to escape and can't take refuge at a country house in France. Even those with wealth cannot easily get themselves or their assets out of Germany. Not many are able to buy Swiss citizenship and Swiss passports."

"Swiss passports? I have a perfectly good French passport as do the children. Whatever would we want with Swiss passports?"

Franz put his finger on her lips and gave her a look of caution. "We have already said too much, my darling. You must trust me and work with me for our new lives."

"But I like my old life and don't want a new life. I want to keep the life I have now."

"The Nazis will never allow you or anyone else to keep the lives we have now. Everything is changing and not for the better. You must come to terms with the fact that you will have to say goodbye to your 'old life' forever."

CHAPTER SIXTEEN

FRANZ AND THEO STOCKER

APRIL 1938
FRANKFURT, GERMANY

F RANZ HARTMANN'S DINGY ONE-ROOM hideout was in a run-down assortment of ancient flats, far from the exclusive suburb of Frankfurt where his family home was located. His elderly landlady, Frau Schnell, was nearly blind and a little bit tipsy on schnapps most of the time. Franz had painstakingly searched for and selected this particular apartment, and the lack of attention from Frau Schnell was one of the most appealing things about the place.

Franz had presented himself in the blue uniform of a railroad worker, a man who shovels coal into the engine, a dirty but important job on the German railway. Franz wore his badly mended blue pants and shirt, covered with coal dust, whenever he went to or from his rented room. Franz explained to his landlady that he worked odd hours on the train and traveled much of the time. He also confided that he spent more than a few nights of his time off with a woman friend at her flat. It was hard for Franz to believe that any woman would want a fellow who looked as disreputable as he did, but he depended on Frau Schnell's cataracts to find his romance credible.

A year ago, Franz had contacted friends in England and the United States, and plans for his escape had been set in motion. He'd been instructed to rent an apartment under the name of Theo Stocker. If he had to disappear quickly, the flat would provide Franz with a place to stay. He could live as Theo Stocker for a while until his contacts abroad could get him out of Germany. These associates had provided Franz with Theo Stocker's German passport and identity papers and helped him find the appropriate apartment. Franz had used the false papers to rent this hiding place. Although the phony documents would probably not fool the Gestapo, they'd been good enough to fool Frau Schnell.

The apartment contained a few "prop" items of a personal nature, and the clothes in the battered armoire were well-used uniforms and ragged underwear. A threadbare suit and a dress shirt hung in the closet as additional camouflage. On one occasion when Franz happened to encounter Frau Schnell, he mentioned that he kept most of his good clothes and import- ant belongings and papers at his fiancée's house.

The basement apartment had its own ancient toilet and small sink. These amenities were behind a flimsy curtain in the corner of the room and were essential. One's own toilet was a rare luxury for a room in this apartment building in this shabby neighborhood and meant that once-upon-a-time, this room had been a servant's quarters. The most important char- acteristic of this one-room flat, the critical requirement, was its separate entrance that opened directly onto the alley behind the building. Franz could come and go without encountering anyone else who lived there, including his landlady.

Franz needed a place where he could receive coded letters and packages important for his escape. He couldn't have these things delivered to his home or his work. And Franz needed a place to hide the valuable documents he'd been photographing.

Franz had begun his preparations to leave Germany years earlier. When the Nazis first passed the Nuremberg laws in 1935, stripping Germans who had Jewish blood of pretty much all of their rights, Franz had not fully grasped that these dehumanizing regulations applied to him. When Franz realized that he was considered to be Jewish because of his grandmother's "suspicious" birth origins, he saw the handwriting on the wall. His alleged Jewish blood put him at risk, and he quietly began making plans to secure his family's future safety and financial security.

While he could still travel outside of Germany, Franz took gems, cash, and other valuables to his bank vault in Zurich. He sold some of his paintings and took others to Switzerland rolled up in a secret compartment in the metal rod of his umbrella. He paid a very good art forger to copy his original art work, and Franz substituted the excellent fakes for his priceless masterpieces so that no one would notice that art was disappearing from the walls of his Frankfurt home. Using holding companies and other legal instruments, he gradually and secretly divested himself of his widespread German real estate holdings and bought properties abroad in countries he thought Hitler would not be able to touch. As a well-connected and wealthy member of cosmopolitan European society, he had the resources to successfully move his assets out of Germany. As he implemented his plans, he worried about his fellow Germans, real Jews, and other "Catholic Jews" who didn't have his financial means.

Because of his work on the Uranprojeckt, the Nazis at first overlooked the fact that he might be one-quarter Jewish, but Franz was living on borrowed time. He wanted to begin his new life with Margot and the children before his situation became desperate, before it was too late. He prepared, with resolution and a heavy heart, for the day when he would have to become a different person in a different country.

Franz had been Albert Einstein's student at the Kaiser Wilhelm Institute in Berlin before Einstein had left Germany in 1933 to live in Princeton, New Jersey. Franz's current work was primarily at the University of Frankfurt. He collaborated with other physicists to unlock the secrets of heavy metal atoms, and as part of his work, he often traveled to the Kaiser Wilhelm Institute and other universities where this important research was being conducted. Franz was certain that Einstein and others would vouch for him with the Brits and the Americans.

Even with all of his foresight and planning, Franz was taken by surprise when he learned from a colleague in the early spring of 1938 that within a few months, he would be relieved of his employment and sent to a special "work camp." Many Germany scientists had already left the country, and others had been sent to these camps, never to be heard from again. Because of the warnings from his friends and the progress of his work, Franz knew the deadline for making his escape was this year's summer holiday. Franz sent a telegram with an emergency alert code to his contacts in England. It was time to leave.

At last a letter of instructions arrived. His escape plan was set. Those who were going to help him leave Germany wanted to know his clothing sizes and other details. They wanted chest and inseam measurements and shoe and shirt sizes. He guessed his rescuers were preparing some kind of disguise, but he could never in his wildest dreams, have imagined what that disguise would be.

A group of school teachers from the United States would visit Germany during the summer of 1938. Franz was told he would make his escape disguised as a woman, a member of that group of school teachers. The plan sounded impossibly Byzantine and full of holes. He didn't know the details, so he had to trust that his friends knew what they were doing and would get him out of Germany. He moved quickly to make plans so that Margot and the children would be safe in Switzerland before he could, in good conscience, give the final go ahead to his British rescuers.

Franz had been working on a project of his own which he felt would make him even more valuable to the British and the Americans. For the past several years, Franz had been making photographic copies of top secret military research plans and drawings with his tiny Minnox camera. He bought precious film for the camera and the expensive photo paper only when he was out of the country. As an amateur photographer, he had his own dark room in the basement of the family's Frankfurt house. He hated to put his loved ones at risk by developing the film at home, but there was no other way. Franz secured the finished photographs in a secret vault in his basement wine cellar.

When he rented the one-room apartment in the name of Theo Stocker, he decided it would be better to store the photos there. Franz built a false back for the flimsy wardrobe that held his clothes in Stocker's flat and secured the hundreds of photographs in this hidden compartment. He'd had a close call with his landlady when he'd been building the secret space behind the wardrobe. The alterations to the heavy piece of furniture had made it necessary to move the wardrobe away from the wall, a difficult and noisy job for one person. Then he'd had to do considerable carpentry work, sawing and hammering to reconfigure the wardrobe's back, to create the hiding place.

He'd made a mess in his tiny room, and there were nails and pieces of wood and piles of sawdust everywhere.

One evening when he was in the middle of working on his project, Frau Schnell knocked on the door. Franz knew she would disapprove of having her furniture altered and the mess he was making. He couldn't let her see what was happening in the apartment, let alone allow her to step inside. She hardly ever wanted to talk to him and seldom came to his door, and he was angry with himself that the noise of his woodworking had attracted her attention. He was frantic to keep her out of the apartment.

He called out that he would be there in a minute, and as he walked to the door, he stripped his shirt, undershirt, and trousers off his body and threw them in the corner of the room. He grabbed a towel and wrapped it around his waist. When he went to the door, his chest was bare, and he appeared to be wearing just the towel. He opened the door and peeked out, enough so that Frau Schnell could see he was almost naked. In spite of her cataracts and the schnapps, she could see that her tenant was undressed. Being the proper older woman that she was, she quickly closed the door and told Theo Stocker she would speak with him later. Franz cleaned up the sawdust and other remnants of his carpentry project as quietly as he could and moved the furniture back into place.

Franz's landlady had keys to all of the apartments in her building. She could let herself into her tenants' rooms when they weren't at home and snoop around. Theo Stocker could not appear to have anything to hide, and Franz took great care to be sure he didn't keep anything in his flat that might arouse Frau Schnell's suspicions.

In May of 1938, Franz received a parcel from an unknown sender at Theo Stocker's "hideout." The package contained women's clothing, all in his size. He realized these special clothes had been carefully tailored to fit him perfectly, including the enclosed bustier with stuffing in all the correct places. The red leather shoes had heels that were not terribly high, but for a man, they were high enough and clumsy enough. He would have to practice walking in them. There was a wig, a woman's suit with a red jacket, a red leather handbag, and a very fashionable red hat with feathers and a veil.

Franz didn't know how far he would have to walk in the red shoes or how long he would have to endure wearing the ridiculous costume. He decided he ought to try everything on and at least make an effort to practice walking in the "high" heels. Putting on the complicated women's clothing took more time and effort than he'd ever imagined. He didn't know how long he would have, when the time came, to get into his disguise. He practiced getting dressed until he felt he could do it quickly. He practiced walking around the apartment in the red shoes and realized it was even harder to do than it looked. He wondered how women ever managed to walk, not to mention look graceful, wearing the tortuous footwear.

One afternoon while Franz practiced getting into his disguise and walking around in the shoes, his landlady knocked on his door. Franz threw a blanket around his shoulders to hide the women's clothing he was wearing, but he forgot about the red heels he had on his feet. When he answered the door, Frau Schnell immediately noticed the shoes. Her eyebrows shot up and her eyes bugged out. She looked at Theo Stocker with a quizzical look, shrugged her shoulders, and said, "I'll come back later, Mr. Stocker. I see you're busy." Whatever she might have been thinking about her tenant's proclivities, she chuckled and went on her way. Franz had to laugh, and he hoped his landlady was the broadminded and uncritical sort. It had been another close call.

Franz was over six feet tall. He wondered where his friends in England would find a woman tall enough to resemble himself. In fact, that very tall, thin woman did exist. Although it was not her real name, she would be known as Eleanor Hammond when she traveled to Germany in the summer of 1938. Her background story said she was a mathematics teacher from White River Junction, Vermont in the United States. There was a real mathematics teacher named Eleanor Hammond who lived in Vermont, but she would be nowhere near Germany in 1938. The tall imposter, who would call herself Eleanor Hammond, would be an essential part of the operation to smuggle Franz Hartmann out of Germany. Franz would put his life in the hands of the pretend Eleanor Hammond, a woman he would never see.

CHAPTER SEVENTEEN

LEAVING FRANKFURT

APRIL 1938
FRANKFURT, GERMANY

MARGOT MOVED SADLY THROUGH HER LAST days in Frankfurt. Franz insisted that Margot and the children leave Frankfurt immediately, even though it meant taking the children out of school early. As she did every year, she instructed the household staff to prepare for the family's summer holiday in France. Clothes, books, toys, and all the other necessities were packed for their summer trip to Beaune. It was amazing how many things had to be considered when moving a household that included an eight-year-old, a five-year-old, and two dogs.

This year, the packing and preparations for their summer vacation had a very different goal, but everything had to appear to be just as it had been every other year. There were quite a few extra trunks included in the piles of luggage and boxes that always accompanied them on their yearly visit to Margot's family estate in Burgundy. Sometimes they went to France by train, but Franz wanted to be sure they had the Mercedes this year. He spent considerable time working on the car in the garage.

Most of the household staff at the Frankfurt house were day workers and had the summers off when Margot and the children were in France. Margot liked some German food but wouldn't have a German cook. She had insisted on having a French cook, and the cook had an apartment in the Hartmann's Frankfurt house. In addition to having studied at the Sorbonne in Paris, Margot had also taken classes at Le Cordon Bleu and was an accomplished chef. Preferring to spend her time with the children and in pursuits other than cooking, she ordered the food and planned the family's menus. She left the actual work of going to the food shops and doing the food preparation to her French cook.

Unfortunately, even though the Hartmanns were almost always happy with their cooks from France, the cooks didn't like living in Germany. In spite of the generous salary and comfortable suite of rooms in the Hartmanns' home, the French cooks quickly grew homesick for France. They rarely stayed in Frankfurt for more than a few months. The latest cook had been persuaded to stay until the family left for the summer, and Franz would be on his own after she returned to France. Besides the cook, only Margot's personal maid and secretary, Lisle, who also functioned as the children's nanny, lived in the house.

This year, both the family's dogs would travel to Beaune with Margot and the children. Cadeau, a tiny Bichon went everywhere with Margot.

"You must take my dear old Zoltan with you to Beaune." Zoltan was Franz's elderly Vizsla. "I will miss his companionship more than ever this year, but I can't bring him with me. He has to go with you. When I escape from Germany, I will have only the clothes on my back." Margot and the children were happy to take Zoltan with them to France.

Franz's goodbye to Zoltan was almost as wrenching as his goodbye to his human family. He walked a distance away from the car, holding Zoltan's leash. He didn't want the children to see or hear what he said to his devoted dog. Franz was afraid he would break down. He could almost not bear the thought of sending his beloved canine away without him. Franz knelt beside Zoltan and held his graying muzzle in both hands. "You have given me great comfort over the years. I will miss you in the weeks to come, and you will also miss me. I pray that God will reunite us, that you and I will have the chance to grow old together in Switzerland." Franz had always believed that Zoltan understood him, and Zoltan rested his head on Franz's knee until he took the dog back to the car.

Margot's final farewell to Franz lingered as the tears ran down her cheeks. He made a remark about salty kisses, but Margot could see the moisture glistening in his own eyes. "You must be brave, Margot, and do everything as we have planned. There is no time or energy to waste on fear or sorrow, if we are to survive." Franz did not want to alarm the children, although he knew they must sense that this leave-taking between their parents was of a different intensity, compared to their previous summer goodbyes. They knew their father was not going to join them in Beaune this year, as he usually did, but they could not know he was afraid he might never see them again. Franz tried not to squeeze the breath out of their small bodies when he hugged them goodbye.

Most of their luggage had been shipped ahead by rail, and the family would drive to France in their large Mercedes touring car. Margot was in the driver's seat, and Lisle rode in the passenger seat with the maps. The children were in the back. Franz directed Zoltan to lie on the floor at Chloe's feet, and Cadeau always rode in the front on Margot's lap. Margot knew this probably wasn't a good idea, but Cadeau wouldn't be denied the driver's seat. A large picnic basket, that held the final lunch prepared by their departing French cook, sat between Frederick and Chloe in the back.

Their departure had been delayed by the protracted goodbyes, but they finally drove away through the beautiful German countryside on a perfect April morning. The family always switched to French when they crossed the border from Germany into France. They made a ceremony of bidding Auf Weidershoen to Deutschland and Bonjour to La Belle, France. After a long day in the car, they reached Margot's family estate near Beaune. It seemed impossible that these beautiful spring days could be overshadowed by terrible things to come. How cruel that these happy times must be ruined by the repellent Nazis and a possible future war. Margot felt as if her life were being stolen from her.

Whenever Margot began to doubt the reality of what was happening in Germany, she thought about Max Meyerhof and his family. She often wondered how Max and Dr. Engelman were doing. Thankful that Franz had been able to help them escape, Margot worried that, wherever they went, they would not be able to stay ahead of the Nazis. Franz had said the German military intended to invade France by advancing through the Ardennes. Most military strategists believed the Nazis would first overrun the Netherlands on their way to France, as they had during the Great War. Whatever way the Nazis chose to advance, when Hitler's army seized Belgium, Max and Margot's favorite doctor would not be safe in Liege. Margot hoped they would relocate to where the Germans couldn't find them, wherever that might be. She prayed they would find a way to save themselves and stay out of the Nazis' clutches. When she thought of Max and Dr. Engelman, she inevitably began to think about all those who would not be saved.

Arriving in Beaune brought back happy memories for Margot who'd spent all the summers of her childhood in this old stone house surrounded by acres of vineyards and farmland. She wanted her children to have the same experiences here and make memories they would cherish. The long days, swimming in the lake, bicycling through the countryside, dining on food fresh from the gardens of the estate, listening to her children play and laugh in the bright morning sun ... all these good things helped to restore Margot's spirit and allowed her to forget, for brief moments, the frightening things that were happening in Germany. As the children read their books, sang French and German songs, and lived the lazy days of leisure that well-off families could afford to do, Margot didn't want to consider that this might be the last visit to her much-loved family home.

CHAPTER EIGHTEEN

FRANZ'S JEWISH GRANDMOTHER

MAY 1938

FRANKFURT, GERMANY

F RANZ PUSHED OPEN THE DOOR TO THE NEARLY
empty library. Exhausted, he collapsed into a chair that
was draped with a dust cover. His family had been away
for just a few weeks, and he missed them terribly. Zoltan had
been his faithful companion and had kept the loneliness at bay
when Franz's family had traveled to France in past summers.
Franz felt Zoltan's absence acutely.

The foreign stamps in the corner of the letter that waited
on the table caught Franz's eye. There was no return address
on the envelope, but it was postmarked from Liege, Belgium.
It had to be from Dr. Engelman, and Franz tore open the
envelope, eager to have news of his friends. Months earlier,
Engelman had sent a short note to Franz. Under the Nazi
censors, all mail received from abroad was opened before

it was delivered to a German address. Likewise, all mail being sent abroad was read before it was allowed to leave the country. Franz and Dr. Engelman knew about the censors and had agreed on a simple code they would use in their communications. The letter Franz had received in January read simply: *"Your order for chocolates has arrived."* This let Franz know that Max and the doctor were safely in Belgium. Franz had heard nothing since. This new letter read: *"Both of your orders for chocolates have been delayed. We expect to ship the dark chocolates within three months."* This let Franz know that Max was still recovering from his wounds and was not yet able to travel. Both Max and Engelman remained in Belgium. The note also told Franz that Dr. Engelman had found a position in England or Scotland and hoped to move there within three months. Franz was delighted to have news, but he was sad it was taking Max so long to heal. He knew Dr. Engelman wouldn't leave until Max had recovered enough to live on his own. Franz was eager to tell Margot the news. He wished he could write back to Dr. Engelman but couldn't take that chance. He didn't know where he would send a letter anyway.

Franz filled his nights and weekends alone packing the family's household goods for storage and transport. Surreptitiously procuring the necessary packing crates and materials hadn't been easy. He'd leased a small warehouse and made nightly trips in the gardener's truck to deliver the boxes he'd packed. Securing his books, furniture, and other treasures and making plans to move to Switzerland gave him a small measure of hope that he would see his family again and that they would someday have a home together.

Franz sold the wine collection he'd spent so much time and effort to acquire. Decades earlier, his father had started filling the extensive wine cellar in the basement of the Frankfurt house with carefully selected and valuable wines. Franz had continued the family tradition, and his wine cellar was now one of the finest in the city. Franz couldn't take his wine with him when he left Germany. Alone in the house at night, he drank a glass or two from his best bottles. In a few days, the agent for the new owner of the wine collection would arrive to carefully pack and remove the thousands of bottles of fine wine from the basement.

The fear and anger he felt about the circumstances in which he found himself were always on his mind. He was being forced to abandon his work, his home, and the life he loved because a grandmother, who had died before he was born, might have had Jewish blood.

Franz's grandmother, Marie Claire, had been left as an infant at a Catholic convent. She had been raised and educated by the sisters of Bon Secours in France. On the night she arrived at the convent, she wore a small gold Star of David on a thin gold chain around her tiny infant neck. The sisters had saved the necklace and given it to her on her twelfth birthday, when they told her the story about how she'd come to live at the convent. She accepted the small necklace from her infancy with some curiosity about what it meant, but in 1850, it wasn't important.

Marie Claire had always thought she would take her vows as a nun, become a member of the order, and nurse the sick. As a young girl, she was spirited and intelligent and asked difficult questions of the other sisters. A voracious reader, she was a grown-up in her own mind at age eight. She wanted to become a nurse and serve those who needed her care. She was well-trained and competent in her chosen field by the time she was sixteen. She felt her destiny, to give her life to the Church, had been decided when she was abandoned as an infant on the steps of the convent.

The mother superior of the order wanted Marie Claire to experience more of the outside world before she took the vows that would bind her to the Catholic Church for the rest of her life. She felt Marie Claire needed to learn more about life beyond the convent. When the young novice was eighteen, she was sent as a missionary to nurse the sick and wounded in the Crimean War.

After a year of working long and exhausting hours in make-shift hospital facilities, Marie Claire fell ill with typhus. Close to death and not expected to live, an angel came into her life in the human form of a handsome young German doctor. He arrived at her bedside, first to save her life and then to fall in love with her. He made sure she received the best of care. Food was scarce, and he gave up his own rations to feed her. As she recovered, they talked for hours about everything. Herr Docktor Franz Von Hartmann was a physician and a well-educated man. He had attended prestigious schools in Germany and knew about many things in addition to medicine. An avid reader, he brought books to Marie Claire which aided in the recovery of her spirit and consequently in the recovery of her body.

During the worst days of her illness, Marie Claire had accepted that she would die in the Crimea, far from her home in France. She had entered a State of Grace with God. Then she had been given a second chance at life in large part due to the kindness and care of her German doctor friend. The old Marie Claire had died, in a way, and a new Marie Claire had been reborn to take her place.

The new Marie Claire talked endlessly with Herr Docktor Franz about her hopes and dreams of taking vows in the Catholic order of Bon Secours. A devout Catholic himself, he had argued that she could make a contribution with her nursing skills and could make a difference in other ways without taking vows. He inevitably told her of his love for her, and both were surprised to learn that she also loved him.

They married and returned to Franz's home in Frankfurt, which was then in Hesse in West Prussia, to raise six children. Marie Claire never mentioned the Star of David on a tiny gold chain. It was not important to her life, and the necklace was found at the bottom of her jewelry box after she died, much too young, at age fifty-nine. The possibility that she might have Jewish ancestry still did not matter to anyone in 1897. This family history ran through Franz's mind every night after he'd finished packing, delivered the boxes to his warehouse, and made himself eat something.

The grandmother he'd never known had influenced his life as a child through her strong religious beliefs. Devout and dedicated, she'd attended mass every day of her life. Even when bedridden by childbirth, and in her final illness, the priest had come to her every day to hear her confession and to give her communion. Marie Claire had instilled in all of her children the belief that daily mass was one of life's duties and privileges. Franz's own father had attended mass every day, and he had lived the life of goodness and devotion his mother had set as an example for all of her children. Franz had fallen away from daily mass attendance, but he was a devout Catholic and lived his life accordingly.

Margot's aristocratic French family had voiced strong objections when she had announced her intention to marry a German physicist. Once they'd met this accomplished and charming man, they grudgingly accepted him and in time grew to love Margot's husband. Margot was an only child, and when her parents were killed in a car accident, she inherited substantial wealth which included a great deal of property in France. While Margot's parents were alive, Franz had spent his August holidays at the chateau near Beaune. The summer tradition in France had continued until the summer of 1938. This was the first year Franz had not been able to accompany his family to Margot's summer home.

Franz fell asleep in his library. The bookshelves were empty. His desk and favorite leather chair and ottoman were safely stored in the anonymous warehouse, awaiting shipment to Switzerland. This was Franz's last night at his home in Frankfurt. Tomorrow he would leave this house that had belonged to his father and his grandfather and move to Theo Stocker's apartment. His escape from Germany was scheduled to take place during August, and Franz had several more weeks at work before he took his summer holiday. He'd openly expressed his unhappiness that he wasn't allowed to spend his vacation with his family in France. He'd told his friends and colleagues at work that he was going instead to Baden-Baden for a week to take the spa waters and then to a monastic retreat in northern Germany for two weeks.

Everyone knew Franz's Vizsla was his constant companion, and Franz told those who asked that Zoltan's age and health had forced him to put Zoltan down. Franz was able to accept their condolences with real sorrow because he missed his canine friend terribly, even as he hoped their separation wasn't forever.

Franz's boss, who cared about what happened to Franz and had no love in his heart for their Nazi masters, had warned him that he would to be sent to a "work camp" as soon as their current research project was finished. His boss had done some small favors for Franz regarding money transfers and the sale of properties but didn't want to know the details of his plans to leave Germany. Franz and his boss managed to string out the work of their project to make it last until Franz's August holiday.

CHAPTER NINETEEN

GENEVA AND EDWARD ARGUE

MAY 1938
GENEVA (BELMONT, OHIO) ON THE PHONE
WITH EDWARD (CAMBRIDGE, MASSACHUSETTS)

"PLEASE, DON'T GO," EDWARD BEGGED GENEVA over the telephone. This discussion had previously been conducted through their written correspondence. That Edward would spend the money for a long distance telephone call from Boston spoke volumes before he even said a word. "I'm worried about your safety."

"You're overreacting. I'll be fine. The trip is sponsored by Columbia University. They wouldn't let us go to Germany if they had any doubts about our safety. This is the chance of a lifetime for me, and it's not costing me anything. This is my opportunity to see the world and work on my master's degree."

"Geneva, you don't know anything about Hitler and the Nazis. The American public hasn't been given the whole story about what's going on over there."

"I know you're still angry about the Olympics, and so am I. But I'm just visiting Germany. I'm not going to work there or live there or do anything dangerous."

"Yes, I'm still angry about the Berlin Olympics. Jesse Owens is one of the world's greatest athletes, maybe the greatest of all time. Because I'm from Ohio, of course I'm disturbed about the way Hitler treated him. Hitler's an extraordinarily evil man. He's taken over Germany with lies, chicanery, and pure arrogance. His Nazis have committed unspeakable crimes." Edward was adamant.

"You're getting carried away and letting your fury about those gold medals make you irrational. I read magazines and newspapers and listen to the radio. I've even heard Hitler speak over the short wave. Of course I don't understand German, but he sounds like a squeaky little man who shouts and struts around to make himself seem bigger. He doesn't have any hypnotic effect on me, and he's more than a bit hysterical. I don't know what all the fuss is about, but I've heard people say he's so charismatic. I even heard somebody say that, when they hear him speak, they felt a tingle go up their leg. I mean, who would even say an utterly ridiculous thing like that?"

"He's certainly done a masterful job of hypnotizing the German people. I don't think you realize what it will be like to visit a society like Nazi Germany. You are used to freedom and the kind of life we have here in the USA. You're not used to having the government restrict where you can travel and what you can do and what you can say. You will have to present travel documents everywhere. German citizens have to carry their identification papers with them when they run to the corner store for a bottle of milk or a loaf of bread. No one can travel freely inside Germany, and many aren't able to leave the country now without the Nazis' permission. You don't have any idea what kind of a place Germany is today."

"I don't mind having to present my papers. Visas are required to visit lots of foreign countries. You still haven't told me anything that makes me think I won't be safe there." Geneva was standing firm.

"I wasn't going to bring this up because it's something I myself can scarcely believe is true. One of our professors at the medical school traveled to Germany a few months ago. He was born in Germany and still has family there. His niece was a Mongoloid child, and she died in a special facility where she'd been sent on the orders of the Nazi government. This professor's family is full of medical people, and when they tried to get information about how the little girl died, they found out some things they weren't supposed to know. The Nazis are rounding up and euthanizing retarded children, the mentally ill, as well as deformed and crippled people. My colleague's family knows this to be absolutely true, and unbelievably, there are some people in Germany who think it's a good idea." Edward paused. Geneva said nothing.

Edward continued. "I don't blame you for being speechless. I was in shock when I heard it. Apparently, it's a policy of the Nazi government, a secret policy. Hitler wants to rid the German population of those he considers undesirable, imperfect, or weak. He's killing anybody who isn't 'a perfect German.' He has written openly about 'cleansing' the German race as part of his vision for Germany's future."

"How can you be sure that story is really true, and what does any of this have to do with me?"

"Look at Austria and the Rhineland. Hitler just walked into those places and took them. Not a single country in the world made any objection; they all just let him do it. Look at the most recent fuss over the Sudetenland. Do you really believe any of the pretenses Hitler has given as reasons for taking over other countries? What if he decides to take over more territory in Europe while you're there? Like Czechoslo-vakia? Do you think the rest of Europe and the world will continue to sit back and let him have his way? You're traveling to a country that could go to war at any time."

"What makes you think anybody will stand up to the Nazis if they take over more territory that doesn't belong to them? Nobody has stood up to Hitler about anything so far. He's taken whatever he wants, and the whole world has just accepted it. What makes you think European countries will behave differently in the future, no matter what Hitler does? The British want peace at all costs, and FDR is totally against going to war. Every world leader has repeatedly promised there will be no war. I will be perfectly safe visiting Germany. I'm not in danger."

"I don't want you to go. I'm afraid for you. You're my girl, and I want you to be safe."

"You're the one who encouraged me to work on a graduate degree and to travel abroad. Whatever happened to that kind of talk, Edward?"

"I just never dreamed you would want to travel to Germany. To go there now is madness. You're walking into a den of wickedness."

"Well, I am going, no matter what you say."

CHAPTER TWENTY

LAST NIGHT IN BELMONT

MAY 1938

BELMONT, OHIO

ALL OF HER SIBLINGS WOULD BE AT THE FARM for dinner tonight. Her mother had set the table with a white linen tablecloth and matching napkins that were freshly starched and ironed. Mae had brought out the good china that usually only made appearances at Thanksgiving, Christmas, and special birthdays. The garden was in its prime, so all the food was fresh and homegrown. They sat down to Geneva's favorite wilted lettuce salad and her mother's homemade yeast rolls. The lettuce had been picked from their kitchen garden less than an hour before it was served, as had the sliced scallions in the salad. The crisp, crumbled bacon came from their own hogs, and Geneva's father had made the cider vinegar for the salad dressing from the apples they grew in their orchard. Geneva knew she had the best of life here in

Belmont and sometimes wondered why she wanted to leave this place and go so far away?

Geneva's father said an especially long grace before the meal, making a heart-felt plea to the Heavenly Father for Geneva's safe travels and return to Belmont.

Talk around the table was about what was happening in Germany and about Geneva's trip. Her brother Arnold admonished her not to flirt too much during her trip abroad. "Are you going to find yourself a German boyfriend when you get over there, sis?"

"Of course not, silly. Edward is my one and only love. We're going to get married. You know that."

"What about Lloyd Dermott and that other doctor you said you were going to marry, the one you met at Muskingum? Am I going to have to learn German to be able to talk to the fellow you bring back with you from the Third Reich? Will he be a Nazi?"

"Stop, Arnold. I know I'm a terrible flirt, and I like to have a good time. But I've changed my ways, and now I am forever faithful to Edward."

Geneva's married sister Bea told Arnold he should take his own advice once in a while. "You should talk, Arnold Burkhart. You always have more girls on the string than Carter has liver pills. You have no room to tease Geneva." Bea knew Geneva liked men and loved to dance the night away when she had the chance. Bea was happily married to Warren, the scholar. Warren knew all about what was happening in Nazi Germany and whether or not there was going to be a war. He wanted to educate his in-laws who were gathered at the table, and he made a valiant attempt to divert the conversation from the volatile topic of Geneva's boyfriends.

Geneva's older sister, sweet Martha, begged, "Please come home to us in one piece." Martha wondered why Geneva hadn't married and settled down. Geneva had attracted many suitors over the years. As soon as they asked for her hand, she turned them down, except for Edward. "I don't understand why you want to go so far away, all the way to Germany. I'm perfectly happy here at home and don't want to go anywhere else, except maybe to Wheeling once in a while."

Platters of fried chicken and bowls of mashed potatoes and gravy circled the table. Green beans, asparagus, candied carrots, and new English peas kept the family quiet for a few minutes at a time. The warm rolls were topped with butter churned in the Burkhart Dairy and strawberry jam made in the farm's kitchen. Geneva and her family devoured the rhubarb and strawberry pies topped with homemade vanilla ice cream. Pitchers of iced tea and lemonade made the rounds as this American farm family feasted on the bounty of their hard work and toasted their loved one who was about to embark on an adventure.

After dinner, Arnold, always the joker, goose-stepped around the porch giving the Hitler salute and saying "Sieg Heil" in a hilariously phony German accent. He played a terrible German-sounding polka on his harmonica and asked "die Fraulein" for a dance. He trotted Geneva around the floor as he played an off-key tune on his harmonica with one hand and saluted with the other. The Burkhart clan convulsed in laughter.

Geneva enjoyed it all with the rest of them, but sobered when she remembered the things Edward had told her. Edward was so serious about everything. He wouldn't have found Arnold's antics funny and probably would have been offended by the "Heil Hitler" posing and prancing. Geneva begged off from the hilarity, saying she had packing to do. She kissed and hugged them good-night and said her goodbyes. None of them could know that, when she left home, she would be traveling into the world's worst nightmare. Daddy would drive her to the train early the next morning. There was no station, just a platform next to the tracks where the train stopped. Geneva would leave Belmont and head for New York City, the first leg in her travels.

It would be weeks before she would again sleep in her own familiar bed. She put her head down on the clean white pillowcase. It smelled of her mother's homemade laundry soap, sunshine, and the iron her mother had used to smooth out the wrinkles. At the farm, all the bedclothes were hung outside to dry. The sweet fragrance of fresh air and clean linen brought back a flood of memories of Geneva's youth and her small-town life. She wondered what the pillowcases would smell like in New York and in strange hotels in Germany.

When she left Belmont the next morning, she would be leaving behind what remained of her childhood. She would return home more experienced and worldly. Within the year, she would become officially engaged to Edward, and they would marry. She would no longer be a girl. She would be a more sophisticated woman. She cried a little into her pillow as she grieved for the country lass she was at this moment. That young woman would disappear forever into the past as Geneva set out on the next part of her life's journey. She would be homesick for the farm, for her family, and for dear Edward. She would return to this place she loved, inevitably changed, a different person. She realized these things would happen, but she could not know how profoundly altered she would be.

CHAPTER TWENTY ONE

GENEVA AND ELSIE BECOME SISTERS OF THE SOUL

JUNE 1938
NEW YORK

O N THEIR FIRST MEETING, ELSIE FARROW and Geneva Burkhart immediately recognized each other as allies. Although Elsie, a teacher at a private school in Connecticut, was a decade older than Geneva, Elsie was out-spoken and high-spirited in a way that made her seem younger than her years. A serious mathematician and excellent school teacher, Elsie came from a wealthy and well-connected New England family.

When they were introduced, Elsie immediately sensed that Geneva was a fellow iconoclast, a woman who had stepped outside the expectations the world had for her and made her own choices about what she wanted to do with her life. Elsie was perceptive about human nature, and although she acknowledged Geneva's obvious youth and naiveté, she immediately wanted to know her better. She knew Geneva was smart; everyone in the group was smart. Elsie could see that Geneva was unsophisticated, and the fact that this basically homegrown country girl from a small Ohio town had chosen to apply to Columbia University for a scholarship to travel to Nazi Germany, not the safest place in the world in 1938, told Elsie a lot about Miss Burkhart's courage and sense of adventure.

Elsie's own rebellion had been against the prospects her very correct and haughty mother had for her. Elsie was not a great beauty, and she loved academics. She'd always preferred studying and reading to attending the silly cotillions with the foppish young males of her own upper class. The thought of marrying one of these superficial and spoiled men filled Elsie's heart with despair. She would rather be dead than live her life with one of those wastrels as a husband. To have to talk to such a man on a daily basis and to see one of them at the breakfast table every morning was about a life consigned to hell for Elsie. She decided to become a teacher, and her profession gave her time and an excuse for the reading and learning she loved.

Her mistake had been in attempting to be honest with her mother who was, in spite of Elsie's declaration that she would never marry, relentlessly trying to find her a mate. Her mother was always planning social activities for Elsie to attend, events which put Elsie together with the eligible bachelors of her mother's choosing. Because Elsie would have none of it, she was alienated from her parents and her two sisters, who had acquiesced to their mother's demands. They'd both married worthless husbands who spent their time in leisure pursuits — drinking, playing the horses, and spending their summers in Newport.

Elsie had a teaching job, and Elsie's grandmother had left her a substantial trust fund which allowed her to buy good clothes and live in a nice apartment without seeking financial help from her estranged immediate family. Elsie loved and prized her independence, and she could see this streak of individuality in Geneva Burkhart. They agreed to be roommates for the next three months.

Dr. Veere had said at one of the orientation meetings, "I want you to find another member of the group with whom you feel compatible and keep the same roommate for the duration of the trip. This will make my life much easier. When we have bed check at our hotels, you will know if your roommate is missing."

What he didn't say was that his "special" teachers needed to be paired with each other. The "cover" members of the group, Veere's innocents, had to be kept in the dark about the secret assignments of the others. The women would travel and live together closely for several weeks. A complete lack of communication among them was neither possible nor desirable, but it was necessary to protect the women with special assignments as well as the women who knew nothing about these secret agendas.

Geneva was thrilled to be sharing with Elsie, and they became friends during the orientation in New York. Elsie had very proper manners and knew her way around every possible situation. She took Geneva under her wing and gave her helpful tips about what to do. Geneva felt lucky to have Elsie as a guide and mentor. The two youngest in the group, they found many things to giggle about, including how mannish some of the other teachers were with their dowdy clothes and brown lace-up shoes. Geneva was sure at least one of the woman was in her 50's, almost as old as Geneva's own Mother and Daddy. Another woman wore what Elsie and Geneva were sure was a blonde wig. They couldn't imagine why someone wanted to wear something that was so obviously fake and at the same time so unbecoming. It was a mystery they wanted to solve.

Although at first a few of the women in the group seemed standoffish in reaction to Geneva's open Middle Western smile and outgoing personality, most welcomed her warmly. Edward, who had lived in Boston for four years, would have understood their aloof New England composure. The group as a whole was lighthearted, friendly, and eager to embark on their journey. No one spoke of politics or Hitler or possible dangers that might arise.

Orientation in New York was busy. The women bunked in the dormitories at Columbia and met with Dr. Veere for several hours every morning. Afternoons and evenings were free for sightseeing and having fun. Geneva had climbed to the crown of the Statue of Liberty, ridden on the Staten Island Ferry, been to the top of the Empire State Building and the Chrysler Building, and seen as many other sights as she possibly could. Elsie knew all about New York City and was thrilled to show off her favorite spots to Geneva. Several women in the group were familiar with New York, so they knew what to do and where to go for the best food.

"We are taking you to a real New York deli today for lunch." The delis in New York were famous, and Elsie was eager to introduce Geneva to this unique regional cuisine. "I know how much you love to eat, and we are treating you to a corned beef on rye. Some people say deli food from New York is the best food the USA has to offer. You will love it."

Geneva wasn't quite used to the bustle of New York and the sometimes brusque manners of the people she encountered, but she was over the moon about the corned beef on rye. "It's like ham but spicier, and it's much more delicious with the Swiss cheese, the coleslaw, and the Russian dressing. This is my new favorite sandwich, and I want to come back here every day for lunch."

"There are other delis you might like to try."

"No, I want to come back to this very same deli and sit at this very same table and eat this very same sandwich tomorrow. It is heaven."

"Tomorrow we are going to Mama Leone's, and you'll be crazy about that restaurant, too. It's Italian, and I'll tell you what to order. After dinner, we have tickets to see a performance of *Our Town*, a play on Broadway. *Our Town* was written by Thornton Wilder, and it's playing at the Morosco Theatre. The play's very popular, and you will like the performance. It will be great fun." Elsie and the others loved Geneva's enthusiasm. Some of them were jaded when it came to New York. Geneva's enjoyment of new experiences allowed them to see things they'd taken for granted through her fresh eyes.

On the first morning of orientation, Dr. Veere handed out itineraries that told them exactly where in France, Germany, and England they would be traveling. The list included the name and address of each of the hotels where they'd be staying and on what dates they would arrive at and depart from each location. The cities and the universities where they would have their mathematics lectures were included. Dr. Veere had been to all of these places. He went over the itinerary and gave the group a short description of each one. Geneva sent letters to her family and included the dates and names and addresses of the hotels where she would be on every day of her travels. She wanted to share this exciting time with them and also hoped they would write to her. Geneva was so busy having a grand adventure in New York, she scarcely had a minute to write about it in the journal she'd promised herself she would keep.

Dr. Veere discussed each of the lists he'd sent to the members of the group. Traveling abroad, especially for those who had never been outside the United States, required them to become familiar with the way things were done in other countries. There were different laws and different customs. Dr. Veere knew the ropes, and he was doing his best to prepare his group for whatever they might encounter.

He spent one entire morning discussing the political situation in Germany. Under the Nazis, neither German citizens nor visitors enjoyed the rights and freedoms those who lived in the United States took for granted. He tried to be tactful and not critical, but the women could tell that, when he warned about some things they absolutely must not do when visiting the Third Reich, he was often speaking through clenched teeth.

He urged them to be discreet. He cautioned them that their hotel rooms, the restaurants, the lecture halls, and the telephones at their hotels probably all had listening devices. The women should be careful about what they said in public. He told them they would have a Nazi "guide" assigned to them for the duration of their trip. He would be their driver, translator, and chaperone. Dr. Veere didn't actually say their Nazi would be reporting on what the members of the group said and what they did, but they all got the point. Veere couldn't help but refer to him several times as their "Nazi minder."

Dr. Veere explained how everything would be paid for — hotel rooms, meals, train travel, sightseeing, etc., with vouchers and letters of credit. He told them he would be taking care of all payments and gratuities. It sounded to the women as if Dr. William Veere had a great many things to be responsible for and think about.

When Dr. Veere gave his orientation talks, he treated them all equally. It was essential that he not show deference to anyone. Six of the members of the group were exactly the women they appeared to be. They had no intelligence-gathering or secret responsibilities. They were not spies. They were mathematics teachers who wanted to travel to Europe and work on a master's degree. They were the essential cover for the others. The other four members of the group were operating undercover, did have special assignments, and would be involved in covert operations. It was essential that the authentic mathematics teachers remain completely unaware that some members of the group were traveling and studying with them under false pretenses.

Two Americans and two British women were in the group for very different reasons. The two Americans were specifically trained to get classified information from the professors and others they would meet during the lecture tour in Germany. Dr. Veere would bring back to scientists in the U.S. and Britain, the vital evidence they gathered. These two American women, in fact, spoke and read fluent German, something that had been strictly forbidden by The German Sciences, Education, and Cultural Ministry, the organization with which Veere had .worked so hard to obtain permission for the trip.

The two British women traveling in the group were pretending to be Americans. They had American passports and false but solid American backgrounds. The hardest part of their mission had been to learn to speak without a British accent. Both women were MI6, and one of them would stay behind in Germany to become a "sleeper" spy. She had a significant long-term role to play — influencing Nazi military decisions. The other British woman was in the group to provide the opportunity to smuggle Franz Hartmann, an important German physicist, out of Germany into Switzerland. This was the most dangerous aspect of the secret plans, but it was of the utmost importance.

The trip led by Dr. Veere was, at this time, the only way for the British to get any of their people into Germany. A U.S. sponsored travel group would be able to travel more easily around the country in a way that wouldn't attract the kind of attention a British contingent would.

The German Ministry that was overseeing the trip had requested in-depth biographical material on each of the women in the group. Jack Trevanian had made certain all of the women's backgrounds would stand up to careful scrutiny. He had personally and painstakingly set up the background stories for the "special" teachers. Some of them were using false names, and some were wearing disguises.

As Dr. Veere concluded their orientation sessions, he said a silent prayer that, God willing, after the next twelve weeks traveling outside the United States, they would all return without harm from a country that they really shouldn't be visiting in the first place. He offered another small prayer that the Germans would behave themselves and not move into any more countries for a few weeks — at least until he'd brought the women safely home.

CHAPTER TWENTY TWO

LEAVING NEW YORK

JUNE 1938
NEW YORK

TONIGHT THEY SAILED ON THE *NORMANDIE*, and Geneva could scarcely contain her excitement. She chose her summer-weight blue wool suit, her favorite, and a gray silk blouse to wear as they left New York harbor aboard the ocean liner. After a fancy bon voyage lunch at the Columbia University Faculty Club, the women loaded themselves and their luggage into a van and were transported to the pier where they would board the ship that would carry them to France.

The departure pier was madness. Horns were honking. Taxis and people and cars stood gridlocked in confusion. Geneva's group tried to stay together as Dr. Veere summoned porters to deal with their luggage. With tickets and passports in hand, he guided the women to the gangway to board the ship. Geneva was amazed at the enormous size of the *Normandie* and how many hallways and stairways and tiny elevators they had to navigate to find their staterooms.

Elsie had sailed on an ocean liner before, years earlier on a trip to Europe with her family. Elsie knew what to do and was helpful without ever making Geneva feel as if she were unsophisticated or dimwitted for not knowing something.

Geneva was impressed with the efficiency of their stateroom and awed by the luxury of the public rooms. She made sure all of her luggage arrived. One of the women in the group called from a stateroom down the hall to say that champagne was being poured. Geneva had tasted champagne only once before. Prohibition was no longer in effect, but Geneva's mother was a strict teetotaler. Daddy would sneak down to the cellar once in a while to indulge in some hard apple cider he'd made. Geneva was eager to try champagne again.

A short time later, an official person came through the hallway, announcing that all visitors who remained on the ship had to disembark. The ship was about to sail. The women carried their glasses of champagne to the outside deck. Someone handed out tickertape streamers and confetti, and everyone was shouting and waving. It was quite a spectacle for the small-town girl. Always eager to get with the enthusiasm of the moment, Geneva cheered and waved and celebrated even though she didn't know a single person on the pier. The *Normandie* blew its powerful whistle, and tugboats guided the graceful ship from its moorings. They were launched and on their way across the Atlantic Ocean. It was a night Geneva would never forget.

Geneva was surprised how many people were always around asking if they could help her. Their cabin steward seemed like he was constantly there, doing something important and useful to their room. He knew they were with a group and gave them a card with their dining room table assignments on it. They were assigned the second seating for lunch and dinner. Breakfast was a "come whenever you want to" kind of affair, or it could be served to you in your stateroom.

Every facet of the dining experience on the *Normandie* was quite wondrous for Geneva. The country cooking her mother served on the farm in Ohio was the best in Geneva's opinion, and her experience with restaurants was limited. The quantity and variety of the items on the *Normandie*'s menus and the number of courses at each meal overwhelmed her. She'd never heard of some of the things that were offered. Geneva had studied French in school, but Elsie was indispensable in guiding her away from the sweetbreads and the liver pâtés that Geneva didn't like. Geneva tried snails one evening and decided that even though the sauce was delicious, the snails themselves had no taste at all. They were too chewy, like trying to bite through a rubber band. Elsie laughed and told Geneva she wasn't the first person to compare snails to rubber bands.

The first few days, Geneva ordered way too much food, but she eventually learned to pace herself. And there were so many meals. The breakfast menu included every possible breakfast thing you could think of, plus some things that Geneva usually associated with dinners, like filet mignon and fish. Then there was a mid-morning buffet in the main lounge with coffee, hot chocolate, and tea and at least fifty different kinds of pastries. Lunch, like dinner, consisted of course after course of food. Just when she thought she couldn't possibly eat another thing for days, English tea was served in the afternoon. Tea was Geneva's favorite meal of the day ... or maybe her second favorite. It was a good thing they were scheduled for the later seating, or she would never have had an appetite for dinner. She usually took a short afternoon nap. All the eating was exhausting, she told Elsie.

There were many activities, other than eating, and Geneva made an enthusiastic effort to experience all of them. She found shuffleboard pretty boring and decided duckpin bowling was not her sport. Geneva and Elsie both loved movies and watched as many as they could fit into their schedule. Geneva found her volleyball skills made her a decent deck tennis player, and she and Elsie tried to swim in one of the ship's pools every day. There was never a dull moment.

The group gathered for pre-dinner cocktails. Because Geneva didn't drink alcohol and had decided that champagne didn't agree with her, she ordered Coca Cola. There was sherry, wine, scotch, and martinis for the more sophisticated drinkers. They went into dinner as a group, and the meal always seemed to last for hours. Some nights there were magic shows, comedians, or singers as after-dinner entertainment.

Most nights, Elsie and Geneva went to the ballroom for dancing. Men she'd never met and whose names she didn't know asked Geneva to dance, and she loved every minute of it. Geneva never wanted the music and the dancing to end. None of the men with whom she danced meant anything to her romantically, but she loved to flirt with her dancing partners. She knew she would never see any of them again. Occasionally, one of the men she danced with gave her his card and ask for hers. She didn't have cards and had no idea what to tell them when they wanted to know how to get in touch with her. Geneva liked men and craved the attention they showed her. In spite of the fact that she had to allow all these dancing partners to slip through her fingers, it was wonderful. Geneva wanted to dance all night. Elsie wasn't that enthusiastic about the ballroom dancing, but she stayed late to be sure Geneva didn't get herself into any difficulties.

To top it all off, just when Geneva thought the fun had come to an end for the night, waiters threw open the doors at the end of the ballroom. Everyone was invited into the next room that held an enormous "midnight buffet." Geneva had always had a vigorous appetite and fortunately had an excellent metabolism to go with it, but the midnight buffet was the topper. There was this wonderful thing, on a long table full of wonderful things, called seafood Newburg that was entirely new to Geneva. It was so delicious that one night she ate way too much of it and made herself sick. Elsie helped her through the small crisis, and Geneva gained some perspective on how to handle the abundance of food.

Cleaning one's plate was important on the farm. Food was plentiful there, but nothing went to waste. It was an adjustment for Geneva to be presented with limitless choices and unending volumes of delicacies. Elsie urged her to enjoy it, within reason. She told Geneva that German food would not be as elegant as the French food they were being served on the *Normandie.*

Geneva thought the trip across the Atlantic Ocean and life aboard the *Normandie* was magnificent. She said she didn't care if the food was bad in Germany or what might happen on the rest of the trip. The ocean voyage alone had been an experience Geneva Burkhart never imagined she would have.

CHAPTER TWENTY THREE

ARRIVING
IN FRANCE

JUNE 1938

LE HAVRE, FRANCE

THE ARRIVAL AT LE HAVRE WAS EXHILARATING. Geneva and Elsie hurried down the gangway, trying to stay with the others in the group while keeping Dr. Veere's head in view as it bobbed above the crowd. Thank goodness he was tall. Elsie, who knew something about everything, warned Geneva, "France is always chaotic." The atmosphere was foreign, and the air smelled of salt water, diesel oil, rope, fish, and apples. Everything was loud; everybody was shouting. Geneva couldn't hear herself think, let alone hear what anybody else was saying. But it was thrilling, not only to have her feet on the ground in another country, but also to be standing on another continent. Geneva had spent some time brushing up on her French, but everybody was talking so fast and yelling and gesticulating. Even if she'd been able to hear anything, she couldn't understand a single word.

The luggage had been collected from their staterooms. Dr. Veere had warned them it would be necessary for them to go through customs and passport control as a group. "There will be long lines, and a great deal of patience will be required. The French are not efficient, and you will become frustrated while you wait. We will go directly from customs and immigration to the train for Paris. Please try to keep me in view at all times, and whatever you do, don't become separated from your roommate. Some of you speak French, but that's not going to help you very much today."

Geneva was in a daze. She'd studied the maps of France and Germany so many times; it was hard for her to realize she was physically here in the places she'd dreamed about for months. She wanted to take it all in and experience every ounce of the day.

Dr. Veere had spoken with the customs and immigration people before they inspected the women's papers. This seemed to enlighten the personnel behind the counters, and they gave the passports and paperwork only a cursory inspection. Geneva thought there was an excessive amount of stamping connected with being allowed to visit France. Every official person had several stamps and used them liberally and enthusiastically, stamping everything in sight. Geneva wondered why all of these stamps could possibly be necessary. Elsie muttered something about French bureaucrats and whispered to Geneva, "If you think this is bad, just wait until we have to pass inspection by the Germans." When they'd convinced everyone that they had nothing to declare, the group was given the stamp of approval to enter France and allowed to board the train to Paris.

They found their way to the railway platform and waited beside their enormous pile of trunks and valises. Their trunks had been unloaded from the *Normandie* and would be transferred by rail freight to hotels in cities where the group would spend a week or more — to Paris, Nuremberg, Berlin, and finally to London.

Geneva commented to Elsie. "It looks to me like we have a whole lot more luggage than we do people. In addition to our wardrobe trunk, weren't we each supposed to bring just one large suitcase plus the kit bag we carry ourselves?" Geneva tried to count the bags, picking through the pile to be sure she didn't miss any lying at the bottom. "Where do you think all these extra bags came from?"

Elsie shrugged off Geneva's concern. "As long as our bags are in the pile, don't worry about it. I worry when the pile looks like there aren't enough bags." Elsie was impatient for their train to arrive and couldn't worry about extra suitcases, as long as she saw her own.

They were swept up in boarding the train and finding their seats. Dr. Veere made sure the mountain of luggage was loaded. He counted noses in the two compartments where his teachers were sitting and handed each woman her tickets. He said the trip to Paris would take about three hours. Taxis would take them to their hotel for lunch. Geneva was so excited; she could hardly believe what was happening to her. Sometimes she wondered if she would wake up from a dream and find herself back in the kitchen at the farm stemming strawberries for jam.

Geneva loved sitting in a compartment, so different from the configuration of train seats in the United States. The compartment was cozy and private, and she and her group were sitting together in their own little room. Geneva thought it was a tremendous improvement over the trains in America where a ride on the train was not very different from the ride on a Greyhound bus. She'd been in France for little more than an hour and had already decided European trains were really swell!

The countryside of northern France rolled by the train windows. The farmland could have been in Ohio, and sometimes farmers in the fields waved at the train when it passed. Geneva decided people were a lot alike no matter what country they lived in or what language they spoke. Seeing crops growing and farmers waving as the train went by were things Geneva could relate to. These familiar sights helped to calm the jitters she felt about being in a foreign place and being out of her league in terms of sophistication and knowing what to do. Reminders of her own life's experiences boosted her confidence that she could do this traveling thing. She didn't want to miss a minute of it, but eventually she nodded off to sleep. Elsie woke Geneva as they were entering the outskirts of Paris. "I knew you wouldn't want to miss our arrival in the City of Light." Elsie smiled.

Their train entered the Gare du Nord, and the women were once again plunged into the confusion of arriving in a new place, trying to keep track of each other, and attempting to keep Dr. Veere's head in sight. People ran in every direction. Men and women on the platforms were embracing and kissing. Most of the people who were meeting gave two kisses, one on each side of the face. Geneva stared when she saw women kissing each other on the lips. It seemed that everyone was kissing.

Train whistles blew, and announcements in French about arrivals and departures blared over the intercom system, trying to be heard above the din. The café smelled like strong coffee, and each table held a multitude of tiny cups. Every person in the café seemed to have a crescent-shaped pastry on the plate in front of them, accompanied by large pats of butter and jams and jellies in tiny glass jars. There were market stalls full of fresh fruits and vegetables for sale, right inside the train station. Two women were arguing with each other about the onions. One woman shook a bunch of leeks in the other woman's face. Geneva realized she was hungry. In spite of being distracted by all the new stimuli and wanting to stop and look at everything, she did her best to stay with the group. At last, they were ensconced in taxis and on their way to the hotel.

The streets of Paris were a maze of congestion, and Geneva could only think about how happy she was that she wasn't driving. Her father complained about the traffic in Wheeling, West Virginia whenever he had to drive there. Geneva couldn't imagine how upset he would be if he ever had to drive in this mess. Someone gasped and pointed out the window. Geneva stared and said in awe, without even thinking that she was speaking in French, "La Tour Eiffel." The taxi full of women laughed and congratulated her on her "sightseeing French." After much stopping and starting, incessant honking, and yelling on the part of their taxi driver at other taxi drivers, they arrived at their hotel.

Located on an out-of-the-way street, their hotel was small but comfortable. Dr. Veere said they were in a central location for seeing all the sights. There was a sitting room to the right of the lobby, and a dining room to the left. The rooms all had high ceilings and were elegantly decorated. Geneva had slept overnight in a hotel only once before in her life. She stuck close by Elsie's side.

Their mountain of trunks and suitcases had followed them and appeared in the lobby. Geneva was still convinced that there were too many bags for the group.

They were all seated for lunch at one long table in the middle of the hotel dining room. The ceilings were encrusted with elaborate gold and plaster moldings. Candelabra-style chandeliers hung down over the tables. Even though sunlight poured in through the floor-to-ceiling windows on two sides of the room, all the chandeliers were lit. Geneva had to remind herself that this was only lunch.

All the tables were set with white tablecloths and white cloth napkins. At each woman's place numerous forks and knives were lined up on both sides of the plate, and a cluster of wine glasses sat at the tip of the knives. Geneva was glad she'd read her Emily Post. She studied the silverware and decided she could handle the meal. A few of the women spoke French with the waiters. The waiters actually understood what some of them were saying and spoke French in return. Elsie's French was excellent, but Geneva was too unsure of herself to try to speak to the waiters in French. She could read the menu, however, and was thrilled to be able to point to the items and pronounce out loud what she wanted when the waiter came to take her order. She pointed to the soup of the day, the seafood salad, the loin of lamb, the pommes frites (of course), the haricots verts, and said she would wait until later to order dessert.

The waiter brought loaves of warm bread with small crocks of butter. The bread wasn't sliced, and Geneva watched as the others tore pieces off the loaves and passed them on. She spread her piece of bread with butter from the crock, and after her first bite, she decided the bread was the best she'd ever tasted. Geneva would never tell her mother that the bread in France was better than what her mother made at home, but this bread was quite wonderful. Maybe the butter didn't quite measure up to what the Burkhart Dairy produced, but it was pretty darn good. It would certainly do while butter from Ohio wasn't available.

Several days on the *Normandie* had made Geneva something of an expert at avoiding foods she didn't like, but she was afraid she'd made a mistake ordering the seafood salad. There were things on the plate that Geneva had never seen. One of the women in the group who knew about French seafood told her the unknowns were mussels and whelks. Neither their names nor their appearance made them attractive enough to convince Geneva to eat them.

She hated to sleep on her first afternoon in Paris, but when she and Elsie finally went to their room at 3:30 in the afternoon, they collapsed on their beds for a nap. Their room was cramped, and two narrow beds barely fit into the space. There was a sink in the room, but they had to go down the hall to use the toilet. Dr. Veere had warned them that this would be the situation in several of their European hotels. If they wanted to take a bath or a shower, they would have to pay for an attendant to unlock the bathing room. The length of time they spent in the bath and the amount of water they used would be monitored. Their trunks and suitcases had been brought to the room while they were eating lunch, but they were too worn out to unpack. It had already been a very big day for the country girl from Belmont and the rich girl from Greenwich.

The days in Paris flew by in a whirlwind of sightseeing, walking, and eating. The group went to every famous place Geneva had ever heard of and many she hadn't. She'd never been to a large art museum before, so when she went to the Louvre for the first time, Geneva was awestruck by the size of the building and the countless rooms full of paintings that went on and on and on. She knew if she got lost in this place, she would never be found. Every room was crammed with art work, and there were statues of naked women on the landings of every staircase. One of the statues of a naked woman didn't have any arms.

Dr. Veere had arranged two tours for the group at the Louvre. One tour was the masterpieces of the Louvre, and the other was of the French Impressionist painters. Several of the women in the group were quite knowledgeable about paintings and sculpture. Geneva's college curriculum had concentrated on mathematics and preparing her to be a teacher and hadn't included any art history. After visiting the Louvre, she promised herself that if she ever had the opportunity, she would study art history. She was fascinated as their tour guide explained the meaning behind a work of art and talked about the techniques that made each artist's style unique. Geneva hoped someday she could bring Edward to Paris and show him the Louvre. Her visit to the famous museum had opened a whole new world.

Paris had been indescribable, and Geneva didn't want this part of the trip to end. France was chaotic as advertised, but Geneva had become used to the traffic and the honking horns and the taxi drivers screaming at each other. She'd even spoken a few words and phrases in French to French people and hadn't done too badly. Elsie warned her, "Eat up and enjoy the wonderful French food. German food is very different, and the bread in Germany is nothing like the bread in France." Geneva took Elsie's advice and devoured the unforgettable French bread like she would never eat again.

Geneva and Elsie had both observed that one member of their group, Grace Davis from Iowa, was extraordinarily intelligent. But they were worried about Grace's health. They were certain Grace would be able to understand everything that was said in the upcoming lectures and would have brilliant questions to ask. Geneva especially liked Grace because she was from the Middle West, from Iowa, and spoke with a broad, open accent like Geneva did.

Grace had been subdued on the voyage to France and had kept to herself. Once they'd arrived in Paris, Geneva thought Grace had even less energy. She took naps during the day and was often late for breakfast or missed it altogether. She seemed listless at meals and pushed her food around on her plate. Geneva, who loved food, especially noticed Grace's lack of interest in eating. Grace hadn't participated in many of the Paris sightseeing and museum tours and always begged off from the nighttime activities. Geneva wondered if Grace would be able to make it through the trip. Elsie was concerned about Grace's unusually pale skin color.

They were heading next to Germany, and the lectures would begin. It had all been just fun and food so far, and the group was looking forward to the upcoming academics. Geneva had always thought math was fun, but she wondered if she would be able to understand what the German professors were saying. She felt pretty sure she could understand the math part. The German lecturers would be speaking in English, but Geneva worried about their accents. As she took on each new challenge, her anxiety diminished about not knowing what to do in foreign territory. She found herself more than able to handle the unexpected, and she even began to look forward to encountering the unknown.

CHAPTER TWENTY FOUR

ARRIVING
IN GERMANY

JUNE 1938

FRANCE AND GERMANY

"ARE YOU READY FOR THIS?" ELSIE ASKED GENEVA the night before they left France. "I've not been to Germany since the Nazis took over in 1933, but even the Germany of the Weimar Republic was very different from any place I'd ever been. Germany was punished harshly for starting the Great War and for losing it. They suffered a terrible inflation of their currency and had to pay enormous war reparations. During the depression, they experienced devastating unemployment, like we all did. But the situation was even worse in Germany."

Elsie continued. "Hitler manipulated the system with lies, deception, and every kind of skullduggery to seize power. There's not a vestige of democracy or freedom left in Germany. There are many dictators in the world, but Hitler is a crazy, insane, evil dictator."

Elsie knew what was going on in Germany. "I read his book *Mein Kampf* which means 'my struggle.' The man is completely and totally deranged. He's not that smart. He's clever and manipulative, and maybe he's a great orator, although, I personally don't see that either. If *Mein Kampf* is any example of the way his mind works, he's not a deep thinker or even an organized thinker. He's not very well-educated, and he can't write worth a tinker's damn. He can't write a decent sentence, let alone a coherent paragraph. It's disgraceful and doesn't reflect at all well on Austria's educational system. He's quite pathetic in every respect. I know the history behind how he came to power, but I don't get what it is about him that appeals to people. It totally escapes me, and I think he's creepy looking. He's a short, ugly man with a silly toothbrush of a mustache and beady little eyes. He's completely unappealing as a physical specimen. I will never understand it, never!"

Geneva listened to Elsie's political lesson with great interest. "Edward told me some things about what the Nazis are doing in Germany, but I didn't believe he knew what he was talking about. He told me stories about the Nazis killing retarded children and crippled people. He didn't want me to come on this trip at all. For years, he's talked about me getting my master's degree and said how wonderful it would be for me to travel and see more of the world. Then, when I finally have this chance, he's dead set against it. He thinks I'll be in danger in Germany."

"I don't think you or I will be in any danger. If we were Jewish or communists, or if we were British spies or trouble makers, we might be at risk. I think our group of mathematics maidens will be completely safe. What kind of trouble are we likely to get into? Eating too much seafood Newburg?" Elsie laughed.

"I am going to forget you ever said that." Geneva had to laugh, too. "I don't get all the excitement over Hitler and his oratory. He sounds shrill and hysterical to me, and I find his shouting speeches very unpleasant to listen to. He's so loud."

The group gathered in the lobby of their hotel, once again surrounded by mountains of luggage. Geneva made a mental note to talk to Dr. Veere about the small leather valises in the pile. There were so many of them, and they didn't seem to belong to anybody. The women could see Dr. Veere outside the hotel, talking to a man in a uniform and cap. The two were standing in front of a small blue bus. The bus, shorter in length and not as tall as a Greyhound bus, must be their ride. Geneva wondered if all the luggage and all twelve of them would fit into the little bus. It wasn't a new bus, but the color would always be easy to see, wherever it was parked.

Dr. Veere came into the lobby beaming. "It's here, and it's perfect, just what I ordered!" He seemed so pleased with himself, the women couldn't help but be excited about the bus's arrival. "Load it up and let's get on the road." Hotel bellmen moved the great mound of bags outside and managed to stow it all into the little bus, with plenty of room to spare for the people. The women climbed aboard and agreed with Dr. Veere that it was "just right." It would be their home, of sorts, for the next two months. Elsie and Geneva sat together, and the teachers were finally on their way to, as Elsie called it, "Hitlerland."

They all said "bonjour" to Albert, who was French and would drive their bus to the French-German border. Once in Germany, another driver would take over. The miles passed, and Geneva began to sing. Sooner or later, car trips with her family and friends always ended up with singing. Some of the women already knew, "Oh, what did Delaware, boys? ... She wore her New Jersey." Those who didn't know it, soon learned and joined in. Some could sing; others couldn't stay on key. It didn't matter. A few tried to think up new verses, and everybody was having fun.

"Miss Burkhart, you are full of surprises. Who would have suspected that you would turn out to be our entertainment director and leader of the choir." Dr. Veere smiled at Geneva. The women were all so different, oddly bound together by their passion for mathematics and their love of teaching. Thanks to the blue bus and the singing, they were becoming a group.

The bus had decent springs and tires, and the windows went up and down easily. The seats were not too hard and not too soft. The women were having a grand time, and the rural landscape of eastern France rolled by the windows. Dr. Veere, who had traveled these roads in years past, gave his commentary. He pointed out important spots and talked about the battles of the Great War. He told them about the scenery and the towns they were traveling through. It was the middle of June, and it was a perfect day. Although they might not realize the impact of their passage, they were glorying in the last few miles, the last few hours of freedom before they crossed an international border. They were about to go from a place where God was still welcome in people's lives to a country where God was no longer allowed.

Arriving at the French-German border seemed to cause less commotion than their arrival in Le Havre. Dr. Veere presented a letter when the bus pulled up to the first of several inspection stations, and the letter paved the way for their entry into Germany. Dr. Veere handed their passports in as a group, and they exited the bus to go through immigration and customs.

When it was Geneva's turn, a Nazi official carefully compared her passport photo with her face. His gaze lingered as he took in her blue eyes and dark hair. Geneva knew she'd made another conquest, and she tilted her head and didn't exactly wink at the man, but close. Elsie, behind Geneva in line, gave her a poke in the back, and Geneva turned off the charm. These Nazis were serious business, and nobody was going to enter Germany who didn't belong. Geneva claimed her luggage so the customs officials could inspect what she was bringing with her.

She was worried about Grace Davis from Iowa who was ill and lying down on the back seat of the bus. Grace wasn't strong enough to get off the bus today, so German officials climbed on board to inspect her papers. They looked at poor Grace's pale face and compared it to her passport. Grace was obviously not well and was sound asleep. The Germans woke her and began to question her. Geneva and Elsie and the others could hear what they were saying to Grace, and everyone was on edge.

Elsie whispered to Geneva, "I've always wondered what they look for when they go through your luggage. Are they looking for bombs or guns or hashish or a suitcase full of cash and gold? They always ask at customs if you have anything to declare. If I were trying to smuggle something into Germany, and I can't even imagine what that would be, would I say that 'yes, I have ten thousand bottles of French perfume that I am smuggling into Germany and intend to sell in the kiosk I'm going to set up on the Unter den Linden Strasse?' I mean, what kind of dummy is going to say 'yes' to that question about having something to declare. I've always thought customs was a very bizarre hurdle for tourists entering a foreign country."

They finally got everything inspected and repacked and reloaded. Their papers were all stamped and stamped again, and they were cleared and given the okay to enter the Nazi paradise that was Germany in 1938. They met their new driver, translator, and tour guide, Wilhelm Durer. He was tall, dark, and handsome. There was no other way to describe him. He had piercing blue eyes that immediately went to Geneva. Elsie whispered to Geneva, "He's the Nazi minder who's going to keep an eye on our group. Wilhelm will watch us every minute and report on everything we do and everything we say. He's our own personal spy."

No group was allowed to travel in Germany in 1938 without an official from the Nazi party traveling with them to monitor their activities. One of the restrictions placed on the group when they'd been given permission for the trip was that they would accept "a government representative" who would guide them through their stay.

No one could deny that Wilhelm Durer was a dreamboat to look at, even dressed in his Nazi uniform. Geneva didn't think he resembled the fearsome Nazi she was expecting, and he didn't look old enough to be taken very seriously as a minder or a guide. He looked much too young to be a threat.

"Nazis come in all ages and sizes and shapes. They get the little kids into Nazi camps when they're barely old enough to walk. I'm sure this guy was a member of the Hitler Youth and has been working his way up in the Nazi hierarchy for years. No doubt about it; he's here to keep us in line." Elsie wasn't cutting Wilhelm any slack.

Wilhelm introduced himself to the group. "I am delighted to make the acquaintance of all of these attractive ladies from America who are also very brilliant and well-educated. You may please ask me anything about where we are going and what we are seeing. I am an excellent tour guide and can tell you everything you need to know."

"Humble, as well as full of bull," Elsie quietly commented to Geneva.

"There are some rules I must go over with you before we begin our tour of the most beautiful country in the world. You will stay together as a group at all times. It would not be good if one or two of you wandered off on your own. You do not speak German and do not know your way around. For your own safety, I must insist that you inform me if you will not be participating in the group's activities. I understand that someone might be ill and not be able to keep our schedule. I will need to be informed about this whenever it happens." Wilhelm was not making any friends with his rules.

"There's a curfew for your group. Everyone must be in their rooms by ten o'clock at night. If there is any reason you cannot be in your room by ten, I need to know about it ahead of time. I will be determining where we go and at what time we go. So you see, you must come to me for all permissions for whatever you want to do."

None of the women, some of whom were in their 40's and 50's, were used to being told what they could do, where they could go, and what time they had to be in bed. Wilhelm, the young Nazi whippersnapper, was telling them at great length how they were to conduct themselves, and Geneva could see that the women were not at all happy about what he was saying. Wilhelm didn't seem to have a clue about how to interact with them. Dr. Veere finally came to the rescue and took Wilhelm aside. He told him to tone it down and not be so bossy. Looking somewhat apologetic, Wilhelm put on his chauffeur's cap, complete with a Swastika on the front, and sat in the driver's seat. The women rolled their eyes at Dr. Veere. Every one of them was wishing they had Albert back as their driver.

Once Durer got over himself and got the message that he didn't need to be so overbearing, he seemed nice enough. He was handsome and could be pleasant. His English was easy for the women to understand. If he could keep his ego and his enthusiasm for Hitler in check, things might work out. Every time he addressed the group as a whole he looked directly at Geneva. She worried that there might be a romantic interest developing on Wilhelm's part, and she didn't want to attract the attentions of a Nazi, no matter how handsome he was.

CHAPTER TWENTY FIVE

LEAVING GRACE DAVIS

JUNE 1938
FRENCH-GERMAN BORDER

GRACE DAVIS HAD SLEPT MOST OF THE WAY from Paris to the German border. Dr. Veere kept looking at Grace, and Geneva could see he was worried. There was a long bench seat at the back of the bus, and if someone wasn't feeling well, they could lie down and rest. After the German officials had been on board to talk to Grace, Dr. Veere spoke with her, left the bus, and walked to a nearby telephone booth where he spent a long time making a call.

Wilhelm chatted cheerfully with the group, "Ladies, you know I have three sisters, and I know a lot about women." He was trying to win them over after a rough beginning, and although he could have a sense of humor if he tried, he continued to put his foot in his mouth. "I attend art school during the fall and winter. I am thrilled to have this summer job of driving your bus and guiding you on your tour of Germany. Please, each of you tell me a little bit about yourself so I can get to know you. Tell me where in America you are from."

Elsie muttered under her breath, "I'm sure he already knows every detail about every one of our lives from the time we took our first breath. He's just checking to see if we're telling the truth."

Geneva was more forgiving. "He looks young and kind of harmless to me, and he's not at all my idea of what a Nazi spy is supposed to look like."

Veere returned to the bus and told Wilhelm they could get on the road. "We're going to have to stop at a doctor's office." Veere gave Wilhelm a piece of paper that had the doctor's name and directions to the office. "It's only a ten minute drive from here."

When they arrived, Dr. Veere went into the office and brought the doctor out to the bus. The doctor, carrying his medical bag, briefly nodded to the women. He went to the back of the bus and sat down next to Grace. He took her pulse and listened to her heart. The women spoke in whispers to each other, not wanting to disrupt the seriousness of the situation. Finally, the physician and Dr. Veere helped Grace stand and slowly walk to the door of the bus. They helped her down the steps and supported her as she went into the doctor's office. The women were quiet as they watched Grace being almost carried off the bus. Eventually, Dr. Veere returned and told the women what was happening.

"I hate to have to tell you this, but Grace Davis is quite ill. Grace has had a heart condition since she was a child. She has tried to live a normal life. Grace told us about her health when she applied to be a member of our group. She gave us a letter from her heart specialist and was very open about the limitations her condition might have on her ability to take this trip. We felt she was a very strong candidate and decided that, in spite of her disability, we wanted her to participate in the trip."

Dr. Veere continued. "Grace and her doctors in the States knew her heart condition could worsen suddenly and without warning. It is an unknown that Grace has lived with for years. For now, I have arranged for Grace to be driven back to Paris. A heart specialist there is going to examine her to determine if she is well enough to sail to New York. If she receives the okay, she will have a private duty nurse accompany her on the return voyage to the United States."

"Grace wanted me to tell you she's had a wonderful time with all of you and wishes us the best for a successful tour. She is very sorry that she can't continue with the rest of the trip, and she will miss each one of you." Veere motioned for Wilhelm to help him unload Grace's trunk and suitcase from the luggage hold underneath the bus. They left the large pieces on the porch of the doctor's office, and Dr. Veere carried Grace's kitbag inside.

The women received this news with solemn faces. They'd realized Grace was not as vigorous as the rest of the members of the group, and she'd not participated in quite a few of the activities. But no one had known about her heart condition. Everyone was very sorry that Grace was so ill and had to go home.

Dr. Veere looked distressed when he returned to the bus. "Wilhelm, we can leave now. We will continue our journey without Grace." Veere was full of regret and felt terribly guilty that he'd had to tell the women such a depressing story about Grace Davis, especially since the entire account from beginning to end was a complete lie. It was all made up. Grace Davis was not her real name, and she didn't have a heart condition. She wasn't returning to Paris or to the USA, and she wasn't leaving Germany. All of this theatre had been for the group, but especially for Wilhelm. Their Nazi minder would report verbally and in a written report about what had happened today. Grace Davis's name would be dropped from the list of Columbia University teachers on the tour. Wilhelm's reports would state that Grace Davis was returning to Paris and then to the United States.

Grace, meanwhile, was also experiencing considerable guilt about making her fellow teachers feel sad about her health, which in fact was perfectly fine. The "doctor" helped her remove the white makeup from her face, and the much healthier countenance of Gretchen Haldemeyer was revealed underneath Grace Davis's artificial pallor. As soon as the blue bus had driven away, Grace's luggage was brought inside. Gretchen sorted through her clothes that had been purchased in the United States. They would all either be given away or destroyed. Gretchen Haldemeyer's new trunk and new set of luggage with her wardrobe of clothes made in Germany were already packed and ready to go. Gretchen herself had chosen the German clothes weeks earlier and was satisfied that she had everything she needed to begin her life as Gretchen Haldemeyer. Gretchen had altered her appearance for her role as Grace Davis, and it would be a relief to return her hair and eyebrows to their original dark blond color.

Gretchen Haldemeyer fortified herself with food and drink for the next stage of her journey. The "doctor" drove her to the railway station in Saarbrucken. Gretchen was finally home after having spent decades away from her native land. Eager to make a connection with her famous German second cousin and undertake the challenges that would be presented to her, she felt confident she could do her small part to help bring down the madman who was destroying the country of her ancestors, the country of her birth.

Wilhelm was in his element as the bus continued on its way after leaving the doctor's office. "We are now traveling through the beautiful Rhineland which was stolen from Germany after the Great War. In March of 1936, the German people took back the Rhineland, and now it is rightly where it belongs, again as part of the Fatherland. Our esteemed leader Adolph Hitler has been reassembling the Reich to the way it was before the Great War, to the way it ought to be. Germany will be the greatest and strongest country in Europe as the National Socialists regain their rightful lands."

Elsie couldn't stand it any longer, "We don't want to hear about Hitler or about territory the Nazis want. So just skip the political BS and the Nazi propaganda. We don't want to hear it, Wilhelm."

"I cannot possibly tell you about the wonderful history and the magnificent sights of the Third Reich without telling you about the greatness of our leaders. To understand what is happening all around you, it is necessary to hear about the splendor that is Germany today."

"Put a sock in it, Wilhelm." Elsie was determined not to listen to this propaganda for the rest of their trip. It had to stop now. "Let's sing, ladies. Geneva, can you start out for us. 'Oh, what does Delaware?' I am sure we can drown out whatever Wilhelm wants to tell us about the glorious Reich with our loud singing voices."

They sang as loud as they could. Dr. Veere sighed and wondered if Wilhelm realized what a bad impression he'd made. Veere knew his mathematicians had no patience for propaganda. The young Wilhelm was going to have to blather less about Hitler and the Nazis if his tenure as a guide was going to get off the ground.

CHAPTER TWENTY SIX

LEAVING BEAUNE

JULY 1938

BEAUNE, FRANCE

"You must leave France immediately and go to Switzerland. Please don't argue with me, my dearest. I've heard from a colleague that I'm to be taken to a 'work camp' in a few weeks. You must follow my instructions exactly. You and the children are being watched. Be very careful when you use the telephone. If you return to Germany at the end of the summer, you won't be allowed to leave again. Our plan for you and the children to escape to Switzerland must be put into motion immediately. I've leased a comfortable estate a few miles from the small town of Coppet near Geneva. Detailed instructions about what you must do will follow by special courier. I've put a great deal of thought and planning into assuring that your escape will be successful, and I will meet you in Switzerland when I can. Don't worry. I love you, my darling. Yours forever, Franz."

Margot's hands shook as she finished decoding the telegram from her husband. She had laughed at Franz when he'd suggested the need to communicate with encrypted messages. She'd hoped the use of the simple cypher they'd worked out would not be necessary. Now she'd received word that they were in danger. She was afraid for herself and for the children, but she was especially afraid for Franz.

As promised, coded and detailed instructions arrived by special messenger the next day. It would be difficult to organize everything Margot needed to do in a short period of time. Who could possibly be watching her? She knew she could trust her own household staff in France. Claude and Theresa had worked at the chateau for decades and lived in a small cottage on the estate grounds.

Theresa cooked for the family, and Claude bossed the daily garden help who took care of the planting and grooming of the grounds. His high standards insured that even the laziest of young helpers didn't slack off on the perfection he demanded. Claude kept Margot's father's old Renault roadster in working order, although replacement parts were becoming harder and harder to find. Claude and Theresa were a part of Margot's family. They would never be the ones "watching" her and the children.

The nuns at the Abbey ran Margot's family winery and hired workers to tend the vines and harvest the grapes. The nuns had known her since she was a little girl and were also a part of Margot's extended family. The old man who had farmed their fields almost all of his life had died recently. Margot had been dealing with his son for several years. There would be no reason for the farmer or his family to wish her any trouble.

She couldn't imagine who might be watching her in Beaune. She hardly ever went to town or used the telephone except for house business. She had a few friends in the area, but she'd mostly grown apart from them when she'd married and chosen to make her life in Germany. She trusted that Franz knew what he was talking about, and she was uneasy as she tried to figure out who might be a threat.

Margot needed help to prepare and pack for the journey to Switzerland. She knew she could depend on her personal maid Lisle and took her aside to explain the family's secret travel plans to leave France. Thinking of the upcoming trip in terms of an escape sounded silly and overly dramatic when she said it out loud. But for Margot, leaving her life behind was tantamount to going into exile.

She knew Jews and others who had disappeared from their communities in Frankfurt and realized she would not see some dear friends again. She never stopped thinking about how sad she was for all that was lost. She'd heard about the retarded children and the handicapped who'd died suspiciously in government health facilities in Germany. It hadn't been until recently that the danger and the fear had touched her personally. She had only a few days to get ready for this journey so that Margot Hartmann and her children could vanish. This trip had to appear to be a casual, and somewhat spur-of-the moment, summertime trip to a fun spa town by Lake Leman.

Margot worked with Lisle past midnight for two nights packing boxes and trunks that held their clothes and the treasured belongings Margot couldn't bear to leave behind. All of these preparations had to be done in secret. They arranged for several valuable paintings and other works of art to be crated and shipped. They boxed up her family's collections of books and coins and other heirlooms. What she was afraid to send out of France, she had delivered to the Abbey where the sisters would take care of her family's treasures in the dry stone caves beneath the Abbey's living quarters. The sisters had guarded her parents' art work and other valuables during the Great

War, and Margot was certain they would do the same for her if another war came.

Frederick was an observant child and noticed any variation in the daily routine. It hadn't been possible to pack up the house without him noticing what was happening. He demanded answers from his mother. "Why are you and Lisle packing up all of our things? Are we going back to Germany? It's only July. We don't usually go home until the end of August."

Margot hated to lie to her son, but she was afraid to say too much. Chloe was only five, too young to understand or worry about world affairs, but Frederick was old enough to grasp some of what was happening in their lives. He was young and trusting, and Margot didn't want to burden him with keeping secrets. She was afraid if she told him they were leaving France, Frederick might naively tell someone about their impending departure. Margot couldn't allow that to happen, but she was going to have to tell him something. She hadn't yet told the children they weren't going back to Germany at the end of the summer, and now she was going to have to tell Frederick that they were leaving France.

"I didn't want to worry you, but with everything that is happening in Germany since the Nazis came to power, our lives are going to change." Frederick had been three years old when the Nazis came to power, so Germany under the Nazi thumb was the only thing he'd ever really known. "We may have to leave Beaune sooner than we'd planned."

"Aren't we safe in Beaune?" To Margot's children, the estate in Beaune had always been the epitome of a safe and secure place.

"We're all right now, but there may come a time when we have to leave. I'm trying to prepare for that day, just in case." Margot didn't know how much more she dared tell her son about their situation.

Margot continued. "I don't have all the answers, and I'm doing my best to follow through with the plans your father and I have made to keep our family together. You and Chloe are more important to us than anything else in the world. We are doing everything we can to insure that all of us are safe."

"Will father be meeting us there, wherever we go? I miss him and don't understand why he isn't allowed to come to France this year. He always comes to France in August."

"I am also very sad he isn't coming to France this year. It isn't his choice, and I know it's hard for you to understand. Eventually, yes, your father will be joining us. That's what we are working for, to make that happen. There's a great deal I don't understand either. Because I didn't want to worry you and was trying to protect you, I was going to wait to share all of this with you. But you are such a perceptive young man, I've had to tell you more than I'd planned about what's going on."

"I worry all the time anyway because father hasn't been allowed to come on holiday with us this year. Why have the Nazis forbidden him to come to Beaune?"

"The Nazis have said that your father is a Jew because his grandmother might have been Jewish. The Nazis have taken away almost everything from German Jews. Even though the Nazis have decided he's a Jew, your father has escaped persecution so far because of his important job."

"But he's not a Jew. He's Catholic, just like we all are."

"It's very hard to understand, and I agree it doesn't make any sense. But that's what the Nazis say. The Nazis have some very confusing and silly laws, and because they are full of nonsense, your father wants us to find a place that's safe, where all of us can be together and where it doesn't matter what the Nazis think. That safe place has to be somewhere the Nazis can't find him. He and I have been working together to plan our future."

"Where is this safe place that we are going to? When are we going there?"

"I will tell you as much as I can. There are many things your father hasn't been able to share with me for security reasons, and for these same reasons, there are things I can't share with you. And we *must* keep all of this just between us. You can't mention a word I've told you to anyone ... about any of it. And I mean to anyone. Do you understand what I'm saying? Everything I'm doing and everything I'm asking you to do is to try to help your father and to help our family. Because of the work he does, we may have to do some unexpected things, some things we don't want to do, to keep him safe and to keep us safe. We may have to move to a new place. I'm going to need your help and your patience."

Eight-year-old Frederick was grown up for his age, and he took in everything his mother had said. Margot knew she'd upset him, but he had to know at least part of the truth. When he hugged her goodnight, she knew he needed reassurance. She held him tightly and said, "It will all work out. Try not to worry." Frederick didn't say anything, and Margot could tell he wasn't convinced. He was deep in thought as he made his way to bed that night.

With a heavy heart, Margot continued to pack. She prayed the Germans would never come to France as they had in 1914, but she knew it could happen. Franz had told her Hitler would march into France and occupy it within a few years. Margot wondered how long would they be émigrés in Coppet. Would she ever see her beloved country house in Beaune again?

The day before they left for Evian-les-Bains, Margot made a trip to the Abbey to speak with the mother superior who was always delighted to see Margot. Margot told her everything, about Franz and their need to leave Germany and now their need to leave France. The mother superior was shaken when Margot told her what Franz had said about the Nazis invading France. During the Great War, the sisters had transformed the family's chateau into a rehabilitation facility for soldiers. Although Beaune had not been on the front lines of the fighting, soldiers who needed convalescence had been cared for in Margot's summer home. Turning the chateau into a hospital had been a way to protect the house, as well as a way to do one's part to help the soldiers. If the Germans came again, Margot asked the sisters if they would once again move onto the estate and set up a hospital. The mother superior agreed, although she also prayed that war would not come.

Margot and the mother superior discussed at length the finances and business of the winery and the farmlands. Claude and Theresa were not going to be able to take care of themselves for many more years, and Margot made practical and financial arrangements for the sisters to take care of them. The sisters agreed to bring Claude and Theresa to live in the convent, if that became necessary.

Margot was satisfied she'd done everything she could to secure her beloved home in Beaune. She had provided for the old couple who had served her family so faithfully over the years. Margot took one last walk around the Abbey cemetery. Her parents were buried there, and Margot and the mother superior visited the graves where Margot prayed and left a bouquet of roses. Margot cried as she hugged the mother superior goodbye. She left the Abbey wondering what would happen between now and the next time she put flowers on her parents' graves. Would there ever be another visit to the cemetery? When would she again tread these hallowed grounds?

That night, Margot spoke to the children as they sat on the terrace after dinner, listening to phonograph records and eating ice cream. She told them they were going to take a short trip to Evian-les-Bains for a few days. Rooms were reserved at a country inn, and the children would be able to swim and fish in Lake Leman. Frederick asked again, in his shy way, when they would see their father. Chloe, who was five, had many questions about how they would get to Evian, how long it would take to get there, how long they would be staying, what they would do, and if the dogs were coming with them.

"We're driving the Mercedes, and the trip to Evian will take several hours. Yes, of course, the dogs are coming with us."

Margot didn't tell them that in two days, they would take a very short but life-changing trip across Lake Geneva to Switzerland. She planned to delay telling them about that part of their journey until the day it happened. Margot packed valises for a five-day trip and included the children's favorite toys and books.

That night after the children were asleep, Margot made her way to the barn where she removed the German license plates from their Mercedes and replaced them with the license plates from her father's Renault. The roadster was fine for short trips, and Claude had kept the registration current on the old car. Thank goodness for the French license plates. The Hartmanns would attract much less attention if they entered Switzerland as a French family with French license plates on their car. Margot rubbed some mud on the plates. The last thing she wanted was for Frederick, who noticed everything, to realize that the Mercedes was sporting French license plates. Although he was usually pretty quiet, it would be just her luck for him to ask about it or announce the anomaly to a border guard or customs agent. It was better that the license plates remain unremarkable.

The children had French passports because Margot was French. It was important to her and to Franz that they have both French and German passports. The children were fluent in French and German. It was understood that when they were in France, they spoke only French.

Convincing Swiss passport control that they were a French family would not be difficult. When the ferry from France arrived in Switzerland, Margot would tell the officials that they were going to be in Coppet for only one day. If the authorities asked to see the papers on the Mercedes, she would be in trouble. The Swiss were tightening up the rules about who was and was not allowed to enter their country, but Margot didn't think she and the children would receive extra scrutiny. They were exactly what they said they were, a French family on holiday taking the ferry on a day trip across Lake Leman to Switzerland. Margot was blond, as were her son and daughter. Their looks would not be a red flag, but if the car's papers were checked, their careful plans could fall apart.

Margot wondered what it must be like to look Jewish or to actually be a Jew. How wrong it was to dislike or punish people because of how they looked, because of the religion they practiced, or because they had a grandmother who might have been a Jew. It was heartbreaking and made no sense to the kind and logical Margot.

CHAPTER TWENTY SEVEN

LEAVING FRANCE

JULY 1938
EVIAN-LES-BAINS, FRANCE

THEY'D ARRIVED IN EVIAN-LES-BAINS THE DAY before yesterday, in time to take a refreshing swim in the lake. They'd dined on hearty country food at the inn. The children were tired after the day of travel, the swimming, and the late dinner, and everyone went right to bed. Yesterday, the children had again spent the day swimming in the lake. Today was the day Margot and her children would leave France, perhaps forever.

Last night, Margot had dined with the other guests who were staying at the inn. The inn's restaurant had three stars, and Margot splurged by enjoying one evening meal at the grown-up table rather than eating early with her children. The food was magnificent, and talk around the table was all about the international conference that had just concluded in Evian-les-Bains. World leaders had met to discuss what to do about the Jewish refugees who were fleeing Germany and Austria and seeking asylum in the free countries of the world.

When the fish course of turbot, poached and served with a beurre blanc sauce, was served, everyone at the table was being polite and cordial as they debated the controversial topic of the international conference. By the time the grilled stuffed leg of lamb arrived, accompanied by Dauphinoise potatoes and haricot verts, everybody had opinions, and the discussion became heated.

Margot was about to become a refugee herself, and she listened closely to the different points of view. It was difficult to understand how the various factions could disagree so vehemently. She finally had to speak up. "Surely all the countries of the world recognize that the refugee situation in Europe is an international human tragedy."

One man at the table was a cynic. "They all acknowledge there's a crisis, but none of them is willing to do anything about it."

A woman at the end of the table tried to make sense of why the conference had been such a complete failure. "Why call together representatives from the world's richest nations to try to figure out what to do, if they'd already decided ahead of time they weren't going to do anything at all? It couldn't have been just for show, could it, to try to look good in the eyes of the world?"

Another older man who seemed to know the details of what had happened the previous week said, "A few countries agreed to increase their quotas of Jewish immigrants, but most of the participants refused to accept more Jews as refugees. They have quotas for Jews, and in spite of the pressing need to relocate these people, they wouldn't increase their quotas."

The cynical man spoke up again. "I personally know Jews who are fleeing Germany and Austria. The Nazis have stripped them of everything, and the great nations of the world have closed their hearts and their borders to them. Even the United States, the richest of all countries, has refused to increase its quotas and accept more Jews."

Margot had been forced to leave Germany, and now she was being forced to leave France. The insensitivity of the participants at the Evian-les-Bains conference made her angry. She was different from most refugees because she had a plan to escape to Switzerland and a home waiting there for her and her family. She had resources and had not been stripped of her property. She could only imagine how terrible it must be for those German and Austrian Jews who had nothing. And now they were being refused entry into safe countries because of quotas.

When the chocolate soufflé arrived at the end of the meal, Margot was still hoping to learn from the other guests. "Where will these people go and what will happen to them?" Margot asked. No one at the table had a good answer for her. No one could look into the future and predict what would happen in the years to come, but Margot knew the future would be dire indeed for Jews who could not escape the Nazis.

<hr />

At breakfast the next morning, Margot told her children they were going to have an adventure that day. "We're going to take the ferry across Lake Leman to Switzerland and visit a charming little town called Coppet. There's a wonderful hotel on the water where we'll have lunch. The view is lovely, and you can watch the boats sail around the lake. Be sure to have your bathing suits and your books in your knapsacks. It's going to be a long day."

Ducks appeared beside the terrace where they were eating, and Margot crumbled some of her breakfast roll and tossed crumbs in their direction. Chloe and Frederick laughed as the ducks waddled toward the bread and tried to push each other out of the way to be the first to reach the food.

Margot didn't want to let the children out of her sight, and she was suspicious of everybody. This was the last leg of their journey before they made it to Switzerland, and Margot still had no idea who had been spying on her family. She had to put the children's suitcases in the car and settle the bill at the inn. After much deliberation, she decided the elderly couple at the next table looked safe.

"Will you please watch my children while I go back inside for a few minutes?" They smiled and said they would be happy to watch Frederick and Chloe.

Nervous about not being able to keep her eyes on the children, Margot moved as quickly as she could. Their rooms were on the first floor, thank goodness, and she'd already packed her own bags and loaded them into the car. In the children's room, she efficiently scooped up clothes and toys, packed their small valises, and stowed the bags in the boot of the Mercedes. The dogs had been walked, fed, and watered before breakfast and were waiting in the car.

Margot approached the front desk, "Madame," she addressed the proprietress of the inn, "I'm so sorry, but I've just received news about an illness in the family. We have to cut short our stay at your delightful inn. We hope to be able to return soon to enjoy a longer visit. We'd reserved for three days and three nights, and I insist on paying you for the entire reservation."

The proprietor of the inn was concerned, and relief showed on her face when Margot assured her that payment in full would be made, even for the days the family wouldn't be staying there. Margot handed the innkeeper an envelope of French francs and told Madame that any overpayment should be given to the maids and others. Margot knew it was important that the rooms be cleared of their belongings and that the bill be settled. She had to be certain that no one would come looking for the family of three.

Leaving with the appropriate degree of urgency, Margot returned to the terrace to see if feeding the ducks still held the children's interest. She thanked the couple for keeping an eye on Frederick and Chloe and hustled them to the Mercedes. Margot threw a blanket over Zoltan who was asleep on the floor in the back. Cadeau was trying to get used to being in the empty picnic basket on the seat between Frederick and Chloe. The Swiss loved animals, but Margot thought it would cause less of a fuss when they entered Switzerland if she wasn't driving the car with Cadeau on her lap. It was almost nine o'clock when they reached the embarkation point with their knapsacks and two dogs. Margot's heart was in her throat as she drove the car aboard the ferry. Would anyone discover that the license plates and the car's registration papers didn't match? She had told her children a lie when she'd said they would be visiting Switzerland just for the day.

CHAPTER TWENTY EIGHT

ARRIVING IN SWITZERLAND

JULY 1938

COPPET, SWITZERLAND

MARGOT, FREDERICK, AND CHLOE STOOD AT the rail of the car ferry and enjoyed the summer breeze that blew off Lake Geneva, known to the French as Lac Leman. "Remember to continue to speak French in Switzerland today. The people of Switzerland speak three languages, French, German, and Italian. We're going to visit the area around Geneva, and that's in the French-speaking part of the country." As a French family, they drew little interest from passport control as they disembarked from the ferry.

Margot was not a good liar, and when the Swiss border guard asked her how long she planned to stay in Switzerland, she stumbled over her words. "Just for the day." The official didn't find her answer remarkable, but Frederick knew his mother. He gave her a look when she choked out her lie.

Margot drove their car with French license plates to the nearby Hotel du Lac in Coppet. Margot allowed herself a momentary sigh of relief. She hoped no one was following them and that they were safe in Switzerland at last. The dogs were given a quick walk and returned to the car.

The Hotel du Lac was small and comfortable, not fancy. Margot settled the children in the lounge, and they ordered hot chocolate and Swiss tarts full of rich custard. Margot ordered a café au lait. She fiddled with the spoon, swirled the coffee around and around in her cup, and scarcely drank any of it. She scanned the lounge and carefully analyzed each of the groups that sat in the large, sunlit room, enjoying their mid-morning coffee and pastries. No one in the hotel's lounge looked very sinister to Margot, but she couldn't shake the fear that someone was watching them. The children were chattering away, but Frederick looked at her curiously when she repeatedly glanced at her wristwatch.

At exactly 11:00, she left the table and went to the lobby of the Hotel du Lac. She could see the children from where she would make her telephone call. As she dialed the number Franz had given her, Margot looked around nervously, hoping no one would see the number she was dialing or notice that her fingers were shaking. There were several unfamiliar clicks on the telephone line before it started to ring, and Margot almost hung up. Was someone attempting to listen in on her call? They were almost at the end of the journey that would take them to their new lives. Following her instructions exactly, Margot completed the call and returned to her table in the lounge. She watched the doorway anxiously for the woman who would arrive to take them to their Swiss home.

Finally, the woman appeared, wearing the identifying bright green sweater. Madam Theroux was brusque when she introduced herself to Margot. Margot was sure Theroux wasn't the woman's real name. Margot introduced Madam Theroux to the children as their tour guide for the day, but Theroux didn't smile at Frederick and Chloe. Madam Theroux was more than anxious to leave the Hotel du Lac immediately and scolded Margot, "You should not be so public about your arrival in Switzerland." Margot was surprised and annoyed by Theroux's curt warning, but she knew the woman had been sent by Franz to help them and to keep them safe.

The children were silent in the back of the Mercedes, and Margot drove while Madame Theroux sat in the front passenger seat and gave directions. Cadeau was not happy to be kept in the back seat, but Margot didn't want to irritate the stern Theroux any more than she already had. It seemed as if they drove forever, far out into the countryside. Madame Theroux didn't want to talk and didn't answer Margot's questions. After turning off the paved road and traveling for miles on dirt and gravel roads, they arrived at the heavy iron gates of a large estate. They were deep in a wooded rural area and miles from any town. Madame got out of the car, unlocked the gate with a large black key, and threw open the gates so Margot could drive the Mercedes through. Madame closed and locked the gates behind them and climbed back into the car. They made their way up a long driveway and came to a clearing in the trees where they saw a beautiful house made of stone and stucco.

"Here is your new home," Madame announced. The children looked confused. Their eyes grew wide, and they had a hundred questions. Madame Theroux had no time for answers and hustled them out of the car, through the house, and out onto the back terrace. She continued her strict instructions, "You will have new names. You leave your German lives behind. Staff will arrive in two days, and they will do all the shopping. You will not leave the estate or go into town until you have practiced your new identities. Staff will know you only as the DeMarches family from Burgundy who have decided to move to Switzerland." Frederick and Chloe stared at Madam Theroux and then at their mother. Was anyone going to tell them what was going on? Frederick had an idea this was the safe place his mother had told him about, but why hadn't she warned him it was happening today? He felt betrayed.

Madame continued, "Basic furnishings are here. Your own belongings will arrive in due time. You must completely leave behind your old lives and become new people." Madame paused and stared directly at Margot and then at the children, "Your lives and the life of your husband and father will depend on it. He is a well-known man in Germany, and he is valuable to the Nazis. They will look everywhere for him and will kill him, and you, if they find you. His life is in your hands."

The children, their eyes now full of fear, looked back and forth between their mother and Madame. They didn't understand. They were frightened and bewildered. Kill their father? Kill us? What was this cross-looking woman talking about? Madame told them the bedrooms were ready for them, and there was food prepared in the ice box. The food would last for several days, and they were not to leave the estate. The staff would arrive on Monday morning.

From the pocket of her skirt, Madame Theroux took the key that opened the gate to the estate and held it up so everyone could see she had it. After she'd given them their orders, she left through the back door. A few minutes later they heard a car start and caught a glimpse of Madame Theroux as she drove away in a small Peugeot that must have been parked in the carriage house. Madame was gone with the key, and Margot knew they couldn't leave the estate, at least by car. They were locked inside this place, with its beautiful house, pool, pond, and all the rest of it, until someone came to unlock the gates again. They could climb over the wall that surrounded the grounds, but for all intents and purposes, they were prisoners.

Margot walked back through the house and out to the front driveway where the Mercedes was parked. The dogs were restless and delighted to finally be let out of the car. They sniffed and explored, and even the elderly Zoltan romped a bit in the new surroundings. Cadeau ran around the side of the house to find the children, who fell on her as if she were a long-lost relative they hadn't seen in years. Zoltan, too, got lots of extra attention. These two canine friends were living remnants of the children's former lives and as such were to be particularly cherished and adored.

Margot had not told her children their day trip to Coppet was in reality a permanent move and a transition to a new life. Because of their ages, she'd felt it best not to say anything until they were all safe in Switzerland. Margot had wanted to explain to them in her own careful way what was happening, but Madame's lecture to them about new identities and giving up their German lives forever had forced the issue. Margot now worried that she'd made a mistake by not telling them earlier what was going to happen. Frederick and Chloe looked to their mother with uncertainty, anger, and fear. They couldn't begin to understand what was going on in their young lives at this moment.

Margot began the belated, complicated, and perhaps impossible explanation about why they were no longer going to be French or German, but from this day forward were to be Swiss children with a Swiss mother and father. In just a few hours, they had been transformed into a Swiss family.

At first, Frederick and Chloe stared at her, wanting her to tell them everything was going to be all right. They were still in shock from the news and the instructions the blunt and tactless Madame Theroux had thrown at them. This was a conversation Margot had been dreading more than any conversation she'd ever had, and she'd definitely put it off for too long.

She saw the deep hurt and confusion in Frederick's eyes and heard it in his voice. "You said you would tell me what was happening. You lied to me."

"I am so sorry, my darlings. Perhaps I should have told you what was happening, but I made a decision to keep it from you, for several very good reasons. When I tell you everything about why we had to leave Frankfurt and then leave France, I hope you will have a better understanding why I didn't tell you ahead of time that we were going to make this move."

Frederick interrupted her, "So it's true; that Theroux woman was telling us the truth. We are going to stay here?" It was too confusing. Why had their mother not warned them about this momentous change?

"Yes, this is our new home. We are going to live in Switzerland now. Your father and I made this decision so we could save his life and all of our lives. It was the only way. Your father is an important man in Germany, but he found out the Nazis were going to be put him in a concentration camp later this summer. He had to leave Germany. He had no choice. He has people who are helping him escape from the Third Reich, but he refused to leave until he knew we were safe in Switzerland. He only told me a few days ago that we had to leave France."

"Even if he has to leave Germany, why couldn't we all just live in Beaune? The Nazis couldn't get to him there," Frederick wanted to know.

"Your father believes there is going to be a war and that the Nazis will overrun France, as they tried to do in the Great War. He said we would ultimately not be safe in France, and that America and Switzerland would be the only safe places. It took him a long time to convince me that this was the right thing to do. I didn't want to leave Frankfurt either, and it was very difficult for me to understand why we couldn't stay in Beaune. But your father finally convinced me. He loves us very much, and moving to Switzerland was the only way he could figure out for us to be able to live together as a family." This reason seemed to be the only thing she'd said so far that her children could accept. They nodded their heads in solemn understanding.

Margot continued. "Your father found this place and arranged for us to have Swiss passports, Swiss names, and Swiss identities — everything we need for our new existence. We must remember to be Swiss people from now on. He did all of this for us, so we could be safe and be together. Staying in Frankfurt or in France are no longer options for us. I've done my best to follow his instructions, and his instructions were that I couldn't tell you or anybody else ahead of time what the plan was. Frederick, you became suspicious in Beaune when you saw me packing up our things, and I had to tell you something. I told you as much as I could at the time. I couldn't tell anyone about how we would actually make the crossing into Switzerland. It was *very* important that we do it all in secret. I couldn't take the chance that you would mention it to one of our staff in Beaune or say something when we crossed the border into Switzerland."

"You didn't trust me not to say something I shouldn't?" Frederick was trying hard to understand, but his anger was getting in the way.

"I didn't really trust myself either. I was afraid I might accidentally say something and give us all away."

"You lied to the border guard when you told him we were staying in Switzerland just for the day."

"Yes, I lied to him. I had to." It was wrenching for Margot to have to admit she'd lied. To be shamed into such an admission by one's eight-year-old son was a bitter pill for Margot to swallow, but she'd decided she would not hold back anything, now that they were finally safe. "I know all of this is very hard for you to understand. It's hard for me to understand. I loved my home in Frankfurt and hated to leave, but it was a matter of life and death — the lies, the escape to Switzerland, everything. Your father had to get out of Germany, and we made a difficult decision to leave our home behind."

"What is this strange Swiss place that Madame has just told us is our new home?" Frederick wanted answers.

Chloe began to cry, "This house smells funny. I don't want to live here. I don't want to live in Switzerland at all. I want to go back to my play group and my friends in Frankfurt. I want to go home."

"This is our home now, liebchen. We aren't ever going back to Frankfurt, at least as long as Hitler and the Nazis rule Germany."

Frederick was worried about his father and what might happen to him. He desperately wanted to know when Franz would arrive to be with them. "I'm very angry that Hitler and the Nazis have done this to us. I'm so afraid for Father and wonder if he really will be able to get out of Germany and join us. Please, mother, tell me he will be here with us one day." Frederick and his father were very close, and Margot wanted more than anything to promise her son that he would see his father again. The tears began to roll down her cheeks. She had promised herself she wouldn't cry when she told her children that their lives had changed forever.

"There are some very smart people working to get your father out of Germany. He's important to us, but he's important to other people, too. I am praying that he will be with us again soon, and I believe he will be. I wish I could absolutely promise you that he will be safe."

Frederick and Chloe were still hurt and confused. Chloe crawled up into Margot's lap. She was five years old, and it was difficult to find a way to explain to her what was happening. She stuck her thumb in her mouth. She hadn't sucked her thumb for almost two years. Even though Chloe didn't understand the politics of Germany, why her father was in danger, or why he wasn't with them at the moment, she did know that something terrible had happened to her life. She knew things had changed and would never be the same again. The security she had known up until today, was no longer. She put her arms around her mother's neck and clung to Margot. Margot held her as she cried.

"I am devastated that you have had this happen to you, especially as young as you are. Sometimes bad things happen in life, and we just have to do the best we can to deal with these bad things and live through them. We're lucky we have enough money to move to Switzerland. We're lucky your father was able to find this wonderful home for us." Margot didn't know if her children were even listening to her any more. They seemed to have drifted into their own thoughts, their own worlds, as they tried to come to terms with what had happened. Margot could not share with them her fears that Franz might not make it out of Germany. She would not tell them that, even though they had new identities and new lives in Switzerland, they would never be completely safe until the Nazis had been beaten into dust.

"Look at this beautiful blue pool where you can swim every day. I know your father must have insisted on a house with a pool because he knows how much you both love to swim. And look at the lake over there. That's on our property, too, and I think I see ducks swimming on the lake. How fun it will be to watch them. There's a beautiful view of the mountains and not another house or farm as far as the eye can see." Margot was desperately trying to emphasize the positive things about their new home. She felt terribly alone as she struggled to find the right words to soften the blow that today's life-altering disruption had inflicted on her children. What was going on in Germany was a tragedy, and it was impossible to pretend it wasn't. Margot was exhausted and felt as if her explanation to the children had been both too simple and too complicated.

The pastries at the Hotel du Lac had been consumed hours earlier, and Margot knew the children were hungry. "Let's have a picnic out here on the terrace and watch the ducks. I'm starving, and you must be, too. We missed our lunch completely. Madame Theroux said there was food in the kitchen. I'm going to see what I can find, and we will have a wonderful al fresco tea."

Margot carried Chloe into the house, and they found a surprisingly modern ice box. As Madame had said, it was full of food. Margot fixed a tray with a plate of ham sandwiches and glasses of milk. In the pantry, she found a lovely cake with sugary pink icing. She carried the tray outside and put it on the table. Chloe wanted to start her tea with a piece of cake, and today, the usually strict Margot cut a big piece and allowed her little girl to begin the meal with dessert.

They were worn out, and all three of their faces were marked with streaks where their tears had dried. After their picnic tea, the children fell asleep on a sofa in the living room. No one could turn back the clock. They could never go back to life as it once had been. That world had crumbled and lay around them in ruins. Margot knew she would grieve for a very long time, for the life she had left behind, for her children's innocence that she had destroyed today, for so many things that the horrible Nazis had stolen from her and those she loved.

CHAPTER TWENTY NINE

STUDY ABROAD

JULY 1938
GERMANY

THE FIRST UNIVERSITY ON THEIR TOUR WAS Heidelberg, and the group spent four days and three nights in the ancient town. Dr. Veere had booked them at Der Europaische Hof, Heidelberg's famous and historic hostelry. When they pulled up to the entrance, a group of men dressed in quaint uniforms and aprons scurried from the hotel lobby to unload their luggage from the bus. It was quite a sight. Dr. Veere always took care of the gratuities and did everything for the group. They didn't have to handle money, pay anybody, tip bellmen and waiters, or worry about what things cost. Dr. Veere knew exactly what to say and what to do in every situation. What would they ever do without him?

The lobby and lounge at Der Europaische Hof were large and elegant, and a grand staircase dominated the front hall. In spite of the opulence, there was a welcoming warmth to the surroundings and the furnishings that made guests feel at home. The dining room's décor was ornate, and Elsie, who was in the know about these things, thought it was overdone and too dark. It reminded Geneva of a much larger, grander version of one of her great aunt's houses, with the heavy, dark, wood-paneled walls and ceiling. The tables were swathed in white linens; crystal goblets sparkled; silverware gleamed. Geneva couldn't wait to dine in this very European room where old-world elegance reigned.

The food at Der Europaische Hof was exceptional, and service in the gracious dining room was something out of the past. The women savored delicately seasoned spring lamb and potatoes au gratin. The dessert trolley was too beautiful for words. After dinner the first night, those who were up for an evening out accompanied Dr. Veere to the Roten Ochsen, a watering hole patronized for centuries by Heidelberg students. Even though she hated beer, Geneva went along. She loved the atmosphere in Heidelberg, the architecture of the university, the elegance of the Europaische Hof, and the Medieval feel of the Roten Ochsen.

Heidelberg was proud of the fact that it was the oldest university in Germany. Its dark side was that it had been one of the first institutions of higher learning in the country to capitulate to Nazification. It was heartbreaking to realize that this proud icon of free thought had so easily given in to the Nazi scourge. If Heidelberg could fall so quickly, how could any institution stand against tyranny?

July was a month full of mathematics. Almost daily, the group attended a lecture given by an outstanding mathematician or physicist at a historic German university. Occasionally, it was difficult for Geneva to follow what the professor was saying. She understood the numbers, but she did not always understand the words. It always proved to be interesting, and she was thrilled to have this opportunity to learn more about mathematics. Dr. Veere attended the sessions, and sometimes the women had lunch or dinner or went for drinks with the professor who had lectured that day. The group stayed at rooming houses and hotels. Dr. Veere made sure they had plenty of time for sightseeing.

They visited Tubingen, Nuremburg, Marburg, Stuttgart, and Freiburg. Dr. Veere was upbeat and emphasized what was positive about each university town. On a few occasions, he apologized that a number of great minds were no longer available to them. When they visited Tubingen, Dr. Veere asked about a colleague who had been a member of the mathematics faculty when Veere had visited Germany in 1936. The initial response was an awkward silence, followed by fear in the eyes of the faculty member who could not give Veere an honest answer. The man to whom Dr. Veere had addressed his inquiry responded awkwardly, "He's no longer teaching here. He left a year ago." Dr. Veere got the point and didn't pursue it further.

Even before the Nazis came to power in 1933, there had been few Jewish faculty and few Jewish students at Tubingen. Veere heard a rumor that two professors at Tubingen, a mathematician and a member of the religion faculty, had been forced to take early retirement because of the "non-Aryan" origins of their wives. Veere knew better than to ask about any Jewish mathematicians or physicists, but he was surprised and disheartened that so many from other religions had disappeared from the ranks of academia.

The Nazis had moved into all levels of education with their doctrine about what was allowed to be taught. Universities were under pressure to legitimize the policies of the Nazis as "scientific." Faculty members were forced to teach Nazi views on race and to pretend these were areas for legitimate research. University curricula were dictated by the government, and books that were not consistent with the Nazi party line were banned from university libraries. Even more shocking and appalling than banning books was the undisputed reality that the Nazis had burned many books. The Nazi's purge of ideas, known as "political alignment," affected all German institutions of higher learning. The intellectual free space that the university experience had once been, no longer existed. Academic freedom was, for all intents and purposes, dead. The women did not have any experience of Germany's universities before the Nazi regime came to power, so they didn't know what the academic community had been like before 1933. But Dr. Veere knew, and it tore him apart.

The group's itinerary scheduled them to spend more than a week in Nuremberg. Nuremberg meant something special to the Nazis, but Geneva was never quite able to grasp what it was that made the city so important. In 1935, the Nazis had held a conference in Nuremberg that stripped German Jews of their citizenship, their occupations, and their assets. It became illegal for Jews to do almost anything. They could no longer work, and it became increasingly difficult for them to provide for their families.

Geneva had seen the "Juden Frei" signs in other cities and towns in Germany, but in Nuremberg they were everywhere. When she'd first seen the signs, she'd ignored them as she ignored most other German signs. None of the members of the group could speak or read German, so signs were mysterious placards for Dr. Veere to translate and explain.

"These signs are on almost every shop and business here in Nuremberg. Please tell me what they mean and why these shopkeepers have the signs in the window in the first place." Geneva demanded the truth from Dr. Veere.

"The Nazis have banned Jews from most spheres of economic life. These signs let people know that a business is Aryan owned, not owned by a Jew." Dr. Veere was sad to have to tell Geneva why the signs were posted.

The signs were so all-pervasive and obviously important. Geneva needed to talk this phenomenon over with Elsie.

"I don't know much at all about Judaism. Belmont, Ohio is a town of just a few hundred people. We don't have any Jews living there. We don't even have any Catholics. Residents of Belmont are mostly Methodists or belong to local churches that don't have an affiliation with a larger denomination. You must have Jews in Connecticut."

"Oh, we have Jews in Connecticut, but if you ask my family about them, they'll pretend there aren't any Jews living in Greenwich. My mother is a snob about pretty much everything, and she's definitely a snob about religion. But, she doesn't discriminate against Jews. She doesn't like Catholics or Baptists or Presbyterians either. The only reason she admits to having Methodists in the town is because her favorite cousin sings in the Methodist church choir. We don't really talk about it. We ignore it."

"When I first meet somebody, I never know what their religion is, and I don't care."

"Remember the delicatessen in New York City that made those wonderful corned beef sandwiches you loved so much? That deli is owned and run by Jews."

"I still dream of that sandwich and would love to have one every day of my life. I would even become a Jew to be able to eat corned beef every day. The only place I've ever talked to any Jews about their religion was at Ohio University. The few I met there were nice and very smart. I know Jews don't believe that Jesus Christ is the Messiah, but I give them credit for believing in God and for knowing at least half the Bible, the

Old Testament. Just before the Christmas holidays one year, I learned about Hanukkah in a discussion some of us had in the student union at O.U. Some Jews were talking about their custom of lighting a candle and giving a gift on each of the eight days of Hanukkah. We gentiles thought the tradition of lighting the candles and the eight days of gifts was a wonderful way to celebrate. We told the Jews about our tradition of lighting Advent candles during the four weeks before Christmas."

"Hanukkah is a nice way to celebrate. It's sometimes called the Festival of Lights."

"I love to learn about other customs and religions. Edward roomed with a student from Palestine during his college days, and they're still the best of friends. Aouney visited Belmont lots of times and had dinner with us at the farm. Everybody who meets Aouney loves him. He's smart as a whip and really funny."

"I guess you know the Jews and the Palestinians don't get along."

"No, I didn't know that. Who cares anyway? I don't understand why the Germans dislike the Jews and their religion. The Nazis don't believe in God at all. I hate their atheism and feel the Jews are much better human beings because at least they believe in God." Geneva had a simple value system, and she thought it was very unfair to dislike the Jews because of their religion.

"The Nazis are cruel to take away anyone's means of earning a living on the basis of religion." Elsie's views were fair and practical.

"These signs make me angry, and I'm not going to shop in any store that has a 'Juden Frei' sign." Geneva was taking a stand, and Elsie agreed with her. From that moment on, both of them boycotted any business that had the loathsome words posted.

As they were driving into Stuttgart, their bus was caught in a traffic jam. There was a huge Nazi parade that afternoon, and unfortunately, they'd arrived just in time to get stuck in the middle of the mess. They were stopped, and their bus wasn't going anywhere until the parade was over. Forced to wait alongside the road, they had to watch each group of Nazi soldiers as they goose-stepped past. The columns of soldiers with their arms raised in the air, saluting the Fuhrer, seemed endless and endlessly the same. The red and black swastika flags that paraded by were in the thousands.

It seemed to Geneva as if these massive parades occurred every day, everywhere they happened to be. The Germans spent so much time on their parades, she wondered how anyone in the country ever got any real work done. Geneva began to dread having to go into another city because she didn't want to see one more parade or one more flag flying. It wasn't as bad in the smaller towns, but when they were in the cities, the constant and aggressive Nazi presence was suffocating. The swastika was everywhere, and Geneva and the others despised the sight of it.

What made everything worse was how much Wilhelm loved it all. He was thrilled that their bus was delayed by the parade in Stuttgart. He tried to convince the women to get out of the bus with him so they could have a better view. Geneva and Elsie and the others groaned when he tried to get them to stand on the side of the road to watch the parade. All declined and decided to stay in the bus, to nap or read or write postcards to send home to the USA.

But Wilhelm was energized, jumped off the bus, and stood at attention as the loud procession passed. He saluted from time to time and seemed completely enthralled with the spectacle. Geneva watched him from the bus window, and if he hadn't been so serious about his admiration for these ridiculous Nazi demonstrations, she would have laughed at him. She found his devotion to be childish and pathetic. She almost felt sorry for Wilhelm. He'd so obviously been brainwashed.

Geneva was thinking of the parades at home with floats of all kinds and bicycles decorated with colorful crepe paper streamers. She was imagining the local high school marching band playing a rousing John Philip Sousa tune and baton twirlers in short skirts stepping high in front of the procession. These things were what a parade meant to Geneva. Wilhelm was so proud of all the Nazi fuss and symbols. He talked constantly about the achievements of Hitler's regime. He'd been especially obnoxious in Nuremberg. Geneva couldn't grasp what appealed to Wilhelm about these stark militaristic events. How could he be such a fanatic? "How can you possibly enjoy all of these trappings? No matter what town or city we're in, the parades are all alike. Don't you get sick of seeing the same thing over and over again?" Geneva wanted an answer, but Wilhelm didn't have one for her.

Geneva didn't understand how Wilhelm could have a reasonably intelligent conversation on other subjects, but be so thoroughly indoctrinated into the Nazis' crazy ideology. Wilhelm was too young to be such a zealot, but he never tired of defending the National Socialist dream, his wonderful Fuhrer, and the parades and flags.

Wilhelm always accompanied them to their lectures, but he sat outside, smoked cigarettes, and waited for the day to end. "Wilhelm is making sure nobody escapes from the lecture hall to spy on whatever he's so afraid we might spy on." Elsie laughed when she said this, but she wasn't really joking. "If he weren't checking up on us, why wouldn't he just drop us off, park the bus or go somewhere, and come back in the afternoon to pick us up? Why does he have to sit outside the lecture hall like a prison guard?" Elsie liked to point out as often as possible that Wilhelm knew absolutely nothing about mathematics.

Geneva liked men, and she loved music and dancing and amusement parks. Geneva was the only woman in the group who wanted to go out in the evenings. Wilhelm invited everyone to go, but more often than not, it ended up that it was only Geneva and Wilhelm who wanted to go sightseeing after dinner. Geneva didn't regard her outings with Wilhelm as dates. Although Wilhelm knew Geneva was promised to her childhood sweetheart Edward, a physician in the United States, Geneva had to admit to herself that their Nazi minder had become romantically interested in her.

Geneva set limits on what was and was not going to happen when she went someplace with Wilhelm. Geneva told him his smoking was a disgusting habit, and when he was with her, he wasn't allowed to bring his cigarettes. Wilhelm told her his smoking was none of her business, but he knew she was serious. He left his cigarettes at home. Eventually, Wilhelm wanted to take Geneva dancing. When Wilhelm tried to dance close with her, the dancing was finished, and Geneva insisted on being taken home at once. She made him promise he wouldn't talk about the Nazis or Hitler or any of that while he was with her. If he did, the evening abruptly came to an end.

When Wilhelm refused to abide by Geneva's rules too many times, she told him she wasn't going anywhere with him again. He moped around and felt sorry for himself. The relationship between Geneva and Wilhelm began to affect everyone and everything about the trip. Wilhelm's moods were so dependent on whether or not Geneva was speaking to him that day or whether or not she smiled at him. It was humiliating for Geneva. Elsie had no kindness in her heart for the boy she called their "egotistical Hitler Youth spy driver minder."

Geneva finally had to go to Dr. Veere for help to diffuse the situation, but Veere told her his hands were tied. "There's nothing I can do about Wilhelm's presence or about his behavior. His role as overseer and 'tour guide' is a condition of our being able to travel in Germany. I'm sorry, but I can't get rid of him or trade him in. Please, Miss Burkhart, try to put up with the poor fellow. We are stuck with him and have to find a way to tolerate him." Dr. Veere didn't sound thrilled to have Wilhelm around either.

Geneva was determined not to let Wilhelm's attentions ruin her trip, and she tried to put him out of her mind and enjoy each new experience. But enjoying anything had become almost impossible with the overwhelming Nazi presence everywhere and Wilhelm always in attendance. The curfews, the rules and regulations about what to do and what not to do that were posted on every wall, and the suffocating authoritarian atmosphere began to wear on Geneva and on all the women in the group. The Nazi specter had become more than an irritation; it had become oppressive.

In 1900 Freiburg University had become the first German University to accept female students. Geneva and the other women were especially excited to visit this forward-looking pillar of higher learning. Geneva had never heard of Martin Heidegger, but some of the women whispered together about the famous philosopher who had once been the rector of Freiburg University and his affiliation with the Nazi Party. All the women in the group were saddened to discover that, even this institution, which almost forty years earlier had broken with tradition and welcomed women, had been seduced by poisonous Nazi dogma.

CHAPTER THIRTY

TOO MANY AND NOT ENOUGH SUITCASES

JULY 1938

GERMANY

DR. VEERE WAS THINKING TO HIMSELF, 'I wanted mathematicians, and of course I got people who think about, love, and live for numbers.' Geneva and Elsie were standing by the pile of luggage in the lobby of their hotel in Freiburg, waiting for the bus to arrive. Dr. Veere watched as Geneva sorted through the bags, and he knew there were going to be awkward questions. She looked closely at the luggage tags attached to the small leather valises, the ones that had no identification on them. Only four of the small leather bags remained.

"Dr. Veere, I think some valises are missing. I know you have many things to worry about, but when we left the hotel in Paris, I'm quite certain there were at least eight, or nine, or more of these small leather ones."

"Miss Burkhart, I assure you I am keeping very close track of everyone's luggage. Don't you see your bag?"

"My bag's there, and all the bags of the group are there. It's all those small leather cases that never made sense to me. There aren't as many in the pile now. Some are missing. There were twice as many of those in the luggage pile when we were loading up the bus in Paris. Now there are only four. They're all locked, and there aren't any names or addresses on the tags."

What could he say to her? She was absolutely correct that there had been ten small leather valises in Paris, and now there were only four. How could he explain this discrepancy to her without revealing things about which she could never know?

He couldn't tell her that each of those ten leather valises held a short wave radio set. Each radio had been carefully packed with instructions, code books, and spare parts into a small and innocuous leather valise. They'd been checked aboard the *Normandie* and transported abroad with the rest of the group's luggage. He couldn't tell her that each of the six valises no longer in their luggage pile had been taken to a left luggage department in the train station of a town along their route. He couldn't tell her he had mailed the left luggage claim tickets to very special people to allow them to claim those valises. That list of names and addresses had been given to him by Sir Nigel Barnaby.

Dr. Veere couldn't tell her the truth. The truth was that when war came, these agents in place, these best friends of freedom and democracy, who were already living in France and Germany, would be their eyes and ears inside countries occupied and subjugated by the Nazis. He couldn't tell her that these brave souls, secretly and at great risk to their own lives, would be sending coded messages to Britain to let the allies know what was happening in countries that were no longer free.

Each time Veere took a small leather bag that held the precious radio to a left luggage department in a railway station and mailed the claim ticket to the person who would turn in that ticket and retrieve the radio, he wondered about these faceless heroes of the future. Were they young or old? Did they have wives, husbands, children? Why had they volunteered to do this dangerous work? Why would they sign up to be part of a war that might not start for years? He thanked them silently and wished them Godspeed. He hoped they would have good luck and long lives, and he knew they would need a lot of the former and probably would not be blessed with much of the latter.

As it turned out, it was not French customs agents, a nosey train conductor, an officious German at the border, or the Gestapo who had caught his deception. It was a member of his own tour group, who had noticed the extra bags he'd hoped would remain "hidden in plain sight" until they'd found their way to new homes. She was asking questions, and she required answers.

"Miss Burkhart, you are so observant. How could you have noticed the number of suitcases in our huge, unruly pile? You are truly a wonder, and you have discovered my secret. I am delivering typewriters. They are very expensive to buy in Europe and much more readily available in the United States. I am taking them to people who need them and can't get them here. This trip seemed the perfect way to transport the type-writers, a much less costly and quicker route than sending each one separately abroad through parcel post. A generous benefactor on the business school faculty at Columbia University purchased these typewriters for colleagues he used to work with in Europe. These typewriters are all gifts. We take our typewriters for granted in the United States and think that of course everybody who needs one has one, but that's not true in Europe. I'm in charge of leaving each typewriter, in its own locked leather case, to our benefactor's friends in need. Your mystery is solved, and I am the one 'who done it.'" He laughed and gave her his most charming and conspiratorial smile.

Geneva acted as if she accepted the explanation about the leather valises, but Dr. Veere knew his face had blanched when she'd first mentioned the missing bags. He'd taken responsibility for the valises, the ones that were still in the pile as well as the ones that had disappeared, but he knew Geneva Burkhart had not entirely believed his fictitious story about typewriters.

CHAPTER THIRTY ONE

SAVING FRANZ I

"OF COURSE HE'S WORTH IT, JACK." NIGEL sounded almost angry. "He was Einstein's student, for God's sake, and he's a brilliant engineer and physicist. He knows everything about what the Nazis are up to with rearmament, but more importantly, he knows all about this atom-splitting thing. He works with Max Planck and Lise Meitner. He's a Nazi treasure." Nigel Barnaby was trying to explain to Jack Trevanian how important Franz Hartmann was and why he had to be saved.

"If he's so important to the Nazis, why does he have to leave Germany?" Jack didn't understand why MI6 and the Columbia University travel group were needed to rescue this man.

"Because the Nazis say he's a Jew, damn it!" Nigel was doing his best to explain the unexplainable. "But he isn't really a Jew; he's a Catholic. It sounds crazy, I agree. Of course, it's crazy, but what do you expect from these psycho Nazi strutters?" Nigel sighed and paused. "I'm beginning to sound like you, Jack, and God forbid that should ever happen. According to the Nazis and their made-up rules, because Hartmann had a grandmother who might have been a Jew, he's now considered to be a Jew. Franz's grandmother was raised by the sisters of Bon Secours and almost became a Catholic nun. I always thought Germans were supposed to be logical, but this is like falling through the rabbit hole."

"You're telling me that because Hartmann had a grandmother who might have been Jewish and who almost became a Catholic nun, he has to leave Germany right now?"

"Yes, that's pretty much what I'm telling you. We have a plan for getting him out, and I need some help from you to pull off his escape."

"Tell me, what in heaven's name do my 'girls,' or rather 'Veere's girls,' have to do with this plan of yours?"

"Eleanor Hammond is very tall, thin, and fair-skinned ... like Hartmann. We put her into the group because of her physical appearance, rather than because of her abilities in math. Her background as a math teacher will stand up to scrutiny, if no one looks too closely. Our man, the one we need to rescue, will be substituted for this tall, thin woman."

"Nigel, please don't tell me the plan is to replace one of our women with a man? That's as goofy a plan as you've ever had. Who is going to fail to notice that a woman, Eleanor Hammond from White River Junction, Vermont, is not really Franz Hartmann, a German man? Do you think the other women on the trip will be fooled? This is absurd, Nigel."

"Just listen, and you'll understand that no one in the travel group is ever going to lay eyes on Franz Hartmann. We're planning to stage a pretend traffic accident on a deserted country road very close to the Swiss border. No one will be

JULY 1938

JACK TREVANIAN ON THE PHONE WITH NIGEL BARNABY

injured in the accident, but we will pretend Miss Hammond has been hurt."

"What about Wilhelm? He knows what Miss Hammond looks like. Won't he be at the scene and notice the accident isn't real?"

"Wilhelm will be driving the blue bus to Munich with the rest of the group as usual. Miss Hammond will say she's ill and stay behind. She won't be on the bus that morning. Veere will stay in Freiburg with her while the rest go on ahead. Albert will drive Veere and Eleanor Hammond in a hired car so they can pretend to try to catch up with the bus. Wilhelm can't be in two places at once, and he'll be with the others. We've got it all worked out."

"You're going to have to give me more of an explanation about how that's going to happen. Remind me again who Albert is." Jack was insistent.

"Albert drove the bus while the group was in France. After the imaginary accident, Albert will hitchhike to the closest town. When he gets to Tengen, he will make a point of telling everyone there's been an accident and that an American woman has been badly injured. He'll pretend to telephone for an ambulance. After he completes his phony telephone call, he will announce that a Swiss ambulance is on its way to take the woman to Switzerland for treatment. The ambulance that shows up at the accident scene will be a fake Swiss ambulance with our people in it. Albert will hitch a ride back to the scene."

"What happens to the real Miss Hammond in all of this? You can't just leave her by the side of the road to fend for herself near some little German town?"

"Hammond isn't her real name, Jack. She's MI6, and she will have her British passport and papers with her in her own name. After the accident, Eleanor will change her clothes and alter her appearance. She'll get rid of her ridiculous red hat and blond curly wig and trade the red jacket, shoes, and handbag for a less conspicuous dark-colored duster, plain walking shoes, and a brown leather shoulder bag. The shoulder bag contains her British passport that shows Eleanor Crockett's photo with the short brown hair that is really hers. She even speaks German, but don't tell anybody. She knows not to draw attention to herself."

Nigel continued. "When he returns from acting his part in Tengen, Albert will drive Eleanor to the train in Ulm where she will buy a second class railway ticket to Koln. From Koln, she will make her way across the English Channel and return to her home in Bexley, England, a suburb of London. Eleanor Crockett lives in Bexley under her real name. She will go back to work at MI6 and will be able to take great satisfaction that she's been instrumental in helping a famous physicist escape from Nazi Germany. Eleanor Crockett will have successfully completed her mission as one of my operatives. She's well trained and will be fine. Our main concern is getting Hartmann out of Germany."

Nigel continued before Jack could interrupt with another objection. "The ambulance that responds to the fake accident will be marked like a Swiss ambulance and have Swiss license plates and a Swiss ambulance crew. They will be waiting in the woods near the accident scene. Hartmann will already be inside that ambulance. He will be dressed in exactly the same clothes Eleanor Hammond was wearing, including the blond wig. He'll be covered with fake blood to make him look as if he's in very bad shape. And he will have an oxygen mask over his face to further obscure his looks. The location of the staged car accident is such that taking the patient to the closest major hospital will mean taking her to a special orthopaedics clinic in Schaffhausen, Switzerland rather than to any place in Germany."

"What's Billy Veere doing while all of this is going on?" Jack asked.

"Veere will be in the hired car with Eleanor, waiting for Albert to return from Tengen. Veere will honk the horn three times, the signal for the fake ambulance carrying Hartmann to drive out of the woods. Veere, who now has Eleanor's American passport and papers in his hands, will climb into the ambulance with Hartmann, and they'll head for the Swiss border. When Hartmann and Veere get to German border control, the Swiss ambulance crew will say they were the first to receive the call about the accident. They'll present Eleanor Hammond's American passport to get Hartmann out of Germany." Nigel hoped he'd made his case.

"Okay, that's all great, if you can pull off the substitution of the man for the woman. Do you think that can possibly work? You say Hartmann's body and clothes will be painted with pretend blood, but won't the German or Swiss border guards compare the face of the accident victim with the picture on Eleanor Hammond's passport? What happens then?"

"That, of course, will be the moment of truth. Hartmann will have blood all over and an oxygen mask to obscure his face. We think it will work."

"Tell me again why Veere will be riding in the ambulance with Hartmann. That seems like a lot of extra risk to take."

"When the Swiss ambulance reaches the border, Veere's role is to impress on the German border guards that the badly injured American woman needs to be taken to the closest hospital with a first-rate surgery department. If he has to, he'll bring out that letter from Bernard Rust at the cultural ministry, the one that authorized Veere to bring the group to study in Germany. We anticipate the Germans will want to turn the ambulance around and send it back to a hospital in Germany. Veere will tell the German guards that the Swiss ambulance was the first on the scene. If the border guards try to stop the ambulance from taking the injured woman to Switzerland, Veere will make a big deal out of the fact that the patient holds an American passport. He will say that precious time is being wasted and will warn the Germans there could be a scandalous international incident if an American woman dies because the German border guards won't allow her get the medical help she needs. When the German guards look at the victim in the back of the ambulance, there will be blood everywhere. When they see how badly injured she is, we hope there won't be too much resistance from the Germans about taking the patient to Schaffhausen, and we're counting on a quick passage into Switzerland."

"This sounds awfully risky to me. Why don't you just dress up the German guy, put him in an ambulance with Miss Hammond's passport, and drive him across the border into Switzerland. Why make it more complicated with the fake accident? This whole thing is impossibly convoluted." Jack was skeptical of Nigel's plan.

"The costumes, the subterfuge, and the substitution with Hartmann dressed in Eleanor's outfit, all of that has been designed to create an illusion in case there are any witnesses and in case the Gestapo later investigates the accident. When we claim there's been an accident and insist on taking an American from our group out of Germany across the border into Switzerland, we need to provide some evidence that there really was an accident. The location of the pretend accident was chosen because it's so close to the Swiss border. Although no witnesses are anticipated on the remote dirt road, we want to make a show, in case a nosy passerby stops to see what's happening. I'll admit, there are a number of tricky parts to the operation. I understand your concerns."

"If this complicated escape plan just happens to work,

what happens to him once he's out of Germany? What is our payoff for rescuing Hartmann?" Jack wanted answers.

"He'll be transferred from the ambulance to a regular car and driven to a safe house in Winterthur in Switzerland. There he will receive a debriefing from you and me and scientists from Great Britain and the United States. Hartmann will share, with Britain and her allies, his knowledge of uranium and all it can do. He will be able to tell us how far along the Germans are in their attempts to make a weapon out of splitting the atom. He also knows about the weapons Germany is developing and how the Nazis are progressing in their preparations for war. He's invaluable."

"What do you want from me?"

"I need a hired car with stolen French license plates. Albert, who will drive the car, has a legitimate French passport, and he knows what to do. I also need an old, dilapidated truck and a man to drive it. The truck has to be an inconspicuous color, brown or black, and covered with dirt. It needs to be the least noticeable truck on the road. You'll have to steal license plates for the truck, too, in case anybody sees them and makes note of them. The truck driver doesn't need to know anything except exactly what he has to do. The less he knows, the better."

"Will Veere be able to carry off the deception? It sounds like he's the one with all the responsibility. I guess I trust you on this, but I don't like to put people in harm's way, any more than we have to." Jack had a bad feeling about Nigel Barnaby's wild and elaborate accident plan.

CHAPTER THIRTY TWO

LEAVING BADEN-BADEN

AUGUST 1938
BADEN-BADEN, GERMANY

FRANZ TOOK THE EARLY MORNING TRAIN from Frankfurt to Baden-Baden where he'd reserved a room at Brenners Hotel. He always stayed at Brenners, but this time, his welcome from the hotel staff lacked its usual warmth. Franz wondered if the Gestapo had been around asking questions about him. Fear might be the reason for the cool greeting he'd received. Franz acted as if everything was fine because his life from this moment on depended on his ability to pretend.

Franz had his luggage taken to room #307, and he lay down for a rest. He couldn't sleep. His mind raced with the details of what would happen in the next few days. Would everything go as planned? Would his disguises and deceptions work?

A few days earlier he'd learned that Margot and the children were safe in Switzerland. He'd telephoned a certain number every day, and until two days ago, no one had answered. Finally, someone had picked up the telephone and said, "Hello, this is Herr Schneider." Those few words were the signal that his family was safe.

Now he had to follow through with his own complicated plan to join his loved ones. He finally drifted off to asleep and was awakened by the telephone. "Herr Docktor Hartmann, sir. This is the concierge desk calling to remind you of your appointment at the baths this afternoon beginning at two o'clock."

Franz thanked the concierge and lay back on his pillow, wishing he could cancel the baths. He was exhausted from the stress of the past few months. The news that his family was in Switzerland had been a huge relief, and it was as if nothing else mattered. He was drained and had to push himself to get ready for his spa appointments. He put on the hotel's cotton terry cloth robe and pulled up the hood. He went downstairs to the lobby of the hotel and walked across the street to the baths.

Herr Docktor Fritz Volk from Koln also arrived at Brenners Hotel that day. When he'd made his reservation, he had requested room #309. Alone in his room, Fritz removed the dark wig, the small moustache, and the wire rimmed eye glasses he'd worn to make his face look like the photo on his identity card, passport, and other travel documents. He removed the padding he wore around the mid-section of his body. Fritz was the man's real name, but Volk was not.

If anyone had bothered to notice, without the dark hair, the moustaches, and the glasses and without the extra forty pounds around his waist, Herr Docktor Volk was very similar in height, weight, coloring, and even facial structure to the man in the room next to his, Herr Docktor Franz Hartmann. Fritz lay down on the bed to rest from his journey, and as soon as he dropped off to sleep, the hotel room telephone rang. "Herr Docktor Volk, sir. This is the concierge desk calling to remind you of your appointment at the baths this afternoon beginning at two o'clock." Fritz put on the hotel's terry cloth robe and pulled up the hood of the robe to obscure his face. He went down the back stairway of the hotel, exited by a side door, and walked to his appointment at the baths.

Fritz's first appointment was a massage, the therapeutic and vigorous kind for athletes and hardy souls. He gave himself up to the stout and muscular Brunhilde who beat, pulled, and prodded his muscles into submission. Then he proceeded to the steam room where he fell asleep. Next he went on to the warm springs and ended his day at the pool. It was important that Fritz keep all of Franz Hartmann's spa appointments and follow the same sequence of activities, today and for the next six days. If Fritz conscientiously kept these appointments every day, Franz Hartmann might be able to leave Germany.

Worn out from the massage, the steam room, and the train travel, in addition to the many months of worry, Franz Hartmann made his way back to the hotel. He put on his silk dressing gown and ordered ice and soda to drink with the bottle of whiskey he'd brought with him. He was too exhausted to think of eating anything but needed to establish a pattern of behavior. He ordered dinner brought to the room. This might be his last nourishing evening meal for a while, so he ordered all the courses — soup, fish, roast, salad, and Black Forest cake for dessert. After dinner, in spite of everything he had on his mind, he fell into a dreamless sleep.

None of the minders who were assigned to watch Hartmann as he kept his appointments during his holiday in Baden-Baden, ever actually went inside the spa. They saw him leave the hotel and enter the baths. They waited outside for him to emerge at the end of his regimen. On that first night, Franz's minder was pleased that Franz was going to eat dinner in his room rather than go to the dining room. This meant that at 9:00 p.m., the minder could leave his post, return to the station, and take the train back to his home in Frankfurt. Another minder would keep watch outside Franz's room during the night, and that minder would be relieved the next morning.

Franz's wake-up call came at 7:00 a.m. Dressed in his walking shorts, knee high socks, and hiking boots, he went down to the hotel dining room and ordered a full English breakfast. He left the hotel carrying a heavy wooden walking stick with a silver top and wearing a green Bavarian hat with a red feather. Franz felt silly wearing the wool hat. It was too hot to wear such a hat in August, but many hikers wore them. The hat was an important, if despised, part of the subterfuge, so he put it on. Franz headed for one of the numerous walking paths in the Black Forest foothills of the Vosges Mountains near Baden-Baden.

Franz's minder for the day had taken over at breakfast. Franz knew he was there and allowed the man keep him in sight when he began his climb into the mountain foothills. At a specific spot in the woods, Franz stepped off the walking path and lay down in a grove of trees for a break and a drink from his canteen. A few minutes later, a man of Franz's size, shape, and coloring, and dressed in clothes identical to those Franz had put on that morning, picked up the walking stick, the canteen, and the hat with the red feather. He stepped out from Franz's resting place, back onto the walking path, and continued the hike that Franz had begun. Franz's minder, who was expecting to see Franz emerge from his short rest in the secluded spot in the shade, saw exactly what he was expected to see. The minder followed the hiking clothes, the walking stick, and the hat with the red feather.

Franz, still in his hiding place in the woods, took a heavy

brown monk's robe out of the cloth bag that was concealed under a bush. He wondered how the poor religious fellows could manage such an outfit in the heat. He took off his hiking clothes and pulled a woman's flesh-colored stocking over his hair. This attempt to make him look bald might work from a distance. He stuck the gray monk's-style beard on his chin and replaced his knee-high socks and hiking boots with thick gray socks and leather sandals. Before donning the monk's robe, he strapped on the "stuffing" that added quite a few pounds to his middle and made him look like a portly and very much older cleric. Finally, he pulled on the robe and tied the rope around his now very wide waist. He drew the hood of the robe up over his head. Leaving the shelter of his hiding place, he was now a monk in a brown wool cassock, carrying a Bible and a cloth sack full of colorful hiking clothes. He headed toward the railway station in town. There was no minder waiting for him, so Franz assumed the man who'd been watching him had followed the substitute Franz in the hat with the red feather, just as had been intended.

Once at the station, Franz, wearing his monk's outfit, boarded a train for Freiburg im Breisgau. He kept his head down, read his Bible, and completed his journey in the second class compartment. In Freiburg, he collected a valise from left luggage and went to the room he'd reserved at the station hotel.

Leaving Brenners Hotel, Franz's daytime minder followed the man who wore the hat with the red feather and carried the heavy walking stick with the silver top. The minder followed Franz to the copse in the woods and lost sight of him for a moment when he ducked into a resting spot. A few minutes later, the hiker reemerged to resume his walk through the Black

Forest foothills, and the minder followed the man he assumed was Franz. The hiker met no one and talked to no one. The minder followed the man as he walked back to his hotel and ordered lunch brought to room #307. The minder waited for the man he believed was Franz to emerge from his hotel room.

Shortly before 2:00 p.m. that afternoon, a tall, thin man with light hair wearing the hotel's terry cloth robe left room #307 and walked to his appointment at the baths. His schedule today was the same as it had been the day before with massage, steam room, warm springs, and pool. The minder watched as the man he believed was Franz Hartmann entered the baths. The minder settled down to wait for him to finish his day at the spa.

At 2:00 p.m., the muscular Brunhilde greeted her client as Herr Docktor Hartmann because this was the same man to whom she had given a very vigorous massage the day before. "So, Herr Docktor, how did the muscles feel after I worked on them yesterday? Are we going for the same pressure today? Or something less? Or perhaps more?"

"Why don't we go with a little less pressure today? It was a wonderful work out yesterday, but my muscles began talking to me last night. I think a little lighter today, and then tomorrow we can work it up again." She smiled broadly. Herr Docktor wondered if it was his imagination or had he detected a slightly sadistic glint in her eye.

"As you wish, Herr Docktor." She began to pummel him.

The call from room #307 came at 6:00 p.m. "Please bring up a bowl of ice and some soda, just as you did yesterday. I will order my dinner now, and you can bring everything together. I'll start with the chicken soup, followed by the sauerkraut garnie with an extra garlic wurst grilled, please, the plum tart, and the cheese plate. I would also like two bottles of your best local dark beer." When the waiter knocked on the door of Room #307, a voice from the bathroom told him the door was open and to bring in the food and drink. The waiter set up the meal on a small table. The room's occupant was just finishing in the shower. The waiter called to him that everything was delivered and thanked Herr Hartmann for the gratuity left on the bedside stand.

Herr Docktor did not hike the following day but stayed in his room and ordered breakfast and lunch sent in. Franz's minder wondered why his target was spending so much time in his room but was reassured when Hartmann again left the hotel just before 2:00 p.m. to attend his spa appointments. Herr Docktor ate dinner in his room again that evening. The minder settled into the dull and repetitive routine of watching, and inevitably he let down his guard.

Every morning, rooms #307 and #309 looked like all the other rooms the chamber maid had to clean. There were damp towels in the bathrooms and newspapers in the wastebaskets. The beds had been slept in. The maid changed the sheets and cleaned the rooms. She made sure the connecting door between the rooms was securely locked. Rooms #307 and #309 could be combined, if necessary, to make a two-bedroom suite. Each door could be locked and unlocked from its own side. The maid had once forgotten to check that both doors were secured. A very drunk guest in room #309 accidentally stumbled into #307 where a couple was sleeping. The drunk man began to shout in anger that someone was in his bed. The chambermaid never again forgot to check the locks.

On the fourth day, a man with a hoarse voice called the concierge from room #307 to say that he was ill. He gave her a telephone number to call to ask his doctor to come to the hotel. He ordered chicken soup, some crackers, and a tisane sent to the room. Notified by his contact in the concierge's office, the minder was alerted to the illness of the guest in room #307. Franz's minder, already becoming a bit lazy at his job and lulled into complacency by the sameness of his target's daily routine, watched the physician enter room #307, stay a while, and speak a few words to Herr Docktor Franz Hartmann as he left the room.

The physician spoke with the concierge and told her that Herr Docktor Hartmann was sick with the flu and needed bed rest, plenty of liquids, and whatever food he could manage. To ward off pneumonia, the physician recommended that Herr Hartmann not leave his room for several days, until the physician could return to listen to his chest again. Requesting that bottled water and ice to be delivered regularly to room #307, the physician ordered special meals for his patient and left detailed instructions with the concierge.

The minder was delighted that his target wouldn't be leaving his room for several days, and he wasn't paying attention when, just before two o'clock, the thin, tall man with light hair walked down the back stairway and left the hotel wearing a terry cloth robe to keep his appointments at the baths.

Little notice was taken when Herr Docktor Fritz Volk, who had been staying in room #309, checked out of the hotel. Wearing the dark wig, the small moustache, the wire rimmed eye glasses, and the bulky padding stuffed under his suit, Volk paid his bill at the end of the week and left Brenners Hotel in a taxi for the train station. When he arrived at the station, he went to the men's toilet and removed the disguise he'd worn as Herr Volk. He put on a different wig and different clothes and checked Volk's valise at the left luggage room. Exiting the station, he walked back to Brenners Hotel, entered the hotel by a side door, walked up the stairs, and let himself into room #307.

On the last day of Franz's vacation, Fritz Volk put on clothes the real Franz Hartmann had abandoned in his room a week earlier when he'd left Baden-Baden as a monk. Fritz packed Hartmann's things and left room #307 dressed as

Hartmann. Because he didn't want to interact with any of the hotel's employees, he left an envelope filled with Reichsmarks at the front desk. The envelope included a note thanking the hotel staff. Hartmann had overpaid the bill with instructions to distribute the extra money to the maids and waiters who had made his stay so enjoyable.

Knowing Hartmann's minder would follow him as soon as he left the hotel, the tall, thin man with blondish hair, wearing Franz's clothes and carrying Franz's luggage and briefcase, left Brenners and took a taxi to the station. His passport and travel documents had Franz Hartmann's name on them. He picked up Franz's tickets at the Baden-Baden station and boarded the train. Few people realized that the real Franz Hartmann had left Baden-Baden after spending only one day at Brenners Hotel. Hartmann's disappearance would not be noticed until he failed to return to work in September.

Franz Hartmann had scheduled seven days for his holiday in Baden-Baden. Weeks later, when the Gestapo began their investigation into Hartmann's disappearance, they would find that all of the scheduled spa appointments made in Hartmann's name had been kept.

When questioned by the Gestapo, the masseuse and the other employees who worked at the steam room, the springs, and the pool would verify that Herr Docktor Franz Hartmann had kept all seven appointments for his spa services. He had generously tipped the masseuse and several of the towel boys on his last day at the baths. They all remembered him well. When shown a photo of Herr Docktor Franz Hartmann, the towel boys were pretty sure, although not absolutely certain, that the man in the photo was the person who'd kept the daily spa appointments. He looked very like their generous Dr. Hartmann but not exactly like him. The man who had visited the spa looked a little older perhaps, but they couldn't be sure.

Brunhilde, the masseuse, however, was very certain. She didn't like the Gestapo, and if she could figure out what answer they wanted, she would always say the opposite, whether it was true or not. She told the investigators that she was absolutely sure the man in the photo was Herr Docktor Franz Hartmann who had kept his massage appointments with her every day for a week. She hardly glanced at the photograph.

Curiously, the hotel concierge reported that Hartmann had become ill with the flu and spent a few days in his room recovering. The concierge and the hotel maids were questioned about the man who had claimed to be ill in room #307. The doctor who'd been summoned to treat Herr Hartmann could not be located. The concierge had either misplaced or thrown away the physician's telephone number and couldn't remember his name. It was a dead end.

CHAPTER THIRTY THREE

LEAVING ELEANOR

AUGUST 1938
IN GERMANY NEAR THE SWISS BORDER

"**A**RE YOU READY FOR THIS, MISS HAMMOND?" "Don't fuss, Dr. Veere. I know what to do, and I know how to take care of myself after you leave in the ambulance and I'm off on my own. I've been trained for this kind of thing, you know." She allowed just a bit of her British accent to creep into the flat American speech she'd affected for the past several weeks while she'd played the part of the American woman Eleanor Hammond. "I have to say, though, I will be very, very happy to get rid of this damned wig. It's so uncomfortable and way too hot to wear in the summer. It itches like the devil."

The rain was pouring down as they climbed into the back seat of the hired car. Miss Hammond was wearing a red jacket over her white dress. She had on red leather shoes with medium-high heels and carried a matching red leather handbag. The red hat, complete with veil and red feathers, was really too dressy for traveling, but she'd been told to wear it just the same. Her wig of long blond curls was not quite the right hairstyle for someone as "long in the tooth" as Eleanor Hammond, but she carried it off with confidence. She was not really as old as she'd made herself look when she'd been pretending to be an American school teacher.

The car stopped on the side of the narrow, winding dirt road several miles south of the town of Tengen. This location had been chosen for the pretend accident because it was only a few kilometers from the Swiss border. Today the road was all mud after hours of rain.

"Don't get out of the car, Eleanor. There aren't any other cars or people anywhere around to witness anything. Our truck isn't even here yet. Maybe it won't show up." Veere didn't want Eleanor to have to climb out of the car and get wet.

"At the very least, I have to get a little bit of rain on my hair and outfit. What if someone comes by? I'll need to be ready to lie down on the side of the road and moan." Eleanor got out of the hired car, walked a few steps down the road, and stood there holding her handbag while the rain soaked her hair and clothes. She turned around and was headed back toward the car when a dilapidated brown truck appeared over the crest of the hill. The truck slowed down, and then it unexpectedly sped up, only to slam on its brakes and go into a skid. It hit a patch of water on the road and fishtailed dangerously. The driver lost control, and the truck slid into Eleanor's back, smashing her to the ground. She never saw it coming. After striking Eleanor, the truck veered off the opposite side of the muddy road into a ditch, just short of the trees.

Dr. Veere and Albert raced to where Eleanor lay on the road. Blood covered her lower extremities, and she wasn't moving. Her legs were crumpled at unnatural angles. Her elbow was obviously dislocated and maybe broken, but otherwise, she appeared to be uninjured from the waist up. She was in a great deal of pain and shaking with cold, a sure sign of shock. Veere didn't think she was mortally injured, but it was very serious.

Veere sent Albert to help the truck driver get his vehicle out of the ditch. Veere ran to the boot of the car for blankets and a first aid kit. He wiped the blood from Eleanor's legs, certain both were broken. In spite of all the blood and the obvious broken bones, her exterior lacerations looked superficial, but he was worried she might have internal injuries. He put pressure on the wounds until he was satisfied she wouldn't bleed to death. She tried to speak, but Dr. Veere hushed her and told her she was going to be fine, that there was an ambulance on the way.

Of course there was an ambulance on the way, but it was not a real ambulance. It was a phony ambulance, painted to look like a real ambulance in order to smuggle a man out of Germany. Dr. Veere couldn't believe what had happened. Apart from his disbelief that there had been a real accident, he was acutely aware that more than one human life depended on what happened in the next few minutes. His thoughts were in disarray, but he had to think clearly and quickly if he was to get everyone successfully out of this calamity.

The original plan, for Albert to hitchhike into Tengen to report a fake accident, wasn't going to happen. Instead of pretending to call an ambulance for an American woman, he had to call a real ambulance for a British woman.

Veere spoke urgently. "This is very important, Albert. We can't waste time waiting for you to hitchhike to Tengen. The truck will drive you. When you get there, you have to call a real ambulance to come to the scene. The victim is now a British woman by the name of Crockett, Eleanor Crockett. You've got to remember that name and the fact that she's now British, not American. You will meet the ambulance in Tengen and ride back here with it — to show it where to go. I don't want it to get lost and be wandering around the countryside, looking for Eleanor. The ambulance you bring will be a German ambulance, and we will insist that Crockett be taken to the best German hospital in the area. The closest ambulance will probably come from as far away as Freiburg, and that's where they will want to take her for treatment. One more thing, and this is critical. While you're in Tengen waiting for the ambulance, you must call Nigel Barnaby and tell him what's happened. Here's the number to call." Dr. Veere handed Albert a piece of paper. "Be sure he understands that I will be sending the package headed for Switzerland as planned. Do you understand your instructions?"

Albert nodded. There couldn't be any delay in bringing the ambulance for Eleanor, and he had to telephone Nigel Barnaby.

Veere continued. "When you return with the German ambulance and Miss Crockett is on board, I will ride in the ambulance with her. You will follow us in the car and pick me up at the hospital in Freiburg. I'll explain more about all of this later when I've had a chance to think about it. It will all work out if you do exactly what I've told you to do."

Veere climbed on the running board of the truck and looked inside the cab to see if the driver had been injured. The driver was physically fine but terrified. Veere shook him and told him to pull himself together.

"It was an accident. I saw the whole thing. It wasn't your fault it's raining and the road is muddy. The truck skidded and ran into her. You couldn't avoid it, but you can't think about that right now. She's been badly hurt and needs to get to a hospital. You're to drive my man into Tengen so he can get to a telephone and arrange for an ambulance. Can you do that? Do you understand me?"

Albert climbed into the truck beside the driver. Veere was struggling to direct the actors in this rapidly shifting drama in which the roles were changing by the minute. Veere spoke again to the truck driver. "After you've dropped this fellow in Tengen, drive your truck away from there, as far and as fast as you can. Get rid of the license plates, and don't get stopped for reckless driving. Don't come back here. If anyone asks me, I'll tell them the driver of the vehicle that caused the accident was frightened and left the scene. Lose the truck and lose yourself. I don't care where."

It had seemed like a good idea to fake an accident in the remotest possible place, but when confronted with a real accident, it was a catastrophe to be in the middle of nowhere.

When the truck was gone, Veere knelt beside Eleanor. He reassured her that everything would be fine and told her again that an ambulance was on its way. This ambulance would be a real one. Veere's heart pounded as he tried to keep his nerves under control. He had to figure out what he was going to do about Franz Hartmann and the fake ambulance that was waiting a few hundred yards away in the woods.

Nothing had gone as planned. Dr. Veere found himself in an impossible predicament. He had to get Eleanor Hammond's American passport and other travel documents into the hands of the man in the fake ambulance so Franz could be smuggled into Switzerland as the badly-injured Eleanor Hammond. Veere looked around for the red leather handbag that held those precious pieces of paper.

The handbag wasn't near Eleanor's body, and Veere didn't see it anywhere. It was essential and had to be found. He mentally replayed the accident in his mind. Where had Eleanor dropped the bag when the truck had run into the back of her legs? Soaking wet, Veere searched through the weeds in the ditch beside the road and slogged through the wet grass and mud. Veere knew he was wasting precious minutes looking for Eleanor's handbag, but everything would be for naught without the documents. The red handbag was chosen because it could be easily seen and remembered by witnesses. Finally, he found it in a ditch. It wasn't red any longer, but brown, covered in mud. No wonder he'd not been able to see it. The clasp had come undone and some of the papers were spilling out. Because of the rain, Veere was worried that the passport might be wet or damaged.

The ambulance with Swiss license plates was still waiting in the woods. Veere honked the horn of the hired car three times, the signal for the fake ambulance to make its appearance. When the ambulance arrived, Veere opened the back to find Eleanor's double lying on the stretcher inside. He had the blonde wig on his head and was dressed as a woman wearing red shoes, a red jacket, and a red hat. As planned, the pretend accident victim was generously painted with convincing-looking blood. Veere reminded the attendant to keep the oxygen mask over Hartmann's face and handed him the mud-covered red handbag. He told both the "victim" and the attendant it was vital to keep track of the bag because of the important papers it contained.

Veere didn't have time to explain to anyone what had gone wrong. "Drive the patient to the border and tell the German border guards you're headed to the clinic in Schaffhausen. Everybody knows the clinic. It has a reputation all over Europe. I won't be riding with you as planned. You're on your own. Now, leave! Immediately! Hurry, and good luck."

As the fake ambulance pulled away, Veere picked up the soaking wet red hat that lay in the middle of the road and ran to where Eleanor lay, now unconscious. She was going downhill rapidly. He brought the valise from the hired car with Eleanor's change of clothes. Veere could hear, in the distance, the beep of the siren as the German ambulance approached from Freiburg. The fake ambulance had to be out of sight before the real ambulance arrived. He'd told them to hurry, to get going at once. Why was the Swiss ambulance moving so slowly? It was going to be a close call.

Veere gently removed the blonde wig from Eleanor's head. Afraid to take her arms out of her red jacket, he carefully put the dark duster on over the jacket to keep her warm. He bundled the hat, the wig, and the red shoes into the small valise and left the brown walking shoes lying on the ground next to Eleanor's bent and broken legs. He looped the strap of the brown leather bag securely around the shoulder and wrist of her uninjured arm. The shoulder bag contained the British passport and other papers she'd intended to take away with her as Eleanor Crockett. Veere returned the valise that held Eleanor's wet and bloody disguise to the hired car.

Veere was devastated he couldn't complete his role according to Nigel Barnaby's original plan. He should have been riding in the fake ambulance with the scientist to make sure he made it across the border. Now Veere had a real accident victim waiting to be taken to the hospital, and his first priority, in his mind, was to be sure Eleanor got the medical care she needed.

CHAPTER THIRTY FOUR

SAVING ELEANOR

AUGUST 1938

IN GERMANY NEAR THE SWISS BORDER

T HE AMBULANCE HEADING FOR SWITZERLAND had just disappeared around a corner when the real ambulance from Freiburg came speeding down the road. The departing Swiss ambulance had come very close to being seen by the approaching German ambulance. Veere almost collapsed with relief that the two hadn't met.

An efficient medical crew came to Eleanor's rescue. Veere stood back to let them do their work and spoke to the ambulance driver. "I believe the injured woman is British. I looked in her handbag, and that's what her papers say. She's very badly hurt. I know you usually take an accident victim to the closet hospital, but can she get adequate medical care there? Maybe you should you take her to a more specialized hospital? What about taking her to Schaffhausen? There's a first-rate orthopaedics clinic there." He didn't think the German ambulance driver would be open to the idea of leaving Germany, but he asked, to see how the driver would react.

The driver, as expected, was insistent, "Any medical care in Germany is just as good if not better than one can get in Switzerland. And there are all the formalities and paperwork if one tries to cross an international border. We don't want an unexpected delay. Time is of the essence, so it's much better to take her to Freiburg. Freiburg University has a fine hospital and excellent surgeons."

Albert had accompanied the ambulance to the accident scene and now waited in the hired car. Veere ran to the car to find out if Albert had talked to Barnaby. "Were you able to reach Barnaby?"

"He wasn't there, but I told Jack Trevanian everything that's happened with Eleanor. He gave me another telephone number and told me to call at two o'clock, exactly. That's twenty minutes from now. Jack said Barnaby will be waiting by the telephone to talk to me, and he emphasized the importance of calling at exactly two o'clock. Do you want me to leave now?"

"Yes, leave now. You'll have to find a telephone along the way to make the call. I'm going to accompany Eleanor in the ambulance. Meet me at the hospital in Freiburg. As soon as I have Eleanor settled there, you will drive me to Switzerland." Albert drove the hired car away from the scene of the accident.

The ambulance people spent some time stabilizing Eleanor's legs before they lifted her onto the stretcher. At last, Eleanor was in the ambulance. Veere climbed into the back beside her, and they left for Freiburg with lights flashing and siren beeping. Dr. Veere held Eleanor's hand and talked to her as they raced back the way they'd come on the narrow, muddy road.

"You are on your way to the hospital. You're going to be all right." Veere wondered what he would tell the other women in the group about the accident. The original plan had been to say that Eleanor was at a hospital north of Zurich where she was doing fine, and Veere decided to stick with that story.

But before Veere ever got to Switzerland, he would receive emphatic orders from Nigel Barnaby. Albert stopped on his way to the hospital and made the call to Barnaby. Barnaby was very upset that Veere had accompanied Eleanor in the ambulance.

"You have to keep Veere from going into the Freiburg hospital with Eleanor." Barnaby screamed at Albert over the telephone. "You *must* catch up with the ambulance and get Veere away from Eleanor Crockett. Veere, out of the kindness of his heart, has associated himself too closely with Eleanor Crockett, and his actions have put her in grave danger. Veere has spoken with the ambulance driver and the attendant. These conversations may already have compromised Eleanor's British identity. I understand that Veere wants to get her the help she needs, but he has to immediately distance himself from the accident victim. Veere is a novice in the spy game, but I hope he will grasp the situation quickly and understand what you're saying to him." Nigel Barnaby, the master of spy tradecraft and the man with a mind for details, was frantic.

Already delayed because he'd stopped to make the telephone call to Barnaby, Albert was several minutes behind the ambulance that was heading to Freiburg at full speed. When Albert returned to the car, he pushed it to its limits, trying to overtake the ambulance. Just as it pulled onto the hospital grounds, Albert caught up and stopped the hired car close to the rear doors of the ambulance.

As the stretcher was lifted out of the ambulance, Albert approached Veere, indicating that they urgently needed to talk. Veere tried to put Albert off until Eleanor was taken care of. Albert stood in Veere's way and grabbed him by the coat and pulled him away from the stretcher. Veere pushed him away.

"What are you doing? Leave me alone. I have to get Eleanor inside and make sure she's getting emergency treatment." Veere was furious when Albert tried to keep him from going into the hospital.

"I insist you come with me at once. Barnaby's orders."

"Let go of me! I have to go into the hospital with Eleanor."

"You can't go in there with her. You have to leave with me … now!" As discreetly as possible, Albert tried to convey Barnaby's orders. He kept his voice low so no one else could hear what he was saying to the stubborn Dr. Veere. "You're putting her life in danger if you go into the hospital. You can't be seen with her. It's dangerous for her and for you." Albert did his best to make Veere listen. "I just spoke to Barnaby, and he says you cannot, I repeat cannot, under any circumstances stay with Eleanor. I have to get you away from here, and Barnaby told me to do whatever I have to do to make sure you comply with his instructions. You must leave with me, right now! You've already put her in jeopardy by riding in the ambulance with her, and you may have already blown the whole operation."

"I can't just leave her here. Somebody has to be sure she's being cared for and gets into surgery. I owe it to her; I'm responsible for her."

"Barnaby will take charge of her medical care. He's sending his own surgeon and has someone coming to the hospital with a cover story about who Eleanor is, what's happened, and what's going to happen. He'll explain everything to you when he sees you, but first we have to get you away from Freiburg. Barnaby is furious and wants to debrief you about exactly what you said to the ambulance driver and the attendant."

Albert steered Veere toward the rental car and pushed him into the passenger seat. He slammed the door behind the angry Veere and climbed into the driver's seat. Veere was upset but didn't try to get out of the car to go back to the hospital. As the two made their way toward the Swiss border, the reason for their quick exit from the hospital grounds began to sink in with Veere.

"I made a big mistake by riding to the hospital with her, didn't I?"

"Barnaby wasn't happy that you spent any time at all with Eleanor Crockett."

"Maybe the ambulance people will think I was just being a Good Samaritan."

"Maybe they will."

Albert and Veere presented their documents at the German-Swiss border. The car had French license plates, and Albert had a French passport. After the formalities were dispensed with and the German border guards had scrutinized their papers, they were allowed to approach the Swiss border guards. Finally, they crossed into Switzerland.

Barnaby, wearing a black raincoat and holding a large black umbrella, was there, standing in the rain just outside the Swiss border control kiosk. Veere thought the man finally looked like the spy he really was. Veere couldn't believe how quickly Barnaby had been able to meet up with them. Then he realized that Barnaby had been at the border crossing, not to meet Albert and himself, but to be sure that Franz Hartmann's entry into Switzerland went smoothly. As it turned out, that border crossing had not gone smoothly at all.

CHAPTER THIRTY FIVE

SAVING FRANZ II

AUGUST 1938
GERMAN-SWISS BORDER

NIGEL BARNABY WAS A SEASONED SPYMAS-
ter, and he had kept his cool through the Great
War and countless dangerous and secret operations
since. He had lost people he cared about, and not all of the
missions during his years with MI6 had been successful. Nigel
Barnaby wanted to go to the border crossing to do what he
could to facilitate Franz Hartmann's entry into Switzerland
but doubted he could do anything but watch.

Barnaby couldn't go into Germany. The Nazis knew him
and knew he was MI6. He was not welcome in the Third
Reich. He had to stay clear and allow others to do his bidding
inside Hitler's domain. This was galling to Barnaby who
wanted to be in the field and in the thick of things. The trouble
with spending many years as a successful spy and living long
enough to tell the tale is that you eventually become known
to everybody.

Barnaby would like to have been waiting for Franz Hartmann at the German border. He wanted to be there to jawbone the Nazi border guards and threaten them if they refused to allow "Eleanor Hammond" to cross into Switzerland to be taken to a clinic in Schaffhausen for medical treatment. But that wasn't going to happen, and Barnaby had to wait on the Swiss side of the border. His presence at the Swiss border crossing was superfluous. The Swiss knew him, too. If the Germans let the ambulance leave Germany, there wouldn't be any problem getting into Switzerland. But this was his operation, and he was determined to be there, as close as he could possibly get to the point where he knew there would undoubtedly be trouble.

Barnaby was able to watch the German border checkpoint from where he was standing on the Swiss side. He waited and waited. A timetable for this operation had been established, but he had no way of knowing that events in Germany had not gone according to plan and that the schedule had collapsed. When the ambulance was two hours late arriving at the German-Swiss border, Barnaby, who never got nervous about anything, began to sweat. What had happened to the ambulance? What had happened to his carefully constructed plan? The difficult hurdle to overcome with the German border guards was still to come. The ambulance had not even shown up yet.

Finally, he thought he saw the ambulance that carried Franz Hartmann approach the barricades on the German side of the border. Barnaby knew the license plates on the Swiss ambulance were stolen, and he knew the ambulance itself was not a real Swiss ambulance. He wasn't really worried about the ambulance passing muster. The ambulance crew was the real thing. He'd insisted on that, and he'd paid a lot of money to procure a real Swiss ambulance driver and a real Swiss ambulance attendant.

The ambulance had its lights blinking and its siren beeping. The German border guards spoke first with the driver, and Barnaby could tell they were arguing. The Germans were shaking their heads and pointing back toward Germany. Barnaby knew they were telling the ambulance crew to turn around and go back the way they'd come. It looked as if the ambulance was not going to be allowed to pass. The driver jumped out of the ambulance and began to argue with the border guards. Then the driver and the two guards went around to the rear of the ambulance. Barnaby watched as they opened the doors and climbed inside. He held his breath.

Where was Veere? He was supposed to be in the ambulance to expedite the crossing. He was supposed to have a letter from the Minister of Culture and something-or-other that explained about the group of American women who were traveling through Germany. Veere was supposed to make this happen. Why wasn't he the one arguing with the German border guards? What in the world had gone wrong? It was a disaster.

Barnaby couldn't see inside the ambulance from where he was standing, and it was driving him crazy to be out of the picture, not to know everything. It seemed like the German border guards were inside the ambulance for a very long time. This was the moment he'd been dreading. He was sure they were comparing the American woman's passport picture with Franz Hartmann's face. This was where it could all go wrong.

Finally, they climbed out of the back of the ambulance. The driver and the attendant were now standing beside the ambulance arguing with the two border guards. They were all shouting at each other, and there was a great deal of pointing and posturing and waving of arms and shaking of fists. Nigel Barnaby could barely keep his cool and stay on the Swiss side of the border. He wished the ambulance would just make a run for it and break through the barriers that kept it in Germany. It was that important to get Franz Hartmann to Switzerland.

The attendant climbed back into the rear of the ambulance, and the driver got into the front seat. The ambulance started backing up, and Barnaby's heart sank. It was over, and he had failed.

He thought all of his planning and all of his work to save Franz Hartmann's life were going down the drain. Then the ambulance stopped backing up. The attendant jumped out of the rear doors. He had papers in his hands and waved them in the faces of the border guards. One of the Germans grabbed the papers from him and began to read. The other German guard looked at the papers and shrugged his shoulders. He shook his head and turned his back on the Swiss ambulance attendant. The attendant climbed back inside the ambulance.

The ambulance drove forward and approached the barricades for a second time. One of the border guards raised his gun and pointed it at the ambulance as it approached. The ambulance kept going and didn't stop this time. At the last minute, the second guard raised the barricade, and the Swiss ambulance raced through. Its lights were still flashing, and the siren was still beeping. The Swiss border guards waved the ambulance through without stopping it.

The driver made sure he was far enough away from the border before he stopped the ambulance. He didn't want the German guards to be able to see what happened once they'd made it safely to Switzerland. Barnaby ran to the rear of the ambulance, and before the ambulance had come to a complete stop, he was banging on the doors. The attendant who was riding inside with the patient knew he was now in Switzerland, and it was safe. Barnaby jumped in when they'd finally stopped. He almost collapsed with relief to see Franz lying there, covered with fake blood and wearing the blond curly wig and red hat.

Barnaby addressed the ambulance attendant. "Bring the car. I want him on his way to Winterthur immediately. Then I want a complete debriefing from you and the driver." The attendant left the ambulance and motioned to the driver of the waiting car. Barnaby took Hartmann's hand, removed the oxygen mask from the man's face, and pulled him into a sitting position. "Dr. Hartmann, I'm Nigel Barnaby, MI6. Welcome to Switzerland."

"So, I am finally out of the Nazi hell hole and safe at last." Franz Hartmann had tears in his eyes.

"It almost didn't happen, but you are indeed. You are indeed, safe at last."

"Are you the person I have to thank for saving my life?"

"Oh, no. Not just me. There were many of us who conspired to save you. I will tell you all about it when we get to Winterthur. The car is here to take you there now. Get rid of that silly hair and hat. Leave it here. How will you walk in those shoes?"

"I practiced walking in these shoes. Just watch me." Barnaby watched as Franz climbed down from the ambulance and teetered on the red high heels as he walked toward the Mercedes that would take him to the safe house in Winterthur.

Nigel Barnaby had to smile as he watched the brilliant physicist, dressed in women's clothing, drive away from what could have been a complete debacle and the end of the man's life. They'd all known it would be risky, but it had been much more difficult than anyone had anticipated. Barnaby wanted to hear everything from the driver and the attendant.

"Where the heck is Dr. Veere, and why were you so late? Veere was supposed to be with you. What happened? You are more than two hours behind schedule."

The ambulance driver had seen some of what had happened at the accident scene, and he spoke up first. "We don't know exactly what happened, but something went very wrong. Somebody was badly hurt, for real, in a pedestrian accident. There wasn't time for your man Veere to tell us who was hurt or what had happened. As soon as he gave us the handbag with the passport and papers, he told us to get out of there as quickly as possible. He was in a panic, and he had blood, real blood, all over him. There was a woman lying beside the road. We couldn't see much, but it looked very serious. She was in very bad shape. Veere said he was staying with the woman who'd been hurt and that he intended to ride to the hospital with her. He told us he wouldn't be coming with us. He wished us good luck and kept telling us to hurry."

Nigel Barnaby never liked to show that he was surprised by anything, but he was shocked by what the attendant had said. "Did Veere tell you the name of the person who was hurt?"

"No, he didn't say."

Barnaby knew he would have to call Jack Trevanian as soon as he could get to a telephone, but he wanted to hear the rest of what the Swiss ambulance crew had to report.

The driver, who had interacted most with the German border guards filled him in. "First thing, they wanted to turn us around and take the patient to a hospital in Germany. They said we couldn't cross. They wanted to know why a Swiss ambulance had gone into Germany in the first place, and they got all hung up on why a Swiss ambulance had been called to rescue someone when a German ambulance would have been much better. They wanted to know where we'd crossed over into Germany on our way to the accident. They knew we hadn't entered Germany here, at this border crossing, where we were trying to exit."

The attendant spoke up. "There is always tension between the Germans and the Swiss. The Germans never want to admit that the Swiss might be better in any way. The German border guards finally accepted that the Swiss ambulance had been the first to respond to the accident, but they argued again that we turn around and take Eleanor Hammond to a hospital in Germany. It was really more a matter of national pride than it was any suspicion on the part of the border guards. I don't think they ever gave a thought to the fact that we were trying to smuggle somebody out of their country."

Barnaby understood this issue. "We anticipated that was going to be a problem. The Germans always want to believe their medical services are superior to those of the Swiss. So how were you able to convince the German guards to let you through?"

The driver responded. "It's a good thing we were a real Swiss ambulance crew. I've gone from Germany into Switzerland at this border crossing a couple of times before, and I'd almost convinced one of the guards they needed to let the ambulance pass. But the other guard refused and drew his gun on us. I acted angry and very distressed about the delay, concerned that the patient was in danger of dying if she didn't get to a hospital immediately. I screamed at them about wasting time and putting the victim in danger, and all of that."

The attendant picked up the story. "Then the border guards had to get into the ambulance and look at our patient. I kept the oxygen mask over his face, but of course the border guards wanted to compare the face with her passport. I did my best to keep them from moving the oxygen mask out of the way. I told them it might be fatal to deprive the victim of oxygen. I told them her death would be on their hands."

Barnaby nodded his head and commented, "This was always going to be our bete noire, the critical moment when our man would either pass for Eleanor Hammond or he wouldn't."

"Yes, and it was a very near thing. I think it was the wig that did it for us." Barnaby smiled when the attendant mentioned the wig. Everybody had hated that wig, and everybody had told him the wig was a terrible idea. Eleanor especially had hated wearing it for as long as she'd had to wear it, and Franz had also protested that it was hot and uncomfortable.

The attendant continued. "One of the border guards actually touched the wig when he was looking at Eleanor's passport. Your man, who was dressed up as a woman, was brilliant, though, when the border guard touched his hair. He pretended to have some kind of a seizure episode. When he began having the seizure, I screamed at the border guards and ordered them out of the ambulance. I told them they were putting the patient in danger, and they would be responsible if the American woman died. I told him there would be a scandal, and it would be in all the newspapers. It would become an international incident. I said it would be the big news about how German border guards had denied life-saving medical care to an American woman traveling in Germany, etc. Even after they compared the female passport picture with the man's face, they didn't seem suspicious. I think they were just miffed because we were breaking the rules and, in their view, not respectful of the medical care in Germany. They said they weren't going to let us into Switzerland and told us to turn around. So we got in the ambulance and started to back up."

"Then I looked in the red handbag Veere had given me, the purse that had the passport and other papers in it. There was a copy of a letter in there from some Nazi minister that said a group of women from the United States had permission to travel in Germany and to extend them every courtesy, and so forth. I got out of the ambulance again and showed that letter to the guards. One of them read it, but the other one wouldn't. We'd decided to run the barricade anyway, if we had to." This explained to Veere the backing up and then the aggressive driving toward the border.

"Whatever you did, it worked. Things don't always, if ever, go as planned. We had a good plan, but those damned Nazis ...! It was touch and go, but you performed magnificently. The free nations of the world are forever in your debt." In the end and in spite of everything, Franz Hartmann had made it to Switzerland.

Nigel Barnaby hurried back to the kiosk at the Swiss border. There was a telephone there, and he called Jack Trevanian who was in Winterthur.

"Hartmann made it out. He's safe and on his way to you. But it almost didn't happen. There were major screw ups all the way around, and I don't have any idea what's happened to Billy Veere. Tell me what you know."

"Albert called, and there's bad news." Jack proceded to tell Nigel what Albert had told him about Eleanor's accident. When Jack got to the point in his story where he said Veere had accompanied Eleanor Crockett to the hospital, Nigel started to scream at Jack over the telephone.

Jack interrupted him. "Don't scream at me. I know you're upset, but you need to get your message to Veere himself. I told Albert to call you on the Swiss border kiosk telephone at exactly two o'clock. I assume you're calling me from that number. So hang onto your britches, Nigel. That's just ten minutes from now. Wait by the telephone, and Albert will call you — if he can find a telephone to call you from in the middle of nowhere. I'm getting off now. Calm down. Our man is free. Mission accomplished. Give yourself credit for that." Jack hung up, leaving Nigel fuming and holding the receiver in his hand.

At exactly two o'clock the telephone in the kiosk rang, and it was Albert. Barnaby screamed his instructions at Albert, and Albert assured him that he would get the job done. He would get Billy Veere out of Freiburg. Albert cut Barnaby off by stating the obvious, that he had to get back in the car and race to catch up to Veere who was riding in the ambulance with Eleanor.

Barnaby decided to wait at the Swiss border kiosk to talk to Veere and Albert when they came through. While it was still fresh in Veere's mind, the master spy wanted to grill the American college professor about everything that had happened.

When they entered Switzerland and Albert stopped the hired car beside the kiosk, Barnaby slid into the back seat. Barnaby was not exactly shaken, but his usual calm demeanor was more than a bit ruffled. He was usually so controlled and hardly ever showed any outward sign that he was worried. Today, he was very angry that Veere's good intentions might have compromised Eleanor Crockett's life. Veere knew Barnaby was unhappy and realized it was all his fault. His decision to accompany Eleanor Crockett to the hospital in Freiburg was the reason for Barnaby's anger. Eleanor Crockett was Barnaby's agent. Veere had put Crockett at risk, and it had been a bad mistake. Barnaby had to be concerned that his MI6 operative was seriously hurt, but he seemed to be a great deal more worried that Veere had been seen in the company of the British woman than he was about her injuries. Dr. Billy Veere was crushed about what had happened to her.

Barnaby's first words were not about Veere's faux pas. "The border crossing was a near thing, and we almost didn't get Hartmann out of Germany." Barnaby was pleased to tell them that Franz Hartmann had at last made it safely into Switzerland. In spite of the fact that nothing had gone as planned, the whole reason for the elaborate subterfuge had been to rescue Franz Hartmann, and that had been accomplished. As soon as Barnaby had reported what had happened with Hartmann, he turned to Veere and began his interrogation.

Barnaby wanted to know every detail about what had gone wrong and grilled Veere the rest of the way to Winterthur. Barnaby tried very hard not to lose his temper with Veere. "I'm sorry Albert had to get rough with you to keep you from going into the hospital, but to protect Eleanor Crockett, I had to get you away from her. You can't have anything more to do with her. Eleanor *Hammond* was one of your teachers and therefore under your care. Eleanor *Crockett* is a British citizen and has nothing to do with the American group. From now on, she has no connection to you, no connection whatsoever. Do you understand that? The ambulance driver probably won't remember much of anything about you, but the attendant will certainly remember you because you sat with him all the way to Freiburg. That's more than an hour on the road. Please try to remember everything you did and everything you said to the attendant, especially what you said about yourself."

"I don't remember what I said. I was so rattled and terribly worried. I was mostly reassuring Eleanor that everything was going to be all right, that I was going to be sure she got the best medical care available. She was in shock and had an oxygen mask over her face. I think she was unconscious most of the way, so I really don't think she heard anything I said. I remembered to say her name was Eleanor Crockett, not Hammond, and I told the attendant that her travel documents were in her shoulder bag. I don't think I said anything at all about myself. I know I didn't give my name. I don't think he was paying much attention to me. The attendant was trying to keep her blood pressure stabilized and deal with the shock. He was focused on his patient, as he should have been. He thought I was just a Good Samaritan who'd happened on the accident by chance."

"You did absolutely the right thing by sending away the truck that struck Eleanor. I'm concerned that the truck drove

Albert into Tengen, but you had to get to a telephone and call an ambulance as quickly as possible. It makes sense that the driver would leave the area when he had the chance. The Germans don't like loose ends. They will try to find the truck, but they'll never find it."

Eleanor Crockett had paid a very high price for her participation in the operation. Her injuries were unexpected collateral damage, but in the end, Franz Hartmann's escape had been a success.

CHAPTER THIRTY SIX

SAVING FRANZ III

AUGUST 1938
SWITZERLAND

THE NEXT DAY, NIGEL BARNABY DECIDED TO bring Veere into his confidence to a greater extent. As a college professor, Veere wasn't trained as an intelligence agent, and Barnaby felt the amateur needed to know more about what was going on with the overall project involving Franz Hartmann.

"You aren't trained as a spy, Billy, and we have expected a great deal from you ... perhaps too much. You are obviously intelligent, and you're also a very quick study. I only have to tell you something one time, and you know what to do. But you're also a nice guy, and you almost compromised the operation to rescue Franz Hartmann because you were thinking like a college professor and a kind, responsible human being, rather than like a covert operative." Nigel Barnaby felt Veere needed to know some things about tradecraft. "We've put a lot on your shoulders, and we don't want you to make any more mistakes by trying to save the day on your own. Good thinking, by the way, for getting her out of the Hammond costume so quickly and making sure her British passport and papers made it into the ambulance with her."

"If I'd figured it out more quickly, I wouldn't have ridden in the ambulance. I'll worry about that until Eleanor is completely recovered and safely home in England."

Barnaby knew Veere felt terrible about what had happened to Eleanor Hammond/Crockett.

"You will be happy to know that Eleanor Crockett came through surgery successfully, and we have a team monitoring her recovery. She's going to be fine. The Gestapo don't seem to be particularly suspicious about the accident in the countryside outside of Tengen. Right now they're obsessed with tracking down the truck that hit Eleanor. I hope you understand why we can't ever have anyone connect Eleanor Crockett's injuries to Eleanor Hammond's accident." Barnaby looked at Veere to see if this was registering with him. Veere nodded that he understood.

"I'm so relieved to know that Eleanor Crockett's surgery was a success." Dr. Veere was feeling very down on himself. He continued to be fixated on Eleanor Crockett and the accident and seemed almost not to care anymore about Franz Hartmann's escape.

Barnaby wanted Veere to know the details of the subterfuge. "The driver of the Swiss ambulance that carried Franz Hartmann and the attendant will file a report that they picked up an accident victim in Germany near the Swiss border and brought her to a hospital in Schaffhausen. The paperwork will indicate she had only minor injuries. A doctor was consulted, and since her legs were mostly scraped and bruised rather than broken, he decided not to admit Eleanor to the hospital but to send her to a convalescent clinic."

Barnaby continued. "There are a number of very private

clinics in Switzerland. Records at one of these clinics will show
that an American named Eleanor Hammond, matching Eleanor
Hammond's description, was admitted after a pedestrian auto-
mobile accident in Germany. The clinic's medical records will
show she stayed for six days and then returned to her home
in the United States. The Swiss are proud of the secrecy they
provide in the field of banking. They also afford strict privacy
in medical matters. It would take significant time and effort
for the Gestapo or anybody else to get information out of our
particular Swiss clinic. We don't think they will bother."

Barnaby continued. "If anyone tries to track Eleanor
Hammond back to the United States, they will find that there
is a real Eleanor Hammond who's a math teacher at the high
school in White River Junction, Vermont. However, the Eleanor
Hammond of the Columbia University study group looks very
different from the Eleanor Hammond who actually lives in
Vermont. The real Eleanor Hammond is Trevanian's niece by
marriage. She's been camping in Canada all summer and will
let Trevanian know if anyone comes around asking about her
activities during the summer of 1938. Chances are extremely
remote that will happen, and it may be silly to tell you all of
this detail. I'm going into all of it to impress you. We have gone
to great lengths to protect identities and people, as well as to
protect our operations. But we don't think anyone will take
the trouble to look into Eleanor Hammond's background."

"I'm duly impressed, with everything you've done to be sure
these deceptions are convincing. I now understand why you were
so anxious for me not be seen with Eleanor Crockett. I hope I
haven't endangered her. I was just trying to do the right thing."

"You couldn't have known. You handled yourself with
tremendous poise and rationality in an unexpected and dangerous situation. I think we're going to be okay. The problem
is that she has to be taken care of in Germany, and she has

serious injuries. It isn't as easy to falsify records and lay misleading trails in Germany, where the Gestapo investigates every hangnail and drop of blood. The Germans want everything recorded in triplicate. The good news is that we still have a few connections there. We called in some favors, and Eleanor Crockett's status as a foreign national may work in her favor."

Dr. Veere didn't say anything, but his shoulders visibly relaxed as Barnaby told him everything that had been done to take care of Eleanor Crockett.

Barnaby wanted to reassure him even more. "When Eleanor regained consciousness after surgery, we had someone at her bedside to tell her what had happened and what she was to say when she was questioned. The story is that you were just a kind passerby who came along by chance. You didn't see the accident and arrived after Eleanor had been hit. You didn't see the truck that struck her. Before she went into shock and couldn't speak, the woman told you her name and that she was British. As a concerned citizen, you stayed with the injured woman and took care of her until the ambulance arrived. You very kindly rode with her to the hospital. Americans are like that, known for wanting to help out whenever they can, and you played your part completely in character. You did everything anyone could possibly have been expected to do. Once you were sure Eleanor Crockett was in good hands, you continued on your way. As far as we know, no one took down any names or license plate numbers, and if anyone remembers what you looked like, it doesn't matter. I think we're clean as a whistle on this one, or almost that clean."

"You really have thought of everything."

"We intend to transfer Eleanor as soon as possible to a very discreet private clinic. A few private clinics still operate in Germany. High-level Nazis use them. They won't find the truck or the driver, no matter how hard they try, and we don't think they'll spend a lot of time on this case. A truck hit a British woman who was crossing the road. Her papers are in order. Her passport has all the necessary stamps to document that she entered Germany as a student a couple of weeks ago. She's headed for a private clinic. She will soon be back in her home country and will no longer be the concern of the National Socialist government. Even Nazi bureaucrats are sometimes glad to have a problem taken off their hands."

"I'm relieved to know Eleanor is being cared for. I messed things up, but it seems you were able to fix it."

Barnaby smiled. "Part of my job is to fix things. I try to set things up from the outset so that nothing goes wrong, but of course something always does go wrong. You quickly learn, in my business, to also be a fixer."

Barnaby was second guessing the Eleanor Hammond operation and wondered if his own obsession with its details had been counter-productive. He needed to do some debriefing of himself on this latest debacle, but he felt he had to fill Veere in on just a bit more of the big picture.

"I have more to tell you about what we've done to protect the person who is the reason for all of this."

"Trevanian told me that Franz Hartmann is an important scientist with valuable information."

"Hartmann is very important. You will meet him later today. He wants to thank our team for getting him out of Germany. His debriefing will take several weeks. More than anything, we hope no one in Germany will realize he has disappeared until he fails to return to work at the end of his August holiday. That day is a little less than three weeks from now. When he doesn't show up at his job, everyone will know for sure, at that point, that he's left the country. Then the Gestapo will begin to hunt him down in earnest. The last thing the Nazis want is for Hartmann to escape from Germany and tell the British what he knows. Because of his work on their Uranprojeckt, Hartmann knows a great deal about Germany's nuclear weapons program. Because of his previous work as an armaments engineer, he has information about all aspects of Germany's military weapons programs. Once the Gestapo realize he's gone, they will do everything they can to find him and kill him, no matter where he's living."

"Would they go into another country to kill him?"

"Yes, to keep him from talking as well as to make an example of him. We must protect him, and there can be no holes in the cloak of deception we have woven around his disappearance. We can't have the Nazis looking for Franz and his family in France or Switzerland or anywhere else. "I argued against Hartmann taking part of his holiday in Baden-Baden because it was so close to both the French and Swiss borders. But Hartmann was familiar with Baden-Baden and the area around it. We decided it was better to have him disappear successfully from a place he knew, close to the border, than to get lost in a place he didn't know.

Barnaby went on to explain to Veere what else had been done to obscure Hartmann's true whereabouts and confuse the Gestapo, who would eventually begin examining every detail of his disappearance. An elaborate plan of deception, that included a variety of red herrings, had been put in place. A multitude of false clues were being left to fool the Germans.

Nigel Barnaby was re-examining in his own mind the operation that had resulted in Eleanor Crockett's accident. Should he have chosen a less complicated way to smuggle Franz Hartmann out of Germany? Barnaby wondered if he'd been guilty of overthinking how things would play out. He didn't often doubt himself, but the consequences of this most recent operation forced him to wonder if he had gilded the lily and overdone it this time with his elaborate duplicity.

CHAPTER THIRTY SEVEN

GENEVA'S JOURNAL:
THE ACCIDENT

AUGUST 1938
MUNICH, GERMANY

We had a dreadful thing happen to one of the members of the group today. Eleanor Hammond, a teacher from the public high school in White River Junction, Vermont, was late for the bus this morning. She's remarkably tall and thin, and very, very nice. I guess she wasn't feeling well, so the rest of us went on ahead in the bus without her. Dr. Veere stayed behind and said he would hire a car to drive her to meet us when she was feeling better. We expected them to overtake us on the road, but they never did. When we stopped in Ravensburg, Wilhelm came to the table and told us he had some bad news. Dr. Veere knew where we would be stopping to eat lunch, and someone had called on the telephone at the inn to leave a message for us.

There was an accident on the road from Freiburg. Eleanor was hit by a truck and very badly hurt. Exactly how it happened wasn't clear. The way Wilhelm told the story, it sounded really horrible. Wilhelm could have been mixed up, and it wouldn't be unusual for him to get it wrong. We found out more later tonight after Dr. Veere called and gave Wilhelm some details. Eleanor is in very serious condition, and both her legs and her arm are broken. For some reason, Eleanor was walking along the side of the road when she was hit by a truck. That part of the story sounded pretty farfetched to Elsie and me. Why would she have been out of the car, walking in the rain? The ambulance drove her across the border into Switzerland. There's an excellent orthopaedics hospital somewhere north of Zurich, and it was the closest place that could adequately treat the serious injuries she sustained.

Elsie and I have thought from the beginning that Eleanor didn't quite fit in. We are a motley crew, and each of us is very different — age, economic status, style, where and how we've grown up, and the kinds of schools where we are teachers. Our common ground is mathematics and our interest in how it's taught. Whenever we discussed our teaching experiences and shared with each other what worked for us and what didn't, Eleanor didn't participate in the conversation. She was a good listener and paid attention to what we said, but she never contributed her own opinion. On most other subjects, Eleanor had lots of opinions and talked at great length. It seemed odd to me, since we're all mathematics teachers, that Eleanor never wanted to talk about teaching mathematics.

My suspicions were aroused, and I always felt that something was "off" with Eleanor.

Also, I don't think Miss Hammond was enjoying the lectures very much. She seemed to enjoy the scenery and the sightseeing, but she was bored with the professors' talks and actually fell asleep at a lecture last week. That was embarrassing! She definitely wasn't as interested in the math and physics as the rest of us. She teaches advanced algebra and trigonometry in Vermont. We took up a collection to send flowers to the hospital, and all of us signed a card.

Dr. Veere told Wilhelm that Miss Hammond won't be returning to the tour this summer because she will require several more surgeries and a lengthy convalescence. We're all very sorry about that. Someone from her family is coming from the U.S. to stay with her at the Swiss clinic. We are down one more member of the group. We are falling like flies.

Besides the fact that Eleanor Hammond was hurt, Wilhelm told us there's a flap about the accident. The Nazis are very keen on investigations and paperwork, and the truck that struck Eleanor left the scene. It's disappeared completely. All that anyone knows is that the truck was old and dirty and a dark color. How many of those do you think there are around? Thousands and thousands! Leaving the scene of an accident is VERY NOT ALLOWED in Nazi Germany!!!! I pity that truck driver if the Gestapo ever gets hold of him. One can hardly blame him, though. If I'd been involved in an accident and had a chance to escape without getting involved in some kind of Nazi investigation muddle, let's just say, it would be tempting.

Because she's an American and was in the country on a travel visa, there's even more paperwork. These people with their paperwork and their travel documents and entry and exit papers and every other kind of permit and the stamping and the seals and all the rest of it, it's ridiculous. Dr. Veere has one large briefcase, a suitcase really, that he uses to carry all of our various permits and passports, tickets, and lodging and food vouchers. I don't know how he ever keeps it all straight.

Dr. Veere is staying with Eleanor until she has her surgery, and we're to remain in Munich until he rejoins the tour. This will mess up the lecture schedule a bit, but it's just one of those unexpected things in life that can't be helped. We are all impatient to have Dr. Veere back so he can give us the details about what happened. We are all hoping, and I am praying, for Eleanor's recovery.

I always wondered about her blond hair. It was much too young a hairstyle for her. She dressed like an older woman most of the time, although I couldn't say for sure how old she really was. But that hair was too much. It didn't look right on her, and I could swear it was a wig. Why she would choose such an ugly wig is beyond me. I tried to get up close behind her a couple of times and give her hair an "accidental" tug to see if it was a wig. Elsie agrees that the hair style didn't suit her, either the blond or the curls, and Elsie also thinks it was a wig. I guess now we will never know. Whatever her hair style, I hope she gets better and isn't in too much pain. When my mother broke her back in a car accident in 1932, she was in a lot of pain for a really long time. I hope Eleanor heals quickly, hairdo and all. I will never forget this fateful day.

On a less serious note, I've struggled with the food here in Germany. Some of it I love, and some of it I really don't like at all. I've always loved hot dogs, and at home I eat at least one whenever I go to a baseball game or a football game. Sometimes I eat two hot dogs. I like my hot dogs piled high with everything there is to put on them. In Germany, there is no such thing as "just a hot dog." Here, there are a hundred kinds of "hot dogs," and they are all called wurst. They come in some unimaginable varieties. Elsie told me to avoid the blutwurst and the black sausage (also full of blood -- ugh!) and the ones made out of liver. Thank goodness for Elsie and her knowledge of the worst wurst! But they're not all bad. Some of them are quite delicious, and I've grown fond of several of the wursts and order them frequently -- with senf. That's mustard. If I can get sauerkraut with my wurst and senf, I order it that way. Sometimes, we just walk up to a vendor in the street and order our lunch-time wursts. I love eating outside and standing up.

For dinners and more formal meals, I adore the veal schnitzel and the pork schnitzel and have it almost every night for dinner. I also like the German potato salad, hot and cold. In fact, I prefer the potato salad in Germany to the potato salad served at picnics in Belmont. Everyone in Ohio puts eggs in their potato salad. I don't eat eggs, so I never eat potato salad at home. I love the sweet and sour potato salad of Germany. No eggs! And I love the cucumber salad and the tomato salad. I want to learn how to make these wonderful salads so I can fix them when I go back to Ohio. Tomatoes are in season now, and I always order tomato salad. There aren't a lot of green things on the menu in Germany. I also don't care for sauerbraten; it's too sauer. I almost always manage to find something I like to eat, and I am definitely not one to go without a meal.

CHAPTER THIRTY EIGHT

SAVING FRANZ IV

SUMMER 1938

JACK AND NIGEL IN SWITZERLAND

"JACK, YOU'VE BEEN SAYING THAT I'VE LEFT YOU out of the loop and you don't know what's going on. Now that Franz Hartmann is safe in Switzerland, I feel free to share more with you about what is happening. I'm going to tell you how the subterfuge surrounding Hartmann's disappearance will continue to be maintained and why the ongoing deception is necessary."

"It's about time, Nigel. You always want my help, and you are using my Americans to make all of this happen for you. But you never want to tell me anything. I'm listening with all my ears."

"Before Franz Hartmann left Frankfurt, he told everyone he would spend the second and third weeks of his holiday at a monastery in northern Germany, on Rugen Island in the Baltic Sea. This part of his vacation was purposely planned to lead the Nazis, once they've figured out that Franz has left the country, to look for him in northern Germany, far away from the Swiss border. We chose the monastery on Rugen Island because Franz's father had a past connection with the monks there. Franz's father went there for religious retreats from time to time, and we made sure Franz told his colleagues at work why he was going to Rugen Island. He talked about his father's lifelong relationship with the Rugen Island monks and about the beauty of the scenery. Franz went on about how pleasant it would be to spend some time by the water and enjoy the island's pleasant sea breezes, away from the hot summer in the rest of Germany."

Nigel continued. "You probably don't need to know all of his, but I want you to realize how much effort has gone into making Franz Hartmann disappear, and not just from Germany." Jack gave Nigel a quizzical look. Nigel was excited about this part of his operation and wanted to share it. "Remember that all of this will take place in the future. It may not work out exactly as we've planned, but this is what we hope will happen.

"At the end of Franz's week in Baden-Baden, the man who everyone believes is Franz Hartmann and who is being followed by Franz's Gestapo minder, will go by taxi from Brenners Hotel to the train station. A reservation was made several weeks ago for Franz Hartmann to take the train to Stralsund, a town in northern Germany. From Stralsund, Franz's double will go to nearby Rugen Island to spend two weeks at the monastic retreat.

"One risk to our plan is the long train ride between Baden-Baden and Stralsund. Someone who knows the real Franz Hartmann might be on the train and discover that the man posing as Franz is not really Hartmann. Therefore, his route north will be through Munich to Berlin rather than through Frankfurt to Berlin. There will be less of a chance for him to run into someone he knows if he travels through Munich rather than through his hometown of Frankfurt. He's traveling overnight in a private first-class sleeping compartment, so his double can spend much of the trip in seclusion. He will not go to the dining car for meals. We want Franz's escape from Germany to be seen by Gestapo investigators exactly the way we want them to see it.

"When the train arrives in Stralsund, a car will pick up Hartmann's double and drive him to the monastery. Because the monks on Rugen Island have never met the real Franz Hartmann, they will believe that the man who arrives for the retreat is Franz. His double will stay at the monastery for the scheduled two weeks of religious contemplation and then be driven back to the train station in Stralsund."

Nigel enjoyed telling the story to his friend, and Jack was always fascinated by the spy's elaborate tradecraft. "Our deception will be helped tremendously because the man who is pretending to be Franz Hartmann is carrying a genuine German passport in the name of Franz Hartmann. The photograph on that passport, however, is the double's own photo. We're hoping that by the time the look-alike reaches Stralsund, his minders won't remember the real Franz Hartmann's face.

"Sometimes a minder rides the train with the person he is watching. More often, one minder hands off his 'target' to another minder when the target is on the move. Franz's double will be adhering to the Hartmann itinerary. We think the minders will have stopped paying close attention and will be so used to watching Hartmann's substitute, they'll feel confident they're following the right person.

"A train reservation was made weeks ago, in Franz Hartmann's name, for his trip from Stralsund back home to Frankfurt. The man with Franz's papers will pick up the tickets in Stralsund and board the train. This," Barnaby told Trevanian, "is the point at which we want the Gestapo to believe that Franz Hartmann begins to take steps to leave Germany. Remember, all of this will happen about three weeks from now. As you know, the real Franz Hartmann left Germany yesterday. The elaborate substitution of a look-alike will keep alive the illusion that Franz is still in Germany, currently enjoying his week in Baden-Baden and then his two-week religious experience on Rugen Island. Gestapo investigators are intended to see the train trip home to Frankfurt, three weeks from now, as the 'jumping-off point' for Franz's attempt to leave the country. We've designed a tangled web of possible escape routes Franz might take once he leaves the train that's headed to Frankfurt.

"Rugen Island is on the Baltic Sea, not very far from Sweden as the crow flies, or as the boat sails. Because he was vacationing so close to the Baltic Sea and the ferry to Sweden, once the Germans realize Hartmann is gone, we're hoping that initially they'll think he might have tried to make his escape during or immediately after the religious retreat. We want the Nazis to waste time and resources chasing Franz in that direction, on the ferry to Sweden. We want them to pursue that line of inquiry for a while, but it's a dead end. Their investigation will shift when they discover that a man carrying a passport in Hartmann's name bought a ticket and boarded the train in Stralsund, headed for Frankfurt by way of Hamburg.

"The man impersonating Franz will get off the train at the Hamburg train station and purchase two tickets. This will be the first sign to the Gestapo that Franz Hartmann does not intend to return to Frankfurt. One of these tickets will be on a local train headed for a small town close to the border with Poland. Another man resembling Hartmann, a second double, will use that ticket to travel to a German-Polish border town where he will leave the train and disappear. We want the German authorities to believe Franz might have sneaked across the border on foot and is now in Poland. That trail will ultimately result in another dead end.

"The other ticket Franz's double will buy in Hamburg is for Bremerhaven. That double will travel to Bremerhaven and secure passage on a cargo ship in the name of Sven Nordson. The ship is scheduled to leave for Norway the next night, but Sven Nordson won't show up.

"A day or two later, a man resembling Franz Hartmann will be seen visiting a neighborhood in Hamburg known to cater to the underbelly of the city. It's an area where prostitutes and criminals ply their wares, but it also has a community of forgers and counterfeiters. With enough American dollars or Swiss francs, one can buy a passport from any country, in any name, with one's own photo on it. Franz Hartmann's double will pay a visit to one of these 'document specialists.' The tall, thin German with whitish hair will present the forger with a photo of the real Franz Hartmann and leave a fifty percent deposit on a Norwegian passport. When the tall German returns the next day to pick up the Norwegian passport in the name of Sven Nordson, he will take a thick wad of British pounds out of his wallet to pay for the passport. He will handle his cash less discreetly than he should, and the cash will be noticed, as it is intended to be, by the 'businessman' who forges illegal documents."

Nigel briefly told Jack about the corpse dressed in Franz Hartmann's clothes that would be found, several weeks from now, floating in the Elbe River. Barnaby said his hope was that, after following the trail of carefully laid clues, the Gestapo will reach the logical conclusion that they'd found Franz Hartmann's dead body in the Elbe.

"As long as the Germans believe Franz is alive, they will never stop looking for him. Only in death can Franz Hartmann and his family be secure in their new lives. It's vital the Gestapo be convinced that Hartmann is the decomposed body they will find floating in the water. To protect our valuable human resource, you can see that MI6 is going to great lengths to prove that Franz Hartmann died in the Elbe."

CHAPTER THIRTY NINE

LEAVING DACHAU

AUGUST 1938
MUNICH, GERMANY

"WE CAN GO OUT FOR THE EVENING AND stay out until midnight." Wilhelm's excitement was obvious in his voice.

"That's way past my bedtime, Wilhelm. I'm an early to bed, early to rise girl."

"I know some fun things to do in Munich. The Hofbrauhaus is here, and this is the birthplace of National Socialism. There are many landmarks that commemorate the rise of our beloved Hitler and the Nazi Party."

"The last thing I want to see is anything that commemorates Hitler and National Socialism. What's with that name anyway? I thought you Nazis hated socialism. Why is it a part of the name of your political party and your government? I don't want to visit any loathsome Nazi landmarks, Wilhelm. I won't go with you if you try to show me any of that. If you can't find something fun to do, I'm staying home."

"I will take you to a biergarten, and you will think it is very fun. There is wonderful food, and not all wurst, either. There is music and dancing and many bands and beer."

"You know I hate beer, but all the rest of it sounds like the kind of fun I'm talking about." In spite of her promise to herself not to go out with Wilhelm again, Geneva loved to go dancing. She was curious about the biergarten and agreed to spend the evening with Wilhelm. She warned him not to talk about the Nazis.

They rode the tram, and it started out to be the evening Geneva had hoped for. They had delicious chicken roasted on a spit over a fire. Geneva had never had chicken cooked that way, and she loved the potato salad and thinly sliced cucumbers in vinegar that were served with it. She gave Wilhelm points for his choice of restaurants.

They ate at a long table with people they didn't know. There were families, children, and old people, all sitting together. Some of the people in the biergarten wore native Bavarian costumes. Seeing the little girls in their dirndls and the men in their lederhosen allowed Geneva to pretend she was visiting Germany in another era. The quaint and colorful clothing was such a relief from the all-pervasive Nazi uniforms. Some of the families brought their own food. Geneva couldn't speak German, so Wilhelm translated for her. She was curious about what real German people would bring to the biergarten for a picnic and tried not to stare when they opened their baskets and unwrapped their sandwiches.

There were bands playing, and Wilhelm wanted to dance every dance. Wilhelm thought he was a terrific dancer, but Geneva thought his dancing skills were mediocre. He had a great deal of enthusiasm and loved the polka, but his efforts at the waltz and other slow dances failed the test in Geneva's eyes.

The families with small children eventually left to take them home to bed, and Wilhelm and Geneva were two of the last people remaining. There was a Nazi curfew, and most Germans were afraid to disobey it.

"I've had a good time, Wilhelm, but I'm exhausted and have to go home." Geneva wasn't happy with the amount of beer she'd watched Wilhelm consume during the evening.

"We're not going to leave until the last song is sung." Wilhelm slurred his words. It hadn't been as noticeable when they were dancing, but when they sat down at the table, it was obvious Wilhelm was drunk.

"I'm leaving. You're very drunk. You know it makes me angry when you drink too much. We need to go!" Geneva was disgusted.

"You can't leave without me. I am the boss here. I am the only one who can speak German and get you safely back to your hotel." Geneva was in no mood for Wilhelm's attitude. She got up from the table and began walking toward the exit. Wilhelm stumbled along behind her, bumping into the empty chairs and tables, trying to keep up with her.

She walked quickly and with purpose, heading for the tram. She didn't speak German and was pretty much lost without her guide, but she was furious with Wilhelm and determined to get away from him. Why had she agreed to go with him again when she knew it always ended in trouble? She needed to have her head examined. She would find her own way. She got on the first tram that came along, and the heck with Wilhelm.

She tried to ask the conductor how to get to her hotel, the Bayerischer Hof. He gave her a blank look and shrugged his shoulders. She kept looking out the window, hoping to see something familiar that would let her know when to get off. When they reached the end of the line, she had no choice but to exit the tram. She sat in the station alone; it was very late.

The next tram reached the end of the line. Wilhelm got off and found Geneva sitting there. He looked relieved and seemed to have sobered up a little.

"What do you think you are doing, going off by yourself like that? Dr. Veere will never forgive me if you get lost."

"You should have thought of that before you drank so much beer."

Geneva suspected that Wilhelm didn't know where they were. Munich was not really his city. There was nobody to ask for directions. Wilhelm lied to Geneva that he knew how to get back to the hotel. All the trams were down for the night, so she followed Wilhelm onto the next interbahn train that came along. He seemed very sure he knew where they were going, but Geneva was beginning to have her doubts.

After they were on the train, Geneva realized she'd made another bad decision. "This isn't the way we came. We didn't ride on the interbahn or any train like this. Are you sure you know where we are?"

Wilhelm's bravado was enhanced by the quarts of beer he'd consumed, and he shouted back at her, "I do know." They were the only people in the empty train car. Geneva's wrist watch said it was after midnight. She was tired and getting nervous because they were out past the curfew. The train was some kind of express because it kept running on and on. It didn't stop at any local stations as they'd expected it would. When the train slowed down, Geneva and Wilhelm moved toward the door of the car, hoping to get off the train even if it wasn't at the right station. The station sign outside the window said "Dachau" which Wilhelm knew was a small town northwest of Munich. They were very far away from where they wanted to be.

The train began to slow down as if intending to stop, but continued on, creeping very slowly past the Dachau sign.

It finally stopped at a platform that was several hundred yards beyond the station building. Geneva and Wilhelm pushed on the doors of the car, but they wouldn't open. They pounded on the doors. Even though there were lights along the platform, no one came to let them out of the train car. They sat down in a compartment close to the exit doors and waited for help.

A truck pulled up to the platform, and men in military uniforms got out of the back. They pushed and pulled a group of about ten prisoners, who were attached to each other with ankle and waist chains, out of the truck. The soldiers had their weapons drawn and prodded the men with their guns as they hurried the chain gang toward the train. Some of the poor souls in the human chain weren't able to stand and were dragged along on the ground by the others. Geneva and Wilhem were silent as they looked out the window of their compartment and watched the brutal display. The Nazis loaded the prisoners onto the railway car just behind theirs. Some of the soldiers boarded the train to guard the chained men.

Geneva was frightened and could see that Wilhelm was frightened, too. She'd never before seen fear in his eyes. He put his finger to his lips. What were they going to do? Geneva pleaded with her eyes for Wilhelm to do something, but it was clear Wilhelm didn't have any idea what to do. They didn't know where they were and had no idea how to get back to a safe and familiar place.

"Whatever happens, don't say a word. It will be worse if the authorities realize you are foreign." Wilhelm motioned for Geneva to stand on the seat and climb up into the overhead luggage rack. Geneva was small and could hide herself above the seats. "Draw up your legs and hide your feet." Wilhelm draped his jacket over her to try and cover her. "Be absolutely silent." They waited. The train was still not moving.

A soldier pushed open the door of their compartment. He pointed his gun at Wilhelm and started to yell at him. Wilhelm presented his papers. Geneva imagined that the soldier was demanding to know what Wilhelm was doing on this train and why he was out after the curfew. Geneva peeked briefly out of her hiding place and saw the guard punch his gun into Wilhelm's stomach. She wondered if Wilhelm was going to be arrested. She saw Wilhelm reach into his pocket for another card.

Geneva tried desperately not to breathe or move or make a sound. She willed herself to be silent and prayed she wouldn't sneeze or cough. She couldn't understand the words that Wilhelm and the soldier were shouting at each other, but knew that she and Wilhelm were in serious trouble.

Wilhelm was pleading with the soldier. Geneva risked another look from her hiding place. The soldier looked at the card and threw it and the other papers back at Wilhelm. He waved his gun in Wilhelm's face, said a few departing words in disgust, and left the train car.

Wilhelm collapsed onto the seat with relief. "Don't move or make a sound," he whispered. The train began to move. It was heading back to Munich, but it crept along at an incredibly slow speed. There were no other people in their car. This was not a scheduled run for the train. Geneva's muscles were cramped, and she had to go to the toilet.

After what seemed like hours on the train, they reached the tram station. The doors of the car wouldn't open. It was very early in the morning. It was going to be difficult to explain why they were at the tram station at this hour and what they'd been doing on the train from Dachau. Wilhelm didn't want to attract attention, but he knew they desperately needed to get off and end any connection between themselves and this train.

Wilhelm helped Geneva climb down from the luggage rack. She was tired, uncomfortable, and furious. Wilhelm couldn't find the emergency door latch. There was always a way to open the door manually from the inside to let passengers out of the car, a safety feature in case of an emergency or a power failure. "Here," Geneva said and pulled the emergency lever. The door opened, and they escaped from the train into the station.

They were back on the platform where they'd been hours earlier. They walked to where the tram would leave on its first run of the morning. Sitting on the wooden bench, Geneva fell asleep against Wilhelm's shoulder.

They were both rudely awakened by the station master who gripped the front of Wilhelm's shirt, pulled him to his feet, and yelled at him in rapid, angry German. Geneva was sure the official wanted to know what they were doing here at this hour of the morning, and she wondered the same thing. What were they doing here, wherever here was, at this hour of the morning? Geneva said nothing and tried to look German.

Wilhelm showed their tram tickets to the official who threw them on the ground and shouted more abusive remarks at Wilhelm. Wilhelm looked frightened again. The interrogation continued, and he took out of his pocket what he later told Geneva was his old membership card from the Hitlerjugend, the Nazi youth group he'd joined when he was a teenager. He presented the card to the official who examined it and compared its picture to Wilhelm's face. Satisfied that Wilhelm was who he said he was, they had a lengthy conversation during which Geneva recognized the words "frauline" and "biergarten" and a few others. Wilhelm took some money out of his pocket and gave it to the station master. The official led them to the ticket window, went behind the counter, and issued them two new tickets. He gave Wilhelm one last scowl and a final scolding. Wilhelm said some conciliatory words, allowed that he had been beaten, and was contrite.

Geneva started in on Wilhelm as soon as the railroad official left them. "Why are you so frightened? Why, for heaven's sake, are you acting like we're in trouble? I want to know why getting lost is a criminal act, because that's how you've been acting, like we are criminals."

Wilhelm was obviously shaken by the night's events. "We should not have been out after the curfew, and we should never have been in Dachau. We shouldn't have been on any of the trains we were on, and we shouldn't have been at the tram station before it opened in the morning. We should not have been out all night. We could be arrested by the Gestapo and taken to jail."

"Arrested for what, Wilhelm, arrested for what? We didn't do anything wrong. Nothing at all."

"But we did do lots of things wrong. We rode the tram to the end of the line, and we didn't have tickets to go that far. We went to a place where it is forbidden for anybody to go, to the secret train stop near the camp at Dachau. The station master found us asleep here early in the morning, without proper tickets. All of that is against the law and punishable by arrest. Fortunately, he had no idea we'd been on the train and ridden it to Dachau. We would be arrested or sent to one of the camps if anyone found out we were on that train. No one must ever know we were in Dachau, on the camp platform, or that we traveled without tickets or permission to a place where no one is allowed to go. We were at the Dachau concentration camp stop and saw prisoners being loaded onto the train. Luckily only one soldier saw us, and I was able to talk him out of reporting our mistake. If I'd not been able to convince the soldier that we'd gotten on the train by accident and didn't see anything, he would never have allowed us to leave. We would have been sent to prison for a very long time. We were lucky that the train returned to the tram station, and we were able to get off."

"I don't understand any of this. We made a mistake by getting on the wrong tram and then on the wrong train. We weren't trying to cheat the railroad out of a ticket or do anything wrong or break the law or anything like that. What we did was completely unintentional. We didn't *want* to go to Dachau or spend the night in the tram station. What's wrong with this country anyway?"

"You must not question the Reich. We were breaking lots of the laws of the land. We are lucky to escape with just buying new tickets. If it hadn't been for my Hitler Youth card, we would have been in very serious trouble. I saved that card all these years, and thank goodness for that."

"Why is it such a bad thing that we went to Dachau? What is Dachau concentration camp station anyway, and who were those poor people all chained together and being dragged to the train? It was disgusting to see the way they were treated by the guards, even if they were criminals. They were being treated worse than anyone would treat an animal."

"You must never mention the name Dachau or that we were ever there or anything about those prisoners. Dachau is where the Jews and socialists go. The retarded, the insane, gypsies, and those who work against the German Fatherland are sent there. It's where enemies of the state are taken and where those who threaten our Aryan purity and racial superiority are imprisoned. If anyone finds out we were there or saw anything, we ourselves could end up there."

"For doing what? Wilhelm, how can you possibly be an advocate for a system like this? It's a smothering, horrible, repressive society run by criminals. We aren't the criminals here. The criminals are the ones enforcing laws that nobody knows exist, laws that anyone can break without being aware they're breaking them. This is no kind of society to live in, let alone brag about. I can't for the life of me understand what you think is so wonderful about the Nazis. They are just thugs and bullies, and they've gotten control of an entire country by frightening and threatening people. I'm sick of it all."

"You must not judge my country, Geneva. It is the best country in the world and will surpass all other nations in the future. There are rules for a reason, and the enforcement of the rules is why our Fatherland is so successful and so full of perfection."

"Tell me, what makes you so full of bull, Wilhelm? How can you defend this place after what we've been through tonight? You're impossible. I'm not going to talk about it anymore, and I'm never going anywhere with you again. Take me home, right now! Dr. Veere will be furious. I'm sure Elsie has raised the alarm that I'm not back in the room, and there will be trouble for you."

"You're the one who ran off and took the tram without knowing where you were going. You're not allowed to do that. That's why I'm here, to keep you from going off on your own and getting lost and causing trouble."

"Just wait until I tell Dr. Veere the truth about you, about all the beer you had and how drunk you were. He'll go to the Minister of Science, Education, and Culture and ask that you be removed as our driver and minder. Yes, minder! I know that's what you really are, Wilhelm. You're assigned to our group to keep an eye on us for the government, and you're not fooling anybody. Your Nazis are not fooling anybody. You've tried to put a wolf in sheep's clothing, and nobody likes what they see!"

CHAPTER FORTY

THE ADLON HOTEL

AUGUST 1938

BERLIN

T HE TOUR GROUP HAD RESERVATIONS AT THE
Adlon Hotel in Berlin. It was a famous and very expensive place to stay. All the women wondered how the
budget for the trip could possibly allow such luxury. Their
bus arrived at the entrance, and several porters appeared and
unloaded their luggage. Geneva walked into the lobby of the
ornately decorated and opulently furnished landmark. It was
breathtaking and overwhelming. She was excited to be there,
and it would have been perfect if there hadn't been so many
Nazi uniforms and so many red and black swastika flags
everywhere. Elsie wondered if they would see William Shirer,
the American journalist who supposedly spent a lot of time
at the Adlon bar.

Dr. Veere announced that they were going immediately to
the lounge for tea. Lunch had been sketchy, just bread and
cheese and fruit on the bus. The women were road weary, but

the enticement of a lovely afternoon tea kept them headed for the lounge. Dr. Veere was treating them to something special. The women were happy to have Dr. Veere back with them. They'd missed him when he'd supposedly been spending time with Eleanor Hammond in Switzerland.

Silver tea pots arrived at their table, and each woman was asked what kind of tea she wanted. The multi-tiered trays of tea sandwiches were tempting. Geneva knew to avoid the tongue, always a sandwich selection in this part of the world. She helped herself to the delicious Westphalian ham she'd become so fond of and her favorite, tomato and cheese. The watercress with cream cheese looked especially good. She loved the way the crusts were cut off. So much effort had gone into making these small, delicate finger sandwiches. They were elegant, and most of them were delicious. Then came the scones, which were very British. Apparently, they were also a favorite of the Germans. The scones came with clotted cream, honey, butter, lemon curd, and apricot jam. Warm and full of currents, some of the scones were topped with cinnamon and sugar. Just when she thought she couldn't eat another bite, more tiered trays arrived loaded with luscious pastries. Geneva decided to eat the fruit tarts at the table, as they wouldn't travel well. She carefully wrapped several other tempting treats to take to her room.

Everyone in the group was groaning from the sumptuous spread, and Dr. Veere loved to see them enjoy themselves. He made the point that they were in Germany's capital city and would have to be on their best behavior. He said the Gestapo were particularly plentiful and watchful in Berlin. He reminded them that their hotel rooms and telephones might be monitored and urged them to be careful about what they said anywhere about the Nazis or Hitler and other high-ranking government officials.

"I know many of you have strong opinions about how the Nazis are running things in Germany, but we need to be respectful." He looked straight at Miss Burkhart when he said this. "Our trip has gone very well so far, and I hope to be able to make my shortwave broadcast on August 11th. I will be allowed to do this only with the permission of the German government."

"That's what's wrong with the rules here. You shouldn't have to ask permission from the government to make a broadcast ...." Miss Burkhart was getting tuned up, and Veere thought all the uniforms and flags were partly to blame for her irritability. The lavish tea had been a kind of bribe, a nice way of asking the women to be discreet and not to say out loud what most of them were thinking about their Nazi hosts.

"There are no First Amendment rights in Germany, Miss Burkhart, and even though we are used to a very different way at home, we have to live by Germany's laws while we are here." He admired Miss Burkhart's spirit, but he prayed every day that her questions and outspoken criticism of the Nazis would not cause an incident. He wished he could tell Miss Burkhart how much he agreed with the things she said, but there was so much more at stake than just the lecture tour or credits toward a master's degree. He couldn't share with the women in the group the secret objectives he and his colleagues hoped to achieve. Their dangerous agenda always occupied his thoughts. "Just keep in mind that we're guests in a foreign country."

They would leave Germany in three weeks. Veere continued to be shaken by what had happened here since he'd last visited in 1936. The lectures had been a great success, and he'd already handed over a suitcase full of intelligence about Germany's rearmament progress and the German economy.

He'd transferred critical materials to Trevanian and Barnaby when he was in Switzerland. Information that both the British and Americans had wanted badly was now in their hands.

Even though he was no longer carrying around as much secret paperwork, he still wouldn't leave his briefcase in the hotel room. In Nazi Germany, everybody knew and accepted the fact that somebody went through suitcases, papers, and everything left in hotel rooms when their occupants were out sightseeing or in the dining room. Miss Burkhart was justified in objecting to this behavior. It wasn't right to search a person's things without their permission or a warrant, and it wasn't right to run a society based on fear. Veere agreed with her, but he had to find a way to keep her from saying it out loud in the wrong places. Veere had no idea about Miss Burkhart's ill-fated visit to Dachau with Wilhelm, so he could not know she had observed Nazi brutality first hand. He didn't realize that, because of her frightening encounter, she might be less out-spoken in the future.

The group was resting after the wonderful tea. An important person in the Cultural Ministry was going to join them tonight for a late dinner in the Adlon dining room. Miss Burkhart certainly could charm the man, but Veere hesitated to seat her anywhere near him for fear she would start to ask her awkward questions — like whether or not he believed in God and what exactly did the Nazis have against the Jews.

The women had been asked to wear their best clothes for the dinner in honor of someone who'd been instrumental in obtaining approval for their group to travel to Germany. As they dressed in their gowns, Elsie muttered about "bowing down to the almighty Minister of Something-or-Other" who no doubt was in charge of making sure you flushed the toilet. "I don't know why I have to waste my time going to dinner with somebody so I can kiss his hide-bound Nazi behind." Geneva laughed as she always did, but after what had happened in Munich, she was more guarded.

"Be careful what you say," Geneva warned.

"What's with you?" Elsie wondered why Geneva, usually outspoken and challenging everything, was all of a sudden telling her to be cautious. "I thought you would be the first one to ask Herr Minister about the grand opening of the latest concentration camp and where all the Jewish math professors have gone."

"I've just decided to be more careful about what I say. That's all." Geneva hadn't told anybody about Dachau. She'd not even written about it to Edward or put it in her journal. She would never tell her parents because she didn't want them to worry. She usually spoke freely in her letters to Edward, or at least she had until Dr. Veere had warned them that he was sure their letters were being opened and censored before being allowed to leave Germany. Spending time in an authoritarian country, the kind of place Germany had become, where freedom definitely did not ring, had made Geneva appreciate the USA in ways she never had before. In another few weeks she would be home in America, America the Beautiful, America the Wonderful, America without Nazis.

CHAPTER FORTY ONE

TROUBLE
IN NUREMBERG

AUGUST 1938

BERLIN

D R. VEERE HAD MADE HIS SHORTWAVE RADIO broadcast from Berlin the night before, and it had been a huge success. Each of the women had given him a few lines to read over the air. Geneva had sent love to Edward and to her parents and brother and sisters. She told them she was eating her way through Europe but had so far kept her girlish figure because she walked so many miles every day. She had sent them the time and frequencies of the short-wave radio broadcast beforehand so they could listen. It was important to Geneva that her family hear from her and know she was thinking about them. The radio broadcast was a link with her home in Ohio, a connection with the known, and a reminder that there were still places in the world that had not lost their innocence. It was exciting to think her family might be listening to a message from her at the same moment it was being sent.

They were scheduled to go to the Wilhelm Kaiser Institute that day, and the group assembled in the lobby of the Adlon as they did each morning. Dr. Veere had not been at breakfast which was unusual. He was such an efficient leader, the women really didn't know quite what to do when he wasn't there. They wandered into the lounge after a while and ordered coffee while they waited for him.

Finally, Dr. Veere arrived. He had a very serious expression on his face. Something was terribly wrong. He sighed deeply and then he spoke. "I have bad news. There's been a tragedy in the city of Nuremberg. The synagogue at Hans-Sachs-Platz has been destroyed. You will remember I pointed it out to you. We drove by it quite a few times and admired its architecture. It happened night before last, and I have only just received word."

"This is not only the loss of an important cultural and historical treasure, it is also a very disturbing and frightening event which defies understanding. The demolition of the synagogue was not an accident. It was a deliberate act by an evil man, Julius Streicher, Nuremberg's mayor, who decided the synagogue didn't fit in with the landscape of Nuremberg. Streicher ordered the building destroyed on his own personal whim, and he's bragging about having done it. It's difficult for me to comprehend this act of senseless destruction, and I am sure it must be difficult for you as well."

Geneva and the others were as moved by the impact this tragedy had on Dr. Veere as they were by the tragedy itself. Geneva could tell he was questioning his judgment about having brought them to this place, this Germany so full of vicious hate.

She spoke up for the group, hoping to reassure Dr. Veere. "We're all stunned and saddened by this news, Dr. Veere. It's disheartening to encounter a cruel and deranged person anywhere. How can one explain such an irrational act? Even though it makes me very angry and I can't begin to understand why it happened, I think we have to go forward with our lectures and our learning."

The women nodded in agreement, and Dr. Veere seemed to be buoyed by this vote of confidence and the group's determination to continue with their schedule. Dr. Veere looked tired. None of them could know that in a few weeks, on a night in November that would forever be known as Kristallnacht, meaningless violence against Jews would be acted out all over Germany. Shop windows would be shattered; synagogues would be burned; people would die. The August incident in Nuremberg would scarcely be remembered, but it was a harbinger of things to come, a foreshadowing of what would befall Germany's Jews. The violence in Nuremberg was a warning, and the terror of "the night of broken glass" yet to come, would be just the beginning of the Nazi's pogrom of death, Germany's "Final Solution."

"Go ahead without me to the Institute. I'll be along later." But Dr. Veere never joined them that day.

As they were leaving the lecture hall, the elderly professor who'd just given the talk approached Geneva. "What is your name, young lady? I hope you enjoyed learning about the philosophy of mathematics."

"I'm Geneva Burkhart, and mathematics is my passion. I've loved every minute of my studies here at the Institute." Professor Hilmar Beck was very frail and grabbed hold of Geneva's arm as if he might fall. She took hold of his elbow to steady him. "Are you all right? Maybe you should sit down?" The others had already left the auditorium, and Geneva was alone with the professor.

"No! I am not all right, my dear. Nothing is all right. Everything is terrible and getting worse every day. Please, you must take some important papers back to Dr. Veere for me. I thought he would be here today, and what I have to give him and say to him is of the utmost importance. I'm going to be taken to a 'relocation camp' because I don't accept the Nazi garbage that they spew out of their mouths in unending streams. I probably will not be here tomorrow, and it's essential that Dr. Veere have this information to take to his contacts outside of Germany. The world needs to know what these Nazis intend to do to the Jews." The old man's English was heavily accented and at times difficult for Geneva to understand.

She was surprised to hear someone speak so openly about something the Germans usually tried to hush up and keep hidden, especially from the eyes and ears of visiting foreigners like herself. Professor Beck wasn't sugarcoating anything. The women had been repeatedly cautioned against talking about certain subjects. They suspected that the professors who'd given their lectures had also been warned not to mention sensitive topics. There were many things one was no longer allowed to say in this country of lies and propaganda.

Wilhelm came to all the lectures. Everyone realized from the beginning that he didn't know anything about advanced mathematics, and it was pretty obvious to Geneva and the others that one of the reasons he attended was to be sure the professors stuck to the script and avoided areas that were verboten. Wilhelm was a spy.

This afternoon Wilhelm had already left the building to bring the bus around to pick up the women after the lecture. Geneva thought this was why the professor had approached her.

"Your little Nazi minder has gone to get your bus, so he will not see what I am going to have you put into your satchel with your notes from the lecture today. That weasel snoop will not be here to listen to the most important thing I have to say to you about these papers. Dr. Veere will understand, so you must say to him exactly what I am telling you, word for word. These papers explain about a common chemical that is currently used in Germany and all over the world. Zyklon B is manufactured by the chemical conglomerate I G Farben, and at this time it's being used to fumigate against insect and rodent pests. It's for delousing and debugging and to control rats on ships, stores, factories, and so forth. But that's not the most important part." Beck seemed to run out of breath and the energy he needed to continue speaking.

Geneva sensed that what this poor man was saying to her might be the last words he would ever speak. He was at the point of collapse, but he continued with what sounded like a last gasp. "It's not just what's in these papers that is important. The important thing is who is asking and making inquiries about this chemical, this Zyklon B. It is Himmler and Heydrich and a man named Eichmann who are studying Zyklon B. They are doing research about how much of it is necessary to kill a sheep, a pig, and a cow. They are asking questions about how expensive it is to produce and how much one factory at I G Farben could manufacture in a year. Remember to tell Veere that it is Himmler, Heydrich, and Eichmann who are asking the questions. Can you remember those three names? It's vital that you do." He collapsed in a chair and waved Geneva away. "Go get your bus. You must tell Dr. Veere, even if you don't understand what I am telling you or why it's important. He will understand."

Geneva was concerned for the old man's health. "Please let me get you a doctor, Herr Dr. Beck. You don't look at all well. Can I call someone for you?"

"Leave now. I'm old and it doesn't matter what happens to me. You must tell Veere. Promise me that you will."

"I promise I will tell him everything that you've said to me, but please let me help you."

"The only thing you can do to help me is to leave at once before that disgusting Nazi bus driver starts to wonder why you are staying behind and talking to me. Get out! Leave now!" He started to yell at Geneva who turned on her heels and ran from the lecture hall.

She was shaken when she reached the bus. "What were you doing in there, Miss Burkhart?" Wilhelm demanded to know. "You know you aren't allowed to get separated from the group and go running around all over the place on your own. Where were you? I will have to report this. You have delayed our departure for the hotel."

"I had to use the bathroom, if you must know, Wilhelm. Put that in your report. I'm sure your superiors will be very curious about it." She gave him a disgusted look, and he slammed the door of the bus. He ground the gears and stalled the bus as he headed out of the Institute parking lot.

Geneva tried to suppress a giggle when he stalled out, but she had a straight face when Wilhelm turned around and glared at her. He'd heard the giggle and was daring her to cross him.

When they returned to the hotel, Geneva went immediately to Dr. Veere's room before returning to her own. When Veere answered the door, it was obvious he'd been asleep. Geneva apologized for waking him but said she thought it was important to speak with him as soon as possible. She handed Veere the papers from her satchel and repeated almost word for word what Professor Hilmar Beck had said to her. Geneva told Veere it was very important to the old man that she communicate every word as exactly as possible.

"Thank you, Miss Burkhart. I'm sorry you had to get mixed up in the middle of my relationship with Professor Beck. Thank goodness he had the excellent judgment to trust you. You have discharged your duty with speed and precision."

"What's it all about? I don't understand what's so important about this, but it was definitely a matter of life and death to the professor. He spoke as if he were uttering his last words on earth. He was so frail and sick, terribly sad and frightened."

"You don't need to think any more about it. I'll take care of things from now on. You are exactly correct; it is a matter of life and death, perhaps more than you or I can imagine. I fear that the professor, one way or the other, will not live to give another lecture. You have, however, done him and others a great service, and I am very grateful."

"I know that Himmler and Heydrich are very high-ups in the Nazi party, but I've never heard of Eichmann. Do you know who he is?"

"I don't know his name either, but I expect that we will find out who he is sooner or later."

CHAPTER FORTY TWO

GENEVA'S JOURNAL:
HOMESICK

AUGUST 1938
BERLIN

This place gives me a headache, and I can't wait to leave. The marching in the streets never ceases, going on from dawn until dark and frequently into the night. It continues day in and day out. How can anyone stand to listen to it? The red and black flags are everywhere, on every street of any importance, and going on and on, as far as the eye can see. The endless marching and the endless flags are so exhausting. I can't even begin to mention the constant "Seig Heils" and "Heil Hitlers."

The German people have been just as polite and hospitable as they can be. As hosts they are impeccable, but dear me, how dreadful all of this must be for the ordinary man or woman who isn't tied up with the military, the government, or the Nazis.

I'm more than ready to go home. It will only be a few more weeks now. I miss Daddy and Mama and Edward and the farm and Arnold's bad jokes and his harmonica. I miss dear sweet Martha and her goodness. I miss my little sister Bea, and I miss Warren's serious analysis and his knowing everything about everything. And he really does know about everything. He's such a scholar and a scientist; he's thinking and figuring things out all the time. I treasure my wonderful family and miss them so much.

I want to ride on the tractor with Daddy. I want to eat homemade peach ice cream on the porch and walk in the orchard holding hands with Edward. I have seen enough of the world. I love my little corner of it, now more than I ever did. I love Belmont and the store where Martha works. I want to go in there and sit on the stool in front of the counter and eat the little bits of Colby cheese rind she likes to share with me. I want to ride my horse and stop and let her drink cold water from the stream. I want to go to Edward's parents' house and eat his Mama's wonderful homemade noodles in chicken broth and her chocolate cake with the double chocolate icing. I never want to see or eat a wurst again. I want to help with threshing and pitch the hay bales up into the barn. I want to pull weeds in my mother's vegetable garden, pick the ripe tomatoes, and eat one on my way back to the house. I want to see my students at the Lampsville School. I even want to see those rotten McClarren boys who are always causing trouble. I want to go to Chestnut

Level Church and sing and sing and never stop singing. I don't think I've heard a single hymn since I came to Germany. I want to go to the library and take out any book I see. I can't wait to have Edward take me to Wheeling and dance all evening at the Epworth Pavilion. I want to be anywhere but here. I want to be home again. I want to return to my own free country.

CHAPTER FORTY THREE

ONE LAST NIGHT OUT

AUGUST 1938
BERLIN

"AFTER WHAT HAPPENED IN MUNICH, WHY would I ever go anywhere with you again? You were disgustingly drunk and almost got us arrested. Why would I want to repeat that experience? How can you even suggest such a thing? You're totally responsible for every bit of the trouble we've had. I can't trust you."

"I've told you many times how sorry I am about what happened in Munich. I promise I will never again take a drink of beer or spirits, if that's what you want. If I take this vow of temperance, will you please go to the amusement park with me this evening?"

"I don't believe for a minute that you won't drink any beer, and how many times have I told you my heart is already promised to my doctor in America. I won't have a romance with you."

"You have indeed told me all of that many times, but you cannot deny me a chance to try to win your heart. You know that I care for you and admire you beyond the moon."

"There's not a chance on earth that you can win my heart, and it's cruel to give you false hope. I could never love any man who doesn't believe in God. You can never win my love, and your Nazi system can never win me over. You're all evil, because you're all Godless."

"Geneva, you know what a kind and charming fellow I am. I am the farthest thing from evil. You must admit that I have the best of manners, and I have the highest personal regard for you and for your beauty. As for Germany and National Socialism, you will see that we will succeed in the world. In a few years, you will be proven wrong. National Socialism will take all of Europe, and eventually, we will own the world. We have in Adolf Hitler, the greatest ruler of all times. You will see that and will have to acknowledge us as rulers of the world."

"Oh, Wilhelm, you are so full of horse hockey; I can't stand it. First of all, you are not such a kind and charming fellow. Furthermore, your Nazis will never rule the United States of America. I know that as well as I know my own name. We're a country based on belief in God, and we are ruled by a Constitution that protects our rights, basic human rights that your Nazis deny their people."

"I stand by my statement that we have the most powerful leader and the most outstanding system. We are the Thousand Year Reich. Let's not argue this again. Let's just go out and have a nice evening. I'm going to buy you a very special dinner and take you on all the rides in the amusement park."

"I won't go anywhere with you. Your precious Hitler is a little pipsqueak of a man who 'struts and frets his hour upon the stage and then is heard no more.' He shouts and flails his arms and makes the whole country jerk their arms up to salute him. He has a silly mustache and says silly things. He's a joke, Wilhelm, just a joke. It's theater for the absurd, and you just can't see it for what it is."

"You mustn't say things like that in Germany. I will not report you for saying this, because I realize you have not been educated enough yet to realize the truth and the strength of National Socialism. But you could get into a lot of trouble if you say these things to the wrong person. You will see that our goals and our system will purify the Aryan race, of which, I must say, you are the finest example I have ever known."

"Dear me, more horse hockey. I don't like your attitude, and I don't like smelly beer breath ... two good reasons not to go anywhere with you." Geneva stormed out of the lounge at the Adlon and went to her room.

When someone knocked on her door later that afternoon, Geneva almost didn't answer because she was afraid it was Wilhelm, begging her again to go out with him. She was surprised to find Dr. Veere at the door.

"I'm sorry to bother you, Miss Burkhart, but Wilhelm just came to my room in quite a state. He claims he is desperately in love with you, and you've said you won't go anywhere with him ever again. He says he wants to take you to the amusement park tonight to ride on the roller coaster and the Ferris wheel. He seems to be trying to make amends for something, although I don't know exactly what. He says he just wants to show you a good time, Miss Burkhart."

"I'm not going with him anywhere, ever again, Dr. Veere. I can't stand to be around him, and I can't stand to hear any more about how wonderful the Nazis are. I know he makes a terrible fuss when I won't go with him, but I'm sick and tired of Wilhelm. I can't do it. The last time I went out with Wilhelm, he got very drunk. We became hopelessly lost. We took the wrong tram and the wrong trains, and we had to stay out all night. I'm not setting myself up for that again." Geneva wanted Dr. Veere to know how strongly she felt about not going anywhere again with Wilhelm, but she didn't dare tell him about Dachau.

"I'm going to ask you to do me a very big favor, Ms. Burkhart. I understand your dislike for Wilhelm, and I respect your decision not to go anywhere with him again. But, just this one last time, can you go with him tonight? Our trip is almost at an end. When we leave for England, you will never have to see Wilhelm again. To keep things running smoothly until our tour is finished, I am asking you to go to the amusement park with him. I know this is an imposition on you, and I don't want to beg you to do it. But just this one final time, Miss Burkhart. I hate to have to say this to you, but it's important to smooth the waters for a few more days."

Geneva was surprised, even shocked, that Dr. Veere would insist she do something she had so vehemently stated she did not want to do. For him to intervene and try to talk her into going on a date with Wilhelm was completely out of character for Dr. Veere. Geneva didn't know what to say. She loathed Wilhelm, and the last thing she wanted to do was go to the amusement park with him. Even the temptation of rides on the roller coaster and the Ferris wheel were not enough to make her want to see him again. But she was impressed by Dr. Veere's plea. It seemed very important to him that she go with the horrid Nazi, just this one last time. Dr. Veere looked so tired, as if he were on his last legs. Gevena didn't know why he looked so tired, but she felt sorry for him. If it was going to be helpful in some way for her to go out with Wilhelm tonight, she would go. "If I agree to go with him, you must promise me you will never ask me to go anywhere with him again."

Veere sighed with relief. "I promise you. I will never ask you to go anywhere with him again after tonight. Thank you Miss Burkhart. I am forever in your debt."

Geneva was as puzzled by Dr. Veere's excessive relief and gratitude as she was by his plea that she go with Wilhelm. She couldn't figure out why it was so important that she go tonight, but she was very fond of Dr. Veere. She would make the sacrifice and put up with Wilhelm for one more evening, but only if he didn't drink any alcohol. She would despise every minute she spent with him. But what could go wrong at an amusement park?

Dr. Veere felt terrible that he'd pressured Miss Burkhart into spending the evening with Wilhelm. Things had gone considerably downhill between the two of them, even before they'd arrived in Berlin. But Veere had an important ulterior motive for insisting that Miss Burkhart to go out with their Nazi minder one last time. Veere couldn't tell Geneva that she was needed to keep Wilhelm occupied. Tonight of all nights, Wilhelm had to be busy and out of the way. Veere couldn't take the chance that Wilhelm would have a free evening on his hands and decide to follow him. Wilhelm had to be distracted, charmed, and entranced by the woman he loved. Dr. Veere was taking a big risk of his own tonight, meeting with his secret Lorenz contact for their final and unscheduled appointment. The last thing he needed was to have to worry about Wilhelm keeping an eye on him, following him, or asking him to account for his whereabouts.

CHAPTER FORTY FOUR

VEERE'S CONTACT WITH LORENZ

AUGUST 1938

BERLIN

GENEVA AND ELSIE HAD THOUGHT FOR SOME time that Dr. Veere looked unusually tired, and they were concerned. They'd grown fond of the tall, thin academic from Columbia University. He had organized their trip and taken the teachers under his wing as he might have his own daughters. He was kind and respectful. He'd done a nearly flawless job of handling all the reservations, hotel vouchers, railway tickets, meal arrangements, and the other hundreds of details required to take their group on an extended tour of a difficult country. They couldn't begin to imagine all the bureaucratic hurdles and paper-shuffling nightmares he must have had to negotiate to bring them through the maze of Nazi rules and regulations.

Once the tour had begun, his work was ongoing and

demanded constant attention on a daily basis. Their bus had to be maintained in good working order. All of their luggage had to be kept track of and transported from the bus to the hotel, back to the bus, and then on to the next hotel. Besides all of his regular duties, there were the countless unexpected events and challenges that inevitably arose.

Eleanor's accident had been a terrible blow to Dr. Veere. He had been preoccupied with the tragedy. But this most recent fatigue was different. It had become more pronounced every day since they'd arrived in Berlin. One of the women had gone to Veere's room in the middle of the night when her roommate became ill. He didn't answer the repeated knocks on his door. The concierge was notified, and a doctor was called.

Dr. Veere apologized the next day for not being available. Geneva and Elsie, just to each other, wondered if he was meeting a girlfriend. One night they tried to keep watch to find out if he was leaving his room and going to another room in the hotel or if he was leaving the hotel. Their vigil lasted only one night because they couldn't stay awake. They gave up pursuing their curiosity about Dr. Veere and a possible romance.

The truth was that Veere was leaving the hotel after ten o'clock each night to meet someone. But it was not for a romantic encounter, as Geneva and Elsie might have imagined or even hoped. Veere left the Adlon and usually walked the five miles, taking a different route every night, to meet with an engineer who worked for C. Lorenz, a well-known German electrical manufacturing company that sold its products all over the world.

Just that year, Lorenz had come out with a new version of their 1933 Volksempfanger radio, the people's radio that almost every German household could afford to buy. The DKE 38 version of the radio was called the "Goebbels Schnauze."

Veere had heard the joke about the new, cheap "people's radio." The story was that it could receive only three things ... programming approved by Joseph Goebbels, Hitler's speeches, and Wagnerian opera.

Veere had been put in contact with the Lorenz employee by Nigel Barnaby. Barnaby hoped to find out about the latest technology Lorenz was developing and manufacturing for the German military. "I want details and numbers regarding the *secret* production at Lorenz. We need this information to prove that Germany's rearmament progress is farther along than anyone realizes. We suspect the Lorenz factory is making military grade electronics in huge numbers. If we can verify this, there wouldn't be any doubt that Germany is not just making weapons to defend itself but is arming for an offensive war. The manufacture of military components is one thing. The manufacture of huge numbers of technologically advanced components and weapons is another thing entirely." Veere understood that Barnaby and Trevanian needed solid evidence to take back to Great Britain and the United States. They had to prove to their politicians and journalists that Germany was planning for a prolonged and extensive future war of aggression. Because Barnaby wasn't able to travel to Germany and Trevanian chose not to go there, Veere would attend the meetings.

Veere was aware that, during the same week that he was meeting with the engineer from Lorenz, British Prime Minister Neville Chamberlain was in Munich, negotiating with Hitler over the Sudetenland in Czechoslovakia. In spite of all the evidence to the contrary, Chamberlain acted as if there wouldn't be a war. Winston Churchill, currently out of power in Britain, was convinced there would be no real peace in the world until Hitler and the Nazis were gone. Churchill needed specifics — hard information to persuade the doubters in his government that Germany intended to attack more of its neighbors.

Veere was certain Roosevelt agreed that Hitler was a bully and a threat to the world. Roosevelt had to know there eventually would be a war in Europe, but he also realized the American public had no taste for war. Roosevelt had vowed to support and supply Great Britain in the upcoming conflict, but by sending war materials to England, he was already testing the limits of his constitutional authority. Veere suspected, correctly, that Chamberlain would bow to Hitler over Czechoslovakia and allow the little dictator to steal yet another piece of someone else's county from the European map.

Roosevelt needed to be convinced that Hitler's intentions extended far beyond the Rhineland, the Austrian Anschluss, and his current grab for the Sudetenland. Veere wondered if Roosevelt had ever read *Mein Kampf.* Did Roosevelt give any credence to the possibility that Hitler intended to carry through with the plans so clearly outlined in the book? Where was all that Lebensraum going to come from, if not from the countries who were friends and allies of the United States and Britain?

The C. Lorenz Company kept many German secrets. It had been an unexpected gift when one of their young engineers offered to share these secrets with the British. The engineer's intentions were heroic, but at the same time, he was very frightened. When he met with Veere in the Sunday school room of an abandoned Lutheran church, Veere could smell his fear. The man wouldn't tell Veere his name, and he didn't want to know Veere's name. The less they knew about each other, the better, the Lorenz employee said. If either was arrested and interrogated by the Gestapo, neither would be able to expose the other because they were nameless. Neither man could be tortured into revealing what he didn't know. Veere had agreed to this condition.

In his own mind, Veere had named the engineer "Herr Young" because of his youthful appearance. During the nights they met, the anonymous Lorenz engineer gave Veere a mother-lode of information, and Veere took careful and copious notes on each word Herr Young said. As a mathematician, Veere understood much of what his source revealed, but some of it required detailed drawings and in-depth explanations. In spite of overwhelming fatigue, Veere tried to approach each meeting awake, alert, and at his best. He knew the Lorenz information was critically important, but it was also very technical. Veere told himself he couldn't afford to make any mistakes about what he heard or what he wrote in his notebook.

At five each morning, Veere took a surreptitious route back to the Adlon. He was always dead tired when he reached his room. He tried to sleep for a few hours before reporting to his day job, taking care of the mathematics teachers.

Radio communications would be essential in fighting the next war. Herr Young told Veere, "Lorenz has been making vacuum tubes for use in military communications equipment. Production of these vacuum tubes for military purposes has been obscured, cloaked under the acknowledged public guise of making vacuum tubes for the 'people's radio.' The military version of this vacuum tube is very different from the tubes used in the popular civilian radio. What my company doesn't want anyone to know is that Lorenz has been producing highly specialized, military grade radio tubes in huge quanti-ties since 1937."

Herr Young spent three nights explaining to Veere the workings of Germany's advanced radar systems. Veere did not know if German radar was ahead of the radar systems in the U.S. and Great Britain, but he knew this very specific information was exactly what Barnaby and Trevanian wanted from the Lorenz contact. Trevanian had stressed that "straight from the horse's mouth" was the only kind of intelligence that would be credible with decision makers. Veere's job was to document and convey every piece of information Herr Young could provide.

On the night of their last scheduled meeting, Young, who by now looked as exhausted as Veere knew he himself looked, said. "I want an additional meeting … tomorrow night. I want to bring you two machines that I am going to steal from Berlin's Lorenz factory. One machine is the most advanced model of what the British call the Enigma machine, and the other machine is known as the Lorenz cipher teleprinter."

The additional meeting with Young hadn't been authorized, and Veere didn't have time to clear it with Barnaby or Trevanian. Veere was reluctant but agreed. "Tonight was supposed to be our last meeting, but I will meet you again tomorrow night. The electronics you describe are highly prized. The value of having either one of them in allied hands cannot be overestimated. To have the latest versions of these devices, just off the assembly line, would be a huge coup for MI6. But these secret machines must be carefully guarded. Do you really think you can smuggle them out of your factory?" Veere had his doubts about how realistic it was to hope he might be able to get his hands on the precious equipment.

Herr Young answered that he had a plan and thought he could successfully procure the two electronic machines. If Herr Young was able to come through, Veere was already wondering how he would be able to transport the bulky contraptions through the streets of Berlin back to the Adlon.

When Veere left the hotel the next night, he carried two empty valises. He hoped the valises were large enough to hold the stolen machines. He knew, as he walked through the hot August night to his final meeting with Herr Young, that what he was doing was extremely dangerous. But, if he could somehow get these treasures out of Germany, it would be a tremendous coup. Any advantage Veere could gain for the United States and its allies was a risk worth taking. Veere now realized, without a doubt, that many of the free nations of the world would soon be at war with Germany.

Anyone who'd spent one day in Berlin could see that Germany was already at war. Every aspect of the society and the peoples' daily lives reeked of militarism. The marching and the flags, that Geneva and Elsie found so hideously disturbing, and the speeches and shouting over the radio were all-pervasive. How could anyone doubt the intentions that Hitler had for his neighbors, for Europe, and for the world? It was madness to visit this police state, but it was worse to ignore what was going on here. Veere worried that the United States would hide behind its oceans for too long, that his country would not wake up in time to help stop this Nazi evil from spreading. He kept himself going by reminding his exhausted body and psyche that his most important job right now was to get the relevant facts out of Germany. If he could also commandeer some of the Nazi's top-secret electronic devices, so much the better.

On that last night, Veere waited at the Lutheran church for two hours, and then he waited two more hours. By four o'clock in the morning, he realized his Lorenz contact wasn't going to show up. Veere had tried not to get his hopes up. He'd tried not to believe he would miraculously be able to take possession of the most recent model of an Enigma machine and a Lorenz cipher teleprinter. It had been too much to hope for, but he'd fallen victim to his expectations. Now he was crushed with disappointment. He was very worried about what had happened to the young engineer from Lorenz who had never before been late to any of their meetings. Veere had sensed a tremendous depth of commitment from his contact and now suspected that something catastrophic had happened to prevent the young man from keeping their final rendezvous.

Herr Young had always stayed behind after their meetings to replace the chairs and square the table precisely so that the room looked exactly as it had when they'd arrived. He took their small glasses and the bottle of schnapps away with him each morning and left everything obsessively and perfectly neat as only the Germans can make a place look. Veere, likewise, didn't want to leave any evidence that he'd been waiting in the Sunday school room.

As dawn was breaking, Veere gave up and left the church. It had rained hard all night and was still drizzling. The storm hadn't done anything to moderate the heat wave. The rain this morning was hot and sticky, an annoying August rain. It was the kind of rain that doesn't cool things off, but guarantees the day ahead will be insufferably humid and uncomfortable.

As he exited onto the street, two men in long raincoats approached him. They were Gestapo. Who else would wear full-length raincoats on such a hot morning? They were walking straight toward him. He was thankful there were no notes in his pockets this morning as there had been every other morning. He was thankful the valises he held in his hands, as hard as they were going to be to explain, were empty.

CHAPTER FORTY FIVE

MURDER ON THE STREET

AUGUST 1938

BERLIN

WILHELM HAD BRAGGED TO GENEVA THAT, of course, he knew his way around Berlin, but he didn't. Geneva and Wilhelm walked along the sidewalk, still lost and looking for a familiar landmark or a street they recognized. "I'm so tired, Wilhelm. We need to either find a taxi or call Dr. Veere." A few drops of rain began to fall.

They'd left the amusement park hours earlier, and by now, some of Wilhelm's usual bravado had evaporated. He always told Geneva and the others in the group not to worry, that everything was under control. "I can't admit I'm lost. If I had to ask for help to find my way back to the hotel, I would be relieved of my position as your group's guide. I would be punished. I would never work as a guide or driver again."

Wilhelm couldn't bring himself to tell Geneva the truth, that he'd spent all of his money at the amusement park. Even if they could find a taxi, he didn't have enough money to pay for the ride back to the hotel.

"You're being downright stupid, and my feet hurt. I'm getting wet. I want to call a taxi right now and go back to my room. I'm tired of wandering around in circles! Every time I go anywhere with you, it's a disaster. Why am I such a fool? When will I learn you aren't dependable?"

Geneva sat on the curb even though the rain was pouring down. It was after midnight, and she couldn't walk another step. Berlin was a big city, and she wasn't ashamed or afraid to admit she was lost and needed help finding her way. They'd ended up in an area of run-down buildings and factories, and Geneva knew they were nowhere near the Adlon. Taxis didn't cruise this neighborhood for customers. Wilhelm stood beside her, not knowing which way to turn. He saw a place to get out of the rain, and they took cover under the awning of a store front.

They heard a loud noise and then an explosion of breaking glass. Then they heard screaming. Hiding in the shadows and leaning against the wall in an archway, Geneva and Wilhelm could see what was happening directly across the narrow street.

Two rough-looking thugs dragged a young man out of a house. They raised their wooden truncheons and began to beat him. They hit him over and over again without mercy. They were trying to kill him.

Geneva and Wilhelm cowered behind a wall, afraid to make a noise, terrified that even the slightest sound or movement would attract attention to themselves. The boy, covered with blood, collapsed onto the pavement. A woman wearing an apron over her house dress ran out to the street, shouting and waving her arms at the Gestapo. She attacked one of the men, stabbing at him with a pair of scissors and beating on his head with a dishtowel. The injured policeman grabbed his side. Geneva could see the blood, even without a streetlight. He used his wooden club to attack the woman. She fell on top of the wounded young man.

The door of the house opened again, and a little girl rushed out. She looked like she was about six years old. She wore a pink dress and had a big pink bow in her hair. She threw herself down beside her mother, crying and begging her mother to wake up. When she couldn't rouse her, the child went after one of the policemen with both her fists. The injured policeman took a swipe at the little girl with his club and struck her head. The sickening, hollow thud reminded Geneva of the time a watermelon had fallen off the back of the farm pick-up truck and splattered on the road. She knew the child was dead. One of the policemen took a handgun from his holster and shot the young man and the mother, both in the head. There would be no one in the family left alive to tell the tale of what had happened in the street tonight. All three had been murdered. The Gestapo men wiped their bloody clubs on the clothing of their victims, climbed back into their official car, and drove away.

The horror that Geneva and Wilhelm had witnessed was finished almost before it had begun. Geneva couldn't move and couldn't speak. She had never before witnessed a murder. The smell of blood and death reached her, and she stood paralyzed and nauseated, watching the rivers of red as they washed into the gutter with the driving rain. The child's pink bow swam down the street and swirled in the bloody water. When she was able to move again, Geneva ran to the curb and retched over and over until she was weak.

Wilhelm pulled on Geneva's arm and whispered to her that they needed to leave. She resisted. "We can't just leave these people dead on the street. We need to call an ambulance or the police or somebody." Even as she said these words, she knew that calling an ambulance would be a waste of time and calling the police would be worse. It was Hitler's police who had committed this terrible crime.

She could see that Wilhelm was also in shock, frightened and desperate to get away from this place. His voice quavered as he spoke. "You don't understand. The police are the ones who did this. We must leave now or the same thing could happen to us."

"We haven't done anything wrong."

"How can you say that? Do you think that little girl did anything wrong? The only thing that makes you any different from those people is that you aren't a Jew. I've seen this before on the streets, with the Jews," his voice trembled as he tried to choke back the tears, "but I have never seen this happen to a small child. They will be back to clean up the mess. They will be back soon with more men, and we must get away from here as fast as we can, before they return."

Geneva was in no shape to walk anywhere, let alone run. She was shaking uncontrollably and close to collapse. Wilhelm took off his jacket and put it around her shoulders. The rain was coming down in buckets. He grabbed Geneva's hand and tried to drag her along behind him. The rain had washed so much blood into the gutter. As they stepped off the curb, they splashed and splattered bloody water on their shoes and clothes. Geneva reached down beside the curb for two pieces of shiny metal. Then she picked up the little girl's pink bow as it spun around in the water at her feet. She clasped it to her chest. Wilhelm tried to tear the bow out of her hands, but Geneva hung on to it for dear life.

"Don't touch that! Drop it where you found it. It could connect us to this." Wilhelm tried again to loosen the bow from her grasp, but the glazed look in Geneva's eyes let him know she wasn't going to give it up.

There was no time to clean the blood from their clothes. They needed to get as far away as possible from this neighborhood. After almost carrying Geneva several blocks away from the scene of the crime, Wilhem found a telephone booth and fumbled with his few remaining coins to call the Adlon Hotel. He asked to be put through to Dr. Veere's room, but there was no answer. Then he asked to be connected to Geneva's room, hoping he could awaken Elsie. She finally picked up the telephone .

"Elsie, this is Wilhelm. I need your help. Geneva and I are in trouble. We're lost. We can't get a taxi. You need to bring a taxi from the hotel to get us. We've had a bad time."

Elsie was alarmed by the tone of Wihelm's voice. "Is she all right? What's wrong? Is she sick? Why can't you call your own taxi? Where are you? Where do I bring the taxi?"

"I don't have enough money to pay the taxi. I barely had enough coins to make this telephone call." Wilhelm gave Elsie an address he'd just read on a nearby building. "Please come as quickly as possible. She's in bad shape. Bring her raincoat and some brandy if you can find some in a hurry."

Wilhelm guided Geneva to a spot under the roof overhang of an abandoned building and made her sit on the concrete steps. He was afraid she might collapse and he wouldn't be able to get her upright again.

It was three o'clock in the morning when Elsie finally arrived in a taxi. She handed the brandy to Wilhelm and put her arms around Geneva. Elsie gently removed Wilhelm's rain-soaked jacket from Geneva's shoulders and tried not to look at the blood on her friend's wet clothes and shoes. Geneva didn't say a word and never looked at Elsie. Geneva was in another world. She clung to the sopping wet pink bow as Elsie guided her arms into the sleeves of her raincoat. Elsie hurried Geneva and Wilhelm into the back of the taxi with Geneva in the center. She tried to block Geneva from the taxi driver's view. Elsie could see her friend was in a terrible state.

"She needs to see a doctor. We have to take her to the hospital."

Wilhelm vehemently discouraged that idea. "Absolutely not. We can't show up at a hospital with blood on our clothes." Wilhelm tried to make Geneva swallow a big swig of brandy, but Geneva choked and spit out the brandy. Wilhelm took two hefty nips for himself.

Wilhelm tried to explain to Elsie what had happened. When he was nervous or angry, Wilhelm's English became ragged. In the back of the taxi, they were speaking English, but he occasionally lapsed into German. "You can't speak German, Wilhelm. You have to speak English. We don't want the taxi driver to understand what we're saying." Elsie told the driver to deliver them to the side door of the Adlon. They couldn't go through the lobby, even though it would probably be empty at this time of night. Their wet and bedraggled appearance would attract attention from the night concierge. They bypassed the elevator and walked up the stairs to Geneva and Elsie's room.

"You've done enough for one night." Elsie angrily spat the words at Wilhelm. "I can take care of her now, since you won't let me take her to the hospital. Go to your room and get yourself cleaned up." Elsie didn't want the Nazi troublemaker anywhere near Geneva.

CHAPTER FORTY SIX

SAVING GENEVA I

AUGUST 1938

BERLIN

ELSIE STRUGGLED TO REMOVE GENEVA'S raincoat and hung it over a chair to dry. She ran hot water in the bathtub and helped Geneva take off her wet and bloody clothes, shoes, and stockings. Elsie guided her into the hot water, shampooed and rinsed her roommate's hair, and helped her wash away the dirt and blood. Elsie left Geneva alone for a minute while she called room service. She knew how much Geneva loved ham and sweet things, and she ordered what she hoped would be restorative food and drink, for both of them.

Geneva hadn't spoken a single word since Elsie had picked her up in the taxi. Elsie knew Geneva was in shock and in a very fragile state. She'd not completely understood the story Wilhelm had told her about the murders. His explanation about the night's events had been confused and almost too disturbing to be believed. Elsie did know that, whatever it was Geneva had witnessed, it was something so terrible, she couldn't fully allow her conscious mind to grasp it.

Elsie dried Geneva's hair and helped her put on a clean nightgown. Geneva stood over her pile of wet, bloody clothes and gazed down at the jumble. Geneva stared at the pink bow she'd rescued from the death scene. The piece of ribbon soaked with blood and water had partially dried. Elsie handed it to her and led her back into the bedroom. Geneva held the bow gently, as if she were cradling an actual child in her arms. She carefully placed the damp and precious relic on the bedside table.

Geneva sat rigid as a board on the edge of her bed. Elsie was giving serious thought to calling a doctor when room service arrived. Elsie opened the door for the waiter and tipped him after he'd wheeled the food into the room. She rolled the room service cart close to Geneva's bed and poured her a cup of very strong, hot tea. She added several teaspoons of sugar to the tea and fixed a plate of food, hoping that something she'd ordered would tempt Geneva. Geneva held the plate on her lap and stared at it. Elsie sat on the bed beside her and put half a ham sandwich in Geneva's hand. She lifted Geneva's hand to her mouth and told her in a firm but motherly way that she had to eat it. Geneva took a bite and then she took another bite. There was cinnamon toast with butter and sugar. Geneva ate some toast and drank two cups of hot tea. Elsie pushed the table of food away and told Geneva to lie down. Elsie tucked the blankets around her, and Geneva was asleep in seconds.

Elsie decided she would have the concierge call a doctor in the morning. She wrote a note to Dr. Veere about what had happened to Geneva and Wilhelm that night on the streets of Berlin. Elsie told him of her own part in the drama and what she'd done to try to help Geneva. She put the note in an envelope addressed to Dr. Veere, walked down the hall, and slipped the note under his door. It was almost six o'clock in the morning. After doing her best to wash the blood and dirt out of Geneva's soiled clothes, she sadly hung them up to dry. She wondered if her roommate would ever be the same. Elsie finished off the tea and the room service food and fell asleep on her own bed, still dressed in her street clothes.

Someone was pounding on the hotel room door, and after the night she'd spent, Elise was not in the mood to answer the door for anyone. When it occurred to her that it might be Dr. Veere, she rushed to answer it. It wasn't Dr. Veere; it was Wilhelm wanting to know how Geneva was this morning. He tried to force his way into the room, but Elsie wouldn't let him in. She pushed him outside into the hall so they could talk. Wilhelm looked like he'd slept in his clothes and as if he'd finished off the bottle of brandy, and more, from the night before.

"She's still asleep, so I don't know if she's any better this morning. She drank some tea and ate a little bit of food last night. No matter what you or Dr. Veere or anybody says, I'm not going to let you wake her up. She needs to sleep. Sleep is the best way for her to recover from what happened."

"I must talk to her right away. I have to speak with her before she talks to Dr. Veere or to anybody. We need to get our stories straight about last night. This is the most important thing!"

Elsie was furious with Wilhelm. "Getting your stories straight is *not* the most important thing. Geneva's recovery from this ordeal is the most important thing. I won't allow anyone to interfere with that. I don't care about 'getting your stories straight' and all of your Nazi bullshit. I am sick of this place and want to get Geneva and myself home to America, where we can live without being afraid of something all the time."

"You don't understand what we are dealing with here in Berlin, in Germany. Our system is very different from yours, and while you are here in my country, you must realize what has to be done in this dangerous situation."

"You don't tell me what to do. Your rotten system is one reason I can't wait another minute to leave this godforsaken place."

"I must talk to Geneva now. You must wake her up!"

"Go away! You look and smell like a drunken Billy goat. I will take care of Geneva and do whatever I can to help her. I'm going to have the concierge call a doctor. A professional needs to examine her."

"Do not under any circumstances call a doctor. Doctors are required by law to report anything at all unusual that happens to patients they treat. If you will promise not to call a doctor, I'll go away. But I need to talk to her as soon as possible this morning."

"I'll call a doctor if I think she needs one. I don't care what doctors have to report about their patients. Geneva will not get dressed at all today, and you will not be allowed to talk to her. If I can possibly keep her in bed, I will, for as long as I think it's necessary. I'm very concerned that Dr. Veere hasn't come to the room to see her."

"If Dr. Veere finds out what happened last night, I will be fired. I'll be questioned by the Gestapo and probably go to jail. I'm begging you, please don't tell Dr. Veere anything."

"It's too late for that. I've already written him a note explaining what happened last night. I've informed him of Geneva's condition. I delivered the note to his room early this morning before I went to sleep. There's not going to be a cover up, Wilhelm, so just forget that. I expect to hear from Dr. Veere any minute now." Elsie started back into the room.

Wilhelm headed down the hall to Dr. Veere's room. Elsie watched as he got down on his hands and knees and looked under the door. When he couldn't reach the envelope Elsie had slid under Dr. Veere's door the night before, he took some small tools out of his pocket and began to work on the door lock. Elsie knew he was trying to break into the room, to remove her note.

She approached Wilhelm with cold fury in her eyes, "I'm going to report your attempt to break into Dr. Veere's room. Even if you steal the note I've written to him, I will write another and another. I will be absolutely certain that Dr. Veere knows every detail of your misadventure." Leaving Wilhelm to his clumsy lock picking, she went back to her room, closed the door, and secured the deadbolt from the inside. She would have slammed the door hard for Wilhelm's benefit, but she didn't want to wake Geneva.

Geneva was mumbling and restless. Her forehead was hot, and she was shivering. Elsie covered her with another blanket and whispered to her to go back to sleep. Elsie was very worried about Geneva but thought rest was the best way for her to recover. Elsie didn't want to leave the room. She didn't want to leave Geneva alone, and she also didn't trust Wilhem. She couldn't take the risk that Wilhelm, in his desire to save his own skin, would decide he couldn't wait to talk to Geneva and try to break into their room. Elsie was determined that wouldn't happen.

Hotels add on so many extra charges for room service food. One of the rules of the trip was that the women were not supposed to order food from room service without Dr. Veere's permission. Elsie was sure Dr. Veere would approve last night's room service expenditure in the midst of a crisis, but so far today he was still nowhere to be found. Elsie decided she would order meals delivered to their room, until she felt comfortable leaving Geneva alone. Elsie would pay for the food herself, if necessary.

Elsie called one of the other members of the group and told her that neither she nor Geneva would be participating in today's activities. Elsie told Mary Alice from Pittsburgh that Geneva had the flu. Elsie intended to stay in the room with Geneva until she was better.

Mary Alice asked if Elsie had seen or heard from Dr. Veere. "No one has seen him since last night at dinner. He didn't come to breakfast this morning, and he isn't answering the telephone in his room. We're all worried. This isn't like him. He's always the first one in the lobby in the morning, making sure we're all present and accounted for. We were supposed to go back to the Friedrich Wilhelm Institute today for two more lectures, and we didn't go. We can't figure out what's happened to Dr. Veere. Wilhelm is also missing."

"I've been to Dr. Veere's room a couple of times today, and I don't think he's there." Elsie was worried, too.

Mary Alice continued. "Maybe we should call or send someone to the American Embassy? Does anyone have an emergency telephone number or the name of a person to contact?"

Their leader was so organized and in control of everything. Elsie couldn't imagine he would abandon his responsibilities unless he were in some kind of trouble. He'd insisted the members of the group list three emergency contacts in the U.S., with their telephone numbers, but he hadn't given anyone an emergency number to call in case something happened to him.

Mary Alice had an idea. "Maybe we should make a call stateside to Columbia University? I think Dr. Veere's secretary's name is on some of the paperwork I have. Maybe one of the other women has a name or telephone number to call at Columbia. If he doesn't show up by lunch time, somebody needs to call somebody or do something."

"I think we should give him more time, and I absolutely wouldn't call any kind of Nazi police. I don't think they're working to protect the public safety. I think they're the main ones who threaten the public safety." Mary Alice didn't know as much about the Berlin Gestapo as Elsie did.

"Elsie, please don't say things like that over the telephone. Dr. Veere warned us that the Germans listen in on each other as well as to foreigners in hotels." They hung up.

It was almost 10:30 in the morning, and Elise was famished. Geneva was still sleeping when Elsie ordered from room service again. She ordered more hot tea with extra sugar as well as a hearty breakfast for both herself and Geneva. Europeans teased the Americans because they loved their food and would go to almost any lengths not to miss a meal. It was true. Americans turned to food for comfort as well as when they were hungry. They wanted to eat when they were happy or sad or afraid or excited. Food was always on hand to help celebrate and to help commiserate. Elsie thought the food cure worked wonderfully well for many problems.

CHAPTER FORTY SEVEN

DR. VEERE
IS MISSING

AUGUST 1938

BERLIN

T HEIR HOTEL ROOMS WERE TOO SMALL FOR the entire group to gather in one room. Even Dr. Veere's room was not large enough to have everyone there for a meeting. Small rooms were the tradeoff for staying at the Adlon and having a private bath. All the women were very worried about Dr. Veere, and they needed to talk things over. They agreed to meet for tea in the lounge at 3:00 that afternoon.

Elsie woke Geneva and insisted that she eat some breakfast. Elsie gathered all of her common sense, marshaled her few amateur counseling skills, and struggled to remember any and all advice from the psychology books she'd read in school. She talked as Geneva, who was wrapped in her dressing gown and sat on the side of the bed, ate bacon and toast from the breakfast tray.

"You had a horrifying experience last night, and you've been in shock. I need for you to understand that I'm here to take care of you. When you're ready, I want to talk with you about what happened. Please let me know that you've heard me and understand what I'm saying. You've not spoken a single word since I picked you up in the taxi last night. If you don't begin talking to me immediately, I will have to call a doctor to come to see you."

Geneva spoke slowly and without affect, as if she were in a trance. "She was just a little girl, and she was only trying to get her mother to wake up. How could those men think the child was a threat? They killed her with one blow to her head. It sounded like a watermelon falling off the back of the truck." Geneva's voice was flat and robotic, and she had a blank, faraway look in her eyes. She picked up the pink bow, dry now, but stained with bloody rainwater, motor oil, and dirt from the street. She stared down at the bow and turned it over and over in her hands.

"It was a terrible thing for you to witness. I'll help you talk about it when you're ready. I can't turn back time. Although I wish we could, we can't pretend that horrible night never happened. I think you're still in shock. You need to rest. I want to help, but I can't do this by myself. I need your help."

"Wilhelm says I can't talk about what happened, that I have to pretend it never happened, that I never saw anything. He says those people were killed because they were Jews. But I can't pretend I didn't see a murder. A women, a boy, and a little girl in a pink dress ... all were murdered."

"Don't pay any attention to what Wilhelm says or thinks. We know what happened is wrong, as wrong as anything could possibly be wrong. But I don't think we can go to the police or any authorities in Germany about this crime. It was an evil act perpetrated by evil men. What you saw last night would put anybody into shock. Think about taking care of yourself."

"Am I really safe now? Can anybody really be safe when they are in such a terrible place? I feel as if I am traveling through the valley of the shadow of death."

"I think we are as safe as we can be."

"I need to talk to Dr. Veere. I need to tell him what happened. He has to do something about this vicious murder. I want to talk to him right away."

Elsie had been dreading this moment. She knew that sooner or later Geneva would ask for Dr. Veere. Of course she wanted to talk to him. He was charged with their well-being, the person who kept them on schedule and on track, the person who had made a promise to each of their families that he would bring their loved one home safe. Elsie had hoped Dr. Veere would turn up and be in control of things as usual before she had to tell Geneva he was missing. What could she possibly say to Geneva that wasn't a lie? "Dr. Veere is busy elsewhere today, so we can't talk to him right now."

"You have to reach him, no matter what he's doing. He has to know about what happened last night. He would *want* to hear about it right away. He will know exactly what to do. He always knows what to do about everything, and he'll be able to do something to make it right. He has to be made aware of the terrible things that are happening in this country. How can we get in touch with him? Where is he, Elsie?"

Elsie was relieved to see Geneva express some emotion for the first time. Elsie had been concerned because Geneva was speaking in a monotone, expressing no emotion, on her face or in her voice, even when she was talking about the horrific details of the murders.

"I'll do my best to reach him and tell him about what happened." Geneva knew that Elsie was concealing something from her. "I promise to do everything I can to talk to Dr. Veere. You've done the right thing — to try to talk about what happened last night, to allow yourself to acknowledge and confront it. But all this talking has exhausted you. Lie down now and try to rest."

Elsie inwardly cursed the entire country of Germany. Nothing that happened in Hitlerland was normal. Geneva's reaction to the horrors she'd experienced was entirely normal. No human being could witness what Geneva had witnessed the night before and not be traumatized.

"I'm meeting the group in the hotel lounge for tea, but you're not strong enough to go down with me. I'll bring you sandwiches, some cinnamon scones, and the fruit and custard tarts you like so much. When you wake up, all your favorites from the tea room will be here for you to eat." Geneva put her head down on the pillow and pulled the blankets up around her. Before she fell asleep, Geneva had managed a faint smile when Elsie mentioned the dessert tarts.

DR. VEERE
IS ARRESTED

AUGUST 1938
JACK ON THE PHONE WITH NIGEL

"**S**ORRY, NIGEL. I KNOW IT'S SIX IN THE MORNING, but Veere's been arrested. We don't know why. Early this morning, the Gestapo stopped him on the street outside the Lutheran church and put him in handcuffs. We have an eyewitness who says he didn't protest when he was arrested. The Gestapo put him into one of their big black cars and drove him away someplace. He's in Gestapo custody, but we don't know where he's being held." Jack was trying to stay calm, but he finally began to yell. "He wasn't supposed to be at the Lutheran church last night. His last scheduled meeting with the Lorenz contact was night before last. The whole thing with Lorenz should have been finished. I got a call from a secretary inside Gestapo headquarters that an American professor from Columbia University had been arrested. She didn't know his name, but how many professors from Columbia do you think are floating around Berlin right now?"

. . . .

"He was arrested about five this morning outside the abandoned Lutheran church where they'd been meeting. For some reason he was carrying two empty suitcases. That seemed to be important to the Gestapo. Veere didn't tell me he was going to the Lutheran church again. Did he say anything to you?"

. . . .

"Of course, we have to get him out of there, wherever he is. Can you find out anything? The secretary at Gestapo headquarters is working on it. When we find him, we'll try to have Veere transferred to the custody of the Berlin municipal police. We have some people there who could be helpful, but the Gestapo ...."

. . . .

"Your lawyer friend needs to find Veere and get some idea about what's going on. I don't know if having a lawyer is any help to anybody here in this lawless place, but he needs a lawyer anyway. This friend of yours had better be a damn good one! Please call him immediately. And, after he meets with Veere, he needs to get to the hotel, as soon as possible."

. . . .

"I don't know what we're going to do about the women, Nigel. Why don't you tell me? You and Veere insisted on keeping everything compartmentalized. He was the only one who knew the details about what they were doing every day. We have a schedule of lectures they're attending. We know what the members of the group who have 'special' assignments were doing, but Veere was very protective of all of them. They have to have noticed by now that he's nowhere to be found, and they've got to be wondering why. These are smart women, and they're going to raise some kind of an alarm soon. They've probably already done something or tried to call someone. Veere did everything for them in terms of hotels, meals, travel, the lectures, and so forth, so they're probably feeling pretty helpless about now. The Germans wouldn't let him put anybody into the group who spoke German. So now they and all the rest of us are in the dark about what they're supposed to be doing."

. . . .

"He's disappeared, too, damn his Nazi eyes. Veere told me he had a real hard-on for one of the women in the group, for Miss Burkhart, the young, pretty one. Wilhelm says he's deeply in love with her. He's been after Veere to allow him to take her on dates and stay out after curfew. He's a nice enough looking fellow, but he's totally indoctrinated into the whole Nazi baloney business. Deliver us from zealots, especially from Nazi zealots who think they're in love! Could anything be worse than that? I've no idea where he is. No one has seen him."

. . . .

"Yes, I know, on the one day we might have gotten something useful out of that fascist minder, he's nowhere to be found. Damn it! Why does everything have to go wrong at once? Yes, I admit, except for the Hammond catastrophe, things have gone pretty smoothly, especially for an amateur operation...."

. . . .

"Don't get your dander up, Nigel. I know you're not an amateur. But the rest of us are, and we're doing the best we can. This is a disaster we have to deal with right now, today, this minute. Somebody has to tell that group of women their fearless leader is in jail. Who's going to do that? We all agreed we didn't want either you or me to have any contact with the group, so here we are in a fine pickle."

. . . .

"Yes, of course you can handle it. I'm more than happy for you to handle it. But remember these are American citizens, and I'm the one ultimately responsible for them. If necessary, I will call in that pompous Nazi ass kisser Ambassador of ours and see what he can do for Veere. That state department flunky is falling all over himself, apologizing to the world for Germany's bad behavior, so I doubt if he'll do anything to help us."

. . . .

"I know being agreeable is his job, but we all know where his sympathies lie. I know he's doing his diplomat thing. That's what he's supposed to do, to be an apologist for these thugs."

. . . .

"I'll stay focused, and I will be nice in case we need him. But these diplomatic types really annoy the heck out of me. You are patient with me, Nigel, and I appreciate it. Next time you're in New York, I owe you a lunch *and* a dinner at Keens. Let's just hope this German lawyer of yours is able to spring Veere. The lawyer's a German, right? Is he a Nazi? Okay, Nigel, I'll stop fussing and won't ask any more questions. Will we have to send the women home, I mean, if Veere stays in Gestapo custody?"

. . . .

"He's a Count? The lawyer you've hired to get Veere out of jail is a Count? Please don't tell me he's a Count. I didn't think the Nazis allowed anybody to be a Count anymore."

. . . .

"He's a Polish Count? Nigel, please don't tell me he's a Polish Count!"

. . . .

Jack listened while Nigel told him about the lawyer's credentials. "Well, I have to say he sounds smart enough and is certainly well-qualified. The fact that he's spent so much time in Britain gives me some hope, and your assurance that he speaks flawless English is critical. When will he speak with the tour group? He needs to go over to the Adlon immediately, but what can he possibly tell them?"

. . . .

"Okay, I'll leave it to you to arrange things. But these are my Americans, and you have to keep me informed about what's happening. I can't go back to the States and tell the President that I messed up, or worse, that you messed up! This has to be resolved without delay. Veere is an important fellow at Columbia, and I don't want his name under a cloud of suspicion when this is all over."

CHAPTER FORTY NINE

SAVING DR. VEERE I

AUGUST 1938

BERLIN

T HE WOMEN HAD SPECULATED, IMAGINED, AND worried together for more than an hour, and some had even cried as they struggled to understand Dr. Veere's disappearance. Talking to each other and sharing their fears had made them feel somewhat better, but they were operating in a vacuum of information. Not knowing anything in the middle of a crisis is difficult for even the most mature and sophisticated human beings. For a group of women traveling in a foreign country where they don't speak or understand the language, the lack of information was particularly distressing. Dr. Veere's leadership had been absolute, and they'd relied on him completely. To make matters even more mysterious, on the very day that Dr. Veere had disappeared, Wilhelm, their resident Nazi had also gone missing. The group was understandably anxious.

The distinguished and handsome Count von Moltke appeared in the Adlon lounge wearing an elegant and perfectly tailored dark suit and carrying a finely crafted leather briefcase. A tall man with a pale face, his smile and bright blue eyes communicated and encouraged confidence. He approached the table just as the women were finishing the last of their tea. He bowed slightly and made eye contact with every woman who was seated in the lounge.

"I am Count Helmuth James Graf von Moltke. I'm here to talk to you about Dr. Veere. He's fine. He hasn't been harmed, but he has been arrested by the Gestapo. I am Dr. Veere's attorney. Please call me James. I've just come from meeting with Dr. Veere, and I will be working to have him released from jail as soon as possible. My job is to have the charges against him dropped and clear him of any wrongdoing. Dr. Veere is quite concerned that he's not been able to contact you. He would give anything to be here with you now." The Count looked at the troubled faces of the women. They'd not reacted well to his news that Dr. Veere was in jail. They were alarmed and agitated, and two of the women had tears in their eyes. Count James could see they had many questions. Of course they did!

"Dr. Veere has spoken very highly of each of you. I'm honored to know you and to be able to act for Dr. Veere in his absence. He's asked me to move into a room here at the Adlon and be available to you as he has been. I will humbly stand in for Dr. Veere until he is able to return and resume his duties. I don't presume to fill his very capable shoes, so I'm asking for your help. We can get through this crisis if you will honor me with your trust."

The women were upset but relieved to hear any news. They overwhelmed their temporary leader with a flood of questions. They all tried to speak at once. There was so much that was unknown. Dr. Veere arrested? What in the world had been the reason for his arrest? Where was he? When would he be released?

The Count signaled a waiter and ordered a bottle of single malt Scotch whisky and a bottle of brandy for those who wanted a strong drink and more pots of hot tea for the others. He pulled up a chair and drew the group together.

"I will tell you everything I can. Then I welcome your questions and will try to answer them to the best of my ability." Moltke's English was grammatically perfect and almost without an accent. "I've studied international law in several countries on the European continent and in England. I have spent time in London and at Oxford, and I'm quite comfortable speaking English. I even speak some American." A few of the women were able to summon small smiles in response to this remark, which had helped endear the count to them and relieved some tension.

"Dr. Veere was arrested early this morning. He had been working on a project to bring orphaned German children to the United States. He was meeting with a representative of the Lutheran church, and the Gestapo detained Dr. Veere just as he was leaving the meeting.

What Moltke could not tell them was that man who worked at the C. Lorenz manufacturing facility had been arrested and interrogated last night. The Lorenz employee had attempted to steal valuable electronics from the company's Berlin factory. When he was caught and tortured, the employee told his Gestapo interrogators he'd been on his way to meet an American to hand over the stolen goods. The Lorenz employee committed suicide by hanging himself in his prison cell, minutes after being questioned by the Gestapo. The Gestapo claimed the empty valises Veere carried were proof he was conspiring with the Lorenz employee.

The count paused and swallowed a deep measure of brandy. He despised deception and hated to lie to these women. It made him sad that living in Nazi Germany made it necessary to lie about almost everything. Given the secret work that the Count did and the clandestine work that Dr. Veere had been engaged in, it was the only way. It was essential to protect Veere and to protect the valuable information he'd gathered. There was no choice but to tell lies and hope they were accepted as the truth.

The count continued with the lies. "Those of you who know Dr. Veere will understand his commitment to finding homes for orphans." The women nodded. "I expect it's just a matter of some formalities, considerable paperwork, and a little bit of time until Dr. Veere is released. Now please, your questions."

Although eager to deliver the sandwiches and pastries to Geneva, Elsie stayed behind after the others went to their rooms. She wanted to talk with Count James about Geneva and what had happened the night before. Elsie gave him a brief account of the murder of the Jewish family. She told him about bringing Geneva and Wilhelm back to the hotel in the middle of the night. She told the count about Geneva's current state of mind, and he listened with great concern. He asked Elsie if she felt Geneva would be able to talk to him. Count James wanted to hear what had happened to Geneva in her own words. He had a physician friend he intended to bring to the hotel to see her.

CHAPTER FIFTY

SAVING GENEVA II

AUGUST 1938

BERLIN

ELSIE MADE SURE THE RADIO WAS LOUD ENOUGH to drown out their conversation when Count James came to the room. Geneva was awake. "Miss Burkhart, I am Dr. Veere's attorney. Elsie calls me Count James. She's explained to you what the situation is with Dr. Veere and why I'm here at the Adlon. Do you have any questions for me about Dr. Veere's arrest?"

Geneva shook her head, and Count James pulled the desk chair close to her bed. He could see how pale she was, but he was more concerned about her flat affect. Given what had happened to her in the past twenty-four hours, shock was understandable and expected. As a member of the legal profession, Count James had dealt with frightened witnesses and victims of terrible crimes. Geneva was both a witness to and a victim of the tragedy. He felt he could reach her, even as withdrawn and empty as she now appeared to be.

"Elsie told me about the murder you witnessed last night. Even the most hardened human being would find it difficult to understand and accept such a terrible thing. I want you to tell me as many details as you can recall. I'm going to investigate this triple murder. I promise you I will find the perpetrators of the crime, and I won't stop until the men responsible are punished. Do you understand what I'm saying? Can you help me, Geneva?"

"You remind me of my Edward. He is tall and handsome like you are."

Geneva didn't pull away when Moltke reached out to take her hand. He held her hand as she told her gruesome story. Count James gently questioned her and guided her through the ordeal to clarify the facts. Elsie and the Count could see that Geneva was growing tired, but as she spoke, she showed more animation in her facial expressions and in her voice. When the Count promised Geneva there would be justice for the crime, some of her despair fell away. She'd found an advocate with whom she could share her need for, if not revenge, retribution. By telling her story to Count James and trusting in his promise to her, she'd given up at least a part of her burden. It was late when he rose to leave.

"Recounting this tragedy has required a tremendous amount of energy. Although the catharsis has been therapeutic, it has depleted her, physically and emotionally." Count James gave instructions to Elsie. "She needs to eat before she goes back to sleep. Order chicken soup with dumplings or noodles, meat and potatoes, and something sweet. She needs hearty food. She might sleep for many hours, even most of the day tomorrow. That's to be expected, and it's a good thing. Please don't wake her unnecessarily. I'm asking a personal friend of mine, a doctor who doesn't report to Nazi officials, to come to see her tomorrow evening. He's an excellent physician and will be completely discreet."

"Thank you, Count James. I can see she feels better after speaking with you. She regards you as an ally and trusts you."

"Thank you, for bringing Miss Burkhart's story to my attention and for allowing me to speak with her in person. She is fortunate to have a friend as strong and as kind as you."

Just as the Count was about to leave, Geneva stirred, "Wait, I have ... something." Her voice was so quiet, they almost didn't hear her. She struggled to stand up, and Elsie and the Count rushed to help her. Geneva made her way slowly to the wardrobe that held their clothes and found the raincoat she'd worn the previous night. She dug into one pocket and then into the other. Clutching something tightly in her hand, she held it out to Count James and gave him two misshapen pieces of lead. Geneva looked as surprised and puzzled as Elsie and Count James did, as all three looked down at the pieces of ammunition.

"Where did you find these?" The Count was incredulous that he was looking at actual physical evidence of the murder. These small pieces of metal told him many things. These were spent rounds from the type of gun the Gestapo used, so he knew that a Gestapo gun had probably been used in the crime. Because of the distortion of the lead, he could tell that the bullets had done terrible damage to whomever they'd hit.

"I picked them up in the street. The rain washed them into the gutter with the blood and the ..." her voice faltered as the horrible scene from the previous night flashed again before her eyes.

"... the bow." Elsie and Count James both finished the sentence she wasn't able to complete.

"This is important, Miss Burkhart, and it may help identify the specific guns and therefore the very people who fired the guns. By preserving this evidence, you've done a great deal to help bring justice to that little girl and her family." The Count put the lead lumps in his pocket and smiled at her. He shook her hand, and then he held Elsie's hand for a moment. Geneva lay down on the bed, completely worn out.

CHAPTER FIFTY ONE

SAVING GENEVA III

AUGUST 1938

BERLIN

THE NEXT EVENING, COUNT JAMES RETURNED to the hotel with a doctor. Geneva had eaten, slept, and taken a hot bath, and she was looking and feeling better. She was dressed in street clothes and sat on her bed. Elsie again had the radio turned up. The doctor was a small man with white hair and wire-rimmed spectacles. He carried a professional-looking black bag. He spoke good English but had a strong accent. He didn't introduce himself or give his name, but he already knew about Geneva's experience and about her state of mind. He examined her briefly.

"You seem fine physically, my dear, considering everything that has happened. You've made a remarkable recovery so far, and I suspect that has more than a little to do with the very good care your friend Elsie has given you. Acute shock has resolved. Your temperature, pulse, and blood pressure are normal. You are eating and drinking normally. I don't think there is any need, at this point, to give you any drugs to calm you down or help you sleep. For what you've been through, Miss Burkhart, you have amazing resilience."

"Elsie has been force feeding me for the past two days. She believes that food can cure everything, and I'm feeling much better. I'm not shaking or cold anymore, and I no longer want to sleep all the time. Count James has given me hope. He's promised me he will be sure the perpetrators are caught and punished. This has given my spirits a tremendous boost."

"There can be long-lasting effects from experiences such as the one you've just been through. There will be ups and downs in mood. Sometimes you will feel that everything is fine, and the next moment you may find yourself in tears. You might experience flashbacks and nightmares. Be prepared for this uneven pattern of recovery. It always takes more time to heal the mind and the heart than it does to heal the body. Don't be discouraged. This unpredictable path back to mental health is quite normal. Soldiers who experience terrible things in war often go through a non-linear recovery. Shell shock is a good way to describe what has happened to you."

"I believe in God, and I believe there will be justice for the family, even if that justice comes at the pearly gates. My beliefs give me comfort." Geneva wanted the doctor to know she had a positive attitude.

"You are fortunate that your faith is strong and that you can call on it when trouble strikes." The doctor's forehead wrinkled, and a puzzled expression appeared on his face. "Pardon me if I ask you what are these 'pearly gates'?" Count James laughed and spoke a few words to the doctor in German as an explanation.

The doctor chuckled, "Ah, yes, St. Peter, the Gatekeeper, always a very powerful position. I will be leaving now, but you must call me immediately if you begin to feel worse or if the symptoms of shock return. There could be exacerbations of shock. Otherwise, I don't think I need to see you again. I wish you the best of luck."

"Thank you for coming to see me. I appreciate your time and reassurance that I eventually will be my normal self again."

"I understand that you will return from your European tour to become engaged to a physician who just this past June graduated from Harvard Medical School."

"He's my childhood sweetheart, and we'll become officially engaged after I'm home. He's now doing his internship in New Haven, where we'll live after we're married. That will put me close to Elsie who lives in Greenwich."

"I wish you much happiness in your upcoming marriage. Your doctor must be exceptionally intelligent to be both a Harvard man and now a Yale man. You see, I know my United States geography and my institutions of higher learning."

"You certainly do. Thank you again."

When the doctor left, Count James stayed behind. "Dr. Veere's still being held by the Gestapo, but I'm confident he will be released tomorrow. It's complicated in Germany, especially with the Gestapo. I believe we've convinced them they have no case against Dr. Veere. He and your entire group are here because of an invitation issued to you by the German government's Cultural and Education Ministry. Dr. Veere has a letter to that effect, and we are using that letter as one form of leverage to have him released. I don't think the Gestapo will end up bringing any official charges against Dr. Veere, but there's an enormous amount of paperwork that must be taken care of before he's free. I hope that happens tomorrow."

"Do you have any idea if we will continue our trip as planned or if Dr. Veere will want to leave Germany immediately?"

"I can't answer that question. I've advised the others in the group to go sightseeing and enjoy themselves. I told them to be back at the hotel at an early hour, not to go out late at night or even after dinner. The Gestapo doesn't need a reason to stop people on the street."

"Have you heard anything about Wilhelm?" Elsie was still angry with the young man and wondered if he'd been able to break in to Dr. Veere's room to steal her note.

"The Gestapo took him in for questioning, poor fellow."

"Poor fellow, my foot!" Else scoffed.

"Wilhelm was afraid they'd picked him up because of the murders, but the Gestapo is completely unaware that Wilhelm knows anything about that. In addition to keeping an eye on the women during your tour, he was also supposed to monitor Dr. Veere's movements. Wilhelm failed to do that, and the Gestapo wanted to question him about it. I've been advising Wilhelm as well as Dr. Veere. Wilhelm is keeping his mouth shut about the other night. He's talking with officials only about Dr. Veere's activities. I'm certain Wilhelm's report about Dr. Veere will be impeccable."

Elsie rolled her eyes. She'd never liked or trusted Wilhelm.

"He's very young, Elsie, and he's very frightened. He also seems to be very much in love." The Count looked at Geneva.

Geneva frowned and shook her head in denial and disapproval. "His romantic notions are all in his head. I've discouraged him from the beginning, but he's relentless. I don't know what to do." Her frustration was obvious.

"Wilhelm was very worried about you, Miss Burkhart, almost as worried as he was about himself. He truly does seem to care a great deal for you. Way too often, rational thought does not get a lot of consideration where matters of the heart are concerned. I think that is the case with Wilhelm." He smiled at them.

"He tried to break into Dr. Veere's room to steal a note I

slipped under the door. He's a sneaky little Nazi." Elsie was never going to give Wilhelm the benefit of the doubt.

"Don't worry about the note. As soon as I got word that Dr. Veere had been arrested, I sent someone to his room to pack up all of his belongings and papers. They're now secure in my room, and I assure you, I have your note with the other things I am keeping for Dr. Veere. Wilhelm may have succeeded with his set of lock picks, but your note, along with everything else, was long gone from Dr. Veere's room before Wilhelm ever woke up yesterday morning. However, since we've decided not to concern Dr. Veere with the incident involving Geneva and Wilhelm, I've removed your note from Dr. Veere's papers. I will return it to you, and you can destroy it if you wish. "

"Thank you for rescuing my note. Please go ahead and tear it up. I don't want to burden Dr. Veere with it. He has enough to worry about."

Count James said his good-byes and looked hopefully at Geneva. "You could try to go down to the dining room for dinner this evening, if you are up to it."

"I might go to breakfast tomorrow morning. I'm still too tired to sit at the table and talk to people."

CHAPTER FIFTY TWO

SAVING DR. VEERE II

AUGUST 1938
BERLIN

D<small>R. VEERE AND COUNT JAMES MOLTKE</small>
entered the Adlon Hotel dining room and approached
the table where the women were already seated. Dr.
Veere went to one end of the table and Count James went to
the other. The women applauded quietly when Veere sat down.

Elsie raised her glass to Dr. Veere. "All of us are delighted
to welcome you back. We've missed you terribly. You have
always been there to guide us, and I don't think any of us fully
realized how much we depended on you until you were taken
from us. You are indeed a 'sight for sore eyes.' Please tell us
what we can do to help you recover."

Veere nodded to Elsie and the others and smiled his bravest
smile. He was paler and thinner, and the dark circles under his
eyes and deep creases in his forehead revealed how shaken he'd
been by the past few days in Gestapo custody. "I am delighted
to be back with you and apologize for my absence. I would

never have purposely left you in the lurch. I owe a great deal to Count Moltke for getting me released from custody and for taking up the reins as leader of the group."

They ordered all the courses at dinner that night and indulged in baked Alaska as a celebratory dessert. Dr. Veere ate every bite on his plate, as if he'd not had a good meal for several days. In fact, he'd not been offered anything at all to eat during his incarceration. Dr. Veere was exhausted by the end of the dinner and told the women to meet in the lounge for coffee the next morning at ten o'clock. They would discuss rescheduling some lectures and the remaining itinerary of the trip. Each of the women came by and shook his hand to welcome him back. He seemed pleased, touched by their concern and happiness at his return.

Veere and Moltke retired to the bar after the women had gone to their rooms. "They're very fond of you, Veere, and are so relieved to have you back. I know they'll understand if you take some time for yourself or have to cancel some of the remaining lectures. You look like hell, my man, like a ghost. You need to rest and recover. You need to eat. Can you please exercise a bit of good judgment and allow yourself some time to get over this? At least cancel your schedule for a few days. You'll be no good to anybody if you become ill."

"I feel as if I've let them down. I have you to thank for holding everything together. The women considered calling Columbia and the American Embassy when they didn't know where I was. Thank goodness you showed up at the hotel and were able to stop that before it happened. I think if we just keep on as planned, I can catch up on my sleep and on my meals." Veere was worried about something else. "Is Miss Burkhart all right? Has she been ill? She is usually the life of the party, chattering all the time and asking lots of questions. She seemed so quiet at dinner."

Moltke didn't want to keep any more secrets than he had to, but he and Miss Burkhart and Miss Farrow had agreed that everything about the night the Jewish family was murdered would remain their secret. Moltke respected the women's desire for confidentiality. He had argued against keeping the truth from Veere, but Elsie and Geneva were adamant. Moltke finally agreed that the fewer people who knew about what had happened, the better.

"I think Miss Burkhart has been down with a pretty bad case of the flu. She stayed in her room for several days, and I think tonight is the first time in a while she's been to the dining room for dinner. I had a doctor come to the hotel to examine her to be sure she was all right. She needs rest like you do. Don't worry about her. It lifted everyone's spirits to have you back tonight."

"Miss Burkhart just didn't seem like herself." Veere was way too observant.

"The flu hit her pretty hard. She was dehydrated and didn't feel like eating. Miss Burkhart will be fine. You're the one I'm worried about, Veere. I'd like to bring my doctor to your room tomorrow to take a look at you."

"I don't think it's necessary, but I'll agree to see the doctor if that will reassure everyone."

"Well, that's something. You certainly don't look fine."

"I'm exhausted. I know I need to rest, but I have to make it up to the group for being in absentia. I want them to continue their lectures. If I can get things rescheduled, I will send them to the Institute without me. Where is Wilhelm, by the way? He doesn't usually miss any meals with the women."

"Miss Burkhart told him to get lost, and I think that's what he's trying to do."

"He just can't give up, can he? He's way too young to be so completely Nazified. We're going next to Dusseldorf, which is Wilhelm's home town. That's where he will leave us. After Dusseldorf, we leave Germany. War is coming, and I won't be bringing another tour back to Germany, for a very, very long time, if ever. What will happen to Germany, James?"

"What happens to Germany is not your problem. I know you will be glad when this tour is behind you. You've had many unexpected challenges. From the outset, we knew there would be a great deal demanded of you, but we had no idea how complicated things would become."

"My capture by the Gestapo is no one's fault but my own. I shouldn't have returned for another meeting with the man from Lorenz without first checking it with Barnaby or Trevanian. There wasn't time to get their okay, so I agreed to meet with him again. Now he's dead, and I'm under suspicion."

"In a few days you'll be in London, and then you'll be on your way back to New York. Your trip has accomplished more than we'd ever hoped it would. Feel good about all that was achieved. Don't be too hard on yourself for the unfortunate things that happened. They weren't within your control. I envy you, being able to return to a country that's safe and free. Germany is neither of those things now. My work to undermine the Nazis is ongoing and will continue until you and Barnaby and Trevanian can bring in the big guns, literally and figuratively, to save us from ourselves."

"Barnaby told me he's offered you asylum in Britain, and he's offered it to you many times. Why don't you take him up on the offer? There's much you can do from across the channel to help the cause of freedom in Germany."

"I can never leave Germany. I would feel like a traitor if I left now. I know that sooner or later the Germans will march into Poland, which is really the country of my birth. I must stay here to do whatever I can to try to keep the Nazi war machine in check. Perhaps I can influence things so Poland won't be completely destroyed. I must stay to do what I can."

"Every man had to do what he feels is right. You could do great things for Poland and for Germany from afar, but I respect your decision to stay here. I am fortunate to be returning to my own free country. I don't minimize what that means, especially after this trip. It's so much worse here than I thought it would be. In the past, it seemed as if the Nazis tried to cover things up and hide their atrocities. Now they don't try to hide anything. Their arrogance has reached the point that they openly flaunt their bad behavior. Every time Hitler takes a notion and steals another country from its people, he and his thugs are more emboldened."

CHAPTER FIFTY THREE

ARRIVING
IN DUSSELDORF

LATE AUGUST 1938
DUSSELDORF, GERMANY

"THIS IS YOUR LAST STOP IN GERMANY. WE welcome all of your group and hope you have had a memorable visit to our beautiful country. I am proud to introduce myself to you as the Oberburgermeister, the Lord Mayor of Düsseldorf, Dr. Dr. Helmut Otto. We will do everything we can for our American friends to be certain they leave us with happy and joyful hearts."

The Lord Mayor welcomed the women when they arrived at their hotel. He gallantly and graciously shook hands with each member of the group. When he shook Geneva's hand, he seemed to be at a loss for words. He stared at her and caught his breath. Many people were taken with Miss Burkhart's looks and charm, but this Nazi official was mesmerized.

He finally found his voice. "What is your name, my dear?"

"My name is Geneva Burkhart."

The Mayor took another quick breath and asked her, "Are you Swiss? Anyone with your name must certainly be Swiss."

"My father is Swiss. My mother is English. But I am one hundred percent American."

"Of course you are, my dear. Of course, you are." He still had not let go of her hand. "And do you have a middle name?"

"My middle name is Regina."

The Lord Mayor caught his breath again, and this time it sounded almost like a gasp. He acted as if he wasn't sure he'd heard her correctly. "You are Regina, the Queen. Of course you are, my dear. Of course, you are." He kissed her hand, bowed a courtly bow, and continued greeting the others in the group.

Later when Geneva and Elsie were in their room resting, there was a knock at the door. The concierge held an envelope in her hand and said she had a message for Geneva Regina Burkhart from the Lord Mayor. Geneva took the cream-colored envelope. The heavy card inside was thick and smooth. The words on it were hand-written in black ink, using the German Gothic script that was so difficult to read.

Geneva giggled and said, "Elsie, listen to this: *The Lord Mayor of Dusseldorf Docktor Docktor Helmut Otto Requests The Honour of Your Presence at Dinner This Evening at Half After Eight O'Clock.* The first letters of the words are capitalized, and the invitation is written in that old-fashioned German writing. Why do they have to write this way and make it so hard to understand? At least it's in English. On the back it says that dinner will be followed by an evening cruise on the Rhine River and a car will come for me here at the hotel."

"Goodness gracious. I knew he was taken with you, when he kept staring at you and held your hand and wouldn't let it go, but now the old coot wants a date with you. How old do you think he is, and are you going to go?"

"He's way too old for me. He must be at least thirty-five, maybe even older, and no, I'm not going on a date with him."

"You can't be rude. He is the Lord Mayor Docktor Docktor of the town, and he's obviously some important Nazi person, from all the medals and decorations on his uniform. You at least have to answer his invitation, and what in the world are you going to say? And by the way, what is it with all that Docktor Docktor business anyway, other than to make him sound ridiculous?"

Geneva put her head down on her pillow and turned the invitation over and over in her hands.

"I can see right through your head, and your brain is working overtime."

"He is a loathsome Nazi, but I'm going to accept his invitation. I'm going to tell him that I'll come, but only if he includes all of the women in the group in the dinner invitation and the river cruise. What do you think he will say to that? I'm hoping he'll say he won't take all of us. Do you think he will write back and say that what he really wants is to get me alone in a dark corner of the boat? He can't very well say that."

"I always suspected you were brilliant, and now I know it to be true beyond a shadow of a doubt. He has to take all of us, or he doesn't get you!"

Elsie helped Geneva with her reply, and they'd used up all the stationery in the hotel room's desk by the time they were finished. Pleased with the result, Geneva took her note to the concierge and asked her to be sure the Lord Mayor received it as quickly as possible. The concierge eyed Geneva with curiosity. What was it about these American women, she wondered to herself, that they could sweep the German men off their feet without even saying one word?

A response from the mayor arrived, and Dr. Veere was consulted. At 8:30, a Mercedes limousine arrived at the entrance to the hotel. The entire group, eight members plus Dr.Veere, climbed into the long black car. Each woman was dressed in her best formal clothes, now a little the worse for wear from being dragged all over Europe. Geneva looked particularly fine in a bright red wool dress with a low-cut neckline and white lace around the cuffs of her long sleeves. Geneva was not going to be the small-town country girl tonight. She felt safe enough with the entire group around her that she was not afraid to dazzle the Lord Mayor. Always the flirt, her bright red lipstick matched her dress exactly. It would be an unforgettable evening.

The limousine drove them to the harbor where the Lord Mayor Docktor Docktor was standing in full formal dress to greet them. A luxurious mahogany and white yacht loomed behind him in the water. He politely greeted them and said something welcoming to each woman as she stepped out of the limousine. The Lord Mayor's assistant guided them abroad the yacht. The Lord Mayor lingered over Geneva's hand as he helped her from the car. "You are positively splendid in red. It is your color," he gushed.

"Thank you for hosting the entire group on our first night in your beautiful city." Geneva was gracious.

They were escorted to the lounge of the opulent vessel, and a waiter came around with a tray of glasses filled with sparkling wine. The Lord Mayor hovered nearby and urged Miss Burkhart to try just a sip of the wine, which he said was a special Rhine wine. She insisted that she didn't drink alcohol and that sparkling wine tickled her nose and made her giggle. He laughed, finding her witty as well as beautiful.

Dinner was announced, and they went into an elegantly appointed formal dining room. A long table was laid with white linens, silver and china, and many glasses at each place. Hundreds of lavender roses in low crystal vases were the center piece and extended from one end of the table to the other. Even Dr. Veere was taken aback at the splendor of the display. When they'd all found their place cards and were seated, the Lord Mayor raised his glass.

"We are, how do you say, 'putting forward our first foot' to impress our American friends. We welcome you to your finest evening in Dusseldorf. We hope that peace and friendship will always live between our two countries. Enjoy your dinner. We will be leaving the pier at once, and your toastmaster, Herr Captain Dr. Weller, will talk to you over the loudspeaker to give you a speech about everything you will see as we sail along the world's most beautiful waterway, the Rhine River."

A delicious clear broth with tiny dumplings in gold-rimmed soup plates was served with cheese wafers. The meal proceeded with poached fish dressed in Hollandaise sauce, followed by pork loin with roasted potatoes and sauerkraut. Finally there was apple tart and the ubiquitous cheese platter. Wines were served with each course, but Miss Burkhart ignored the alcohol. Seated to the right of Herr Docktor Docktor she kept up a lively conversation during the meal and had him laughing frequently. Finally, there was a dish of dark chocolate truffles which, although she was "stuffed to the gills," she couldn't resist. Docktor Docktor Otto put one in her mouth and then another. His hand lingered close to her mouth, and he caressed her cheek with his hand.

She pulled away from his touch and turned angrily away from Otto, directing her attention to the person seated on her other side. She knew she was a flirt, but it always made her angry when a man flirted back and went too far with her.

Geneva hated herself for accepting this man's dinner invitation. He was a fawning sycophant and a horrible follower of Adolph Hitler. He was repugnant. She hated herself for wearing her red dress and topping it off with bright red lipstick. All the other women, except maybe Elsie, were having a wonderful time, drinking the Nazi wine and eating the Nazi food. Geneva had brought this on herself. She was angry because she knew she should have learned her lesson by now. She should have refused the invitation, but she had wanted an adventure. She'd thought *he* would refuse then she'd insisted the entire group be included. She was disgusted with herself. She wanted to go to the railing of the yacht and get rid of every bite of food she'd eaten that night. She wondered what in the world was wrong with her.

CHAPTER FIFTY FOUR

LEAVING DUSSELDORF

LATE AUGUST 1938
DUSSELDORF, GERMANY

LORD MAYOR DOCKTOR DOCKTOR HELMUT
Otto was on hand to say good-bye when the tour bus
arrived at the train station. When the group boarded
the train today, they would be leaving their blue bus behind
forever. They would travel to Ostend in Belgium. From Ostend
they would board a ferry to cross the English Channel and
then take the train to London.

Otto was loquacious, but seemed sad when he took Miss
Burkhart's hand and said his farewells. "Is there anything,
anything at all, that I can do for you or give to you so you will
always remember your visit to Germany and especially your
visit to Dusseldorf?"

Standing only five feet two inches tall, Miss Burkhart
looked at the Lord Mayor. She had to tilt her head back to

look up at his face, but when she looked straight ahead, her eyes were directly in line with the swastika pin on his uniform. Before she could think about what she was saying, she blurted, "Can I have your Nazi pin as a souvenir?" When the words came out of her mouth, she was as surprised as everyone else. She'd never imagined she would ask for the pin or that he would honor her outrageous request and give it to her.

The Lord Mayor was openly taken aback by her direct and unexpected demand. Some of the other women gasped out loud at Geneva's audacity. Otto hesitated momentarily as he thought over what she'd asked for. He raised his hands to his uniform and began to unpin the swastika from his jacket. He put the pin in Geneva's hand and closed her fist around it. "You are welcome to have my swastika pin, but you must be careful. I would advise you not to wear the pin in public. You are going from Dusseldorf to England. Many in England do not like National Socialism. For your own protection, you must keep this pin hidden during the remainder of your travels, especially when you are in England. Will you promise me that?"

Shocked that she'd asked for the swastika pin, and shocked that he'd given it to her, she clasped the pin in her hand. "Thank you for your hospitality ... to all of us ... during our visit to your city." Geneva's fumbled thank-you sounded hollow to her ears. He bowed gravely to the group and bid them Auf Wiedersehen and a safe journey.

Geneva took seriously the Lord Mayor's admonition that she keep the Nazi pin in a safe place where no one would see it. She made a trip to the WC after they were aboard the train and attached the swastika pin to the inside lining of her suit jacket. She placed it near one of the shoulder pads where she hoped it wouldn't leave an obvious bulge.

The women were seated in two compartments. Elsie and Geneva sat together as always, and both were quiet this morning. All the members of the group were pensive, each alone with her thoughts. They would be leaving Germany today. They would be in England tomorrow. It was a bitter-sweet goodbye. Their great adventure was drawing to a close. The trip they'd all anticipated with such excitement had come to an end. They were going home, back to their regular lives in their own cities and towns, their own schools, their own country, back to freedom.

Geneva's reverie was interrupted when an all-too-familiar face appeared at the door of the compartment. Wilhelm had sent word the night before that he would be at the railway station to see them off, but when he didn't show up, they assumed he'd changed his mind. He'd almost missed the train, and he'd had to run and swing himself aboard as it left the station. After catching his breath, he'd come to find them. He said goodbye to each of the women and kissed hands all around in both compartments.

"I am honored to have had the chance to get to know you. Dr. Veere, you have been an excellent guide and teacher, and I have learned a great deal from you." Wilhelm said all the right things and didn't mention the Nazis. He was trying very hard to be a gentleman today.

When he came to Geneva, he asked if she would walk down the corridor with him. She wanted to tell him she wasn't going down the corridor or anywhere else with him, but after today she'd never have to see him again. Geneva walked with Wilhelm through the train car to an empty compartment. He was carrying something under his arm. They sat down, and he took Geneva's hand.

"I have done and said many things to make you angry. I'm sorry and want to beg your forgiveness for my mistakes. I wouldn't hurt you for anything in the world. I truly love you, Miss Burkhart. I have said this to you before, and my words always made you laugh or made you angry. I know you don't love me. If I thought there was the smallest chance in the world that you might care for me in return, I would fight for you. I will think of you every day for the rest of my life."

Geneva was silent, not knowing what to say.

"I've made something for you. I didn't have time to finish it, but you are leaving, so I must give it to you unfinished. I worked very hard on this gift and hope that whenever you look at it, you will think of me with good thoughts." Wilhelm took a painting out of the cardboard tube he was carrying and unrolled it to show Geneva. "This painting of a boy and girl is a picture of you and me. It is a painting of a farm, with a Bavarian house or maybe even a Swiss house, and a country lane and all the beautiful scenery you will find. There are chickens and flowers. It is created from my heart with love. I wish we could have been this happy pair, but I know you despise me because I do not believe in God. I cannot be what you want me to be. I have to be who I am. And, I cannot ask you to be other than who you are. I really would not change you at all except, if I could change you, I would make you love me."

"It's beautiful, and I'm quite overwhelmed. I never expected a gift. I see you have signed and dated it." Geneva had been caught off guard.

"Please remember me once in a while and think about the man who painted this for you and will always love you, no matter what happens. I fear that soon, our countries will be at war with each other. Germany thinks it has the best system, and the United States thinks it has the best system. I will fight for Germany with everything that is in me. I am a patriot. Even though our countries may be fighting a war. I will never stop loving you. Keep the painting in the cardboard tube. It will fit into your suitcase and protect the painting. I hope whenever you look at it, you will have a smile on your beautiful face." Wilhelm looked at Geneva with sad eyes.

"The train will be stopping at the border in a few minutes. I have to get off and wait until another train comes to take me back to Dusseldorf. I knew you would never agree to go out with me again, but I wanted to have a chance to tell you goodbye alone. Goodbye, dearest Geneva. You are always in my heart." He stood up, squeezed her hand, and was gone forever.

Geneva sat alone in the compartment, until the conductor told her she would have to get off the train with the others to go through German customs and passport control at the border. She retrieved her luggage and put Wilhelm's painting into her suitcase. It had been a strange day. Geneva was always so certain about everything, but today she was not sure she could say, even to herself, exactly what she was feeling.

CHAPTER FIFTY FIVE

THE FRANKFURT HOUSE IS SOLD

LATE AUGUST 1938
FRANKFURT, GERMANY

WHEN FRANZ HARTMANN DIDN'T
returned to his job at the end of August, the
Gestapo were called to investigate. They immediately assumed that Franz had left Germany. He was considered a high security employee, and the fact that he'd vanished
was of urgent concern. Because of his grandmother's possible
Jewish heritage, Franz's arrest and transfer to a work camp
had been scheduled to take place immediately after his summer
holiday. Fearing he might try to leave Germany during his
vacation, he'd been carefully watched, in Baden-Baden and
on Rugen Island.

It wasn't possible for the authorities to watch him every
minute when he was at a religious retreat, but the Gestapo
had placed one of their people in the kitchen at the monastery.

Their contact assured them that Franz had spent every day of the two weeks at the retreat, eaten three meals a day, and departed at the end of August as scheduled.

The people who believed they were watching Franz began to suspect that something was wrong when he failed to follow his planned itinerary after leaving Rugen Island. In Hamburg, Franz purchased tickets to various destinations and appeared to be leaving a conflicting and confusing false trail. He did not return to Frankfurt as scheduled and did not return to work. He disappeared into thin air.

In an effort to try to locate him, the Gestapo went to Franz's home in an exclusive neighborhood of Frankfurt. When they knocked on the door, it was answered by an elderly Catholic nun. She frowned, not happy to see the Gestapo.

"We are here to see Franz Hartmann. We want to come in and speak with him."

The nun gave them a blank look. "There's no one here by the name of Franz Hartmann. I've never heard of this person."

The Gestapo official insisted. "We know that Franz Hartmann owns this house. We demand that you allow us to come inside and speak to Hartmann."

When they interrogated the nun who was in charge, she explained that the house was a retirement home for aged nuns. "Franz Hartmann does not own this house. Our order of nuns owns this house. We care for sisters of the Catholic faith who are retired, sick or crippled in some way, and can no longer do their work. They have no families and are unable to take care of themselves." When the Gestapo searched the house, they found ten elderly nuns in residence. Most of them were bedridden.

The administrative sister told investigators that her religious order had purchased the building in April. "We remodeled the house and installed a lift for the disabled. The renovation work was completed during the month of May, and the home was ready when our elderly residents began to arrive during the first week of June." She showed the Gestapo around to all the rooms. They could see for themselves that the only people living in the house were old women, plus nursing staff, a cook, and other household help.

The Gestapo was completely baffled. What had happened to Franz Hartmann? Why did he no longer live in this house that had been the Hartmann family home for generations? The Gestapo had one of their legal experts look into the property's ownership records. They hoped to trace Franz's whereabouts through the paperwork. If he were merely leasing his house to the nuns, they would find him.

The house had been sold in April, just as the sister said. The transaction had been executed by a bank in Lichtenstein. The Catholic order had paid cash and owned the house outright without any liens or mortgages. No one asked, so the bank in Lichtenstein didn't bother to tell the investigators that, as one of the conditions of the sale, the previous owner had leased the house back from the nuns for the month of May. While the renovations were taking place, Franz had stayed at the house to pack his family's belongings. The only mention of Franz Hartmann the Gestapo could find on any paperwork was on an old deed to the property showing that Franz had purchased the house from his father in 1925.

The Gestapo investigators were forced to accept that Franz had sold the house in April of 1938 and no longer had any connection to his former home. He'd still been working every day during the summer months until the first week in August when he'd left for his holiday. Where had Franz been living after he left his house? Franz was important enough that the Gestapo had to find him, but it looked as if Franz and his family had been way ahead of the German authorities. They had planned their disappearance without leaving any loose ends.

Another mystery the Gestapo was never able to unravel was the whereabouts of Franz Hartmann's wine collection. Married to a French woman who owned a major winery in Burgundy, Hartmann had assembled an enviable wine cellar. Franz's father, who had owned the Frankfurt house for decades before selling it to his son, had also been an avid wine collector. The rumor was that Franz's cellar contained thousands of bottles of fine wine.

The Gestapo made a second visit to the house that was now a nursing home for nuns. They again questioned the nun in charge and insisted on another inspection. They found a few bottles of wine in the basement, but if there had ever been a wine collection at the house, it was gone now.

In April of 1938, a very rich American, who spent part of the year in Portugal and was a serious wine connoisseur, scored a fabulous addition to his wine collection. Always on the lookout for a bargain, he'd received word from a wine broker in Luxembourg that a collection of more than 10,000 bottles of first-rate wine was for sale at a very reasonable price. Whoever bought the wine collection had to pack and move the wine, using their own moving company and at their own expense. All of the wine had to be moved before the end of May. The American was very particular about the way his wine was handled and transported from place to place, and he readily agreed to this part of the deal.

In May, a special team of movers spent several days at the house in Frankfurt carefully crating the massive wine collection and removing it for transport out of the country. It was one of the largest wine collections they'd ever handled. The wine was on its way to a castle near Lisbon before June 1st when the Catholic sisters arrived at the house to welcome their elderly residents.

CHAPTER FIFTY SIX

REUNITED WITH ZOLTAN

LATE AUGUST 1938
COPPET, SWITZERLAND

T HE DEMARCHES CHILDREN WERE TIRED FROM playing outside all day. They'd adjusted surprisingly well to being Swiss children with a Swiss name. They seemed to understand that their safety and their father's life depended on it, so they tried hard to become a Swiss family. Margot was amazed at their resilience and adaptability. She was having more difficulty than the children were, and she'd made a few slips in front of the staff.

The DeMarches family's new lives were comfortable and pleasant, but there was a very large hole at the center of it all. Franz was not with them. They'd heard nothing for weeks. Margot tried to hide her despair from the children. Then she received a post card sent from London, of all places, that read, "Having a wonderful visit. See you soon." It was signed

"Natloz" which was Zoltan spelled backwards. Written in Franz's hand, it gave her hope. She prayed it was true that they would see him soon.

Summer was winding down, and Margot was in a quandary about where the children would attend school in the fall. She was in favor of hiring a tutor to teach them both at home, but they might be able to go to school in the village. She needed Franz to help her weigh the options and make a decision.

Both dogs were resting at her feet. Cadeau had worn herself out playing with the children. Zoltan had watched from the sidelines and slept. All of a sudden, Zoltan's head went up, and he seemed to be listening to something only he could hear. Margot was engrossed in a book and didn't pay much attention. Occasionally, Zoltan would wander around the grounds as if he were searching for something or someone. When Margot saw him wandering, she wondered if he was looking for Franz or merely suffering from old-age confusion.

Zoltan picked himself up from the terrace and headed around the side of the house. The closer he got to the front, the faster he moved. By the time he reached the driveway, he was bounding like a puppy. He ran in the direction of the master he loved, his best friend who'd been gone for such a long time. Franz stepped from the taxi and bent down to welcome his Vizsla. Zoltan put his front paws on Franz's shoulders and lay his head against Franz's chest. After this hug of welcome, he licked Franz's hand and pushed himself so close to Franz's legs that Franz could barely walk. Franz paid off the taxi and put his bags on the front steps. He knelt down again to stroke Zoltan's ears. Franz buried his face in Zoltan's fur, and his tears ran down over the old dog's head. "My dearest Zoltan, I didn't know if I would ever see you again." Zoltan licked the tears from Franz's face. "But you, dear heart, never doubted for a moment that we would be reunited."

Franz wiped the tears from his eyes and hurried to the front door and through the house, more than ready to be reunited with the family he adored. Zoltan kept pace as he walked beside Franz, jubilant to be back in the place he had dreamed about.

The children, who had wondered if they would ever see their father again, were overcome with joy. Frederick burst into tears and ran into his father's arms. Chloe hugged her father's legs and begged him pick her up so she could see his face. She put her hands on his cheeks and looked at him closely. She wanted to make sure this man really was her father who had finally come back to them. Margot watched as Franz embraced his children, and then she threw herself into his arms and wept. She couldn't stop. Her tears were those of joy and relief. The family had traveled a long road to arrive at this day and this place. So many things could have gone wrong, but the final outcome had been achieved. It was a miracle. Franz had been afraid to imagine this reunion and this happiness in his mind for fear it would forever remain a mirage and never be real.

Franz would have to travel back to Winterthur from time to time to confer with British and American officials and other scientists. They were putting pressure on him to move to Britain or the United States. They didn't want to lose his expertise. But Franz needed time right now, time to decompress from what he'd gone through, leaving his occupation and his country behind. He needed time with his family who'd also been traumatized by giving up their former lives.

Franz had carefully packaged the thousands of documents he'd photographed about the Uranprojeckt and other armaments development. Months ago in Frankfurt, he'd removed the back seats of the Mercedes and rebuilt the seats over the boxes of heavy photographs and papers. He'd put special shock absorbers on the car because of the extra weight it was supporting. Margot had known nothing of Franz's plan to smuggle out the precious photos and documents underneath the seats of the Mercedes. She'd noticed that the car had used more gas during their journeys from Frankfurt to Beaune and from Beaune to Evian-les-Bains. She'd written to Franz after arriving in France that the car's acceleration had not been as powerful as she'd thought it should be.

Franz hadn't wanted Margot to know she was smuggling anything out of Germany and out of France. She was not a good liar. The less she knew, the less likely she would be to look guilty. She'd been under enough pressure, just getting herself and the children into Switzerland. Franz would take the seats of the Mercedes apart, retrieve the documents, and rebuild the car so no one would ever know it had once held priceless atomic secrets and designs for guided rockets. After the car had been restored to its original condition, Franz would tell Margot about what he'd done.

Franz knew the intelligence operatives he'd been working with would be delighted when they saw the volume of unexpected information he'd been able to smuggle out of Germany. He was deeply grateful to the people who had saved him and his family.

Franz was thrilled to be able to give Margot news of Max and Dr. Engelman. He'd just heard, by way of Nigel Barnaby, that Dr. Engelman was living in England, happy with his thriving new medical practice. Engelman reported that Max's leg was almost as good as new, although he still used a cane. Because of nerve damage, Max's arm, even after months of physical therapy, would never be completely functional again. Max had recovered his strength, and he'd signed on to a freighter out of Lisbon that traveled across the Atlantic to the United States and South America. Dr. Engelman didn't think Max would ultimately be satisfied with this menial job because Max was so intelligent and, at age eighteen, already had an advanced education.

Engelman knew nothing about Franz's escape plans, and Franz knew he would be devastated if and when he learned that Franz's body had been found in the Elbe River. Franz was sorry for the deception and hoped that someday, when the world was sane again, he would be able to communicate with Engelman and tell him what had really happened. Franz was thankful that a few had been able to flee the clutches of the Nazis, but there were so many who would never be able to escape. What would happen to them? Franz knew enough to be very worried about the fate of the Jews and about what the Nazis would do to those of any faith who spoke out against them.

For the immediate future, Franz would enjoy his family. There would come a day when he would have to do something about those who were being persecuted by the Nazis. Even though he was a Jew by definition only, he knew what it was like to be hunted. He wanted to be part of the fight to help others evade the Nazi menace.

CHAPTER FIFTY SEVEN

ARRESTING FRANZ HARTMANN

LATE AUGUST 1938
NIGEL AND JACK ON THE PHONE

"JACK, YOU'RE NEVER GOING TO BELIEVE WHAT'S happened. While I've been in England preparing our ice man surprise, the Gestapo in Hamburg has arrested someone they say is Franz Hartmann. Of course, we know it can't be our Franz, but the Gestapo is convinced they have their man in custody."

"It isn't Franz's double either. I happen to know he's safely back in Amsterdam." Jack had kept track of the Dutchman who had pretended to be Franz for several weeks.

"We haven't been able to find out very much about the man who's been arrested, but we have to get him out of jail. We have to prove to the Gestapo that he's not Franz. I guess this guy looks enough like Hartmann to be his identical twin. He's

Franz's doppelganger!" Nigel could scarcely believe what he was saying to Jack.

"Where was this fellow when we were trying to find someone to be Franz's double?"

"The story is that this fellow is so terrified, he won't answer any of the Gestapo's questions. He won't even speak."

"It's our fault he's been arrested, Nigel. Neither my fingerprints nor yours can be anywhere on any attempt to get him released, but we're going to have to get him out of trouble. If we hadn't made Franz disappear, the Gestapo wouldn't have gone looking for him and found this poor man."

Nigel had more to tell. "We do have a name, and we have a little bit of information about him. He lives in Bremerhaven and is employed at the ship works there. He went to Hamburg and got drunk in a bar. He got into a fight with somebody, and that's how he came to the attention of the police. There's an alert out for Hartmann, and by now, I'm sure his picture is plastered all over the walls of every police station in Germany. Apparently, when the Kripo took this Bremerhaven guy into the station, he saw Franz's picture hanging on the wall and asked the police why his own photograph was posted there. So that means, even that unlucky chap thinks he looks enough like Franz to fool himself! Can you believe it? Of all the things to happen. He's younger than Franz, I think, but Franz is well-preserved for his age."

"We can't just let them figure this out on their own." Jack was adamant. "If he looks that much like Franz, it will be hard to convince them that he's not Franz. Once the Gestapo gets something stuck up their arses, it takes more than one crowbar to convince them to let go of it. We have to get this man out of jail, Nigel."

"His name is Hans Schluter. According to what I've

learned, Schluter never went past the third grade in school and has a very menial job at the Bremerhaven ship yard. Can you imagine how terrified and confused he must be if the Gestapo thinks he's a world class engineer and atomic physicist? The guy can write his name, but that's about all."

"We want them to think Franz Hartmann is dead, but we don't want them to do the killing themselves. We can't let them continue to believe Schluter is Hartmann and that he's just being uncooperative. That's what the Gestapo must be thinking right now. They could send him to Dachau today or take him out and shoot him. We aren't in the business of harming innocent bystanders, if we can help it." Jack was very worried about the unfortunate Schluter.

"I guess that figuring out what to do about Schluter is my department." Nigel didn't really have time to deal with the Schluter problem.

"We could try to get his supervisor from the ship yard in Bremerhaven to go to Hamburg and vouch for him. The supervisor could go to the jail and tell the Gestapo that the man they have in custody is Hans Schluter. He could say 'this man works for me and lives in Bremerhaven -- and blah, blah, blah.' That's a pretty straightforward solution. But knowing the Gestapo, I'm afraid they'd arrest the supervisor, too, and say it was a conspiracy. Anybody with two brain cells to rub together can see that their illiterate metal worker or pipe fitter or whatever he is, is not a physicist. But whoever said anybody in the Gestapo had more than one brain cell. Ha! Ha! That's my Nazi joke for the day." Jack almost always had a Nazi joke.

"I've been completely tied up lately with the ice man project. I'm more than a little bit worried about what might happen if our corpse turns up in the Elbe, while the Gestapo have somebody in custody that looks just like Franz."

"Can we wait until Hans Schluter gets out of jail before the corpse turns up?"

"We can't. The ice man operation is on a strict time table because of the thawing of the body, the tides in the Elbe, and a number of other factors. We can't delay the discovery of 'Franz's body.' Our timing doesn't depend on whether or not Hans Schluter is still in custody. So, we need to get Schluter out of jail immediately. Can you have one of your people find out the name of Schulter's supervisor at the ship works? Someone has to call and tell him to get himself to Hamburg."

"I could have somebody call Schulter's supervisor and say they saw Hans being arrested in the bar, that he needs help. I hope Hans is a good worker and that his supervisor likes him. It's a lot of trouble to go to for one of your employees, getting involved with the Gestapo and all. I can find somebody to make that telephone call to Bremerhaven."

"Good. Do it today. I've been keeping up with the reports of the Nazi investigators who are searching for Franz. They're chasing their tails and tripping all over each other, just as we'd hoped they would. When the police put out a picture of somebody they're looking for, it's always surprising how many mistaken sightings there are. We set things up so the Gestapo would be following false leads all over Northern Germany, but I love the way the public lends a hand to the confusion with their false reports of seeing the missing person. That occupies a lot of Gestapo time and shoe leather, tracking something down to a dead end. That's exactly what we wanted to happen."

Jack and Nigel were skeptical about Franz's safety if he decided to live in Switzerland long term. The Nazis were everywhere. "You and I and Franz himself did a superb job of covering his tracks. Maybe they will never find him in Coppet, but I wish he'd consider letting us move him to the States. He could be so much help to us there. He could work with Einstein and some of his other old friends who've left Germany over the past several years." Jack wanted Franz to leave Switzerland.

"He might feel differently when war comes. Remember, his wife is French, and they make a very convincing Swiss family. But he can't continue with his work while he's living in Switzerland, or at least he can't publish papers under his own name. He's dead, or he soon will be. I mean, we're working really hard to convince people that he's dead, and we don't want that undone."

"Here's a funny thing you'll appreciate, Nigel. The Gestapo got a big surprise when they went to Franz's house in Frankfurt. Franz told us he'd sold the house and moved all of his family's things out. He sold his wine collection. He did all that on his own through some companies in Luxembourg or Lichtenstein or one of those places. I guess when the Gestapo arrived at the door of the Frankfurt house where Franz's family used to live, they were greeted by an old nun who runs a nursing home there taking care of other old nuns. The Gestapo went into every room and spent a long time questioning the sister who runs the place, but she'd never heard the name Franz Hartmann."

"I'd love to have seen the looks on their faces when that elderly nun opened the door."

"But that's not all of it. Listen to this. The Gestapo goes back a second time to search the house, looking for Franz's wine collection. I guess they went over the cellar with a fine tooth comb and found a few broken bottles and a few bottles of wine here and there. But there was no wine collection anywhere. Supposedly, Franz sold the wine to somebody who came last May and moved more than 10,000 bottles out of the house. If the Gestapo was angry about losing Franz and the family, imagine how furious they were about losing his wine." Jack and Nigel had a good laugh, enjoying the trick that Franz had played on the Gestapo.

CHAPTER FIFTY EIGHT

GENEVA'S JOURNAL:
LEAVING EUROPE

LATE AUGUST 1938
LONDON

Germany is already at war. It's at war with itself and at war with segments of its own society. It's at war with its Jews, its disabled people, its gypsies and socialists. It's at war with any German who doesn't conform to the Aryan ideal. Germany is at war with its neighbors; those neighbors just don't know it yet. The Rhineland, Austria, and probably the Sudetenland are already gone, and who knows what nation is next on the chopping block? Will Poland be given away like a prize at a carnival? Will there be war with France? With England? It's just a matter of time.

Before I came on this trip, I didn't believe there would be another war in Europe. Now I'm as sure of it as I've ever been about anything. Who can watch the incessant parades, the guns and tanks everywhere, and not know what Hitler has in mind for Germany and for the rest of the world? Every part of Germany's population is mobilized and militarized. Youth of every age, women, and workers — all have their own clubs, camps, creeds, mottos, songs and uniforms. The entire economy and society are geared up to fight. The business of Germany is the business of preparing for a wide and long-lasting conflict. Germany's international trade is focused on procuring raw materials for their war machine. The culture, the education, the science … everything is subordinate to the goal of war readiness.

Every person in the country is controlled by the rules and regulations and the endless papers that everyone must carry. The Nazis have the Germans, as well as foreign visitors, under constant surveillance. They're tapping telephones and using listening devices in restaurants, hotel rooms, and everywhere. There are Nazi spies on every block. The block warden keeps track of the activities of his neighbors. Everything that anybody does is recorded and reported. Children and teenagers are taught and encouraged to spy on their own parents and families and inform the authorities about anything negative that is said or done against the Nazi regime. Wilhelm is one of these Nazi spies. The newspapers and the radio constantly spew out lies. It's all propaganda. It's total war.

There's a mind game working against the citizens of the country, and it includes every aspect of their lives. If you haven't seen it for yourself, you could not possibly believe what is happening here. It's just too terrible to comprehend, to accept the totality of the control the Nazis have managed to acquire over the German people. It's as if they've crawled inside the heads of their citizens. There's no freedom, certainly not of speech or movement. Even more frightening, the Nazis allow no freedom of thought. I could never have imagined a society so totally controlled by a band of brutes, and that's what the Nazis are, a gang of bullies and murderers. They arrest and kill with impunity. Guilt or innocence is not the point. Compliance with what the Nazis tell you to do is what matters.

I can't wait to be gone from here. It's my worst nightmare. It will take tremendous determination and resources to stand up to these criminals. This is a government of madmen, led by the craziest degenerate of them all. They are in charge of an entire country. I don't fully comprehend how it came to be, and I don't know if it can be stopped. It's a cancer, as malignant as the worst physical disease you can imagine, and it is metastasizing. Who will stop them? What countries, what people have the will to go to war against them? Who will be able, let alone willing, to sacrifice all that will be required to defeat these Godless villains?

CHAPTER FIFTY NINE

SAVING GENEVA IV

LATE AUGUST 1938
LONDON

THE NATIONAL HOTEL IN LONDON WAS NOT nearly as elegant as the Adlon. Geneva and Elsie had a room with two single beds but no adjoining bathroom. The visit to London was anticlimactic, and as the women prepared to return to their lives in the United States, the excitement of being abroad was winding down. Some were tired of washing out their underwear at night and sleeping in uncomfortable beds. Others were just worn down from traveling.

Geneva unpacked her trunk and suitcase and selected certain clothes that absolutely had to be sent to the dry cleaners before she made the five-day voyage on the SS *Hansa* back to New York City. She thought of Wilhelm's artwork that was carefully rolled in its cardboard container in the bottom of her suitcase. She thought of the family she'd seen murdered at the hands of the Berlin Gestapo. She thought about what a relief it would be not to be barraged with the constant marching and arm raising and the Nazi flags flying everywhere. She thought about everything she was looking forward to at home, especially seeing dear Edward again. She definitely had her mind elsewhere as she sorted her clothes and put them in a bag for dry cleaning.

Geneva and Elsie were happy to be in England where they could speak the language. It was as if a burden had been lifted. Geneva could never forget the terrible things that had happened in Germany. But when she had arrived in London, it was as if those things had happened to someone else, in another time and in another place.

Geneva and Elsie loved riding on the upper level of the red double-decker London buses. They visited the pubs and ate the ploughman's lunch. They saw all the sights. The group had tea every afternoon, and one day Dr. Veere treated them to tea at the Ritz. The tea was lovely, but it was not nearly as extravagant or as "English" as the English tea they'd enjoyed at the Adlon. The women had a good chuckle about the Germans trying to out-do the English, and in such a proprietary area as their afternoon tea!

Geneva woke each morning and dressed quickly so she wouldn't miss the full breakfast that was served to guests as part of the hotel's daily room rate. Geneva was groaning as usual from having asked for extra rashers of bacon. She'd never been exactly clear about what a "rasher" was and had probably ordered too many. She sat in the hotel lounge and picked up *The London Times* as she did every morning.

Her blood ran cold when she saw the headline that screamed from the front page of the newspaper: **"AMERICAN WOMAN SUSPECTED OF BEING NAZI SPY!"** Her heart pounded and her eyes blurred as she read the article:

"A young woman holding a United States passport is suspected of being a member of a Nazi spy ring. The group is believed to be operating both in Hitler's Germany and here in London. Scotland Yard and British Military Intelligence are working a joint operation to identify and arrest members of the secret cell. A number of arrests have already been made and more are expected within the next hours and days."

The article went on and on, talking about Nazi sympathizers in England and how they wouldn't be tolerated.

Terror grabbed Geneva because she suddenly remembered that she'd sent her suit, with the swastika pin in the lining of the jacket, to the drycleaners. She'd completely forgotten that, before leaving Germany, she'd hidden the pin. How could she have done such a thing? How could she have been so careless? What was she going to do now? Where could she go for help? Who would believe she wasn't a Nazi sympathizer? Who would believe the story about how she happened to have a swastika pin? Who would believe it had been a gift from the Mayor of Dusseldorf, Germany? Geneva could imagine the questions the police would ask her. Why had she wanted the pin in the first place? Was she in sympathy with the Nazi cause or the Nazi government? Did she believe in the Nazi ideology and policies? With whom was she working in England? Who else was part of her Nazi spy network?

Geneva felt physically sick and sick at heart. Should she go to Dr. Veere with her confession about the Nazi pin? Should she try to find out where the hotel had sent her dry cleaning? Should she contact the dry cleaning establishment to explain why the Nazi pin was hidden inside her jacket? Why had she asked for the stupid swastika pin in the first place? She lay down on the bed and sobbed.

She told Elsie and the others that she was having a relapse of the flu and was staying in her room for the day. She couldn't face the group. After much soul searching, she decided she had to confide in Dr. Veere. He was their leader and responsible for their well-being. Failing to tell Dr. Veere might put them all at risk. She pretended to be ill and stayed in bed. That night, after she was sure Elsie was asleep, she went to Dr. Veere's room. There was no answer when she knocked at the door. Geneva returned to her room, and with a flashlight under the blanket, she wrote Dr. Veere a note, saying she had to speak with him. It would be a couple of days until her dry cleaning was returned, but the authorities could come to the hotel to arrest her at any moment — even in the middle of the night. Geneva decided to wait until morning to deliver the note to Dr. Veere. She couldn't go to sleep and paced the floor of the tiny room, trying to be quiet.

"What's wrong with you? Are you really sick?" Elsie wanted to know what was happening, why Geneva was so agitated. Geneva made the decision to tell her, to confess all to her roommate. Geneva hoped Elsie would understand and not be too disappointed to hear of Geneva's stupidity. Elsie, after all, had been there when Herr Docktor Docktor The Lord Mayor had given Geneva the pin. She could vouch for Geneva that she really had received the pin as a gift.

"I am sick, Elsie, but not because I have the flu. I am sick with guilt and fear. I could be arrested at any time for being a Nazi spy." There, she'd said it out loud for Elsie to hear.

"What in the world are you talking about? Have you completely lost your mind? Why would you be arrested as a Nazi spy? That's the most ridiculous thing I've ever heard."

Geneva handed Elsie *The London Times*, but reading the

newspaper wouldn't mean anything to Elsie because Elsie didn't know that Geneva had sent her suit to the dry cleaners with the swastika pin hidden in the lining.

"Why are you giving me yesterday's newspaper, Geneva? I read it every morning."

"Do you remember that the Lord Mayor gave me the Nazi pin from his uniform the morning we left Dusseldorf?"

"Of course, I remember. I couldn't believe you had the nerve to ask him for it. You really outdid yourself with that one. Why in the world did you want a Nazi pin, especially considering everything that's happened in the past few weeks?"

"I was being bold and brassy and showing off and being every terrible thing you could ever think of me. I asked him for the pin because I was pushing my luck, because I was trying to outdo myself, because I wanted a trophy to take home and show around to people. I didn't dream he would actually give it to me. I was astonished when he took it off his uniform and put it in my hand. I almost decided not to take it, but I'm greedy and had to have it. Can you imagine what a selfish and stupid woman I am? I am so shallow and so full of myself. I hate myself. Where are my values? Where is my self-respect?"

"Most of the time, Geneva, I love you for your audacity, but you really did go to the limit, asking the Lord Mayor Doctor Doctor for his Nazi pin. It was too much, but it seemed to be all right with him. Who was I to object? I hope you took his advice and hid it. Is that what this is all about? Did you wear it here in London and someone saw it?"

"Worse, much worse than that. I hid the pin in the lining of the suit I was wearing. I tried pinning it several places, but you could see a bump where the pin was. So I pinned it close to one of the shoulder pads where it didn't show a bulge from the outside."

"What's wrong with that? It sounds like you hid it pretty well."

"What's wrong with that is I forgot I'd put it in the lining of the suit, and I sent the suit to the dry cleaners. When they press the suit jacket, they'll find the pin. There's no way they can miss the pin in the lining."

Elsie stared at Geneva trying to grasp what Geneva had just said. "Oh, my God, Geneva. How could you not remember you'd pinned the thing in your jacket? How could you send it off to the dry cleaners? How could you?"

When Elsie expressed her shock at Geneva's folly, it confirmed everything Geneva was feeling. "What am I going to do? What do you think I should do? I went to Dr. Veere's room tonight, but he wasn't there. I've written him a note to tell him I need to talk to him, but I haven't delivered the note yet. I hate to worry him with one more thing. He's been through so much on this trip, and I'm sure he can't wait to see the back of us, especially the back of me."

Elsie was silent, thinking about what Geneva had said. "I don't know what you should do, and I don't know who would be able to advise you. I agree with you for not wanting to put this on Dr. Veere. We did a good job of keeping what happened to you and Wilhelm from him, but you may really need his help to get you out of this one. You'll need his help if you get arrested."

"Why did I have to ask for the stupid pin in the first place?"

"Do you want to know what I think, about why you asked for the pin? You may not like my answer."

"I want to hear what you have to say. I don't understand myself sometimes, why I do things."

"You're young and very beautiful, Geneva. You are a shameless flirt. You like men and the attention men show you. There's nothing wrong with that. I think you love to play the femme fatale, and you enjoy the way men react to you. I think you sometimes toyed with Wilhelm's emotions. He was clearly besotted with you, and you just couldn't leave him alone. I personally think he deserved whatever emotional torture you put him through, but you did manipulate him and lead him on."

"I never led him on. He knew I was always faithful to Edward, and he knew I didn't want to be romantically involved with him."

"But he was romantically involved with you. In spite of telling him you were faithful to Edward, you kept going places with him. You told him countless times you weren't ever going out with him again. Every time the two of you went anywhere together, he always did something to make you mad at him. But you couldn't stick to your promise to say no. The next time Wilhelm would invite you to do something fun, you went with him, even though you'd vowed not to, no matter what. I think this led to confusion and false hopes on his part."

"I am terrible. I do like men, and I like them to make a fuss over me. I love to go dancing, and I love riding the Ferris wheel and the roller coaster. I like to have a good time. I like to go out in the evenings. I'm a shameless hussy."

"Don't be so melodramatic. Of course you're not a hussy. You're a manipulative and flirtatious good-looking young women. It's not a crime, but your behavior has consequences. The only person you really hurt was Wilhelm, and he deserved it. Now you may have put yourself into the worst jam yet. How could you have forgotten that pin was in the suit lining? You must have been very distracted to have done that."

Elsie went to her handbag and brought out an engraved calling card."This is Count James's card, and it has his address and telephone number on it. Of course, the telephone number is in Germany, and I don't think we can call him from England. That would make things even more suspicious than they already are. He may be looking into the murder you and Wilhelm witnessed, and he wouldn't want that to be connected with you in any way."

"I'd give almost anything to talk to him right now."

"We could sent him a telegram. His office address in Berlin is here on the card. What do you think? Should we send him a wire?"

"If I go to prison, you must call him at once. He'll know what to do and be able to get me out."

"I think we need to send him a telegram first thing in the morning, before you're arrested and taken to jail. He'll know how to advise us, and it's better to be ahead of things. He's very smart and very kind. He'll understand why we don't want to bother Dr. Veere with this."

They composed a short telegram to Count James saying that Geneva was in trouble and needed his help. They asked him to contact them directly and not to contact Dr. Veere. They finally fell asleep, exhausted from the night's worry. Elsie slipped out early the next morning and sent the wire to Count James Moltke in Germany. She wondered if the British were as nosy as the Germans and if their telegram would be read by British Intelligence before it reached Count James. Now all they could do was wait to hear from the Count — or to have a visit from Scotland Yard.

Geneva's clothes came back from the dry cleaners two days later. She tore the paper off the suit and turned the jacket inside out. The pin was still there. She nearly collapsed with relief until she realized the pin wasn't in the same place it had been when she'd sent the suit to be cleaned. Someone had moved the pin, probably to press it. They'd unpinned it from where it had been and put it back in a different place. The sick feeling in the pit of Geneva's stomach returned. She wasn't in the clear. The dry cleaning people could have discovered the pin, called Scotland Yard, and put the pin back in the lining of the suit. Maybe Scotland Yard had told them to return the pin with the suit, so Geneva wouldn't suspect she'd been found out. There were any number of scenarios that could be imagined; most weren't good.

When the telephone rang the next day, Elsie answered. It was Count James, and he was in London. He'd come in response to the telegram and to give a report to Geneva about the murders she had witnessed. Elsie didn't want to talk about their situation over the hotel telephone line." Can you come up to our room?"

"I'm calling from the hotel lobby, and I will be right up."

Both women were impressed that Count James had traveled to England in response to their call for help. Geneva explained what had happened with the Nazi pin and showed Count James the suit jacket. She explained that the pin had been in one spot when she'd sent the suit to the dry cleaners and had been moved to a different spot before it was returned.

"Please tell me the story about how you acquired the pin. Who witnessed your conversation with the Lord Mayor of Dusseldorf, and who saw him actually hand the pin to you?" Count James seemed satisfied with her story." I don't think you are in trouble or in danger. But why in the world did you want a Nazi pin, especially after everything that has happened to you and everything you've seen? Why did you want a souvenir that would remind you of all that horror?"

Geneva began to sob. "I really don't know why I wanted the pin."

"I'd have thought that after your experience in Berlin, anything that had the swastika on it would have been the last thing in the world you would want."

"I keep asking myself the same question, and I don't have a good answer, even for myself."

"You're scheduled to leave England on the SS *Hansa* on the day after tomorrow. It's a German ship, but you should go ahead and sail as planned. I don't think anyone from Scotland Yard is after you. I think you're in the clear."

"Thank you for coming. I feel guilty for bringing you all this way, but I was afraid I might be in jail by now and would need your help. You've been such a good friend to Dr. Veere and to all of us."

"Actually, I'd hoped to be able to speak with you before you returned to the United States. I have some news about the events you witnessed in Berlin. I didn't want to write down anything in a letter, so I'm glad you sent me the telegram. It gave me an excuse to contact you again. I told you I would see that justice was served for the murders."

Geneva felt sick to her stomach when she remembered that night and the deaths she'd witnessed. Her face was pale, and she was quiet.

Count James saw that the memory was difficult for her, but he continued with what he had to say. "I can't tell you everything you might want to know about my investigation into this crime. What I can tell you is that the two men who murdered that family will never again hurt anyone. Justice, in the sense of having a trial and a jury and all of that, was not possible. However, the murderers have received justice of a less formal sort. That's all I can say. It may not be a satisfying resolution in terms of legalities and niceties, but the two men are dead. Don't ask me any questions because I can't tell you anything more."

"I think of that family every day and probably will for the rest of my life. Now that I know those two Nazis are no longer a threat to anybody, I'm greatly relieved. What haunts me is my fear that there are a hundred, even a thousand, more where those two came from."

"You haven't seen much of the world, Geneva. Unfortunately, evil is everywhere, and Germany under the Nazis has more than its share. I've devoted my life to working against evil, but sometimes I feel as if I'm going backwards. I wish I could say I will see you in a few years, in a Germany that has cleansed itself of Nazis. Who knows if the wickedness the Nazis represent will be eradicated in a few years? Because of the way I have chosen to live my life, I may not live to see that day, when and if it ever comes. I'm not much older than you are, and I've already seen more evil than any man should see in a hundred lifetimes."

Elsie had been silent until now. She was fond of Count James and was moved and troubled by the dim view he'd expressed about his own future. "Thank you for everything you've done for us and for everything you do to fight against the Nazis. Even one man who stands against what is wrong in the world counts for a great deal." She grabbed hold of his hand and didn't want to let him go. He took her hand and kissed it, and then he kissed Geneva's hand. He bowed to them and was gone. They knew they would never see him again.

CHAPTER SIXTY

KILLING FRANZ HARTMANN

EARLY SEPTEMBER 1938
NIGEL AND JACK ON THE PHONE

"JACK, I'VE RECEIVED WORD THAT THE HAMBURG police have pulled Franz Hartmann's body from the Elbe River. They dragged the corpse out of the water yesterday morning, and it's at the morgue undergoing an autopsy. They found the passport and are treating the body as if they believe it's Hartmann's. Our ice man may have done the trick to convince them that Franz is dead."

"Brilliant work, Nigel. Will they buy it? Will the body stand up to a forensic examination?" Jack Trevanian was always hopeful, but always skeptical.

"When they do the post mortem, they'll find the corpse has three gunshot wounds, one each to the heart, the arm, and the head. The actual cause of death will be drowning. It will be impossible to say exactly when he died because of the decomposition of the body. The length of time the body has been in the water will obscure the fact that it was frozen and thawed before it was thrown into the Elbe. Fish have eaten away part of the face. No one will ever know exactly what this man looked like when he was alive."

"You have people at MI6 who can figure these things out and know all about the decomposition of bodies. I just hope your people are smarter than the German pathologists. The ruse depends on your scientists being better than theirs."

"Of course our scientists are smarter than theirs, Jack. The Gestapo are a blunt instrument. They aren't into subtlety in anything they do. When they dig a bullet out of our corpse's head, they will be able to tell what kind of gun was used to shoot our ice man, but they will never know he lay in a commercial freezer for six weeks awaiting his assignment in Her Majesty's Secret Service! It's a tremendous coup, Jack, if it works, and it looks like it's going to work."

Nigel continued to tell Jack how the subterfuge had been accomplished. "A fake Norwegian passport in the name of Sven Nordson, but with the real Franz Hartmann's photograph on it, was found in an oilskin packet taped to the skin of the corpse's chest, under his shirt. The tape came loose in the water, of course, but the oilskin packet remained intact, held in place by the shirt and suit. The suit and everything else the corpse was wearing belonged to Franz Hartmann. His shoes didn't fit our ice man, but shoes don't usually last long on a body in the water. After some initial swelling, the flesh on bony feet decomposes quickly, and the shoes fall off. Investigators will believe our scenario, that Franz was trying to escape from Germany using a Norwegian passport in the name of Sven Nordson."

"It's brilliant, Nigel, and a coup indeed!"

"There will be rumors among Gestapo informers on the

street that someone who looked like Franz Hartmann was attacked near the waterfront in Hamburg, on or about the date he's thought to have tried to leave the country. The scuttlebutt will be that he was carrying a fat roll of British pounds and was robbed for the money. When he resisted, he was shot and thrown into the river. When the Germans examine the body, of course, there won't be any money."

"That all makes sense in terms of Franz's personality. He would not be very sophisticated about buying an illegal passport. Given what they know about Franz, that's what the Gestapo would believe. He also wouldn't know better than to flash around his wad of cash around. Not a suspicious man by nature, he wouldn't have been as careful as he should have been when prowling around the Hamburg docks."

"Exactly. When they investigate they'll find that someone with the name Sven Nordson booked passage on a ship headed for England. It was scheduled to leave around the time Franz Hartmann disappeared into the Elbe. The steamship captain will report, when questioned, that Nordson never showed up for his berth on the ship leaving Hamburg, so they sailed without him. That's all true and can be corroborated independently, without our doing anything."

"Nigel, once again your audacity and imagination have done the job. I'm thankful every day that you're on my side and not my adversary. By the way, I have some good news to report about Hans Schluter, the man who was arrested and believed to be Franz Hartmann. His supervisor came from Bremerhaven and vouched for him. The supervisor brought pay stubs and even had a photograph of himself and Hans together, taken at a company party. The Gestapo let the supervisor cool his heels in Hamburg for a couple of days and finally had to admit the man they had in custody wasn't Hartmann. Schluter and the supervisor are now back in Bremerhaven making Nazi U-boats, happy as a couple of clams. They're a little the worse for wear, but you know how good it must feel to get your life back when you thought you might not. Now that the Gestapo have the corpse, let's hope they'll decide not to waste any more time searching for Hartmann."

"They'd better decide that. Do you have any idea how much trouble it is to find a dead person that resembles your live person? Franz was extra tall and extra thin, not at all your average overweight Brit who's been eating too many bangers and mash for most of his life and has a paunch to show for it. We were trying to keep the whole thing as close to the vest as possible and involve as few people as we could. We were lucky because a man from Finland, who was in Scotland on a fishing holiday, fell into one of the lochs and drowned. The Finn fell off a cliff outside Tarbert."

"How did you manage to keep the body from the family? That must have required some fancy footwork on someone's part."

"The local authorities in Tarbert got the body out of the water not very long after the man fell off the cliff. Months ago, we'd circulated a very confidential memo that Scotland Yard was looking for a man of a certain physical description. No one knew we just wanted the body; most thought we were looking for a live fugitive. The locals in Tarbert called the Yard immediately, saying they thought they'd found our man. They were so sorry he was dead and couldn't deliver him alive for questioning."

"If they only knew .... We told them we would handle things from there. We sent a man in a refrigerated truck to Tarbert that day to pick up the body. He brought the body back from Scotland, and we had our corpse. After we dressed it in Franz Hartmann's clothes, which was no easy feat, by the way, it immediately went into a commercial freezer in a warehouse we'd rented specifically for this purpose. The Finn wasn't a perfect match to Hartmann's body type, but who was going to be able to tell after the body had been decomposing in the Elbe River? It was the best we were going to be able to do, and we guarded that freezer and that warehouse around the clock. I'm sure the good soldiers who stood guard there were curious about what was in the freezer, but we had it locked up tight. No prying eyes were going to get a look in there. We were afraid the electricity would go out and our prize would thaw, so we had a backup gasoline generator, just in case the warehouse lost power."

"You put a lot of thought and planning into this, and it seems to have worked brilliantly."

"That wasn't the end of it, Jack, not by any means. We had to have a body to turn over to the family of the Finn who'd drowned in Scotland. We delayed notifying them until we had another dead body to substitute for their loved one. The owner of the fishing lodge in Scotland where the Finn was staying had called the family in Finland and told the man's mother that her son was missing. He went out alone with his rod and reel one morning and never come back. "

Nigel continued. "When we got another corpse, Scotland Yard called the relatives in Finland and told them the body had been found. Scotland Yard and the Foreign Office would be expected to take over from the locals in Tarbert because the dead man was a foreign national. We told the family we were certain the dead man was their relative because the man who runs the fishing lodge had identified him. We told them the body wasn't in good shape because of the fall off the cliff and the time it had spent in the water. The man didn't have a wife or children, thank God, so we were talking to his elderly mother. She was, of course, completely devastated by all of this terrible news, but she was not that surprised to hear her son was dead. His mother wanted his body back to bury in his hometown cemetery near Helsinki. She didn't ask too many questions, but we had answers for the ones she asked as well as for the ones she didn't ask."

"Wouldn't she know, when the body got back to Finland, that it wasn't her son?"

"That's why we told her the body was in bad shape. We said the body had been embalmed at a local funeral home in Tarbert. Because of the injuries and the decomposition, we told her we were shipping the casket to Finland sealed and ready for burial. We told her it wouldn't be a good idea for anyone to break the seal on the casket. We said the casket should be buried as is, untouched and unopened. We boxed up all of the Finn's clothes and belongings and shipped them back with the casket. We bought a very nice casket, one anybody would be proud to have as a family member's final resting place. I think the mother was relieved she didn't have to deal with any of the details having to do with the body itself. She could focus on the funeral and having her son interred in the family plot. We expressed our deepest sympathies and sent a floral spray. It was all done with diplomacy, grace, and dignity ... everything you would want to happen if your loved one died in a foreign country. As far as I know, everything went smoothly, and our game of musical chairs with coffins and corpses has worked out without anyone becoming suspicious."

"What would you have done if you hadn't found the Finn who was close to Hartmann's body type? And age? And what did you do about the gunshot wounds?"

"If we hadn't found a suitable body, Jack, I really don't know what we would have done. It isn't exactly our style to go out and shoot a man on the street, just to get a corpse of the right height and weight. As far as the gunshot wounds are concerned, we fired a gun into the corpse. If we wanted Hartmann's death to look like a robbery and a shooting, he had to have gunshot wounds. That wasn't the hard part. The hard part was getting the corpse into Hartmann's clothes. We taped the oilskin packet, with the Nordson passport, around his middle and dressed him before we put him into the freezer. We never would have been able to dress him once the body was frozen. As it was, we struggled with the clothes but finally got the body dressed. The thing about it was, our Finn was bigger and taller than Hartmann, if you can believe it? That won't be a problem in terms of convincing the Gestapo, because bodies lose mass during decomposition, but when we dressed the recently deceased man from Finland in Hartmann's clothes, they really didn't fit. We knew we were never going to get a better match in terms of the body, so we literally stuffed our Finn into Hartmann's shirt and suit. The body did shrink while it was in the freezer, and we knew it would shrink even more once it was in the water and the fish started in on it. All we had to do was get the body to Germany and wait for the right day and the right tides."

"What do you mean, 'all we had to do'? That part of the charade sounds like the hardest part of it all."

"Believe me, Jack, it was the riskiest part of the entire operation. Once we had our tall, thin Finn, dead and stuffed into Hartmann's clothes, of course, everything up to the point of transporting the frozen body had been relatively easy. Do you have any idea how difficult it is to smuggle a frozen man, one who is over six feet four inches tall, into a foreign country, especially into Nazi Germany?"

"Sounds like more than a notion to me, Nigel, but knowing you, I'm sure you came up with a creative way to do it. It's hard to disguise a body in any state, especially a really big one that's as stiff as a board. The Germans inspect everything you Brits send in with a microscope anyway, so I can't even begin to imagine how you did it."

"Just as you said, we couldn't send something that suspicious into Germany from England, but we did manage to send it in from Denmark. We have friends in Denmark. We knew it was better if the corpse thawed gradually, that decomposition would look more natural than if we did a quick thaw. We got the body into a crate, a really big crate, and flew it to Denmark. We put the crate into a refrigerated railroad car full of dairy products headed from Copenhagen to Hamburg. Our ice man was off to Germany in a Danish railroad car full of butter, milk, and cheese. The Germans love Danish cheese, so the shipment passed quickly through customs. The body went to a Danish import company's refrigerated warehouse in Hamburg. By this time, our man was no longer frozen, but he was still very cold."

"We'd given a lot of thought to figuring out exactly when and where we had to put the body in the Elbe. It had to go into the water at exactly the right place and on exactly the right day. Our people can figure out amazing things with regard to tides. We're a seagoing nation after all, and I give them all the credit. The body had to appear to have been thrown into the Elbe off the Hamburg docks within a certain thirty-six hour period. Then we had to have it stay decomposing under the water for a very specific period of time. It had come to the surface to be discovered on just the right day, before it was carried all the way down the river and out into the North Sea. What a waste of work that would have been, if the body had floated out to sea. The Germans never would have had a chance to find it and appreciate our handiwork. Somehow our chaps figured it all out. They made weights, out of something the fish would eat, to hold the body under water for the correct number of days. When the fish had eaten all the food that composed the weights, the body rose to the surface, and there were no weights left to be found. Can you believe it? Is that original or what? Our people also put something on the face of the corpse to attract the fish. We had to be sure some of the face was eaten away. The body couldn't be found with an intact face. There was no evidence to contradict our scenario that the man was thrown into the river by the thugs who robbed him." Nigel was pleased that his elaborate ruse appeared to have worked.

"No wonder the ice man mission has taken so much of your time recently, Nigel. I'm very impressed with the detailed planning and the number of things you had to take into consideration. You've truly outdone yourself this time, my friend. You never cease to amaze me."

"I think we pulled it off. According to my sources inside the Hamburg Gestapo, the corpse's face was gone to the extent that no identification could be made that way. The operation took more of my people than I wanted to involve, but I kept the technicians who participated in the deception isolated from each other. Most of them reported directly to me and only to me. The tides people, the medical-scientific people, the transport people — none of them interacted with each other, just with me. I couldn't risk delegating this project to anybody else. I'm thrilled it seems to have succeeded."

"Are you going to take a break now? I think you need a few weeks' vacation with your boys at Pemberton. Play some croquet. Take some walks. Take some naps. Don't work so hard."

"Are you kidding me, Jack? It's September 1938, and Neville Chamberlain is giving away Czechoslovakia. I expect bad news at any moment. Then my work will really begin. How much more of Europe will the appeasers cede to the little syphilitic house painter from Linz?"

"You work too hard. You're my friend, and I worry about you."

"Several months down the road, a rumor will trickle out, slowly in bits and pieces in Frankfurt, that Hartmann's widow and two children are living in England. No one knows exactly where, but the story will be that she's living there under a name other than Hartmann to protect herself and the children. She left France for England in July of 1938, and Franz was supposed to join them. When he never arrived, Mrs. Hartmann assumed he had died. For a while, she thought he'd been arrested and sent to a concentration camp, but she finally gave up hope that he was still alive. She was certain he would have sent word to her somehow. She's sure the Nazis killed him. Fearful that her husband was murdered, she legally changed her name and the names of the children. She wanted to be sure they could live in England without fear that her husband's killers would come after them. In a few more months, it will be rumored that the very sad and very beautiful Mrs. Hartmann has been seeing a wealthy Englishman or Scotsman and in time may consider marrying again. Franz Hartmann is dead."

CHAPTER SIXTY ONE

GENEVA COMES HOME

EARLY SEPTEMBER 1938

NEW YORK

EDWARD WAS DRIVING DOWN FROM NEW HAVEN to meet Geneva when she arrived in New York on the SS *Hansa* the next morning. Edward was many things to Geneva, but tonight he was her link with her old life, her connection to her own free country, and her reminder that there were still places in the world where reason and sanity prevailed. She wasn't the naive young woman who'd kissed Edward goodbye in June. She was no longer the simple country girl she'd been when she'd left for Europe a few months earlier. And she was no longer the adventuress, setting out on her chance of a lifetime, eating everything in sight, dancing until dawn, and greeting everything new with the embrace of youthful enthusiasm. It seemed like a lifetime ago that she'd left Belmont and her family's dairy farm. Did any part of that girl still exist? Was the Geneva Burkhart who had sailed aboard the *Normandie* at the beginning of the summer, someone that she, these few weeks later, could even recognize?

She was more mature, cynical, and aware of things outside herself. She'd seen only the surface of Hitler's society, but even that superficial, carefully crafted view her group of teachers had been allowed to experience, was unimaginably frightening. Having escaped serious trouble, maybe even prison, she was more conscious of the world around her. She was more in touch with her own actions and words, what she did and said to others. She wondered if this increased self-awareness and becoming more in tune with the rest of the world was what growing up was all about. She wasn't sure she liked it. There were now too many things to question and to fear — things she never could have imagined before her trip to Germany.

Edward would put her on the train in New York tonight, and she would be back home in Belmont by tomorrow. Geneva couldn't wait to hug her family and tell them how much she loved them and how much she'd missed them. At Thanksgiving or Christmas, Edward would ask her to marry him. After everything that had happened to her and everything she'd seen, she wondered if she could go back to the life she'd always assumed she would live. Could her personal future ever be separated, especially in her own mind, from the future of the world, the terrible future she knew was coming? Should she tell Edward he'd been right about the Nazis and the despicable things they were doing? She lay awake until the early hours of the morning critiquing her past and pondering her future.

Her world seemed brighter in the morning sunlight, and she was excited to see Edward. She wanted Elsie to meet her beau, the tall, handsome doctor she was going to marry. She wanted her childhood sweetheart to take her in his arms and tell her everything was going to be all right. But Geneva knew, even as she wished Edward could reassure her, that everything would not be all right.

Geneva was six years old in 1918 when the Great War ended. She still remembered the men who'd returned from the battlefield with missing limbs. She remembered feeling sad for the soldiers who stared ahead at nothing, the vacant look in their eyes. She hoped there wouldn't be another war, but in her heart she knew the military state she'd just visited would stop at nothing until they'd achieved their terrible ends. There would be war, and many brave men and women would have to die before things could be put right again. Geneva had looked into the naked face of evil, and she would never be the same. How could she come to terms with the much wiser woman she'd become after visiting the devil's workshop, after traveling through the valley of the shadow of death?

☙

AUTHOR'S END NOTE

The real person, who painted the picture that serves as the artwork for the cover of *Traveling Through the Valley of the Shadow of Death* and on whom the fictional character Wilhelm Durer is based, survived the war. He fought in the German military; he was married and had a child; and in November of 1945, his family was living in a displaced persons' camp in Germany. Somehow he knew that my mother had given birth to me in 1944. He wrote to her that his new baby girl had nothing to wear, and he asked my mother to send his child some of my baby clothes. My parents debated how to respond to this request. Nazi atrocities were being revealed on a daily basis, and no one in the United States was inclined to give assistance to those who had so recently been in the business of killing Allied soldiers. After some soul searching, my mother and father decided that the German baby, who had not participated in the aggression and was barely surviving in the winter of 1945, could have my clothes. Miraculously, the baby clothes eventually reached Germany and their intended recipient. The war was over.

AUTHOR'S NOTE

ARTIFACTS, ANECDOTES, and IMAGINATION

CHARACTERS

I have used the names of several real people in my story, but all dialogue, thoughts, action, motivation, and everything else attributed to the real people in this story, is made up. Except for their names, they are creations of my imagination.

I know that Dr. William David Reeve was the academician who led and traveled with my mother's group. I researched Dr. Reeve on the Columbia University website and elsewhere on the internet. Dr. Reeve was a professor at Columbia University Teacher's College. His particular interest was the teaching of mathematics, and he published a number of articles and several books (ten, I think) on the subject. Based on what I know about Dr. Reeve and his background, he was the perfect person to lead this group of mathematics teachers.

Dr. William Hoover (1850-1938) was a Professor of Mathematics and Astronomy at Ohio University in Athens, Ohio and an Ohio Master of Mathematics. I don't know that Dr. Hoover ever had my mother in any of his math classes, but he taught at Ohio University during the years my mother was there. He was elected to The Ohio Hall of Fame for Mathematicians and was an exceptional mathematician of his day.

Dr. Hoover belonged to several national and international mathematics organizations. Dr. Reeve belonged to some of these same organizations. It is not a stretch to imagine that Dr. Hoover and Dr. Reeve knew each other through their professional associations. This could be the connection that made it possible for my mother to learn about the Columbia trip and how she could participate in it. Could Dr. William Hoover have recommended my mother for the trip through his professional acquaintance with Dr. William Reeve? It's a possibility.

I have created Dr. William "Billy" Veere (an anagram of Dr. Reeve's last name) as a fictional character who might have played Dr. Reeve's role, and I have created Dr. Cutter as a fictional character who might have played Dr. Hoover's role. I don't know that there was ever any contact or a relationship between Dr. Reeve and Dr. Hoover, but I have made that connection with my fictional characters, Dr. Veere and Dr. Cutter.

Other than my mother's reference to Dr. Reeve on her postcard of July 24, 1938 (see below), I know nothing about what Reeve was like as a person. Everything I know about him, I learned from what was listed on the Columbia University website, from Wikipedia, and from other internet sites. Both the real Dr. Reeve and the fictional Dr. Veere were members of the faculty of Columbia University and led my mother's tour group to Germany in 1938. Their names are anagrams of each other. Anything and everything else the real Dr. William David Reeve might share with my fictional character Dr. Billy Veere, as to personality, motivation, dialogue, actions, looks, and everything else, is entirely coincidental. Dr. William Veere is a fictional character and a product of my imagination.

Although the imaginary character Dr. Cutter is loosely based on the real person Dr. Hoover, anything and everything I have attributed to Dr. Cutter is also purely a product of my imagination.

The character of Wilhelm Durer is based on a real person. My mother's travel group was required to have a Nazi "minder," a young man who traveled with them everywhere they went. My mother told me many stories about this self-proclaimed and enthusiastic Nazi. For privacy reasons, I have decided not to use his real name. He survived World War II, and I know he had a family. I believe he had a long life in post-Nazi Germany. My characterization of Wilhelm Durer's personality is an amalgam of anecdotes my mother told me about her real Nazi "minder" plus what I made up about him.

I have taken a great deal of poetic license with my mother's character, but I believe if she were alive to read this story about herself, she would have agreed with and approved of the Geneva Burkhart who experiences *Traveling Through the Valley of the Shadow of Death*.

Other real people mentioned in the story are members of my family. In addition to my mother, there are her parents, Theodore Frederick Burkhart and Margaret Mae Carleton Burkhart; her siblings, Martha, Bea, and Arnold; and Bea's husband Warren Maywood Davis. I have written these people into the story as minor characters and have tried to accurately portray what they would have said and done. My mother married her lifelong sweetheart, Edward Vernon Turner, M.D. in 1939. He became my father when I was born in 1944. All the people from my mother's family who appear in the story are now deceased.

HISTORICAL FIGURES

There are real dates, places, and public figures referred to in *Traveling Through the Valley of the Shadow of Death*. Some of these are obvious and historically well-known. I freely attribute any and all atrocities to Hitler and his henchman -- without apology or qualification. Other Germans, contemporary to this period with whom the reader might not be as familiar, are:

HJALMAR SCHACHT [JANUARY 22, 1877 – JUNE 3, 1970]
Schacht was a German economist, banker, and liberal politician. He was Hitler's Minister of Economics until Hitler fired him in 1937.

COUNT HELMUTH JAMES GRAF VON MOLTKE
[MARCH 11, 1907 - JANUARY 23, 1945] Moltke was a real person. He was a German jurist/ lawyer of Polish heritage who was anti-Nazi and turned down a nomination for a judgeship because, to accept the position, he would have had to join the Nazi Party. In addition to attending and working at several German universities, he also attended Oxford University in England. He devoted his life to working against the Nazis' human rights abuses, and was a founding member of the Kreisau Circle resistance group. He was executed on January 23, 1945 at age 37 at the Berlin-Plotsensee concentration camp for being a traitor to the Nazi cause. I know only what Wikipedia has told me about him. When I read about his life and his anti-Nazi activities, he sounded like the best kind of hero, and I wanted to include him in my story.

DOCTOR DOCTOR HELMUT OTTO was Lord Mayor and Oberburgermeister of Dusseldorf from 1937-1939. Otto was the real Lord Mayor of Dusseldorf in 1938 when my mother visited that city. He comes into the story through my mother's anecdotal account about her interactions with the Mayor. He is the person who gave my mother the Nazi pin from his uniform.

BERNHARD RUST was the Nazi Minister of Science, Education, and National Culture, the Reichserziehungsminister, in 1938. I am using his name only because of his official position and do not have reason to believe he played any part in granting approval for the Columbia University trip in 1938.

Although the above people's names are real, I again cite the disclaimer that anything in my narrative, other than the name, is entirely a product of the writer's imagination.

ARTIFACTS

My mother brought home these artifacts, souvenirs from her trip to Germany:

1. I have a painting done in 1938 and signed by the travel group's Nazi minder, the real person on whom the character of Wilhelm Durer is based. The painting was a gift to my mother and is the cover of this book. The original painting hung in my mother's bedroom (in all of the houses where she ever lived) for as long as I can remember. The painting always occupied a prominent place where it was the last thing she saw at night before she went to sleep and the first thing she saw when she woke up in the morning. I took it down from her bedroom wall in Columbus, Ohio after my father died in 1997 and brought it with me when my mother moved to an assisted-living facility near my home in Maryland.

2. My mother brought back a numbered lithograph of Nuremberg Castle. After she died, I found the lithograph among her possessions, in perfect condition and still covered with the "flimsy" paper that protected the colors from running or smearing. The lithograph with its flimsy covering were both stored in a simple, heavy, off-white paper envelope, and it appeared as if no one had taken the lithograph out of the envelope since its purchase in 1938. When I took the lithograph to a framing shop in Towson, Maryland, the owner questioned me with great interest about where I'd found such a print. He said the lithograph was quite

valuable and offered to buy it from me. When I told him
the story, he understood why I wanted to keep the print
that represented so much personal history.

3. I have a Nazi pin that was given to my mother by the
   Mayor of Dusseldorf in that summer of 1938. My mother
   kept the round ceramic pin with the black swastika on a
   red background in her jewelry box. Whenever she brought
   the pin out to show me, she always told me the same story
   about how she had acquired it.

4. I have two post cards sent from Germany.

   The first postcard was written by my mother to her sweetheart, Dr. Edward Vernon Turner. It is dated July 24, 1938
   and postmarked from FURTH (SAY). The "picture" side
   of the post card is a black and white photo of Nuremberg's Das Heil Geist-Spital (The Holy Ghost Hospital).
   On the message side of the post card, my mother writes:
   "July 24, Dear Ed, This seems like anything but Sun. Dr.
   Reeve will broadcast from Berlin Aug. 11 at 7:15 a.m. N.Y.
   Standard Time. Shortwave 1974 or 2549. Listen in if you
   can. Geneva." I found this lone postcard mixed in with my
   father's personal correspondence.

   The second post card was written to my mother by the
   man who painted the above-mentioned picture (this book's
   cover) and who inspired the character of Wilhelm Durer.
   It was postmarked December 20, 1938 from Dusseldorf,
   Germany, the real Nazi's home town. The postcard would
   have been written a few months after my mother returned
   to the United States from her trip to Europe. Because
   Christmas was not celebrated by Nazis and the sender of

the postcard was a Nazi, he sent her a Happy New Year's card. On the message side of the postcard he writes: "Dear Geneva, Luck, health, and joyful mind I wish you for the New Year. I am just writing to all members of our group while my sisters are cooking in the kitchen. I taste often to give my opinion. School will finish Wednesday and then I'll make plans for Komographie [?] and the wished drawing. I think you have a grand time as I'll have after Wednesday. Love, *(redacted)*."

ANECDOTES

My mother told me anecdotes about her experiences in Germany during that fateful summer of 1938, and she always told the stories in the same way. Her recollections were consistent from one time to the next and were consistent with my mother's personality. I wish I had listened more carefully and asked more questions when my mother talked about her trip abroad. However, I did listen pretty well and remember most of what she told me. She loved to recount the story about how she talked the Lord Mayor of Dusseldorf into taking her entire travel group for a dinner cruise on the Rhine River.

IMAGINATION

Traveling Through the Valley of the Shadow of Death is not intended to be a true story. This historical novel is not meant to be factual or to portray an accurate account of my mother's experiences. Using my imagination to write the narrative has been an especially fun part of the process, and I've loved creating the fictional characters, plot, drama, and intrigue.

Most of the characters in the novel are not based on any person who has ever lived. Pemberton Manor in Hampshire is a figment of my imagination.

ADDITIONAL THOUGHTS

Traveling Through the Valley of the Shadow of Death is a story woven from facts and artifacts, anecdotes, and imagination, and the work has not been a seamless process. My search for a satisfactory explanation about my mother's 1938 trip has yielded this narrative as one possible answer, and my story, that the trip was used as cover for an unspoken agenda, may be wrong. Perhaps Dr. Veere was gathering material for his next book on teaching mathematics. It could have been entitled "The Constraints of Teaching Mathematics in a Totalitarian Society."

I've often wondered why I never found a journal or any of my mother's letters that might reveal a fuller account of what happened that summer. My mother must have written to my father and to her parents and siblings while she was away from home on this life-changing journey. Maybe one day I will discover a treasure trove of letters written by my mother in the summer of 1938, and the truth found in those letters might completely debunk my hypothesis about her trip. Maybe I will find a journal in which she wrote down her thoughts and feelings about what she experienced. Some of my questions may ultimately be answered.

My mother died in 2002 and suffered from dementia for many years before her death. Having failed to ask my questions in time, I will never know what her answers might have been. I wish I had asked her about so many things while she was still alive and able to answer me in her own words.

Thinking about and writing this book has allowed me to get to know my mother and father better — even though they both died years ago. I wrote my master's thesis in Economic History at the University of Pennsylvania in 1970. I've always been fascinated with the Nazi period in German history, and my thesis was an analysis of the relationship between the

National Socialist party and the leaders of major industries during the 1933-1936 period. I have read more than 100 books as background for *Traveling Through the Valley of the Shadow of Death*. As I make the transition from academic writer to story teller, I have tried to create a semi-fictional narrative that is fun to read.

ACKNOWLEDGMENTS

My dear friend Jane Rogers Corcoran had heard me tell the story of my mother's 1938 trip to Germany many times. In 2014, she said she thought the story was fascinating and unique and urged me to write it down. When I showed her the picture my mother's Nazi admirer had painted for her, Jane said, "This is the cover of the book about your mother's trip." And so my first book was born. Jane has been encouraging my writing ever since that day, when she first suggested I begin to write novels. I was seventy years old. In the last five years, she has read and reviewed every manuscript I've produced.

Another life-long friend, Steve DeVoe, M.D., who is married to my best friend from high school, Kathie Newhouse DeVoe, volunteered to read my story. His editing skills were invaluable, and he spent many hours making suggestions and corrections to my first draft of *Traveling Through the Valley of the Shadow of Death*. Steve subsequently put me in touch with Eric Rickstad, a best-selling author and professional editor, who was critical in holding my feet to the fire and urging me to rewrite large sections of the book. I have learned a great deal from paying attention to Eric's excellent advice.

Peggy and Vaughn Baker were early readers of this historical novel. They both offered major suggestions about how the story could be made more interesting and exciting. Peggy is a dear friend who reads and critiques all my stories.

Judith McFadden also read my first draft, and she asked for more adjectives.

I am grateful to these early readers. The story is more compelling because of their comments and contributions.

Much gratitude goes to David Hetzel and Bettyrose Schwier-Hetzel, my dear friends and neighbors. Their brilliance and editing has made this novel a great deal more credible and readable.

Nancy Calland Hart has edited most of my books. She has been a close friend since we were children, and I am very thankful for her intelligence and editing precision.

My husband, Robert Lane Taylor, was a careful reader and editor. He kept me historically honest, and I am grateful to him for his scrutiny. Because of his attention to the details about when certain slang expressions entered the American lexicon, I had to drop "gung-ho," "cool it," and "lipstick on a pig" from the final version of the manuscript. Accuracy must trump poetic speech.

My daughter Amy Louisa Taylor was also a reader and editor. I can always depend on her for sharp eyes and excellent suggestions about how to improve my manuscripts.

Finally, my granddaughter, Lane Taylor Worthing, was the youngest reader to edit this novel. She is fourteen, and her comments and contributions are worthy of a first-rate professional editor. She is supremely gifted and wise beyond her years.

Writing the manuscript of a story may be a solitary exercise, but bringing a book into printed form is complicated. The process has many stages and involves many people. I am grateful for each of these dear ones in my life who have taken the time and made the effort to read my story and to give me their feedback.

Thanks to Jaime Coston who worked tirelessly with me to perfect the cover. Although the original painting is the work of the Nazi who fell in love with my mother during her trip to Germany in 1938, Jaime took the painting and made it into an intriguing book cover. Jaime is such a talented artist. She is on my wave length and works very hard to make my book covers just the way I want them.

Jamie Tipton is another critical member of my team. She has done the formatting and layouts for all of my books. She takes the cover design and lays it out for the hardcover laminates of the youth books, the paperback covers, and the dust covers of the hardbacks. Her business, Open Heart Designs, has recently expanded, and Jamie has helped me take *Traveling Through the Valley of the Shadow of Death* from manuscript form to final printing. Her work is world-class, and she is also patient and kind.

Andrea Lõpez Burns is my photographer who can take this old lady's face and transform it into a face that beckons readers. I am always thankful to Andrea.

The first question Elizabeth Burke, M.D. always asked me when I saw her in her office was: "What's new and exciting in your life?" I promised myself that one day I would have a good answer for her. Thank you, Dr. Burke.

Thanks to every one of my team for your tremendous help in bringing this first effort of my writing career to fruition. I am forever in your debt. I love you all.